ABOUT SIXTY

WHY EVERY
SHERLOCK HOLMES STORY
IS THE BEST

"An elderly man, I presume?" said Holmes.

"About sixty; but his constitution has been shattered by his life abroad." ("The Boscombe Valley Mystery")

"And perhaps, after all, it is for the best." ("The Speckled Band")

"I have the best of proofs." ("The Final Problem")

"I ask nothing better. I guess the very best case I can make for myself is the absolute naked truth." ("The Dancing Men")

ABOUT SIXTY

WHY EVERY SHERLOCK HOLMES STORY IS THE BEST

EDITED BY CHRISTOPHER REDMOND

WILDSIDE PRESS

CONTENTS

Introduction, by Christopher Redmond 9

A Study in Scarlet, by Susan Smith-Josephy. 12

The Sign of the Four, by Charles Prepolec 20

The Adventures of Sherlock Holmes
A Scandal in Bohemia, by Angela Misri. 28
The Red-Headed League, by Al Shaw. 32
A Case of Identity, by Sonia Fetherston 35
The Boscombe Valley Mystery, by Fran Martin. 39
The Five Orange Pips, by Clifford S. Goldfarb 43
The Man with the Twisted Lip, by Mark Alberstat 47
The Adventure of the Blue Carbuncle, by Monica M. Schmidt. . . 50
The Adventure of the Speckled Band, by John C. Sherwood 54
The Adventure of the Engineer's Thumb, by Tamar Zeffren 58
The Adventure of the Noble Bachelor, by Derrick Belanger 62
The Adventure of the Beryl Coronet, by Christopher Sequeira . . . 66
The Adventure of the Copper Beeches, by Debbie Clark 70

The Memoirs of Sherlock Holmes
The Adventure of Silver Blaze, by Elinor Gray 74
The Adventure of the Cardboard Box, by Resa Haile 78
The Adventure of the Yellow Face, by Amy Thomas 82
The Adventure of the Stock-Broker's Clerk, by Michael Duke . . . 86
The Adventure of the 'Gloria Scott', by William R. Cochran 90
The Adventure of the Musgrave Ritual, by Susan E. Bailey 94

The Adventure of the Reigate Squires, by Ashley D. Polasek. . . . 98

The Adventure of the Crooked Man, by Peggy Perdue 102

The Adventure of the Resident Patient, by Margot Northcott. . . 106

The Adventure of the Greek Interpreter, by Bill Mason. 109

The Adventure of the Naval Treaty, by Bonnie MacBird 112

The Adventure of the Final Problem, by Jim Hawkins 117

The Hound of the Baskervilles, by Anastasia Klimchynskaya. . . 121

The Return of Sherlock Holmes

The Adventure of the Empty House, by William A. Walsh 128

The Adventure of the Norwood Builder,
by Vincent W. Wright 132

The Adventure of the Dancing Men, by Randall Stock 135

The Adventure of the Solitary Cyclist, by Lisa Burscheidt 138

The Adventure of the Priory School, by Denny Dobry 141

The Adventure of Black Peter, by Carla Coupe 144

The Adventure of Charles Augustus Milverton,
by Beth L. Gallego. 147

The Adventure of the Six Napoleons, by Regina Stinson 151

The Adventure of the Three Students, by Rachel E. Kellogg . . . 154

The Adventure of the Golden Pince-Nez,
by Alexian A. Gregory. 158

The Adventure of the Missing Three-Quarter,
by Dan Andriacco 162

The Adventure of the Abbey Grange,
by Meghashyam Chirravoori 166

The Adventure of the Second Stain, by Mary Loving. 170

The Valley of Fear, by Jennifer Liang 174

His Last Bow

The Prefaces, by Christopher Redmond. 181

The Adventure of Wisteria Lodge, by Mark Hanson 183

The Adventure of the Red Circle, by David Lewis 186

The Adventure of the Bruce-Partington Plans,
by Julie McKuras 189

The Adventure of the Dying Detective,
by Nancy Stotts Jones 193

The Disappearance of Lady Frances Carfax,
by Thierry Saint-Joanis 196

The Adventure of the Devil's Foot,
by Diane Gilbert Madsen 200

His Last Bow: The War Service of Sherlock Holmes,
by Thomas Drucker 204

The Case-Book of Sherlock Holmes

The Adventure of the Illustrious Client, by Leah Guinn 207

The Adventure of the Blanched Soldier,
by Richard J. Sveum. 211

The Adventure of the Mazarin Stone, by Jack Arthur Winn. . . . 215

The Adventure of the Three Gables, by Brad Keefauver 218

The Adventure of the Sussex Vampire,
by Carlina de la Cova 221

The Adventure of the Three Garridebs, by Tamara R. Bower. . . 225

The Problem of Thor Bridge, by David Marcum 229

The Adventure of the Creeping Man, by Barbara Rusch 233

The Adventure of the Lion's Mane, by Jacquelynn Morris 237

The Adventure of the Veiled Lodger, by Jaime N. Mahoney . . . 240

The Adventure of Shoscombe Old Place, by Bob Coghill. 243

The Adventure of the Retired Colourman,
by Elizabeth Bardawill. 246

INTRODUCTION

CHRISTOPHER REDMOND

I used to say that my favourite Sherlock Holmes story was "The Red-Headed League". But in those days my own hair was red; now that it's gone white, and now that I reflect more soberly on the cartoonish characters of Jabez Wilson the gullible pawn-broker and John Clay the self-important con man, I have had to look further.

In 1978, in my first orally presented Sherlockian paper, I sang the praises of "The Boscombe Valley Mystery", especially by holding it up to the checklist provided long ago by Monsignor Ronald Knox, who gave scholarly Greek names to the eleven essential parts of the ideal story. My exposition of the matter was mechanical and dull, but there was no doubt, "Boscombe Valley" had almost everything the reader might look for, from the prone detective peering at the grass, to the presumptuous detective acquitting the criminal.

Still, I must have had doubts, because it was as the result of that presentation (subsequently edited for publication in the *Baker Street Journal*) that I first had the idea of a collection of essays presenting the merits of one story after another from the Canon. Indeed, why not all 56 short stories and, for that matter, the four novels? I thought for a while about writing the case for each story myself, but the cognitive dissonance such a project would have required was a greater deterrent even than the labour itself.

Finally, decades later, it occurred to me that the work could be divided, and that sixty different minds would take sixty different approaches to sixty stories that vary dramatically in date, style, familiarity, length, and (by conventional criteria at any rate) literary merit. The Sherlock Holmes stories were, after all, published over a forty-year period, and it would be astonishing if the novel *A Study in Scarlet*, candidly described by its publisher in 1887 as "cheap fiction", could be easily compared with the 1926 short story "The Three Gables", a racy modern tale of scandal. Readers' tastes differ, and some will like one while some prefer the other. The challenge and delight is to learn from both, as one builds up a picture of the characters they have in common, Sherlock Holmes and John H. Watson, and of the long literary saga (some 660,000 words altogether) in which they figure.

Late in 2015 I decided it was time to make the attempt. I wrote to a few people, asking whether they would take part if I could find enough others to join in, and if so, which story they would prefer. Response was slow at first, but then quickly became a torrent. While some of the people I invited (all of this discussion was done by email) had to say no for various reasons, they were balanced by the number of people who volunteered before I had a chance to invite them. I could easily have found authors for another dozen essays beyond the canonical sixty.

The authors who appear in this book are not an intentional representation of the Sherlockian community by any means. I started by inviting some of my friends, then adding friends-of-friends and people I happened to be in touch with on some other matter, and soon the company was mustered. My only intentions were to include plenty of younger or newer Sherlockians—including some who are here being published for the first time—and to keep a rough balance between men and women. I hoped not to have to include prominent Sherlockian writers, who I calculated had enough work to keep them busy already, but a small number of them found their way into the project after all, and I was grateful to have them. The eventual 60 authors come from six countries, but predominantly from the United States, with a healthy representation from my own homeland of Canada. (Authors have for the most part been allowed to follow their local rules about punctuation and spelling, which will explain some inconsistencies through the volume.)

Some writers got their first choice of story; others had to make repeated requests before I could match them with a story that had not yet been claimed. I am particularly grateful to several people who said they'd take up the cause of any story I couldn't otherwise assign. "I think I could argue that every story is the best," said one noted Sherlockian who approaches the Canon (and life) with undisguised love.

When the list of authors was complete, in the final days of 2015, I wrote to them all, phrasing their assignment in this way: "Each essay will deal with one of the 60 stories, and if possible will argue that it is 'the best' tale in the Canon. If you can't do that with a straight face, perhaps you can say that it's the best of its kind, whatever its kind may be. Either way, you will probably devote most of the essay to pointing out your story's distinctive and interesting points, and the reasons why it is a valued part of the complete Sherlock Holmes saga." I told them that plot spoilers "are fine, as necessary. This is a book for people who have read the stories."

As the word got out, and especially after the title was determined, from a phrase in "The Boscombe Valley Mystery" that I wrenched far out of context, enthusiasm seemed to grow. "This is just the best idea," one supporter wrote on Facebook. I received the first essay within a couple of days of sending out that memo—it was summer vacation time in Australia, I was reminded, the perfect time for a Sherlockian author in that country to spend some relaxed time writing. By the middle of April 2016, with the authors' deadline imminent, there was a fierce and good-natured argument on Twitter about which was in fact the best of the 60 tales, and what weapon would be most effective to defend it with.

With all the essays now in place, I am pleased, but unsurprised, to see that authors have taken a variety of approaches to their assignment and written in a variety of styles. Some are clearly Watsonians, playing the traditional Sherlockian game in which the stories are historical documents and Watson their author as well as their narrator. Other essays take an unrepentant Doylean approach and include references to the circumstances in which the stories were written and published. Several authors even take note of Arthur Conan Doyle's own ranking of the stories, though not always agreeing with it.

What they have written is compelling evidence that any one of the Sherlock Holmes stories can be the best; it's all a matter of what the reader is looking for. "I enjoyed the process," one contributor told me as she prepared to send in her text, "and got a new insight into my story, thinking it even more brilliant than I had originally thought."

I am so grateful to all 60 contributors (and doubly so to the few who took on this challenge on very short notice); to many well-wishers; to Jacquelynn Morris, Alistair Duncan, Leah Guinn, and Ashley Polasek for proofreading; to Carla Coupe and Sam Cooper at Wildside Press; and now to those who will read and, I hope, enjoy the essays in this book.

No royalties from the sale of this volume will be paid to either the authors or the editor. Royalties earned will, with the cooperation of the publisher, be turned over in their entirety to the Beacon Society, a not-for-profit organization of Sherlockians with the purpose of introducing young people to Sherlock Holmes through classrooms and libraries.

Oh, my own favourite story? I deliberately didn't take one of the 60 tales for myself in this book, contenting myself with a brief note about the Prefaces, since they, too, are an essential part of the Canon. If you press me, though, I will confess a special affection for "The Illustrious Client" and "A Scandal in Bohemia". Oh, and *The Valley of Fear*, and "The Copper Beeches", and "The Three Students". How many am I allowed to choose altogether?

A STUDY IN SCARLET

SUSAN SMITH-JOSEPHY

A Study in Scarlet hooked me from the start. When I was a 10-year-old bookworm, my parents suggested I read the Holmes stories one Sunday afternoon, when I'd finished all my library books. And as *A Study in Scarlet* was the first story of the sixty, I started with that.

The physical aspects of the book itself were slightly intimidating. It was a hefty red and black hardcover, with staid silver wording on the side: *"Sir Arthur Conan Doyle, The Complete Sherlock Holmes, 1, Doubleday."* It came complete with an introduction by somebody called Christopher Morley. No illustrations, I noted. Surely this would be terribly boring? I couldn't have been more wrong.

Almost 50 years later, time has done little to diminish the physical quality of those two volumes. They are still in good shape, bindings all firm, pages clear and crisp. Good quality stuff which has held up well despite hundreds of readings and rough handling (in bed and in bath).

The content has held up as well, of course. In fact, in my opinion the stories reveal more of their wit and brilliance each time I read them. I became entranced right away with all of the stories, but in particular with *A Study in Scarlet*, which I consider to be the best of all of the Holmes and Watson stories. Just as Irene Adler is The Woman, I believe *A Study in Scarlet* to be The Story. Or, if you like, The Study.

Its position as Doyle's first work featuring Sherlock Holmes makes it unique amongst the stories. It was, as well, enjoyed by the original readers in 1887. Like the Victorians who read the story—which is a little over 43,000 words long—in *Beeton's Christmas Annual* that year, I began the story knowing nothing about what was written. As a child, I knew nothing about Arthur Conan Doyle, nothing about Holmes and Watson, and certainly nothing about the subject or plot of the story.

If the stories are read in the order in which they were published in most collections, *A Study in Scarlet* will be the first story that modern readers will encounter. And, with the exception of stand-alone publications of the longer works, and some other smaller collections, this is usually the case. The 60 stories are published together, and *A Study in Scarlet* always comes first.

It begins with Part I, "Being a Reprint from the Reminiscences of John H. Watson, M.D. Late of the Army Medical Department." Because of Watson's straightforward account, we are intrigued and empathetic to his situation: he's homeless, injured and broke. And the Jezail bullet! "I was struck on the shoulder by a Jezail bullet, which shattered the bone and grazed the subclavian artery," he says. And then he got enteric—typhoid—fever. No wonder he had to convalesce.

Watson describes himself, his medical training, and his short army career, which was beset with 'misfortune and disaster.' He was invalided out to Peshawar, "worn with pain and weak from prolonged hardships." Then, "weak and emaciated," was sent back to England, his health "irretrievably ruined." So we see Watson, right on the first page, as a sympathetic character. Additionally, he is broke, has only a small pension to live on, no relatives and a nine-month convalescent period to bear. We are curious how this doctor who, ironically, cannot heal himself, will deal with his situation.

How shocking was Watson's proclamation about his move to London to recuperate from his injuries? "Under such circumstances I naturally gravitated to London, that great cesspool into which the loungers and idlers of the Empire are irresistibly drained." I was thrilled by this bitter recommendation of my country's capital (I was, after all, a young English girl living in Canada), and felt that this brutal but honest assessment of London boded well for the rest of the story. This would be an exciting read, I thought. It had only taken me a few paragraphs to become a fan. The first page alone should be enough to establish *A Study in Scarlet* as the best Sherlock Holmes story. But there is more, so much more.

We know very early that Watson has a sharp tongue and is a first-class writer. He says, and it is funny reading it now, "I am not strong enough yet to stand much noise or excitement." Well, too bad, Watson. Your life is about to get a lot more interesting. After squandering his money, he decides that a change is in order in his life. It comes with a fortuitous meeting at the Criterion Bar with Stamford, "who had been a dresser under [him] at Bart's." Stamford describes Watson "as thin as a lath and as brown as a nut."

And so in *A Study in Scarlet*, through Stamford's introduction, our two beloved characters meet and form a friendship that is still enduring today.

Who can forget what Holmes says upon meeting Watson? "You have been in Afghanistan, I perceive." Thus he demonstrates his deductive skills to an incredulous Watson. This early meeting with Holmes is just one of the reasons that *A Study in Scarlet* is the best Holmes story.

The first section of the narrative is set in England, where we get to know Watson and Holmes, their personal situations, and professional lives. We feel empathy for Watson, his injury, his despondency, his penury and his boredom. This draws us into the story, and we are kept there because of what follows. We are welcomed into 221B Baker Street, which the two men agree to share. The lodgings "consisted of a couple of comfortable bedrooms and a single large airy sitting-room, cheerfully furnished, and illuminate by two broad windows." So much of our knowledge of Holmes and Watson's private lives come from this text.

Of course we not only learn about our chronicler, Watson, we learn a lot about Holmes, too. Everything we learn about Holmes in these early pages sets the tone and expectation for Holmes's behaviour in future stories in his habits either at home, or out in the field doing detective work. Stamford describes Holmes as "a decent enough fellow" but not "easy to draw out" though he can be communicative enough when the fancy seizes him.

Watson's description of Holmes, which is much more detailed than that of Stamford, has stayed with us all these years, being the base of many a dramatized version of the stories, for stage, television and film. We always go back to these words, to learn about the physical characteristics of Holmes: "Rather over six feet, and so excessively lean that he seemed to be considerably taller. His eyes were sharp and piercing, save during those intervals of torpor to which I have alluded; and his thin, hawk-like nose gave his whole expression an air of alertness and decision. His chin, too, had the prominence and squareness which mark the man of determination. His hands were invariably blotted with ink and stained with chemicals, yet he was possessed of extraordinary delicacy of touch." We learn of his scientific experiments, his willingness to use himself as an experiment, his interest in crime, proving people innocent or guilty.

His successful haemoglobin test is particularly interesting: "Criminal cases are continually hinging upon that one point. A man is suspected of a crime months perhaps after it has been committed. His linen or clothes are examined and brownish stains discovered upon them. Are they blood stains, or mud stains, or rust stains, or fruit stains, or what are they? This is a question which has puzzled many an expert, and why? Because there was no reliable test. Now we have the Sherlock Holmes's test, and there will no longer be any difficulty." Who wouldn't want Sherlock Holmes as a roommate?

Watson observes Holmes because Watson has no friends to visit him and can only go out when the weather is good. He makes a list of Sherlock Holmes – His Limits, one of the best-known passages in the entire Canon:

Knowledge of Literature – Nil
    "   " Philosophy – Nil
    "   " Astronomy – Nil
    "   " Politics – Feeble...
Knowledge of Geology – Practical, but limited. Tells at a glance different soils from each other. After walks has shown me splashes upon his trousers, and told me by their colour and consistence in what part of London he had received them.
Knowledge of Chemistry – Profound...
Plays the violin well.
Is an expert singlestick player, boxer, and swordsman
Has a good practical knowledge of British law

As for Watson, I never understood how people could think of him as a dullard. After all, he was a medical doctor, which took a great deal of intelligence. He was a soldier, which needed wits and bravery. And he was Holmes's chronicler, which meant he was observant, literate and disciplined. He must have been creative and entrepreneurial, because he spun a great yarn, and sold the stories to make money. He was empathetic, diplomatic and was Holmes's best, perhaps only, friend. And that fact alone should be enough to make Watson elevated in our eyes.

A Study in Scarlet was originally meant as a one-off, just a story. But eventually demand from readers resulted in future Holmes and Watson stories being published—first *The Sign of the Four*, then a sequence of short stories in the *Strand*. Unlike now, when we can flip the page after the concluding sentence in *A Study in Scarlet* and go right to the next story, Victorian readers had to wait for the next story and, indeed, the next installment in a few cases when the story was broken up into successive issues of the magazine.

For all that, *A Study in Scarlet* is more than just a precursor or an introduction to the rest of the Canon. It is a cracker of a stand-alone story. The story is the absolute epitome of a Holmes/Watson tale. Watson's chronicle sets the mood, scene and tone not just for this first tale but for the other 59 stories that come after. Events take place in the moody setting of Victorian London in the last years of the 19th century, and yet, for all the gloom and cynicism, there is such hope and possibility.

Watson tells us that Holmes had written an article called "The Book of Life" about the science of deduction and analysis. He is initially derisive and scoffs at Holmes's declaration that he makes his living as the world's first and only consulting detective. As he describes Holmes's "science of deduction", we begin to realize just exactly what a 'consulting detective' does. This reasoning and scientific method are demonstrated when he and Watson go to Brixton, where the body of one Enoch Drebber has been found. Within three days, Holmes has examined the scene, rounded out the characters, and solved the murder. This is a satisfying conclusion.

But it is not left there. Holmes explains his scientific and observational approach to solving the crime: "Now let me show you the different steps in my reasoning. To begin at the beginning, I approached the house, as you know, on foot, and with my mind entirely free of all impressions." Thus Holmes examined the roadway, and determined a cab, rather than a brougham, had been there.

"I then walked slowly down the garden path which happened to be composed of a clay soil, peculiarly suitable for taking impressions. No doubt it appeared to you to be a mere trampled line of slush, but to my trained eyes every mark upon its surface had a meaning. There is no branch of detective science which is so important so much neglected as the art of tracing footsteps. Happily, I have always laid great stress upon it, and much practice has made it second nature to me." Holmes explains how he was able to separate out the footprints of the constables, and see that of the remaining two sets of prints, one belonged to a man with a large stride and the other to a smaller and elegant foot.

"On entering the house this last inference was confirmed. My well-booted man lay before me. The tall one, then, had done the murder, if murder there was." As the dead man had an agitated expression, Holmes surmised that the man had been murdered. Then, after sniffing the dead man's lips, Holmes smelled poison. Because of the hatred and fear on the corpse's face, he deduced that he had been forced to take poison.

"Do not imagine that it was a very unheard-of idea. The forcible administration of poison is by no means a new thing in criminal annals," he says, drawing on his vast background knowledge of crime and sensation. "And now came the great question as to the reason why."

After eliminating the possibilities of robbery and politics, Holmes comes to the conclusion that a woman was the reason for the crimes. He eliminates the word "Rache" written on the wall in blood as a blind. Jefferson Hope later admits this was a ruse to fool the police. Holmes knew that the ring he found meant the murderer was righting a private wrong. "Clearly the murderer had used it to remind his victim of some dead or absent woman."

It goes on: "I then proceeded to make a careful examination of the room, which confirmed me in my opinion as to the murderer's height, and furnished me with the additional details as to the Trichinopoly cigar and the length of his nails." He had already figured out that the blood had come from the murderer, who was 'full-blooded" and would have bled out that way "through emotion"—thus "the criminal was probably a robust and ruddy-faced man."

We are treated to not just how Holmes solved the murder, but why it took place. And that is where the unexpected second half of the story, called "The Country of the Saints", comes in. One thing I enjoyed on first reading *A Study in Scarlet* was the terrifying detachment I felt in the American portion of the tale. Without the solid team of Holmes and Watson, and the comforting feeling of Watson's narrative and Holmes's confident presence, I felt alone and scared, just as the Ferriers felt fear by themselves in the desert after they left Salt Lake City. Jefferson Hope, brave and bold as he was, wasn't enough to save them, and this sent Hope on an international man-hunt to revenge Lucy's marriage to Drebber—but also to redeem himself and his own failure as a rescuer. It was a case of "too little, too late" though, because not only had Hope lost Lucy years ago, his own health did him in at last. Revenge may have been sweet, but it did him little good except for perhaps personal satisfaction.

As we know, Sherlock Holmes tells Watson he found it to be a simple case. "The proof of its intrinsic simplicity is, that without any help save a few very ordinary deductions I was able to lay my hand upon the criminal with three days. I have already explained to you that what is out of the common is usually a guide rather than a hindrance. In solving a problem of this sort, the grand thing is to be able to reason backward. That is a very useful accomplishment, and a very easy one, but people do not practice it much. In the everyday affairs of life it is more useful to reason forward, and so the other comes to be neglected. There are fifty who can reason synthetically for one who can reason analytically."

Holmes's specialty of reasoning "backward" to discover the reasons behind a crime is precisely why *A Study in Scarlet* is written the way it is. The first five chapters of the second half, set in Utah, shows in fine and illustrative detail how Holmes is correct in his deduction. In effect, the Utah portion of *A Study in Scarlet* is the scientific proof that Holmes's deductions were correct. It was necessary to go "backward" and read about Lucy and John Ferrier and their connection to Drebber and Stangerson in Utah, for the rest of the story to make any sense. These chapters are the evidence for the scarlet thread—the scientific "Study" of the title, the background information we need in order to understand and believe Holmes's deductions as they were revealed in the first part of the story.

"In the Country of the Saints" is deliberately written in the third person to make it seem detached, accurate and real, rather than being filtered through Watson's eyes. To bring us back home, however, by Chapter 6 of Part 2 we are back to "A Continuation of the Reminiscences of John Watson, MD." When Watson takes up his pen again, he recounts Holmes's words to conclude the *Study*.

Though Holmes dismisses many things as "not important knowledge", he knows enough about the world and its politics and news to be familiar with certain aspects of American life that have spilled over into London, that scarlet thread, all the way from the remote and terrifying deserts of Utah to the drawing rooms of London. The thread includes far-flung tales of people's pasts coming to haunt them, and inescapable truths leading to the deaths of not only the Ferriers, but the two men responsible for their deaths.

For me, though some readers claim to be bored by the portion of the story that is set in Utah, these chapters are one of the most riveting sections of *A Study in Scarlet*: the desert, the stark setting, the exotic characters and the historical strangeness of it all. The introduction to the grittier aspects of the Mormon religion (however much it distorts historical fact as we now recognize it) is another of the draws of *A Study in Scarlet*. Sure, it's sensationalized and sordid. But isn't all history a little sordid? And isn't that why we're reading in the first place, to dig a little deeper, to understand our past, and get an insight into human nature?

As a child, I found the revelations about plural marriage to be so shocking as to be incomprehensible. Yet, I never did question the subject, and nor did I bring the subject up with my parents, who were both free-thinking atheists. We always had friends of various faiths, almost curated by my father who invited everyone who knocked on our door with religious pamphlets in for a vigorous intellectual discussion. No wonder I loved the Holmes stories!

A Study in Scarlet is something special. Not only do we get the crime solved, we get a most intriguing and in-depth back-story that keeps the reader riveted as it explains and expands on what had initially seemed just a violent and unpleasant murder. With Part 2 we understand the motive and force of the emotion, passion and revenge that Hope held onto, years after John Ferrier was killed and after Lucy wasted away after her short marriage to Drebber. This back-story is no filler; it is vital to illustrate the deductive reasoning that Holmes is exhibiting. This is one more reason that *A Study in Scarlet* is so brilliant. The back-story is so well expressed, and of such a unique subject, one wishes almost immediately to re-read the first section again with fresh understanding.

It is interesting to note that Hope's tracking and search for Drebber and Stangerson took years, if not decades, but Holmes's search for Hope took only three days. Hope spoke of his admiration of Holmes: "If there's a vacant place for a chief of the police, I reckon you are the man for it. The way you kept on my trail was a caution."

A shocking element, for me, and perhaps for some other readers, was the death of the dog. Holmes wanted to test Hope's pills, which the murderer had used so cold-bloodedly, so he used the landlady's sickly old dog to prove that one of the pills found in the death chamber "was of the most deadly poison, and the other was entirely harmless." Using the dog for an experiment shows that Holmes is willing to do a scientific experiment, and risk error, to prove a fact. We can be thankful the dog was somewhat quickly despatched. I realize it's a little gritty for 21st-century readers who are dog lovers.

Some of the themes that hold true throughout the whole Canon are first seen in *A Study in Scarlet*. The police, represented by Gregson and Lestrade of Scotland Yard, come to ask for Holmes's advice. We know, therefore, that Holmes's abilities and intellect far surpass those of the police, a trope that continues right throughout the Canon (indeed, this theme has influenced many writers of detective stories since then).

We are introduced to the world of Victorian London with its varied neighbourhoods, myriad streets and byways, and the cabbies and other characters who inhabit it. The time and place are brought to life so well, we feel that we are there in the cab with Holmes and Watson as they speed towards the scene of the crime. The story is the perfect introduction to the detective, his life, his occupation, his companion, the London police, the Baker Street Irregulars, and so many of the main aspects of the Holmesian world that we expect when we read stories of Holmes and Watson.

I still remember how enthralled I was, at 10, when I first read the story. The thrill of that first encounter with the story has never left me. It surely must have been the same for the first readers of *A Study in Scarlet* when it first came out almost 130 years ago. After all, didn't they clamour for more? And who can blame them. The more times I read *A Study in Scarlet*, the more convinced I am that it truly is the best Sherlock Holmes story.

Susan Smith-Josephy (Quesnel, British Columbia) is a writer and researcher, and a former reporter, curator and sailboat cleaner, who loves historical mysteries, both real and imagined. She has a BA in history from Simon Fraser University, and is currently writing her third book.

THE SIGN OF THE FOUR

CHARLES PREPOLEC

There is a charm, energy and simple elegance to *The Sign of the Four* that sets it apart from so much else in the Canon, but there is also a curious dichotomy bound into its structure that adds to its beauty. It is too short to be a novel, yet it encompasses all the elements of a classic Victorian "romance" novel. We are given a damsel in distress, action, grand adventure, detection, incisive deduction, grotesque characters, an old dark house, a gripping river chase, hidden jewels, an exotic backstory, and best of all, romance for Watson. Too long to be a short story, it nevertheless holds the structure that would largely serve as a template for the hugely popular short stories that would start in the *Strand* magazine nearly two years after it was written. There is the Baker Street sitting room opening; a client, particularly a young woman in need, arrives; the problem is stated; a crime scene is visited; a police inspector ignores advice and goes his own path; Holmes has an idea, dons a disguise, investigates on his own, or uses his Irregulars; the villain is caught, the mystery explained, the Police Inspector proved wrong, and all is well as we're ready to do it all over again in the next story.

It is a continuation of the general set-up and story of the characters introduced in *A Study in Scarlet*, but also something of a reboot or relaunch. In essence, *The Sign of the Four* stands as the first story to feature the fully formed Sherlock Holmes as we recognize the character today.

I suspect it's a tough nut to swallow for the modern reader to learn that the debut of Sherlock Holmes—*A Study in Scarlet*—was a relative dud with the reading public when it was released in December of 1887. Then again, maybe not so difficult a concept, after all, when one considers that the Sherlock Holmes of *A Study in Scarlet* is in many ways little more than a somewhat updated and British knock-off of the first literary consulting detective, Edgar Allan Poe's C. Auguste Dupin. Sure, unlike Dupin, Holmes's sidekick rates a name, and we get a lovely bit of domestic backstory about Watson and Holmes meeting, moving in together, getting to know one another, etc.... and yes, there's a glimmer of the Master there and he's a clever fellow, able to outpace Scotland Yard detectives Gregson and Lestrade in solving a murder. But when all is said and done, by the end of the poorly paced and poorly structured novel our hero is still just a sort of cardboard cut-out proto-Holmes. Happily, for us, young Dr. Arthur Conan Doyle got a second shot at setting things right, and did so with considerable gusto, in *The Sign of the Four*.

But how did we get to such a masterwork from the basic, if largely disappointing, seeds planted in *A Study in Scarlet*? Perhaps a bit of background on how the book came to be is in order, as in some ways it feeds into the making of the story and is a pretty good tale in itself.

After the failure of *A Study in Scarlet* to find a readership, Doyle, being a practical fellow, dumped detective fiction for historical romance and moved on to writing *Micah Clarke*, which would bring him some reasonable attention in London literary circles when it was published in February of 1889. As luck would have it, the managing editor of *Lippincott's Monthly Magazine*, Joseph M. Stoddart, was in London that summer to launch a British version of the popular American magazine. Wanting British writers, Doyle, more popular in the US than England at the time (largely thanks to a proliferation of pirated works), and bolstered with a referral from *Cornhill Magazine* editor James Payne (who rejected *A Study in Scarlet* for being both too long and too short), was invited to attend a dinner at the Langham Hotel, hosted by Stoddart, in August of 1889. Another young upstart writer present at the dinner was Oscar Wilde (who apparently, according to Doyle, had read and liked *Micah Clarke*). As a result of the dinner, Doyle walked away with his first ever commissioned (rather than spec) story sale. After his experience with *A Study*, where he sold the full British copyright to Ward, Lock & Co for £25, the £100 offered by *Lippincott's* for just the magazine publication rights must have seemed miraculous. What about Wilde? Well, his commission resulted in the writing of his only novel—*The Picture of Dorian Gray*—but we'll come back to Oscar and his influence on *The Sign of the Four* shortly.

Doyle, having had some positive feedback regarding his detective character, if not the book itself, chose to write about Sherlock Holmes once more. Never one to look a gift horse in the mouth, Doyle opportunistically pressed *Lippincott's* to reprint *A Study in Scarlet* as well, and they took him up on it. Armed with a contract to produce a story of no less than 40,000 words, Doyle tore himself away from work on *The White Company*, spent the month of September writing a story he initially suggested would be called either *The Sign of the Six* or *The Problem of the Sholtos*, but which, thanks to Stoddart's hand, saw print as *The Sign of the Four; or, The Problem of the Sholtos* in the February

1890 number of *Lippincott's Monthly Magazine* and then in book form as *The Sign of Four*, when it was released by Spencer Blackett in October 1890. (For the record, Doyle preferred the short four-word version of the title.) While the book enjoyed some success, it didn't become a major bestseller until after *The Adventures of Sherlock Holmes* was published in October 1892, when nearly 3,000 copies sold within a week. By 1896, with a new edition of 50,000 printed by the Newnes Penny Library, it became Arthur Conan Doyle's bestselling book at that point in his career.

So what is it that makes *The Sign of the Four* so much better than its predecessor? What makes it stand out from the rest of the Canon? In a word: Heart.

When our young author wrote *A Study in Scarlet* in 1886, he wrote it as a sort of reaction against contrived *deus ex machina* storytelling. Making much of the diagnostic skills of his former medical school instructor, Dr. Joseph Bell, Doyle set out to create a scientific detective, one who uses facts and plays fair with the reader, and relies on "the science of deduction" for results. So while he certainly succeeded on that basic level in *A Study in Scarlet*, his creation lacked depth and warmth. As Watson suggests early on in this second novel:

> "You really are an automaton—a calculating-machine!" I cried. "There is something positively inhuman in you at times."

Of course there's a wonderful irony that pops up a little later when Holmes criticizes Watson's write-up of *A Study in Scarlet*, since the very point Holmes describes as a flaw is the key to what makes this sequel the superior tale.

> "Detection is, or ought to be, an exact science, and should be treated in the same cold and unemotional manner. You have attempted to tinge it with romanticism, which produces much the same effect as if you worked a love-story or an elopement into the fifth proposition of Euclid."

In this instance, romanticism is precisely what was lacking. While I don't specifically mean Watson's romance with Mary Morstan, although it's part and parcel of the whole humanizing process, it's in the addition of details that put flesh on the bones of both the characters and the world they inhabit. Holmes, rather a too earnest, smug, excitable and, let's face it, somewhat annoying figure in *A Study in Scarlet*, begins *The Sign of the Four* languidly discussing the merits of cocaine. A crack appears in the shell of the automaton and he instantly assumes a more identifiably human mien as a result. This is a more sensitive and considerate Holmes, who learns something of tact after rattling off what is surely the single best deductive sequence in the entire Canon, the business with Watson's watch. It is a somewhat chastened Holmes who responds:

> "My dear doctor," said he, kindly, "pray accept my apologies. Viewing the matter as an abstract problem, I had forgotten how personal and painful a thing it might be to you. I assure you, however, that I never even knew that you had a brother until you handed me the watch."

Holmes has also developed a playful side. Surely this exchange must be a gentle joke reflecting his awareness, or amusement, at Watson's obvious interest in Miss Morstan:

> "What a very attractive woman!" I exclaimed, turning to my companion.
> He had lit his pipe again, and was leaning back with drooping eyelids. "Is she?" he said, languidly. "I did not observe."

For a man who must both see and observe to earn a crust, this can only be a joke. But while gentle with Watson, Holmes's humour takes on a delightfully sarcastic aspect with the rather oblivious Inspector Jones:

> "Ha! I have a theory. These flashes come upon me at times.... What do you think of this, Holmes? Sholto was, on his own confession, with his brother last night. The brother died in a fit, on which Sholto walked off the treasure! How's that?"
> "On which the dead man very considerately got up and locked the door on the inside," said Holmes.

In the earlier book, Holmes has no time for anything which doesn't directly influence his calling, and professes a complete ignorance of Thomas Carlyle, yet here he not only references German writer Jean Paul, but is clearly aware of his influence on Carlyle. Holmes becomes less of a cold, scientific policeman and takes on the mantle of Bohemian aesthete (thank you, Oscar Wilde) and we move from the science of deduction to the whole art of detection. His interests and knowledge are much expanded. We meet McMurdo at Pondicherry Lodge and in a few words Holmes's boxing skills are no longer just something Watson put on a list. It's a simple little bit of business, but it instantly expands our understanding of how Holmes is viewed in his world and sets the reader's mind to wondering what other hidden depths there are to this clever young man.

It isn't just Holmes who appears more rounded, but supporting and even incidental characters are far more vividly etched. In *A Study*, a landlady at 221B is mentioned, but she isn't named as Mrs. Hudson until *The*

Sign. The Sholto brothers—well, Thaddeus's home and elements of his personality at any rate—again owe something to the aestheticism of Oscar Wilde. Surely it is Wilde who inspired at least one physical element of Thaddeus Sholto:

> Nature had given him a pendulous lip, and a too visible line of yellow and irregular teeth, which he strove feebly to conceal by constantly passing his hand over the lower part of his face.

Jonathan Small, the villain of the piece, with his grizzled appearance, wooden leg, and wretched history elicits our sympathy. He is a victim of circumstance and poor judgement. Incidentally, Small, Major Sholto's fear of a one-legged man, the map to a hidden treasure, and various elements of the story itself, even the early possible title *The Sign of the Six*, owe more than a little to Doyle's friend Robert Louis Stevenson and his rollicking adventure tale *Treasure Island* (1883). Old Sherman, with his threat of dropping a "wiper" on poor Watson's head, is shaded in with a few strokes. The boatman's wife, Mrs. Smith, and her son, Jack, the latter with his chirpy "two shilling" response in particular, feel real and remain with the reader. Athelney Jones, broad and blustering, but voicing appreciation for Holmes's "theories" and his skill in disguise, give him a life that few of the Scotland Yard men, aside from possibly Lestrade, ever achieve.

Of course there's more than just the humanizing of Holmes that makes *The Sign of Four* the best story in the Canon. There are elements of structure that come into play. While this tale contains a flashback sequence, it doesn't take up a third of the tale as the equivalent did in *A Study in Scarlet*, and the pacing is much improved as a result. As an added bonus, the flashback here adds another layer of mystery, to say nothing of exoticism, to the tale as most of it occurs in India, or the Andaman Islands. Quite frankly, the story really moves along at a deceptively fast, almost cinematic, pace even with the flashback. While the mystery is reasonably strong, and the deductive sequences sharp, *The Sign* is, in modern terms, an "action-adventure" tale. The clock is ticking; there is a sense of urgency as Holmes and Watson must track down Small before he makes his escape. This is driven home to the reader as our heroes, along with the dog Toby, go racing through the streets of London following the creosote trail, and the haste is reinforced again later during the exciting boat chase sequence. That Holmes is at a loss, concerned that he may fail, between the two sequences, simply drives up the tension. There is no other Canonical tale that comes close to the same sort of energy.

While not as obvious as in *The Hound of the Baskervilles*, Doyle's lifelong fascination with horror also heaves into view, and he begins playing around with grotesques, a device he relies on occasionally in later stories, to an amazing effect. Once again we turn to the Sholtos:

> I stooped to the hole, and recoiled in horror. Moonlight was streaming into the room, and it was bright with a vague and shifty radiance. Looking straight at me, and suspended, as it were, in the air, for all beneath was in shadow, there hung a face—the very face of our companion Thaddeus. There was the same high, shining head, the same circular bristle of red hair, the same bloodless countenance. The features were set, however, in a horrible smile, a fixed and unnatural grin, which in that still and moonlit room was more jarring to the nerves than any scowl or contortion.

While the Sholtos are certainly grotesque, Doyle goes considerably further and delivers the most extreme example in the nightmarish presentation of Small's sidekick, the Andaman Islander Tonga:

> There was movement in the huddled bundle upon the deck. It straightened itself into a little black man—the smallest I have ever seen—with a great, misshapen head and a shock of tangled, dishevelled hair. Holmes had already drawn his revolver, and I whipped out mine at the sight of this savage, distorted creature. He was wrapped in some sort of dark ulster or blanket, which left only his face exposed; but that face was enough to give a man a sleepless night. Never have I seen features so deeply marked with all bestiality and cruelty. His small eyes glowed and burned with a sombre light, and his thick lips were writhed back from his teeth, which grinned and chattered at us with half animal fury.

Mind you, it isn't just in description or characters that Doyle reflects a horror sensibility, but in his use of foreshadowing and misdirection to create a frisson of fear.

> "At this instant a horrible change came over his expression; his eyes stared wildly, his jaw dropped, and he yelled, in a voice which I can never forget, 'Keep him out! For Christ's sake keep him out!' We both stared round at the window behind us upon which his gaze was fixed. A face was looking in at us out of the darkness. We could see the whitening of the nose where it was pressed against the glass. It was a bearded, hairy face, with wild cruel eyes and an expression of concentrated malevolence. My brother and I rushed towards the window, but the man was gone. When we returned to my father his head had dropped and his pulse had ceased to beat.
>
> "We searched the garden that night, but found no sign of the intruder, save that just under the window a single footmark was visible in the flower-bed. But for that one trace, we might have thought that our imaginations had conjured up that wild, fierce face. We soon, however,

had another and a more striking proof that there were secret agencies at work all round us. The window of my father's room was found open in the morning, his cupboards and boxes had been rifled, and upon his chest was fixed a torn piece of paper, with the words 'The sign of the four' scrawled across it. What the phrase meant, or who our secret visitor may have been, we never knew."

Later, we are right there with Watson, a shiver running down the spine, when we encounter this:

He held down the lamp to the floor, and as he did so I saw for the second time that night a startled, surprised look come over his face. For myself, as I followed his gaze my skin was cold under my clothes. The floor was covered thickly with the prints of a naked foot—clear, well defined, perfectly formed, but scarce half the size of those of an ordinary man.

"Holmes," I said, in a whisper, "a child has done this horrid thing."

Were it at the end of a chapter, I suspect it would be as oft quoted as "Mr. Holmes, they were the footprints of a gigantic hound!"

Doyle's masterful use of language, however, is not restricted to the horrific. The dialogue sparkles and some of the most quotable lines in the Canon appear in *The Sign of the Four*:

"My mind," he said, "rebels at stagnation. Give me problems, give me work, give me the most abstruse cryptogram or the most intricate analysis, and I am in my own proper atmosphere. I can dispense then with artificial stimulants. But I abhor the dull routine of existence. I crave for mental exaltation. That is why I have chosen my own particular profession, or rather created it, for I am the only one in the world."

"I never guess. It is a shocking habit—destructive to the logical faculty."

"You know my methods. Apply them."

And the single most often quoted and important line in all the Canon, a line that alone would make me adore this tale over all other stories, makes its first appearance:

When you have eliminated the impossible, whatever remains, however improbable, must be the truth.

Quotable dialogue aside, we can go further with the charm of Doyle's language in these pages. The honest introspection and self-doubt surrounding Watson's romantic interest in Mary Morstan is a study in sensitivity. It reaches a pinnacle in what must surely be one of the most delightful and heartwarming passages to appear in any Sherlock Holmes story:

Miss Morstan and I stood together, and her hand was in mine. A wondrous subtle thing is love, for here were we two who had never seen each other before that day, between whom no word or even look of affection had ever passed, and yet now in an hour of trouble our hands instinctively sought for each other. I have marvelled at it since, but at the time it seemed the most natural thing that I should go out to her so, and, as she has often told me, there was in her also the instinct to turn to me for comfort and protection. So we stood hand in hand, like two children, and there was peace in our hearts for all the dark things that surrounded us.

While I wrote previously about the injection of warmth and humanity to the character of Holmes being crucial to the success of the story, Watson too got something of an upgrade in this reboot. Although obviously never as cold as Holmes, from the opening expression of concern over his friend's cocaine use, throughout his wooing of Mary Morstan, it is obvious our Watson too has taken on greater warmth and become a more fully realized character. His romance of Mary Morstan, the only "on-screen" romantic entanglement for either of our leads in any of the stories, gives *The Sign of the Four* more heart than any other. When Watson informs us of the loss of his wife in "The Empty House" it is because of *The Sign of the Four* that we mourn with him. He is us and we are him.

Heart, expressed through the friendship between Holmes and Watson, is the key to the success of the Sherlock Holmes stories. It is what sets them aside from the huge pack of literary detectives that followed and keeps these stories alive in our minds, and perhaps our own hearts, today. That being the case, then *The Sign of the Four*, this rather long short story, with its condensed Victorian romance novel sensibilities, exciting action film pacing, grotesque characters and situations, exotic locations, beautiful language and a myriad of other details, is where it all began. As the fixed starting point in an ever changing world, to paraphrase some clever fellow, it is the true heart of the Canon, and for that it is surely the very best Sherlock Holmes story of all.

Charles Prepolec (Calgary, Alberta) is co-editor, with J. R. Campbell, of five Sherlock Holmes anthologies, as well as works about Professor Challenger and other science fiction. He is a member of the Bootmakers of Toronto and other societies.

A SCANDAL IN BOHEMIA

ANGELA MISRI

Sherlock Holmes, by his own admission in "The Five Orange Pips", was bested only four times in his career as a consulting detective. Only one of his adversaries did it with just 25 words. And she was a woman. The Woman. The incomparable, unforgettable Irene Adler. So how can any canon story hope to outshine "A Scandal in Bohemia"? Three features set this story apart: The Woman, the mystery as a backdrop rather than focus, and the rare insight into the emotional side of Sherlock Holmes this remarkable short story presents to its readers.

The first Holmes short story, published in the *Strand* magazine in June 1891, it was also the first to feature illustrations by Sidney Paget. Though it had been preceded by two novels—*A Study in Scarlet* and *The Sign of the Four* —it has made its mark on the Sherlockian universe in a way no other tale has.

Its author was well aware of its distinctiveness. In its June 1927 issue the *Strand*, which enjoyed one of the most symbiotically successful relationships with an author, asked Arthur Conan Doyle to pick his favorite Sherlock Holmes stories. This is how he explained his reasoning for including "Scandal" in that list: "I think the first story of all should go in, as it opened the path for the others, and it has more female interest than is usual." Presumably he was talking about the female readership of the *Strand*, and in paying heed to their oft-ignored interest, ACD took a calculated risk that has paid off with his readers for more than a hundred years.

At the time of the story's publication, Victoria was still a queen in mourning, and women in the United Kingdom did not yet have the right to vote, but they were making advances in their struggle for equality. Contemporary issues of the *Strand* magazine carried advertising clearly aimed at the women readers—from Dr. Tibbald's tonic for pimples to Trilene tablets to battle "stoutness." The ads feature images of pretty women and written testimonials from satisfied female clients.

Conan Doyle himself was surrounded by the women he loved—his mother, Mary Foley, to whom he was very devoted, his wife Louise, whom he married in 1885, and his first daughter, Mary, born in 1889. Was this changing environment, both inside his home and out, what influenced his creation of The Woman?

Irene Adler appears only once in the original 56 stories written by Conan Doyle. She speaks 25 words aloud in the entire short story (by comparison, her adversary, the King of Bohemia speaks 761 immediately forgettable words). Adler is described by the King as an "adventuress" having "the face of the most beautiful of women and the mind of the most resolute of men." Various definitions of the term "adventuress" all refer to the pursuit of money as one of the key identifiers in such a woman. In other words, the King is doing his best to cast Adler as the criminal in the affair, bent on evil revenge against him. Holmes and Watson (and indeed even the reader) begin the story with that vision of her in their heads.

But it doesn't take long for all of us to reverse that initial impression and realize that between the two, it is surely the King who deserves our disdain. He makes a failed attempt at disguise, made even more pathetic by Adler's success at disguise later on in the story. He admits that he has broken into her home five times to recover his photograph, and failed every time. He claims that she has threatened to destroy his prospective marriage, but we have no evidence of that save his words, and based on her actions —she gets married the very next day to Godfrey Norton—I very much doubt the King's accusation. Confronted with the fact of her marriage, he acts like a jealous lover, in disbelief that she could love anyone but him. Finally, when her letter is read, the King is fully satisfied, proclaiming, "I know that her word is inviolate," which contradicts his claims of her evil nature.

Adler plays one of Holmes's own favorite tricks on the great detective, risking discovery to say good night to him as he stands outside his Baker Street office. How can you do aught but admire The Woman?

But it is the letter she leaves for Holmes that best underlines her importance to the Canon. She writes that "your client may rest in peace. I love and am loved by a better man than he. The King may do what he will without hindrance from one whom he has cruelly wronged. I keep it only to safeguard myself, and to preserve a weapon which will always secure me from any steps which he might take in the future." Thus she reveals that she has been hurt by the man who hired Holmes, and in that moment of discovery, no one is more keenly aware of that than the great detective himself. He was taken in by his client and outsmarted by his prey, who turned out to be a self-rescuing victim. To outsmart Sherlock Holmes is no mean feat, and more than that, to actually make him change his mind is something his best friend Dr. Watson marvels at. "He used to make merry over the cleverness of women, but I have not heard him do it of late."

"A Scandal in Bohemia" is the most humanizing of the canonical stories. Watson's voice and words are fairly dripping with love and admiration, and the only story that even comes close to that level of emotion is "The Final Problem". Watson goes out of his way to describe their joyful reunion at the beginning of the story, writing of his friend, "His manner was not effusive. It seldom was; but he was glad, I think, to see me." Of his own reaction he writes, "I was seized with a keen desire to see Holmes again."

Many have speculated on the condition of Watson's marriage from the first paragraphs of this tale, but I would instead use it to highlight the significance of Holmes's reaction to Adler. Watson explains: "It was not that he felt any emotion akin to love for Irene Adler. All emotions, and that one particularly, were abhorrent to his cold, precise but admirably balanced mind."

This story gives an unusual view of the great detective's emotions, one that is only possible because the mystery itself is a backdrop rather than a central part of the narrative. Holmes himself admits that his strategy to fake a fire and see what his prey protects is an old one. "I have more than once taken advantage of it. In the case of the Darlington substitution scandal it was of use to me, and also in the Arnsworth Castle business." There is nothing new about his methods, and he goes through the motions with minimal thought or adaptation. This allows the actual retrieval of the letter to become a backdrop to the more important work of developing the three main characters—Holmes, Watson and Adler.

This is actually a well-known strategy for authors, especially in a continuing series where you know you will have ample opportunity to focus on different aspects of your larger story. The author needs to provide more than a good mystery—she or he must also offer a reason to care about the characters, something about them that pulls a reader into their corner. That's what we find in "A Scandal". The reader is manoeuvred to admire Adler and pity the way she was treated by the King. Equally, the reader finds themselves admiring Holmes for his skills and then sympathizing with him for his defeat (not an easy thing to do with so arrogant a main character).

Conan Doyle takes the time to open up about the great detective—to give him some depth, which is vital if the author wants an audience to continue to follow one character through a series. Here in the first short story in a series published in a popular magazine, it was a good strategy for Conan Doyle to employ, and made him a fan favourite for the *Strand* magazine.

And that is why "A Scandal in Bohemia" eclipses and predominates all others.

Angela Misri (Toronto, Ontario) is an author, journalist, designer and podcaster. She is the creator of the Portia Adams Adventures, a popular pastiche series featuring a 19-year-old detective in 1930s London who inherits 221 Baker Street.

THE RED-HEADED LEAGUE

AL SHAW

I ask myself: What is it that puts "The Red-Headed League" in everybody's Top Ten list or even Top Five? More to the point, why is it *my* favorite story? The answer: It assembles all the components and signifiers that we have come to love in a quintessential Sherlock Homes story.

This story is an actual mystery that requires an actual investigation (i.e., a visit to scope out the scene of the crime, sidewalk tapping and all). There is none of this "something feels wrong," "he is behaving oddly," "I am being watched," feeling. There is no leaping up from chairs, exclaiming, or ejaculating (although Watson ejaculates in this story). But that is not why this is my favorite story.

Perhaps it is because this was the first time I read about a scam, a hustle, a persiflage, a canard, in essence a con. It is conceivable that this may even have been the first time the concept of the "long con" was ever used in a detective story. As part and parcel of this concept let us not forget originating the soon-to-be-copied (in real life) "the old digging next door to break into the bank trick" (previous line delivered in the voice of Maxwell Smart). But that is not why this is my favorite story either.

In the initial encounter, in the Baker Street sitting room, Holmes does his trademark Bellian observation and deduction of the visitor, Jabez Wilson. "Beyond the obvious facts that he has at some time done manual labour, that he takes snuff, that he is a Freemason, that he has been in China, and that he has done a considerable amount of writing lately, I can deduce nothing else." And of course once explained, the visitor replies with the usual, "Well, I never! I thought at first that you had done something clever, but I see that there was nothing in it, after all." But that is not why this is my favorite story.

It is in this deduction above that Holmes gives us one of his little self-promotions, like the monograph on 140 varieties of ash and all the rest. Holmes teases us with, "The fish that you have tattooed immediately above your right wrist could only have been done in China. I have made a small study of tattoo marks and have even contributed to the literature of the subject." But that is not why this is my favorite story.

We have, in "The Red-Headed League," the colorful categorization of the super-criminal that has led to so many wonderful toasts at Sherlockian club meetings. Toasts like: "To The Napoleon of Crime. The organizer of all that is evil and nearly all that is undetected, I give you Professor Moriarty." Or, "He is the second most dangerous man in London, the most cunning and dangerous criminal in London... Colonel Sebastian Moran." Or, "To the worst man in London! I present Charles Augustus Milverton." And now from this story I give you, "With a white splash of acid upon his forehead, royal blood in his veins, the grandson of a royal duke, he is the fourth smartest man in London and he may even be the third. We toast... John Clay!" Here we have yet one more reason to raise a glass. But that is not why this is my favorite story.

In fact, it is not even the fact that the story is an early popularization portraying redheads—which these days seem to be everywhere. No, it is the following passage which upon reading, resonates with readers so strongly that it remembered with other famous Sherlockian passages like "The dog did nothing in the night-time." "That was the curious incident," and "Mr. Holmes, they were the footprints of a gigantic hound!"

In "The Red Headed League" we are treated to this:

> "What are you going to do, then?" I asked. "To smoke," he answered. "It is quite a three pipe problem, and I beg that you won't speak to me for fifty minutes." He curled himself up in his chair, with his thin knees drawn up to his hawk-like nose, and there he sat with his eyes closed and his black clay pipe thrusting out like the bill of some strange bird. I had come to the conclusion that he had dropped asleep, and indeed was nodding myself, when he suddenly sprang out of his chair with the gesture of a man who has made up his mind and put his pipe down upon the mantelpiece.

As a Sherlockian and pipe smoker, who has himself published a monograph or two on the subject of Holmes and pipe smoking, this was the Blue Carbuncle of the story for me. *A three pipe problem* is a phrase so familiar to us that it has even entered the vernacular of the non-Sherlockian populace. It has been so often quoted to describe a particularly knotty problem that many who utter the phrase are not even aware of its origin being from the Canon.

A three pipe problem: that phrase has entered all the Sherlockian papers and debates on Sherlock Holmes's pipe smoking habits and preferences. "How can he consume three pipes in fifty minutes?" "His pipe was small like sixteenth century clay?" "He smokes a black clay pipe. It stuck out like the bill of a bird, ergo Holmes only smoked a straight pipe? Wait, perhaps it wasn't his only pipe." "Why was it black?" "Black from use?" "Black clay?" After all, what is Holmes without his pipe? (Probably a television show.) This is a three pipe problem indeed—and I love it!

> 'Twas The Red-Headed League
> Of John Clay tried to rob them,
> But it was Sherlock who solved
> The three pipe problem.

Or, as Jay Finley Christ wrote in 1947:

> Good Sherlock took full many a crook
> In Adventures beyond compare;
> And the best of the lot is the crafty plot
> Of the man with the flaming hair.

Al Shaw (Chicago, Illinois) has been since 1971 a member and officer in many Sherlockian societies, including Hugo's Companions and the Hounds of the Baskerville (sic). He creates still life cards and calendars from his collection of pipes and Sherlockiana.

A CASE OF IDENTITY

SONIA FETHERSTON

There are a lot of ways to go about predicting the future. Clairvoyants rely on spiritual visions. Astrologers study the heavens. Diviners interpret omens and portents. Numerologists seek out patterns. "Extispicers" (confession: I've *always* hoped for a chance to use that word) read the entrails of dead animals. Seekers of what's-to-come consult pendulums, spirit boards, tarot cards, crystal balls, tea leaves, coffee grounds, runes and more. And Sherlockians? For us the answer is simple. To predict the rest of the Canon you just put your nose into the short story Arthur Conan Doyle called "A Case of Identity."

That's because although it is only the fifth Sherlock Holmes account ever published (*The Strand Magazine*, September 1891), this great little tale sparkles as a perfect example of literary prognostication. For the remaining fifty-five Holmes stories "A Case of Identity" proves itself a highly accurate fortune-teller. With its rich atmosphere, iconic props and amusing characters, this story is the wellspring for so much of what defines Holmes, Dr. Watson and their world. It is a remarkable achievement coming so early in the Canon, almost as though the author somehow penetrated the mists of time to anticipate how he would manage his creation for the next thirty-seven years. This makes it simply the best.

With its appearance in "A Case of Identity," 221B Baker Street becomes fixed in our collective consciousness. Outside is the "dull neutral-tinted London," while inside readers join Holmes and Watson in colorful, comfortable surroundings. So many Canonical tales will be launched from this sitting room—"The Six Napoleons," "The Five Orange Pips," *The Valley of Fear* and "Wisteria Lodge," to name but a few. Holmes and Watson are seated on either side of the fireplace, where flames will again dance for "Charles Augustus Milverton," "The Copper Beeches" and "The Resident Patient." Some of the Canon's most recognizable props are arranged around the room. The pipe rack, as in "The Blue Carbuncle" and "The Empty House," stands at attention on the mantelpiece. Holmes selects an old clay pipe this time; we'll see it again in stories like "The Priory School" and *The Hound of the Baskervilles*. On a nearby table the magnifying glass awaits the Master's touch. He will use it not only in "A Case of Identity," but in a handful of upcoming stories, including "The Norwood Builder," "The Golden Pince-Nez" and "Black Peter." Off to the side are his chemical experiments, reeking of hydrochloric acid. It's so like the "malodorous" experiments that linger in the air in "The Dying Detective," "The Naval Treaty" and "The Dancing Men." Visitors are ushered in and out by "the boy in buttons," identified in no less than four subsequent stories by his proper name: Billy. From the lad's presence we may infer the possibility of Mrs. Hudson, though regrettably she does not look in on this particular day.

In "A Case of Identity" Sherlock Holmes is wreathed in tobacco smoke. His fingers are steepled. He natters about monographs. These are all aspects of the detective that we will see time and again as the Canon unfolds. Here Holmes employs the technology of his day—in this instance a typewriter—to solve the problem at hand. Applying modern tools to crime fighting will occur again in "The Second Stain" and "The Six Napoleons" (photography), as well as "The Norwood Builder" (fingerprints). In "A Case of Identity" we're also treated to an early *tour de force* "reading" of a client. Following a trial run in the earlier story "The Red-Headed League," Holmes here deduces Mary Sutherland's short-sightedness (the dint of a *pince-nez* on her face), that she's a typist (an impression on her sleeve), the fact that she left her house in a hurry (her unmatched boots and a spot of ink upon her finger) and so on. This foreshadows other readings he will one day perform, such as upon the person of John Hector McFarlane in "The Norwood Builder," not to mention the hat of Henry Baker in "The Blue Carbuncle" and the pipe of Grant Munro in "The Yellow Face." Watson marvels at this feat, but Holmes simply dismisses it. "All this is amusing, though rather elementary," he shrugs.

Best of all is a magnificent example in "A Case of Identity" of one of those odd reveries to which Sherlock Holmes is periodically prone. He says to Watson:

> If we could fly out of that window hand in hand, hover over this great city, gently remove the roofs, and peep in at the queer things which are going on, the strange coincidences, the plannings, the cross-purposes, the wonderful chains of events, working through generations, and leading to the most *outré* results, it would make all fiction with its conventionalities and foreseen conclusions most stale and unprofitable.

This precedes other eccentric musings in "The Cardboard Box" ("What is the meaning of it, Watson? What object is served by this circle of misery?"), "The Naval Treaty" ("What a lovely thing a rose is"), "His Last Bow" ("There's an east wind coming") and more.

There are intriguing unchronicled tales: Dundas and his false teeth, along with a matter of some delicacy undertaken on behalf of Dutch royalty, are referenced in "A Case of Identity." Scores of other such accounts, noted but never fleshed out, are found elsewhere as the Canon continues on its way. We're shown means by which the powerful express their gratitude to Sherlock Holmes; the golden snuffbox and jeweled ring in "A Case of Identity" portend other gifts, such as the emerald tie-pin to be given by a certain gracious lady at the conclusion of "The Bruce-Partington Plans." The detective spouts a half-dozen classic Holmes-isms ("The larger crimes are apt to be the simpler," "Never trust to general impressions, my boy," "Oscillation upon the pavement always means an *affaire de coeur*") as he does throughout the balance of the Sherlockian chronicles. A most unconventional ("like a full-sailed merchant-man") damsel in distress, Mary asks Sherlock Holmes for help. Scan the horizon and there are several more unlikely maidens each in search of a champion, including bike-riding Violet Smith ("The Solitary Cyclist"), bruised-but-defiant Helen Stoner ("The Speckled Band"), and freckled-'n'-bobbed Violet Hunter ("The Copper Beeches"). Finally, this mystery turns on a disguise, anticipating that this device will be used in forthcoming Sherlockian stories such as "The Man With the Twisted Lip" and "The Solitary Cyclist."

Quite often disguises conceal bad people. Enter James Windibank. While he doesn't rise to the level of a Moriarty, Windibank nonetheless does a fine job preparing the way for a slew of other villains: Jephro Rucastle, James Wilder, Grimesby Roylott, Professor Presbury, Jacky Ferguson, Jack Stapleton, Josiah Amberley and Mortimer Tregennis, to name a few. Just like these fellows, Windibank is a member of the family he seeks to harm. When Windibank really rankles Sherlock Holmes, the detective reaches for a whip, as fiercely as he reaches for a cane when faced with the deadly adder in "The Speckled Band."

To be sure, "A Case of Identity" is more accurate at predicting the Canon's future course than are horoscopes, runes, or even entrails. As querents—those who seek to know what comes next—readers find that this brief tale foresees the larger, as-yet unrevealed, Canon. It shimmers impatiently on the verge of the Great Impending. There is simply none better. This is a superb starting point from which to explore other Sherlockian writings. For the same reason, it's also a satisfying place to end the journey.

Sonia Fetherston (Salem, Oregon) is a veteran Sherlockian scholar and a Baker Street Irregular. She received the Morley-Montgomery Award for 2011, and the BSI published her book *Prince of the Realm: The Most Irregular James Bliss Austin* in 2014.

THE BOSCOMBE VALLEY MYSTERY

FRAN MARTIN

As every Sherlockian knows, there are seventeen steps leading up to the famous rooms of 221B Baker Street. I have calculated that each adventure in the original Canon possesses a certain number of "steps" or elements which dictates its success as a classic Sherlock Holmes story. The more steps it contains, the better the story.

Without skipping any of these steps, "The Boscombe Valley Mystery" contains all the features we need to reach the landing with ease and ultimately seek out Sherlock Holmes and Dr. Watson to aid in a successful conclusion. Very few of the original stories can make such a claim. Let us climb the famous staircase together as we ponder each step from the initial invitation to the "view halloo" to the resulting revelation.

And so our climb has begun, and continues with the use of a telegram which Holmes has sent summoning Watson to join him on a case in the countryside. The message is short and to the point, and Holmes is confident that Watson will acquiesce. How could he refuse an adventure to where "air and scenery" are perfect?

Watson, who at this time is married and in active practice, packs a bag in no time at all, thanks to his campaign experience in Afghanistan, and is off to the station, with, of course, Mrs. Watson's encouragement and approval. (Although we are not told Mrs. Watson's first name, we can assume it is Mary, nee Morstan.)

Visualize, as this adventure will allow us to do, Holmes and Watson racing off to the scene of the crime in a private carriage at fifty-three and a half miles per hour. The carriage is littered with papers, and Holmes relates the facts of the case to Watson, his "conductor of luminosity". Holmes's attitude towards Watson is here shown in a favourable and welcome light. We are all, in a way, Watsons, and to be treated with respect and honour makes us beam. We, like the original Watson, are often left in the dark. We hear what Watson hears and see what Watson sees. Watson is not only a chronicler of the case, but a valued companion and friend. Holmes admits his reliance on Watson, and tells him that he values his advice.

We see Holmes don the "close-fitting cloth cap", which most people refer to as a deerstalker, and a long grey travelling-cloak. These items, which were worn only on excursions outside the city, have come to be iconic symbols, easily identifying Holmes to the Sherlockian and non-Sherlockian alike.

Holmes's belittling attitude towards the official police force is evident in this case. He is called in by Inspector Lestrade, the "pick of a bad lot", who admits that he is puzzled over the case. Lestrade does, however, display enough intelligence to call in the world's first and foremost consulting detective, despite Holmes's assurance that he and Watson may hit upon some obvious fact which may be not so obvious to Lestrade. Indeed, he goes so far as to say that Lestrade often "finds it hard to tackle the facts". Holmes has even less confidence in the local constabulary, stating that they are "either worthless or else biased."

Whether quoting or paraphrasing the Bible, Greek philosophers or Shakespeare, Holmes's many literary references are profound. How many times have we, ourselves, quoted or perhaps misquoted his words? He is the source of words which are recognized and readily attributed to him and often repeated elsewhere in print or other media. This story contains several well-known quotes: "Circumstantial evidence is a very tricky thing... moonshine is a brighter thing than fog... there is nothing more deceptive than an obvious fact."

Another element, or step, is the mention of a monograph. Sherlock Holmes has written several, and being an avid smoker himself ("I have a caseful of cigarettes here which need smoking"), it does not surprise us to learn that he has written a monograph entitled *Upon the Distinction Between the Ashes of the Various Tobaccos* in which he states that he is able to identify 140 varieties of tobacco ashes. By examining a cigar, he is able to discern whether a holder was used and if the cigar end was cut off or bitten.

Holmes enjoys astounding clients with his on-the-spot deductions upon first meeting them. In this case, he makes deductions upon Watson's appearance, not so much to impress him, but to demonstrate that he is able to observe details which would elude Lestrade.

Yet another appealing aspect of this story is its background. The plot originates in Australia, a seemingly lawless territory where criminals abound, a dark background rife with corruption, woe, secrets and mysterious signals that have followed its characters across the ocean to Mother England. This past keeps a tight grip on its players and refuses to let go, even after death—a past sullied with lies, deception, robbery, indiscretions, blackmail and murder.

How can we not tread on the step which mentions Watson's eye for the fair sex? Watson's descriptions of the women in the Canon are quite detailed and almost always flattering. It is surprising how many beautiful women pass through the pages of his writings. In "The Boscombe Valley Mystery", Watson paints a lovely picture of Miss Turner, noting her sweet facial features, her violet eyes and her pink cheeks, not to mention those lips! He goes so far as to call her "the most lovely woman I have ever seen in my life." Surely he has not forgotten the Mrs. back home?

The next step is the actual examination of the crime scene—a crucial step, one that we look for in each of the adventures of Sherlock Holmes. We can easily imagine a bloodhound on the trail of its prey. He is on the scent feverishly dashing about reading the herd of footprints left strewn about the scene of the crime. Heels, soles, square toes, twisted feet, feet firmly planted, pacing or racing, speak volumes. Let us linger upon this step as we become witness to a brilliant display of detection at its best. Let us watch as Holmes employs his exemplary powers. It is through careful observation that a series of deductions can evolve and ultimately bring a successful conclusion.

The use of the iconic magnifying lens is key. It is an instrument that every Sherlockian holds in their possession, a quintessential symbol of detection. Once this lens is taken out of the pocket, we know that even the minutest of details will be discovered. Criminal beware! Sticks, stones, leaves, nothing will go undetected and all are subject to scrutiny.

Having collected and sorted all the data, having pulled together all the clues and become satisfied as to the result, Holmes hands his findings to Lestrade. The response? Laughter. But we must forgive the Scotland Yarder for now. He has had little opportunity yet to work with Holmes and is unfamiliar with his methods.

We have now reached the landing, having explored each of the seventeen steps, stopping on each one to examine its significance, identifying how each one has a purpose and plays an integral role in the success of the story. We stand in awe before the great door. Sherlock Holmes has revealed all: Who had committed the crime, why and how it was executed. The result? Right has triumphed. What more could one ask?

This is a true mystery story in every sense of the word. After all, this is the only story in the original Canon that actually contains the word "mystery" in its title! But whether a story has seven of these steps or seventeen, every one has its merits. Who better to climb the staircase with than another Sherlockian?

Fran Martin (Vancouver, British Columbia) is an administrator in an accounting firm, a grandmother, a Master Bootmaker, and president of the Stormy Petrels of British Columbia as well as keeping up links with Sherlockians on the west coast of the United States.

THE FIVE ORANGE PIPS

CLIFFORD S. GOLDFARB

To make my point that "The Five Orange Pips" is the best of the Canon, not only must I disagree with my 59 fellow contributors, I must also disagree with Arthur Conan Doyle himself, who rated it as his seventh best: "though it is short it has a certain dramatic quality of its own" ("My Favourite Sherlock Holmes Adventures", *Strand*, June 1927). Other readers have consistently rated it lower. It was listed as 23rd in a poll of the 56 short stories in "Rating The Canon" by Randall Stock in the *Baker Street Journal* in 1999. Isaac Asimov, in a rather humourless essay in *The Baker Street Dozen* (1987), picks apart every aspect of the story, from its opening to its plot to its consistency—in my mind totally missing the spirit of the tale. It seems to have reached its high at number seven and has been declining in popularity ever since. Nevertheless, I am not entirely alone in my task—Richard W. Clarke has written that the case is one of the finest ("The Story I Like Best", *Baker Street Journal* 1948).

This lack of respect may be because Holmes, after having correctly theorized the reason for the two earlier deaths and the nature of the looming death sentence on young Openshaw, and having determined the location and travel methods of the killers, then shockingly fails to take the simplest of precautions, resulting in Openshaw's murder. "The Five Orange Pips" in fact may be Holmes's greatest failure. But what a glorious vehicle Conan Doyle has contrived to carry this tragic negligence!

It amazes me how little respect this story has garnered from otherwise discerning readers. It is clearly one of the most underrated cases in the Canon. It has atmosphere enough for any other two stories. It has, more than almost any other case, all of the required canonical elements, including one of the best openings, with three separate but complete passages, any one of which would be sufficient.

It begins with a list of some of the most intriguing unwritten cases: "the adventure of the Paradol Chamber, of the Amateur Mendicant Society, who held a luxurious club in the lower vault of a furniture warehouse, of the facts connected with the loss of the British bark Sophy Anderson, of the singular adventures of the Grice Patersons in the island of Uffa, and finally of the Camberwell poisoning case." The last of these may be unique, in that Watson goes on to explain how Holmes solved the case—"by winding up the dead man's watch, to prove that it had been wound up two hours before". As a bonus later in the story there is yet another unwritten case, the Tankerville Club scandal. Following this classic opening, we then have not one, but two more scene-setting passages, beginning with one of Conan Doyle's finest "atmospheric" openings:

> It was in the latter days of September, and the equinoctial gales had set in with exceptional violence. All day the wind had screamed and the rain had beaten against the windows, so that even here in the heart of great, hand-made London we were forced to raise our minds for the instant from the routine of life and to recognize the presence of those great elemental forces which shriek at mankind through the bars of his civilization, like untamed beasts in a cage. As evening drew in, the storm grew higher and louder, and the wind cried and sobbed like a child in the chimney.

In case this is insufficient, it is in turn followed by yet another classic passage, with rare biographical information about both men:

> Sherlock Holmes sat moodily at one side of the fireplace cross-indexing his records of crime, while I at the other was deep in one of Clark Russell's fine sea-stories until the howl of the gale from without seemed to blend with the text, and the splash of the rain to lengthen out into the long swash of the sea waves. My wife was on a visit to her mother's, and for a few days I was a dweller once more in my old quarters at Baker Street.
>
> "Why," said I, glancing up at my companion, "that was surely the bell. Who could come to-night? Some friend of yours, perhaps?"
>
> "Except yourself I have none," he answered. "I do not encourage visitors."

In later published versions "mother" became "aunt", both words inspiring generations of Sherlockian scholars to speculate on the marital adventures of John Watson. We also learn what we had begun to suspect, that Holmes is misanthropic. In fact, given the number of comments by Sherlockian scholars on this case, it is clearly one of the most read, even if not the most enjoyed, tales in the Canon.

A few paragraphs later this pair of classic openings is followed by "I have been beaten four times—three times by men, and once by a woman." Of course, here Holmes is beaten again—pipped at the post, as it were—by a group of men. A few lines later we have another fine Sherlockismus: "I am the last court of appeal."

Once we get into the case we are rewarded with fairly lengthy references to two earlier tales, *A Study in Scarlet* and *The Sign of Four*—it is unusual to have that many (although the same two tales are briefly mentioned in "The Cardboard Box", and "A Case of Identity" happens to mention the same two plus "A Scandal in Bohemia"). Then, towards the unfortunate climax, to round out the already generous supply of classical canonical elements, we are given this memorable Sherlockismus on Holmes's method of reasoning:

> "The ideal reasoner... would, when he had once been shown a single fact in all its bearings, deduce from it not only all the chain of events which led up to it but also all the results which would follow from it."

A reference to the great zoologist, Georges, Baron Cuvier (1769-1832), founder of comparative anatomy and palaeontology, completes this little demonstration of Holmes's observational and reasoning powers.

This is only the seventh Holmes tale in order of publication—we are still seeing Conan Doyle molding Holmes and Watson into their fully developed characters. At this point, we would not even need a story to conclude that this is one of the best of the Holmes tales. But there is a story, one which offers something for every category of reader:

- For those who prefer their Holmes tales to have actual crimes, there are three separate murders here—all of which are found by coroners' inquests to be either suicide or accidents.
- For mystery lovers, the reclusive uncle, Elias Openshaw, with his locked attic room.
- For believers in the infallibility of Holmes, his total and inexplicable failure to protect the life of his client—in fact, like Nero, he fiddled, while Openshaw drowned.
- For history lovers, a passable, if truncated, history of the first manifestation of the Ku Klux Klan.
- For librarians and bibliophiles, the revelation that Holmes's bookshelf contained the rare and previously uncatalogued *American Encyclopaedia*.
- For lawyers, Fordham (from Horsham, in Surrey), a supposedly competent solicitor who allows a potential beneficiary to witness a will, thereby probably invalidating the intended gift (and incidentally, for me, the source of my investiture in the Baker Street Irregulars).
- For technology buffs, the introduction of the Openshaw unbreakable bicycle tire.

- For lovers of classic detective fiction, the unlikely plot that members of an essentially defunct criminal organization would need to commit three serial murders, just to recover possibly incriminatory papers from the victims, who obviously had no intention of using them; that they would still want the papers 14 years after the event; and that they would make no attempt to actually recover the papers.
- And finally, for all of us, the disappointing use of a *deus ex machina*—if we can apply such a term to "equinoctial gales" (and how many short stories have two references to "equinoctial gales"?)—to bring the villains to justice.

Clifford S. Goldfarb (Toronto, Ontario) is author of *The Great Shadow: Arthur Conan Doyle, Brigadier Gerard and Napoleon*, and co-author, with Hartley R. Nathan, of *Investigating Sherlock Holmes*. A Baker Street Irregular and Master Bootmaker, he is chairman of the Friends of the Arthur Conan Doyle Collection at the Toronto Reference Library.

THE MAN WITH
THE TWISTED LIP

MARK ALBERSTAT

"The Man with the Twisted Lip" is not only the best story in the Sherlockian Canon. It is the best story Conan Doyle wrote, and he wrote a lot. The story has everything: Watson's comfy home life; damsels in distress; a midnight ride with Sherlock Holmes; the seedier side of Victorian life and Victorian London; and a grand reveal at the end of the story. What reader, Sherlockian or otherwise, could ask for anything more, or have more delivered in only 9,000 words?

This is also a mystery in which the reader can follow along and match wits with Sherlock Holmes. This is a true fair-play story. In 1930, during the so called Golden Age of Detective Fiction, a group of well-known novelists, Agatha Christie and Dorothy Sayers among them, created a nine-point list of ways a mystery story must provide fair play. Conan Doyle wrote this story decades before this group formed or even thought of the idea. This story is not only the best; it is ahead of its time. In this Holmes adventure there are no facts hidden from the reader, no inside or arcane knowledge that only Holmes has, and no conversations with informants or sources that we are not privy to. In this story, first published in 1891 in the *Strand Magazine*, Watson and Holmes lay out the facts of the case and ask us to solve it alongside Holmes.

To Sherlockians reading the story today, the opening scene is familiar: a Victorian sitting room with Watson enjoying an evening at home. The address, however, isn't the expected 221B Baker Street, but Watson's house after his marriage to Mary Morstan and the establishment of his own home and practice. For readers in 1891, this was only the sixth Holmes story to be printed, and they were not yet familiar with the caneback chair, cigars in the coal scuttle and other items in the Holmes and Watson sitting room we now know so well.

Doyle makes this story relevant and real when in the opening two sentences he mentions the Victorian interest in opium and a well-known book on the subject, Thomas De Quincey's 1821 *Confessions of an English Opium Eater*. Watson also tells us the tale began in June 1889. These three points are another aspect that helps elevate the story from the rabble to the great. This opening firmly places us in Victorian times, an era all Sherlockians love; many of us read the stories specifically to be taken to that time and place. This adventure also takes us to the real Victorian world of opium dens, beggars and the growing sprawl of suburban London. It isn't the perfect 1895 that some Sherlockians like to think about, although it is as illusory as an addict's dream.

The damsels in distress in this story are Kate Whitney and Mrs. Neville St. Clair. Kate Whitney is the wife of Isa Whitney, the only opium user we actually meet in this story that is so heavily focused around an opium den. Although usually, in our favourite dynamic duo, Holmes is the man of action, this story begins with Watson showing he is far from a second fiddle. When Watson learns that his friend Isa Whitney is missing and most likely in an drug-induced haze at a seedy opium den called The Bar of Gold, Watson does not call for Holmes, as Holmes often does for Watson, but strikes out alone to the "vile alley, lurking behind the high wharves" of London's east end. Showing us Watson as a man of action, and not the passive follower, has to be another distinction for this story, more evidence that it is the best.

The story also reveals the deep trust and friendship that has developed between Holmes and Watson by this time. When Holmes asks Watson to accompany him on his latest adventure instead of returning home to his wife and comfortable home life, Watson writes a quick note to her and the pair set off for Kent. Watson not only trusts his friend but must also crave the excitement, mystery and companionship that another exploit with Holmes will surely entail.

There can be no doubt that one of the attractions of all the stories for Sherlockians and readers around the world is the relationship between these two Victorian gentlemen. Despite Watson's initial act of courage in rushing to The Bar of Gold to retrieve his friend, he has very little to do in this adventure other than be Holmes's companion. Before Watson comes along, Holmes has made no headway in the mystery. For some unknown or unstated reason, he is staying in Kent at the home of the missing man. Holmes takes the opportunity of the seven-mile drive to bring Watson up to date on the case and recite and order the details in his own mind.

Overnight, with Watson asleep in a bed beside him, Holmes sits on "a sort of Eastern divan, upon which he perched himself cross-legged," and is able to see through the clouds of the mystery—and the haze of his own tobacco smoke—to the solution. With Watson by his side, asleep or awake, Holmes is a better detective. Watson clarifies Holmes's mind and the detective is once again able to form the deductions for which he has become famous. This story clearly illustrates that Watson is far more than a biographer; he is the whetstone that sharpens Holmes's mind.

The final point that makes this story the best is the final reveal. This story shows Holmes at his showmanlike best, at least for these first few opening adventures. With two quick rubs across the beggar's face, Neville St. Clair is revealed, the mystery solved, the onlookers left gasping and Holmes standing in triumph.

It is all of these points, combined into one story, one adventure, firmly settled in Victorian England, that makes "The Man with the Twisted Lip" the finest Sherlock Holmes story penned by Conan Doyle.

Mark Alberstat (Halifax, Nova Scotia) is founder of the Sherlockian society there, the Spence Munros, and co-editor of *Canadian Holmes*, the quarterly journal of the Bootmakers of Toronto. He has written extensively about Sherlock Holmes and sport.

THE ADVENTURE OF
THE BLUE CARBUNCLE

MONICA M. SCHMIDT

When I was five years old, I picked up a well-worn book from my family's home library: a children's edition of *The Mysteries of Sherlock Holmes*. The volume included slightly abridged versions of three stories: "The Blue Carbuncle," "The Speckled Band," and "The Red-Headed League." These tales were selected as being the most user-friendly for younger readers, and incidentally are among those that many Sherlockians identify as being among their favorite short stories. As I read, I became enthralled with the yellow fog of Victorian London and this singular sleuth who was a little prickly on the surface, but ultimately kind-hearted enough to help those in need by solving their problems. These stories captivated my interest and sparked a life-long love affair with "the man who never lived, and so can never die" (as Vincent Starrett wrote).

"The Speckled Band" and "The Red Headed League" are tales that rank among the favorites of Arthur Conan Doyle and Sherlockians alike. But although it is rated highly by Sherlockians, Conan Doyle did not have much love for "The Blue Carbuncle." This is where I diverge from his views: for me, the story is exceptional. It's accessible and easily re-readable. The story is the origin of minutiae that is of particular interest to devotees of Sherlock Holmes. Unlike many other cases, the trail of clues is easy to track. But, ultimately, the narrative contains the best illustration of how Holmes's moral code is a balance between justice and compassion. All of this blends together seamlessly and illustrates why "The Blue Carbuncle" stands above all other Sherlock Holmes stories.

Holidays have a way of motivating a person to ritualistically revisit their favorite stories time and time again. An example of this is the annual Christmas-time airing and viewing of *A Christmas Story* (1983) or *It's a Wonderful Life* (1946). As the events of "The Blue Carbuncle" are set two days after Christmas, revisiting the story or the Granada television episode during the winter holiday has become a widely-adopted Sherlockian tradition. I have subjected my family and friends to Christmas day viewings of the Granada version for 23 years and counting—a ritual that began long before my knowledge that other Sherlockians were doing the same. No other Sherlockian narrative ties itself so specifically to a season and invites repeated readings or viewings.

In the opening paragraph of "The Blue Carbuncle," Watson identifies Holmes's dressing gown as being purple. But Holmes has a blue one in "The Man with the Twisted Lip." In "The Empty House," and "The Bruce-Partington Plans," Holmes owns a *mouse*-colored dressing gown. Sherlockians, by their nature, like to focus on the minor details found in the Canon, and a bit of trivia like this can come in handy when attempting to best others at a test of knowledge. Beyond that, this seemingly innocuous bit of information has great significance to those within the Sherlockian community. The three colors of Holmes's dressing gowns were adopted by Christopher Morley as the official colors of The Baker Street Irregulars.

In "The Blue Carbuncle," we see Holmes at the height of his deductive prowess—inferring facts about the life of Henry Baker from the hat brought to him by the commissionaire Peterson. While some of his deductions seem a little outlandish on the surface ("a man with so large a brain must have something in it"), everything is precisely on: intelligence, a sense of foresight, that the man had fallen on hard times, and that he and his wife were on the rocks. There's not another passage in the Canon that better displays not only how minor details that most would overlook can provide insight into the inner workings of a person's life, but why Holmes might possibly have been burned as a witch if he had lived during an earlier time period. It also serves as a proper foreshadowing of how Holmes's attention to detail will help bring forth a satisfactory conclusion to the mystery of the jewel in the crop of the goose. (Geese don't actually have a crop, a pretty significant forensic blunder for our great detective.)

This story highlights a full proper investigation by Holmes. Watson (and the reader) can easily follow the trail as Holmes tracks various leads and clues. Peterson presents Holmes with the mystery of the beautiful blue carbuncle found in the goose that formerly belonged to Mr. Henry Baker. (Carbuncles, or garnets, appear in many colors, but blue is not one of them.) The investigation begins with finding and questioning Henry Baker and following any leads that will bring Holmes closer to discovering to the origin of the goose, which should, in turn, shed light onto the identity of the thief. The trail leads first to the Alpha Inn where Baker got the goose, and then to Breckinridge, the man who sold the goose to the

Alpha Inn. When questioning Breckinridge, Holmes relies on the same deductive reasoning showcased in the opening paragraphs of the story: he reasons that Breckinridge is a gambling man when he observes a betting slip in his pocket. By posing his questions in the context of a bet, Breckinridge inadvertently betrays the name of the woman who raised the geese. This is a vital clue Holmes and Watson intended to follow up the next morning, and one that most likely would have led them to the true culprit.

That is, until Holmes and Watson observe another man attempting, much less successfully, to elicit information from Breckinridge. This shows Watson (and the reader) that Holmes is not too proud to capitalize on the occasional stroke of luck. The interchange between Holmes and this fellow, James Ryder of the Hotel Cosmopolitan, produces two of the most quotable quotes from the Canon. "It is always awkward doing business with an alias," says Holmes when James Ryder initially gives him a false name. When Ryder wonders how this stranger knows all these details about theft, Holmes replies with authority, "My name is Sherlock Holmes. It is my business to know what others do not know." (That phrase is enough to send shivers down the spines of evildoers everywhere!) After confronting Ryder, Holmes gives him an opportunity to explain the full story. And then, Holmes makes a decision that we did not expect: he lets Ryder go free despite knowing he is the true culprit.

What is noteworthy for me is that "The Blue Carbuncle" is the first story in which Holmes exhibits his own concept of justice. He follows the spirit, rather than the letter, of the law, and ultimately true justice prevails. As Holmes tells Ryder to get out of his sight, he tells Watson, "I am not retained by the police to supply their deficiencies"—that is, because he is not officially connected with the police, he is under no obligation to bring the culprit to full legal justice. By not turning Ryder in, Holmes is technically committing a felony (as is noted in the story), but he recognizes something that the punishment-focused criminal justice system often forgets: compassion and mercy.

Punishment for a crime should be exacted if there is malice aforethought and the potential for recidivism. Holmes recognizes that Ryder did not intend to harm Horner when he accused him of the theft. He accepts that Ryder's act of thievery was an impulsive and opportunistic crime—not something that he had been planning or scheming for weeks. And he acknowledges that Ryder is very unlikely to commit another crime of this nature—the fright of being caught by Holmes is likely to set Ryder on the straight path for the rest of his life. By showing compassion, Holmes ensures that the legal case against the falsely accused Horner would fall apart for lack of evidence and eye-witness testimony.

In the decision to let Ryder go, two lives are saved instead of one. Holmes takes it upon himself to give Ryder another chance—making a judgment that no societal good will be served by entrenching Ryder in the system and making him a jailbird for life. A lesser man than Holmes would have followed the letter of the law and made sure Ryder was punished for his wrong-doing. Holmes exhibits justice tempered with mercy, and his actions at the end of "The Blue Carbuncle," indicate that he answers to a higher moral code. And this is a trait for which we should all look in our protagonists and personal heroes.

When all of these examples are combined, the reader is left with a nuanced mystery, with an increasingly complicated protagonist, that is fun and interesting at multiple levels of analysis. This narrative passes the test of time for both novice and seasoned Sherlockians, as well as casual readers. And that is why "The Blue Carbuncle" is my favorite.

Monica M. Schmidt (Solon, Iowa) is president of the Younger Stamfords in Iowa City and a member of the Adventuresses of Sherlock Holmes, the Hounds of the Baskerville (sic), and other societies. She works as a mental health counselor specializing in substance abuse.

THE ADVENTURE OF
THE SPECKLED BAND

JOHN C. SHERWOOD

Sir Arthur Conan Doyle told us which Sherlock Holmes tale was his best. "There is the grim snake story, 'The Speckled Band.' That I am sure will be on every list," Doyle wrote in response to the *Strand Magazine*'s 1927 request for his view. We now propose to explore whether he was correct. (Spoiler alert: *He was.*)

The Baker Street Irregulars voted with Doyle in 1944 and again in 1954, as Bliss Austin relates in *The Baker Street Dozen* (1987). Doyle's 1892 story led to his own stage version. Other dramatizations followed in all known media excepting the clay tablet. Individual results vary, but for innumerable readers "The Speckled Band" became the gateway tale to Sherlockiana.

The scion society Watson's Tin Box annually challenges Maryland seventh-graders to read this story, and publishes their best essays in its journal. The students heap praise on the rocketing pace, that distant whistle, the locked-room death, burst-open door, bent poker, repulsive stepdad, cheetah, baboon, dark vigil and lethal climax. How could they not?

Of course, seventh-graders don't recognize this jewel's more, shall we say, adult facets. The biggest baboon in the room is Grimesby Roylott, an immoral slab of beef whose intimate authority over his stepdaughters' fate looms dangerously large in minds alert to his sexual menace. There's also that deliciously awkward, deliberately racy moment when Holmes blithely announces his plan to spend the night in Helen Stoner's bedroom. What's more, after all is revealed, the psychic symbol of a snake having slithered toward the chaste maidens in their boudoir lingers in the mind, potent and unsettling.

These features combine to make this tale the most vivid, compelling and memorable of the shorter chronicles, even after 124 years. Reflect, please: When your friends have asked where to start their individual

Sherlockian journeys, haven't you recommended this story? Its brevity, clarity and appeal are undeniable.

Or are they? You're wise to be skeptical, so it's time to confront—and mend—your own personal disappointment with "The Speckled Band."

Face it, you were bothered when you learned there is no "Indian swamp adder." After all, it's a fictitious creature with impossible skills that Doyle admittedly devised to serve the plot. It may be the only objective reason why you might dismiss this story as the best.

The Baker Street Dozen even includes a cluck-clucking, Great Game-style apology, musing that Watson misidentified the snake. It's as though this otherwise mighty Sherlockian titan had an Achilles heel tripping up its believability and ratiocinative worthiness. But that alleged weakness is no such thing. It's essential to what gives the story its enduring power and a fixed niche in the pantheon. It presents Holmes exactly as Doyle came to see him, and makes "The Speckled Band" the best polished lens through which we can view Holmes's reason for being.

My thesis: After testing Holmes's evolving character in two novels, Doyle's storytelling skills reached their apex when he conceived this updated gothic legend, in which a perfect knight for the modern age triumphs over supernatural terror and restores divine justice.

Doyle's luck was to be born into a Roman Catholic family, so he couldn't avoid the iconography of Catholic belief, history and symbolism. He broke with traditional faith while in his 20s—as Daniel Stashower related in *Teller of Tales* (1999)—but the Church's values and imagery remained etched on his mind. Almost from the start of Doyle's writing career, he manipulated themes drawn from his former faith. Traditional symbols emerged in his work persistently, looming up as apparitions with lasting subliminal impact. Today, we can peek beneath the surface of some of our favorite canonical scenes and find these robust, archetypal foundations.

In *A Study in Scarlet* (1887), the youthfully defiant Doyle criticized intense faith through a hero with no tie to faith whatever. This early Holmes—glib, outgoing, scientifically informed—represented reason and law in contrast to a form of faith depicted as irrational and savage. Three years later in *The Sign of Four*, Doyle re-invented Holmes as a monkish recluse who rises above his personal failings to fight sinister outward forces, leaving his friend Watson to win the maiden's hand. These ideas were rooted in a literary tradition Doyle declared outright:

> "It is a romance!" cried Mrs. Forrester. "An injured lady, half a million in treasure, a black cannibal, and a wooden-legged ruffian. They take the place of the conventional dragon or wicked earl."
> "And two knight-errants to the rescue," added Miss Morstan.

Knight and squire, more precisely. The faith on which Doyle was reared had produced this heroic emblem, and in his youth he'd seen endless artworks representing the persistent battle between good and evil— the soldier of God spearing a terrible serpent to rescue maiden purity from corrupted evil. This ancient formula boiled with a heady mix of chivalry and high-minded motifs. After the invention of his first novels, Doyle tested the short-story format by developing his original champion and fitting him into that world, bit by bit.

In "A Scandal in Bohemia," Doyle declared Holmes's mastery over carnal passion; in accord with chivalric tradition, no woman in distress should fear him. A saintly hero would require another enemy worthy of *Study*'s religious zealots and *Sign*'s death-breathing Tonga. Now, with this shorter story, we've no evidence to show whether he drew motifs from some unconscious wellspring or from personal research, but the picture he drew is familiar to anyone who's studied the lineage of the dragon family.

In Joseph Campbell's *The Hero with a Thousand Faces* (1949) is an image of a 9th century B.C. Assyrian sculpture, showing a man-like sun-god hurling lance-like thunderbolts at a dragon. In content it's the same as an Egyptian depiction of the sun god Ra, who morphed into a cat and knifed the demonic snake Apep while traveling nightly through the underworld. Reptile, cat, weapon—all re-emerged in the myth's European versions. There, the saintly knight and his loyal squire typically would meet bizarre creatures before entering a cave to spear a dragon. (See *Yvain, the Knight of the Lion,* by 12th century poet Chrétien de Troyes.)

To bring this ancient notion into the 19th century, it was necessary to imagine a serpent with weird, fakir-induced abilities. The snake should breathe in an airless safe, drink indigestible milk, hear its master's musical commands with deaf ears and destroy its victims without detectable marks. It had to be supernatural.

Doyle's knight and squire would summon their courage, approach the forbidding estate guarded by bizarre creatures, and stand ready in the grim chamber to await the Unknown. In single combat, the knight would drive the serpent back against its master. The tyrant would be thwarted and the intended victim restored to her legacy of marriage and fertility.

At story's end, Holmes makes no logical quip. Instead, he paraphrases Ecclesiastes 10:8 and Proverbs 26:27. He'd begun literary life as faith's challenger, but "The Speckled Band" transforms him into a soldier of God, championing the divinity of reason. The secular avenger has become a spiritual messenger, too.

This is *myth*, replete with all the flavors of the ancient recipe nourishing the human spirit. It's an exercise in emotional education through the fairy tale, as described in Bruno Bettelheim's *The Uses of Enchant-ment* (1976). This story's innovation is that it's a swiftly related, forensic detective story—but symbolically remains the Canon's most crafted moral fable.

Through some marvel, Doyle anticipated Bettelheim and molded this rough psychological magic with concise, instinctive cunning. As a result, this amazing story leaves readers universally satisfied, inwardly changed. Its benediction lets us switch off our nightstand lamps and face the dark without fear.

No other canonical tale achieves this so powerfully. That's why Doyle declared it his best, and why fans have tended to agree for gener-ations. Down deep, we all fear that demons may devour us. "The Speck-led Band" reminds us that they can be driven back to their doom—and that we have a friend who knows how.

John C. Sherwood (Marshall, Michigan) has been a professional Sherlock Holmes impersonator since 1987. This thesis was presented initially in articles that appeared in *Irene's Cabinet*, the annual publica-tion of Watson's Tin Box of Ellicott City, Maryland, which he served as Gasogene XVI.

THE ADVENTURE OF THE ENGINEER'S THUMB

TAMAR ZEFFREN

"I will bite my thumb at them; which is a disgrace to them, if they bear it." (Romeo and Juliet I.i)

"The Engineer's Thumb" does not shrink from asserting itself. Its opening sentence claims distinction: the "problem... of Mr. Hatherley's thumb" is one of two "problems" that Watson industriously brings to the attention of Sherlock Holmes. Ensconced in domestic life, having resolutely "returned to civil practice and... finally abandoned Holmes in his Baker Street rooms" (doth the Army doctor protest too much?), Watson takes pains to establish his distance from the remarkable exploits he enjoyed with the world's premier consulting detective. However, that distance collapses almost immediately when the doctor's maid taps on the window, to arouse him to a patient in need.

Watson's longstanding expectations—and rhetoric—of suspense surface almost immediately upon this summons. He prepares in haste, since "railway cases were seldom trivial." En route to his consulting room, Watson passes the guard. He notes that the guard refers to the as-yet-unseen patient as if he "was some strange creature which he had caged up in my room." And indeed, our first encounter with the patient, "Mr. Victor Hatherley, hydraulic engineer," affords readers the impression of a barely-mastered hysteria. The patient is "quietly dressed"—which then vividly contrasts with the hysterical laugh he unleashes. This laugh, "a high, ringing note" that galvanizes Watson's medical instincts, summons up, for this reader, the imprint of a hyena's maniacal chortle. "[S]trange creature" does not appear to be wide of the mark.

The unvarnished title ensures that there is no ambiguity about the nature of the client's injury. The wound he presents to Watson shakes even the good doctor's "hardened nerves." The visceral reality (in every sense of the word) of Hatherley's missing thumb, "hacked or torn right out from the roots," heightens this story's primal texture. The juxtaposition of primal behavior with expected comportment in the public sphere—deployed later to distressing extremes in "The Creeping Man"—finds subtler but no less chilling purchase in our present tale.

This story finely plays upon the ramifications of Hatherley's disfigurement. To wit: an engineer in Victorian-era England was associated with a profession that accrued tremendous prestige. Its sphere of influence, as one of the bulwarks supporting Great Britain's ascension to the most influential trading nation in the world at this juncture, was capacious. Contrasted with the exponentially expanding scope of his chosen profession, Hatherley the engineer, shorn of one of his opposable digits, embodies not only acute physical distress, but as well the despairing portrait of a specialist facing the possibility that his future utility is compromised, perhaps permanently.

Applying this reading effectively underscores the aptness of Watson's immediate suggestion to his patient to relay the bizarre circumstances of his injury to Sherlock Holmes. Once ensconced in Holmes's study, Hatherley, the engineer *sans* thumb, declares that he "has felt another man" since undergoing Watson's attentions. But the specter of emasculation recedes for the moment as he finally describes his harrowing experience to Holmes and Watson, who "listened in silence to the strange story."

Of note is Hatherley's opening description of himself as "an orphan and a bachelor," which further underscores his isolation and the stark ramifications of the injury he has suffered. While the reader may respond that losing a thumb pales in comparison with more comprehensive wounds, the narrative of "The Engineer's Thumb" economically limns the potential bleak outcome for the victim. An unmoored man whose professional prospects have been damaged is a pitiable character indeed. Hatherley's unhinged laughter demonstrates that he is already severely aware of the fate that could await him. The account does not flinch from that sad consequence—and in so doing, this irregular episode acquires an additional timbre of poignancy.

Hatherley's first encounter with his new client, Colonel Lysander Stark, presents some interesting features. Stark is an unsettling amalgam: fleshless but seeming not ill; flattering to the young entrepreneur but then making seemingly capricious demands. The trace of a German accent that Hatherley notices strikes another note of unease, perhaps intentionally thematically linking this story with "A Scandal in Bohemia," published the previous year, and its notably mediocre King of Bohemia.

Colonel Stark, like the absurd King, floridly insists on secrecy: "absolute and complete silence, before, during and after." Here again, the motif of the ridiculous yet sinister German appears—and this story demonstrates its thematic coherence with other canonical installments, including "His Last Bow."

The specter of foreignness is deployed again when Hatherley arrives at what he has been informed is Colonel Stark's estate in Eyford. When he enters the estate, he glimpses a woman, who addresses the Colonel in "a foreign tongue." Now, the unease occasioned by hearing a foreign tongue is tempered somewhat by the speaker, a pretty, well-dressed woman. I take this interchange as a stylistic nod towards Dr. Watson's tendency to be attracted, and even distracted, by a feminine presence. When the woman passionately warns him to leave before it is too late, Hatherley's subsequent rationalization of the woman's behavior as potential "monomania" adds another facet to the treatment and depiction of women in the Canon. When this same woman rescues him, Hatherley's description of her deservedly changes to "the same good friend whose warning I had so foolishly rejected." This story is of interest alone for this rendering, providing as it does an instructive contrast to Holmes and Watson's possible behavior in such circumstances.

The hydraulic press, the monstrous object of Colonel Stark's obsession, and the intended torture and murder device of Victor Hatherley, adds a peculiar insult to the engineer's pronounced injury. An expected instrument of Hatherley's profession is turned against him, to near-fatal effect. To make matters even worse, this grievance comes at the behest of outsiders. "Who were these German people," Hatherley wonders aloud in his recollection, "and what were they doing living in this strange, out-of-the-way place?" While at Eyford, Hatherley is even unable to distinguish cardinal directions. Stark does not just present an uncanny visage and behavior; he and his co-conspirators are even able to disrupt the British engineer's sense of direction, by driving horses six miles in, and then six miles back over the same route.

The presence of the dastardly and murderous German is problematized by the selfless actions of this unnamed foreign woman—and, though Hatherley never witnesses it, the presumed actions of the other man at the estate, Mr. Ferguson (who the narrative assumes is also English). The various manifestations of Hatherley's latent (and then not-so-latent) xenophobia in this story contribute to its compelling effect.

Fittingly for a story in which Holmes's solution includes the insight that the victim was conveyed around in circles to create confusion, this account concludes by returning to the anguished fate that likely greets this client. Holmes's response to the beleaguered engineer, after they and the Scotland Yard inspectors have discovered the estate in ruin and the villains absconded, is a near-glib assertion that now Hatherley easily has "the reputation of being excellent company for the remainder of your existence."

Hatherley's mutilation, the loss of the promised funds, his forlorn professional prospects (bare even prior to his injury!), will likely continue to exercise significant control over the remainder of his existence. The narrative does not trouble further with Hatherley's grave concerns. This final denial of even patent sympathy from Holmes to the engineer exemplifies this tale's bracing, even brutal, candor about the ramifications of such a criminal act and the inadequacy of even a successful criminal investigation to remedy such ills. And, thus, much like the besieged protagonist, "The Engineer's Thumb" clamors for deserved attention among its canonical brethren.

Tamar Zeffren (New York, New York) is a digital archivist, a member of the Adventuresses of Sherlock Holmes and the Baker Street Babes, and an inveterate volunteer for the Baker Street Irregulars Trust.

THE ADVENTURE OF THE NOBLE BACHELOR

DERRICK BELANGER

The quintessential Sherlock Holmes story has to include all the aspects we love about the world's first consulting detective. It must have a mystery set in London, it must have Holmes act like Holmes and solve that mystery using his seemingly otherworldly genius, and it must be told by Dr. John H. Watson, his Boswell. Going a few steps further, the absolute best Holmes stories have a sense of humor, whether it is from the detective (the hysterical quote about the curious incident of the dog in the night contained in "Silver Blaze" is an excellent example) or from another character (no character is perhaps more comic than the bumbling Jabez Wilson in "The Red Headed League"). The very best also have a strong sense of social justice, of Holmes taking on royalty or the upper class and knocking them down to size while lifting up those who are socially maligned by society (such as lifting up Irene Adler and knocking down the King of Bohemia in "A Scandal in Bohemia"). Not all Holmes stories include all aspects of the quintessential Holmes story—indeed only a handful do—and of that handful, the one story that rises to the top and should be noted as the best of the Canon is the delightful tale known as "The Noble Bachelor."

The story of the "Noble Bachelor" follows the Arthur Conan Doyle formula for a great Holmes adventure. We begin the story at 221B Baker Street, where a client brings a case to Holmes and retells much of the action of the story. The case appears to be a puzzler which leaves a representative of Scotland Yard (this time Inspector Lestrade) drawing a completely wrong solution to the crime. Holmes investigates the scene of the crime (this time around Hyde Park, though interestingly enough, he addresses matters not by going to the actual location but by hearing retellings of the case from persons involved), and, by using his powerful reasoning skills, is able to show that what appeared to be a complicated matter had a rather simple and routine solution.

While "The Adventure of the Noble Bachelor" follows the ordinary pattern of a Holmes tale, it is the plot and details of the narrative which allow it to rise to the extraordinary. As in all the best Holmes stories, the tale begins at Baker Street, this time with Watson laid up, his war wound affected by the rainy London weather. Watson notes an envelope upon the table with a crest from a noble correspondent. Holmes informs Watson that the envelope is from his client, one of the highest of the aristocracy. Watson congratulates Holmes on this, but Holmes dismisses his friend and says, "I assure you, Watson…, that the status of my client is a matter of less moment to me than the interest of his case." As always, status means very little to Holmes, and as illustrated in this story, the class system often finds itself the loser at the end of an adventure.

As the narrative develops, we learn that the client, Lord St. Simon, is trying to discover the whereabouts of his American bride, Miss Hatty Doran, who mysteriously disappeared on the morning of their wedding. Lord St. Simon is described by Watson as having dress which "was careful to the verge of foppishness," and comes across as a pompous stuffed shirt. St. Simon describes his wife as *nouveau riche* ("twenty before her father became a rich man"), and also "a tomboy, with a strong nature, wild and free." The implication is that he has taken this wild lower-class woman who stumbled into her money and tamed her, and that she is "at bottom a noble woman." Yet, she has vanished. Perhaps Lord St. Simon was not so great at taming as he thought he was?

The only lead the police are following is that of Miss Flora Millar, a woman who made a disturbance at Lord St. Simon's wedding. We learn from Lord St. Simon that Miss Millar was a dancer at the Allegro, and that they had an affair in the past. Lord St. Simon confesses that despite tossing Miss Millar aside for the wealthy Miss Doran, she has "no just cause of complaint against me." He dismisses Flora Millar as "exceedingly hot-headed and devotedly attached to me." He sees nothing wrong with his actions; after all, in his eyes, Miss Flora Millar is merely a dancer, unworthy of his name, certainly without the wealth to share his title. While she is not included in the story's conclusion, in some ways, as will be revealed, she unknowingly is avenged.

We also get the trademark Holmes humor both in the pomposity of Lord St. Simon and in the occasional remark from Holmes. For example, when Lord St. Simon laments to Holmes that solving this case will take "wiser heads than yours or mine," Holmes responds with a laugh: "It is very good of Lord St. Simon to honor my head by putting it on a level with his own." The humor is not left to the noble lord alone, as Inspector Lestrade is also in this adventure. When Holmes tells Lestrade that "Lady St. Simon is a myth," Watson writes that the inspector "looked sadly at my companion. Then he turned to me, tapped his forehead three times, shook his head solemnly, and hurried away." Of course, Holmes is correct in his statement and it is Lestrade who once again appears dimwitted.

In the end, Lord St. Simon receives his comeuppance when it is revealed that Hatty Doran had left him because she was already married to Frank Moulton, a man she had believed killed during an Apache attack on his miners' camp. Mr. Moulton had not died in the raid, had gone on to strike it rich, and had sought out Miss Doran as he had promised to find her when he had made his fortune. Here we have Miss Doran choosing her original American husband, a man who started out quite poor but rose up through his own volition, in preference to Lord St. Simon, a cad who received his title from his birth and put no effort of his own into accruing his now-dwindling fortune. Lord St. Simon finds himself in the same position in which he put Flora Millar: cast aside for a more suitable partner. But he does not catch any of this irony. He is rigid throughout the explanation of Miss Doran's background, and when she asks him to shake hands in forgiveness, he "put out his hand and coldly grasped that which she extended to him." Londoners must have thrilled, as audiences still do today, to see this boorish aristocrat rejected for a now-wealthy commoner.

After Lord St. Simon leaves Baker Street, Holmes explains to Watson how he solved the case from two facts which appeared obvious to the detective, that "the lady had been quite willing to undergo the wedding ceremony" and that "she had repented of it within a few minutes of returning home." He knew something had occurred to change her mind, and from that knowledge plus the clues provided by the tale of Lord St. Simon, he was able to do what no one else was able to do, puzzle out the rest of the case and follow it to its logical conclusion.

It is that conclusion which makes this story rise above that of "A Scandal in Bohemia," another Holmes tale which fits all of the requirements for the quintessential Holmes tale—all save one. Although the adventure involving Irene Adler is far more popular than that of the noble bachelor and contains much of the same ingredients of a perfect Holmes story (humor in Holmes subtly making fun of the King of Bohemia, Irene Adler rising above her station in life), Holmes does not actually win in that story. While that makes for one of the best endings of any short story ever written, it puts it out of the running for the quintessential Holmes story because Holmes does not end up as the victor. Therefore, out of all the stories in the Canon, "The Noble Bachelor" best illustrates the perfect Holmes adventure.

Derrick Belanger (Broomfield, Colorado) is co-owner of Belanger Books, a publishing company focusing on children's books, new Sherlock Holmes stories, and steampunk. He is the author of *Sherlock Holmes: The Adventure of the Peculiar Provenance*, the *MacDougall Twins* series, and many other works.

THE ADVENTURE OF
THE BERYL CORONET

CHRISTOPHER SEQUEIRA

Let us say that the most important Sherlock Holmes tales are those that recount significant aspects of the protagonists' lives (such as the origin of the Holmes-Watson team, their closest brushes with death, their most personally revealing encounters). Accepting this, then, and looking at the remaining canonical tales, "The Beryl Coronet" may be the greatest exemplar of what a classic Sherlock Holmes story is from the second-level tales because it contain so many, crucial, Holmesian features—features that I shall discuss under five categories.

Structure and Settings. The structure of this tale is that of an ideal, identifiable (nay, desirable) Sherlock Holmes story. We open with a Baker Street scene: Holmes makes armchair deductions about an approaching stranger, that new visitor, Mr Alexander Holder, makes a dramatic entrance, and then an amazing case, full of intrigue and import, is set out for us. This inciting episode propels our adventurous duo to head to a crime scene, via that quintessentially Sherlockian conveyance, the Victorian-era railway carriage.

When they reach their destination we are presented with a house full of suspects, these being a family torn apart by scandal and intrigue, with very clearly a pall cast over that house through some terrible lie, concealment and betrayal. In the midst of this there is a wrongfully accused culprit—Mr Holder's son, Arthur—whom we just know can't be responsible for the crime that has been committed. Holmes carefully investigates the surroundings, quizzes the suspects, makes canny observations and comments that tantalise us, and then it's back to Baker Street for our next act.

Once back at digs, Holmes pulls out an example of disguise—a formidable, familiar weapon from his investigative armoury—and is off to avenues that the good Watson will only slow him down in pursuing; more likely, his presence would rob us of any surprise for the reveal and dénouement! Those climactic scenes are also replete with most that we have come to want from a Baker Street finale: The client shows up, despairing; Holmes plays with him like a fish on a line, extracts a penance from him, and sees to it that the wrongly accused will be allowed to rejoin family and society via a dramatic return of the missing item. We are satisfied, because although the client is slightly wounded by the revelation, Mr. Holder's world is restored. In this case that world also includes the dignity of the very Crown itself—for we know the beryl coronet belonged to "the very noblest in the land".

So, structurally, this story hits most all the beats a Holmes *aficionado* could desire, with but perhaps one deficiency that I will mention later.

Holmesiana Veritae. What a marvellous catalogue of Sherlockiana this story is! There are a number of elements and tropes present that send a frisson of excitement through us, and that provide the *authentic* signal that the game is afoot, the hunt is on! We have the props and devices: dressing-gown, railway system, magnifying lens. We also have a hat that I argue might well be a deerstalker (or at the very least a "travelling cap"). For, if Holmes spends much of the train journey sitting "with his chin upon his breast and his hat drawn over his eyes, sunk in the deepest thought" surely said hat must be a deerstalker, for presumably one doesn't adopt such a posture with a stiff-brimmed Homburg!

We also have, as far as the content of the story goes, the unnamed illustrious client (in this case, a sub-client if you will), mysterious trace evidence in the form of footprints only Holmes properly interprets, references to an odd, wooden-legged suspect, and, as mentioned, Holmes in disguise.

Even off-stage activities suggest classic Holmes paraphernalia: Holmes voices words that demonstrate he has had recourse to some sort of in-depth profile on the evil Sir George Burnwell, and knows well the man's true criminal nature. Thus can we imagine him poring through his extensive criminal catalogue files, although we don't witness him doing this first-hand. And what would an adventure be without Watson recording deathless insights uttered by the world's foremost detective? Most fascinatingly, there is not just a philosophical maxim stated relating to the art of detection, but perhaps *the* Holmes maxim, repeated from *The Sign of the Four*. This is truly significant; of all Holmes's methodological standards, this is the one that sums him up—it should thus appear more than once in sixty records, and so here it is repeated!

There are also pleasing little displays of Holmes's famed physically distinctive capabilities; his exceptional strength (in the fingers), and his quickness with reflexes (used to get the drop on Sir George Burnwell). Finally, a story cannot live without a pulse, and this tale's heart is Holmes himself acting as a moral compass for the client (more on this below), something we have come to truly admire about the Master.

The Human Condition. This tale shines a light on a dynamic that is not one-dimensional, not simplistic. The tragedies, the losses and the wrongs committed against players in the drama, are multiple, and criss-cross between the main characters, but they are all bound up in the most fundamental types of human interactions: parent-child relationships and sexual relationships. Mr Holder is too trusting of his "pseudo-daughter", his niece, Mary, and fails to trust his son; that son desires Mary; and Mary betrays all for her desire for Sir George Burnwell. It is a neat knot these characters are in; the virtuous ones driven to deceive and betray or sacrifice by their desires; the less virtuous, well, we can guess what they are motivated by! In a lesser scribe's hands the complications could be farcical, but here we have no doubt of the seriousness of things.

Holmes is, as I have said, the moral compass for Alexander Holder and his entire family, and he knows the banker's heart is unfortunately linked to coin of the realm—so, what better punishment for the banker than to have to pay an exorbitant fee to get a result at the end; it's not as though he will miss the money! Therefore we see this human tragedy is not without slight, leavening, comic touches, too.

Villainies Revealed and Withheld. Great stories need great villains. This story has two, for Mary Holder is quite the twisted, manipulative character, and we must acknowledge that she puts Holder and his son through a horrible ordeal, fleeing only when she knows discovery is imminent; she was prepared to let her cousin rot in gaol!

Mary enables the other antagonist, Sir George Burnwell, and we have no less an authority than Holmes himself confirm that Sir George is a serious matter, for we are told he is a most "dangerous man" (an epithet that I have speculated in the past is a coded reference to Holmes's belief the assignee has ties to Moriarty's criminal operations; Sir George might have had the Professor in mind as a recipient of the coronet if he'd secured all of it). Sir George is also a physical as well as strategic menace, trying to cut Holmes down with a life preserver, and his reputation for violence clearly ensured Holmes was armed and ready. This villain has a shortcoming, however, that I'll cover in my final observations.

Baker Street Irregularities. It is one thing to have a Sherlock Holmes tale that functions as a perfectly good detective story, but to deserve a place of distinction it needs to also provide fertile ground for those who play the Great Game. There need to be inconsistencies in this tale, that we Sherlockians can pore over at length, and which might send us scurrying to the research shelves. And this tale has the goods, because, despite Holmes solving the case, we all still ponder some questions: Why on

Earth does the Crown need to borrow money? What possessed a banker to not just take it home, but to keep it unsecured and tell his family, including his frequently financially inconvenienced son? Where on Earth does a crook think one can sell a beryl coronet of such fame safely? Who paid Sir George for the broken piece? Wasn't it too hot an item?

A Final Word. Considering that this tale contains so many fundamentally Holmesian elements, including a genuinely engaging human drama, why is it not more read, more anthologized, more referred to, or more adapted to television and cinema? I think that must come down to its signal deficit: the malefactor(s) are dealt with off-screen at the end. Regrettably, in "The Beryl Coronet", there is not only no chance for the audience or reader to witness the perpetrators meet Holmes's justice, but we are also deprived of seeing Holmes risk injury or life to apprehend a villain. This lack of closing action—payoff, if you will—makes Holmes and Watson navigators of the mystery, and not crusaders, as they are in the greatest cases. So, notes for any adaptors: Let's see Holmes (yes, and Watson) risk their necks to capture the evil Sir George in a real skirmish, and then you've got a first-level Sherlockian story!

Christopher Sequeira (Sydney, Australia) is a long-time member of the Sydney Passengers and a horror, mystery, science fiction and superhero writer and editor. He is editor and a contributor for Echo Publishing's forthcoming anthology *Sherlock Holmes: The Australian Casebook.*

THE ADVENTURE OF THE COPPER BEECHES

DEBBIE CLARK

This story has just about everything one could hope to have in a Sherlock Holmes story, and then some! The story opens in the cozy domesticity of the Baker Street rooms. There is a thick fog outside and a warming fire inside. Holmes is holding forth on some of his favorite themes: that he practices Art for Art's sake and for the love of the game; that the public lacks appreciation for the finer points of observation and deduction he presents; that "Crime is common. Logic is rare"; that criminals have lost "all enterprise and originality" and that "the days of the great cases are past." He specifically states that his practice is "now reduced to giving advice to ladies from boarding schools." However, this situation is about to change.

Holmes tweaks Watson about the cases his friend has written up for publication. This becomes a recurring theme throughout the Canon. He also compliments Watson for choosing "those incidents which may have been trivial in themselves but which have given room for those faculties of deduction and of logical synthesis which I have made my special province." But he chides Watson for having "degraded what should have been a course of lectures into a series of tales" and for "attempting to put color and life into each of your statements, instead of confining yourself to the task of placing upon record that severe reasoning from cause to effect which is really the only notable feature."

Watson counters by saying he thinks he's done justice to Holmes and his methods and has, for the most part, avoided sensationalism. This is also a recurring argument. Holmes then compliments Watson on his handling of recent cases involving Mary Sutherland, the King of Bohemia, the twisted lip, the noble bachelor and the blue carbuncle. Compliments from Holmes are scarce, but perhaps he knows he's struck a nerve in Watson. Unhappily, it is too early in the partnership for Watson to tantalize us with unpublished cases.

Enter a client, with an interesting case! Miss Violet Hunter, an unemployed governess, describes Jephro Rucastle's unusual job offer. Holmes acknowledges that her story has some very "novel features" and is the most interesting problem he's had in some time. He then dispenses advice. Ultimately, Holmes does not succeed in dissuading Miss Hunter from taking the governess position offered by Rucastle at the Copper Beeches even though he cautions her that it is "not the situation I should like to see a sister of mine apply for" and it is "not a nice household for a lady."

They acknowledge concerns regarding Mr. Rucastle's requests that Miss Hunter take charge of one six-year-old boy (who enjoys killing roaches!), acquiesce to the Rucastles' peculiar fads and fancies (wearing an electric blue dress, sitting in certain places), and cut off her long "artistic" chestnut hair... for which she will be paid three times the normal yearly salary of a governess, even one with five years of experience. With this background, Holmes promises to come to Miss Hunter's request for aid, day or night.

Within a fortnight, that telegram arrives, and Holmes and Watson travel to the scene. They meet Miss Hunter in Winchester and her story takes on characteristics of Gothic horror (another genre where Arthur Conan Doyle excelled). The setting is an old house, the Copper Beeches, which stands in a beautiful area with a group of copper beech trees in the front of it, but is itself "stained and streaked with damp." (This could easily represent the 'rot' inside the house.) There is an abandoned wing with locked doors and covered windows. It is also isolated, five miles from Winchester. (Holmes says the five miles of country concern him, since there are far fewer people to be aware of a problem than in a town, and they may be loath to intervene.)

Beyond all that, there is a Gothic atmosphere of fear and threat. Mr. Rucastle clearly has some secret he is keeping locked in the empty wing (and it's not photography). Once Miss Hunter is found snooping in the wing, he makes it clear that if it happens again, he'll throw her to the mastiff. She admits to being afraid of the house, the Rucastles, the servants, and the child.

There are also surly, unhelpful servants. Mrs. Toller is the housekeeper, and Mr. Toller (who is frequently drunk) does the outside work and takes care of the vicious mastiff. There is a disturbing discovery or portent: Miss Hunter finds a coil of hair in the exact shade of her own locked in a drawer and wonders at its significance. Women are threatened by a tyrannical male. Mrs. Rucastle is described as a "sorrowful nonentity", "colorless in mind as well as in feature", but devoted to her husband and son. Rucastle's daughter, Alice, did not get along with the new wife, and ostensibly moved to Philadelphia. However, one wonders if it was not primarily to get away from Rucastle himself. Miss Hunter becomes aware of the dark side of Rucastle's nature when she starts exploring the empty wing and finds the locked room. He demonstrates that he can switch from bluff good humor to rage in an instant.

As for women in distress, we eventually learn that Alice had met a man who would become her fiancé, and her small inheritance would come under his control when Alice married. Alice had been badgered by her father to turn over control of her money to him. Rucastle locked her away in the attic and told people she had gone to Philadelphia. His constant badgering ultimately led to brain fever and her hair had to be cut off.

In short, as the Gothic demands, there is terror. Jephro Rucastle terrorized Alice and Violet Hunter psychologically and with the threat of bodily harm as well. This may also account for Mrs. Rucastle's colorless personality.

Meanwhile, Holmes deduces. With Holmes and Watson on the scene we are treated to some interim deductions. (Usually those are only shared at the very end.) Here, Holmes deduces from the coil of hair found in the dresser drawer that Violet Hunter has been brought in to impersonate someone, most probably Alice, because of her physical resemblance, even down to the hair. Holmes reasons that Alice had some illness requiring her hair to be cut; hence Miss Hunter had to cut hers too.

Holmes infers the presence of a young male friend, possibly a fiancé, who was seen in the area and was supposed to be warned off by Miss Hunter's unknowing impersonation of Alice. Miss Hunter wore Alice's electric blue dress, and appears to laugh happily at Mr. Rucastle's stories. Holmes notes the mastiff is let loose at night to prevent anyone from coming onto the grounds (and rescuing Alice). He also deduces the cruel character of Mr. Rucastle from Miss Hunter's observations of the son. ("I have never met... so ill-natured a little creature.... Giving pain to any creature weaker than himself seems to be his one idea of amusement and he shows quite a remarkable talent in planning the capture of mice, little birds and insects.")

But then Holmes gets it wrong. This is rare! Holmes accosts Rucastle who returns unexpectedly, and accuses Rucastle of spiriting Alice away via the skylight. (In fact, it is the fiancé, Mr Fowler, who has rescued her with the help of the Tollers.)

The denouement: Rucastle looses the starving mastiff which turns on him. Watson shoots the dog (foreshadowing of *The Hound of the Baskervilles*?) and treats Rucastle's wounds until his wife and the surgeon return. Mrs. Toller explains the backstory of Alice, her money and her fiancé to Holmes, et al. At the end, Holmes and Watson take Miss Hunter back to Winchester and they return to London.

As mentioned earlier, this story has everything: a glimpse into the domestic arrangements of Baker Street, some discourse on Holmes's philosophy and Watson's writings, a rather bizarre problem, a decaying house which harbors more than one secret, one damsel in distress and another locked in an empty room, a bipolar villain, some deducing by Holmes, some doctoring by Watson, and a dog that did something in the night-time!

What it doesn't have is much actual deduction. Early on, Holmes forgets to share deductions he most certainly made about Miss Hunter when she entered. Watson says Holmes was "favorably impressed with [her] manner and speech" (so much so, that Watson is disappointed when Holmes shows no more interest in her once the case is concluded. But then, we know Watson is at heart a hopeless romantic). And his assumptions about Alice's departure have to be explained by Mrs. Toller. ("Data, data, data! I cannot make bricks without clay!")

That said, I still think it is the perfect story to conclude the first collected volume of Sherlock Holmes's adventures.

Debbie Clark (Frederick, Maryland) is a longtime member and past Gasogene of Watson's Tin Box (of Ellicott City) and registrar of the annual Scintillation of Scions convention, as well as a member of the Adventuresses of Sherlock Holmes and other societies.

THE ADVENTURE OF SILVER BLAZE

ELINOR GRAY

There are three reasons that "Silver Blaze" is the best short story in the entire Sherlock Holmes collection: first, Sherlock Holmes is at his best in this story, making some classic deductions, gallivanting across the downs, and in tearing spirits all the while; second, this story is the source of some of the most famous moments in the entire Canon, both textual and visual, which are repeated over and over in scholarship, adaptations, canonical quizzes, and popular culture; and third, it contains the very pinnacle of Arthur Conan Doyle's inventiveness when it comes to villains: the Murder Pony.

Sherlock Holmes is, in this story, at his very best. He is having so much fun with this case, from start to finish. In the introductory scene in Baker Street, Holmes says he is "afraid" he will have to go to King's Pyland and assist with the case, but it is clear that he is excited to get involved. He is in good spirits and begs Watson to come along for a good time. On the train, he shows off his great brain by telling their speed by the telegraph posts, and then gets into the details of the case with relish and amazing detail. Upon their arrival at King's Pyland in the presence of Colonel Ross and Inspector Gregory, he has to be roused from his "day-dream," his eyes gleaming with the solution to the mystery on the horizon. Almost as soon as he has completed his examination of Straker's body, he is acting on clues (to Mrs. Straker, "You wore a costume of dove-colored silk"), and he drags Watson across Dartmoor in search of hoofprints. He already knows the answer; he only has to confirm his suspicions.

We see a classic example of Holmes's sense of humor in this story, and of his desire to hold all the cards until the final reveal. Watson does guess that Silas Brown has Silver Blaze in his keeping—he would be a dull companion indeed if he did not draw that conclusion—but he doesn't know what Holmes plans to do next. Holmes is in control: of all the facts, of all the players, and of the end of the story. This is Holmes at his absolute brightest.

Outside the story itself, there is the context into which "Silver Blaze" falls. This is the first story in *The Memoirs of Sherlock Holmes*, initially published in 1892. Conan Doyle demanded an outrageous £1,000 for the twelve stories in this collection, expecting to be denied, and received it. Holmes's popularity had exploded between *Adventures* and *Memoirs*, so "Silver Blaze" is the first in a series of widely-anticipated stories that *Strand* readers were mad for. Holmes is at his peak both in the story and in the historical moment of the story's creation.

Some of the most famous moments of the Canon come from this story: the scene in the train car as Holmes and Watson travel down to King's Pyland, the remark about the dog in the night-time, the ill-advised and certainly illegal running of an unidentified horse in the Wessex Cup, and, at the end, the reveal of the horse as the killer of his own keeper.

The scene in the train car is an iconic moment, both textually and visually. In this scene, Holmes and Watson engage in their classic period of exposition, catching Watson and the reader up on the mystery *du jour*. This exposition is essential to the success of Sherlock Holmes, as it establishes Holmes's importance as a detective but also Watson's as a writer: it gives the story its flavor of truth, reported as it is from one character to another. This is not something Watson has made up, the reader is to understand. It is Holmes's work. Simultaneously, this is a widely repeated visual moment: Sidney Paget's illustration of the train car repeats itself twice more in the Canon itself ("Thor Bridge" and "The Naval Treaty"), but also in several famous adaptations. The Granada series mimics this visual very deliberately in the "Silver Blaze" episode, and the BBC's *Sherlock* echoes it in a diner booth. This mirroring creates continuity across the Canon and adaptations, linking them inextricably, and it originates in this story (for more on the importance of illustrations, see my essay "'Your Picturesque Account of the Matter': Bitextuality in Sherlock Holmes" in *The Watsonian*, spring 2015).

"The curious incident of the dog in the night-time" is perhaps the most repeated Sherlock Holmes quote, short of the erroneous "Elementary, my dear Watson." This is classic Holmes, noticing details upon which other people do not remark. That the dog does "nothing in the night-time" is a brilliant detail, and is the final tumbler necessary to unlock the mystery.

The running of a disguised Silver Blaze in the Wessex Cup is, as other Sherlockians have noted, incredibly illegal and would never have been allowed. But Conan Doyle was never one for fact-checking if it got in the way of a good story, and he operated at his best when he has so thoroughly suspended belief that readers do not question the workings of established institutions, logic, or sense. The mysterious horse must run for Holmes's joke (and wager) to work, and so it runs.

His joke, then, is the final entry in this list of classic moments. Conan Doyle has done it before in "The Man with the Twisted Lip", and understandably so: introducing a character and then wiping their face clean with a giant sponge to reveal that it is, in fact, the character we have been missing all along. It's cheesy and unbelievable, and is therefore the perfect climax to this perfect story.

Silver Blaze himself is one of the best murderers in the entirety of the Sherlock Holmes Canon. There are plenty of stories in which Holmes lets the culprit go free for one reason or another, be it that no crime has actually been committed (as in "A Case of Identity"), or that he is "not retained by the police to supply their deficiencies" ("The Blue Carbuncle"), but this one is so good it cannot be overstated. The horse is led out to a dell in the company of a person it knows and trusts, but the moment it senses it is threatened it brings its considerable strength and independent will to bear and eliminates the threat with one swift kick. Silver Blaze does not know the petty human motivation for the neatly avoided attack, and feels no remorse for the entirely justified action. He simply wanders off into the night to be gathered up by benevolent, if misguided, neighbors.

Holmes draws this reveal out as long as possible, going so far as to confirm his suspicion and beg Silas Brown at Mapleton to keep the horse until he can play his practical joke on Colonel Ross. He loves that the murderer is a blameless horse, and his "he's right behind you" gag is full of smug amusement. He gets grudging admiration out of Colonel Ross, and genuine astonishment, his most-desired form of payment, from Watson and the others.

Furthermore, the sheer cheek of naming the story after its culprit is so splendid that Conan Doyle should be congratulated for giving away his ending before it had even begun, not that anyone was paying attention.

As the reader can conclude, "Silver Blaze" is the best story of the Canon, due to a combination of its classic moments such as the exposition in the train car and the silence of the dog in the night-time, Holmes's peak performance as a detective and as a character, and the unsurpassable Murder Pony. Other stories may come close, but from start to finish, "Silver Blaze" is a perfect example of Conan Doyle's skill as a short-story writer, and it does him great credit as the creator of Sherlock Holmes.

Elinor Gray (Portland, Oregon) co-founded the Retired Beekeepers of Sussex in Brighton, edits the bi-annual journal *The Practical Handbook of Bee Culture*, and is the author of *Compound a Felony: A Queer Affair of Sherlock Holmes*.

THE ADVENTURE OF
THE CARDBOARD BOX

RESA HAILE

"The Cardboard Box" is the unwanted child of the Sherlock Holmes Canon—removed from here (*The Memoirs*), squeezed in there (*His Last Bow*), its opening Frankensteined onto another story ("The Resident Patient"), and rejected by its creator, much like the famous creature. This is fitting, as it is a horror story—a remarkable one, in fact, the best in the Canon.

Published in January 1893 in both British (the *Strand Magazine*) and American (*Harper's Weekly*) periodicals under the series *The Memoirs of Sherlock Holmes*, it was removed when the first English edition was published in London the following year, although it did appear in the first American edition—which was quickly replaced by a revised American edition without it.

Edgar Allan Poe is explicitly mentioned in the story, not as a master of the macabre but as the progenitor of detective fiction. However, Poe's horror tales often feature an unreliable narrator, and there is an incident early on (and connected to Poe) which gives us pause regarding the reliability of narrators. In the "mind-reading" scene, in which Holmes is able to follow Watson's thoughts accurately by watching his actions and facial expressions, the account of the famous duo's discussion of Poe and Dupin appears to contradict an earlier one given by Watson in *A Study in Scarlet*.

In one of Poe's non-detective stories, "The Tell-Tale Heart," the narrator assures us he is not mad while detailing his premeditated murder of someone he claims to love—all because he cannot bear to look upon the man's repulsive eye. It is a tale of horror but not of the supernatural, a tale of the tortures conscience can bring to bear upon the perpetrator of horrific deeds. And so is this one.

Although Watson maintains his role of narrator throughout the investigation, and Lestrade briefly narrates the killer's capture, we are given an account of the crimes from a statement by the murderer, Jim Browner. Browner offers up the tale as a modern retelling of "Othello," casting his sister-in-law, Sarah, as Iago, and his wife, Mary, as Desdemona. Sarah, according to Browner, sets out to destroy his marriage after he rejects her advances. She poisons his wife's mind against him and throws her together with another man, inflaming Browner's jealousy and leading to the final tragedy.

That Sarah has a temper is corroborated (in advance of Browner's claim) by an interview with her other sister, Susan, the unfortunate recipient of an unmatched set of severed ears in a cardboard box. Clearly, Browner also has a temper.

In Browner's confession—the narrative of his story that he presents to the world—he says that it is Sarah's fault. Sarah, in her role of Iago, the spoiler, has destroyed his idyllic marriage. It is not that he wants to clear himself, he hastens to assure us. He admits that he had begun to drink again, "like the beast that [he] was." Browner says that he "saw a great deal of [Sarah]," who at this time was effectively living with him and Mary when he was at home from the sea, often on the weekends and sometimes "for a whole week at a time."

His description of his sister-in-law is arresting. She is "a fine tall woman, black and quick and fierce, with a proud way of carrying her head, and a glint from her eye like a spark from a flint." He adds: "But when little Mary was there I had never a thought of her, and that I swear as I hope for God's mercy." This is a rather fine bit in the narrative. When someone relating a story arrives at a certain point and swears to the truth of it, it demonstrates that he particularly wants the listener to believe that part. And it makes the listener wonder why. Did Browner really have no thought of Sarah when Mary was around? And what of when she wasn't? Examine his description of his sister-in-law, the detail of it—quite detailed indeed, from a man who never gave her much thought, at least when his wife was around.

Browner tells us that Sarah liked to be alone with him and to "coax [him] out for a walk with her." He doesn't say whether he goes on these walks; however, one evening, quite to his surprise and when his wife is out, Sarah makes an advance upon him. According to Browner, he is unhappy and restless because Mary is not there, and Sarah complains that he can't "be happy for five minutes without [her]." Browner then puts a hand out to Sarah in a "kindly way" and offers a few words of comfort, but she grabs his hand in both of hers. He reads the passion in her eyes; she reads the rejection in his, and from then on, she hates him. This is the slight that leads to his destruction.

If we consider that Browner may be an unreliable narrator, we must ask if this situation could be other than what he has related; yet we must seek the clues within his statement, and it is admirably set up for us to do this. Is it possible that he carried on a relationship with his sister-in-law? Or could it have been he who made the advance to Sarah and she who rejected him? Browner states that in letting Sarah continue to stay with them after this incident, he was "a besotted fool." He adds that he never told Mary as he "knew it would grieve her," but is it reasonable that he is talking about being besotted with his wife here?

Although she doesn't immediately move out, Sarah begins avoiding him while becoming ever closer to her sister. Mary, however, who had been "trusting" and "innocent," is now "queer and suspicious, wanting to know where [he has] been and what [he has] been doing, and whom [his] letters [are] from, and what [he has] in his pockets, and," as Browner puts it, "a thousand such follies."

Mary suspects Browner of infidelity, whether from something Sarah has told her or for other reasons—perhaps something she found in his pockets or a letter he received. He begins to drink again. By the time a sailor named Alec Fairburn arrives on the scene, originally to see Sarah, Mary is already disenchanted with her marriage. Sarah seemingly encourages this relationship. To Browner, this is her vengeance upon him for his rejection or possibly a ploy to turn him against his wife. Whether Fairburn becomes a romantic interest for Mary or offers her the solace of a friend, she is visibly disappointed one day upon realising it is Browner and not Fairburn who has come into the parlour. This leads to a row that culminates in Fairburn's being banned from the house and Sarah's moving out.

Browner also promises to send Fairburn's ears to Sarah as a keepsake if he comes near the house again. On another occasion, after finding Mary at Fairburn's, her husband threatens to kill her if he finds her there again. By Browner's own account, Mary has gone from loving him to hating and fearing him, yet, when he comes home for an unexpected visit after a mishap with his ship causes a delay, he thinks "what a surprise it will be for [her]" and hopes she may "be pleased to see [him] so soon." He is not, of course, thinking he may catch Mary with Fairburn. Is he?

That, of course, is what happens, and Browner follows the pair with intent. He has a heavy stick and a heavy awareness of it. He "sees red" at first, but then becomes "cunning." He follows, hanging back, but "never more than a hundred yards," as silent as Sherlock Holmes. They rent a boat, and he does the same.

Unlike many of the killers who tell their stories in the Canon, Browner is not avenging the death of a loved one or defending another. His account is a horror story narrated by the monster, his description of the murders chilling. He "crushe[s] Alec's head like an egg," decides against mercy for his wife, and, as Sarah is not there to join his victims, he cuts an ear off of each to send her, an act which gives him "savage joy."

Like the unreliable narrators of "The Tell-Tale Heart" and *Lolita* (which also takes inspiration from Poe), the monster in "The Cardboard Box" tells his own story, pleading with us to believe that, whatever he has done, he is the victim of forces beyond his control. Just as Poe's killer hears that beating, beating under the floorboards, as Humbert Humbert is troubled by Dolores Haze's stolen childhood, Jim Browner is haunted by his victims' faces. "The Cardboard Box," this dark and grisly tale of jealousy, guilt, and betrayal, is both the greatest horror story in the Sherlock Holmes Canon and one of the finest examples of the unreliable narrator in fiction.

Resa Haile (Janesville, Wisconsin) is the co-founder of the Original Tree Worshippers of Rock County and the Studious Scarlets Society, as well as a member of the Notorious Canary Trainers of Madison and the Hounds of the Internet. Her work has been published in the *Baker Street Journal*.

THE ADVENTURE OF THE YELLOW FACE

AMY THOMAS

"'Watson,' said he, 'if it should ever strike you that I am… giving less pains to a case than it deserves, kindly whisper "Norbury" in my ear, and I shall be infinitely obliged to you.'" Holmes enthusiasts often give less pains than they should to appreciating "The Yellow Face," a story that reaches the apex of the Victorian Gothic, while also subverting and modernizing its traditional components. This complex interplay of elements, along with its rare example of Holmesian failure, makes it a masterpiece of short fiction and Arthur Conan Doyle's finest gift to his readers.

To subvert the Gothic, a story must first include its traditional elements. Among those possessed by "The Yellow Face" are the presence of an overarching fear, a woman of mysterious past, a hero, the exploration of character psyche, and a strongly influential mysterious setting.

The fear element is presented almost immediately, through the character of Grant Munro. Before he utters a word of his story, Watson uses the words "restless," "half dazed," and "jerky" to describe him. Without knowing why he's come, the reader is already informed that something serious is amiss. Munro is not presented as a ridiculous or delusional man, rather as a sensible one driven to dire straits, thereby increasing the reader's dread.

The woman of mysterious past is, of course, Grant's wife Effie, the catalyst of his desperation. After three years of apparent marital bliss, he says of her, "I find that there is something in her life and in her thought of which I know as little as if she were the woman who brushes by me in the street." Suddenly, what was once familiar has become strange, and an amiable woman becomes a mystery with a past and depths of which her husband is unaware. As the tale unfolds, the fact that this strangeness is directly tied to Effie's past becomes increasingly evident.

One of the notably unique qualities possessed by "The Yellow Face," though not one completely absent elsewhere in the Canon, is the presentation of a decidedly heroic character other than Holmes. This is none other than the above-mentioned Munro, the beleaguered husband who finds out that his suspicions about his wife's infidelity are instead the subterfuges of a desperate woman who, justifiably considering the mores of the time, expects him to reject her multiracial child, the progeny of a previous marriage. Instead, Grant wholeheartedly and instantaneously forgives his wife's deceit and accepts her child as his own. Effie is an independent and formidable character, but in this sense, Munro acts as a hero-rescuer, who eliminates her shame by lending his credibility to her situation.

Another Gothic marker that is amply present in the story is the exploration of character psyche, an element present in several Doyle stories but in one of its most overt and complete forms in this one, where it is seamlessly entwined with the action. "Mr. Holmes, Effie loves me. Don't let there be any mistake about that," says Grant Munro, as Doyle, through Watson, shows the reader his desperate, emotionally-driven desire for this to be the truth—in other words, he obviously protests too much. Munro's eventual heroic behavior can be seen as a triumph over his initial insecurity. Effie's psyche is also explored, first through her behavior as described by her husband: "My wife had always been a woman of a frank, open nature, and it gave me a chill to see her slinking into her own room." Later on, her own perspective is given voice, when she explains the weakness that caused her to reject her child, the all-consuming love that caused her to change her mind, and finally her horror at exposure. Even though Effie informs the reader of these psychological factors after the fact, they inform and back-influence the plot, the instigating reasons for the entire affair. At a time when modern psychology was in its infancy, Doyle did not merely present characters performing unmotivated actions. He provided ironclad reasons for their behavior and, in so doing, followed a Gothic pattern that heralded an age of psychological fiction.

Finally, the thickly atmospheric element of the Gothic, which is present in many of Doyle's stories, provides the eerie backdrop to the action of "The Yellow Face." At first, the mysterious cottage around which the action centers seems like a pleasant enough place, a "neat little homestead," but then Munro sees something in a window, a face he describes as "unnatural and inhuman." Suddenly, an innocent setting is imbued with a sense of Gothic horror, as the reader is tantalized by just enough information to feel the hero's terror. From that point on, the cottage is no longer a benign home; it is fear personified, as if a supernaturally malevolent evil is within.

These elements could unite to fulfill, simply, the requirements of a well-written Gothic tale. However, Doyle chose not to stay within the confines of the traditional, choosing instead to subvert the expected in order to form something different, a post-Gothic tale that uses recognizable elements to craft something progressive and new. He did this through his defiance of gender and cultural stereotypes.

As pointed out previously, Grant Munro functions as a hero in the story, accepting his wife and her child against expected prejudices. The even more heroic character the story presents, however, is Effie herself, who says, "Though I knew the danger, I determined to have the child over." A woman who had established a comfortable life with a new husband, far from a child society considered inconvenient, chooses to risk her respectability and throw off her veneer of perfect Victorian womanhood by symbolically acknowledging and embracing her past choices and literally embracing the product of the choices, her daughter Lucy. Unbeknownst to the reader, Effie begins the story as the bold widow of a man she chose to marry against the world's disapproval, and she ends it as a heroine who ultimately chooses to be true to herself and her child, regardless of society's expectations. Doyle is not the only author to have used the Gothic to explore feminine empowerment; the Brontës are another notable example. "The Yellow Face," however, is unique because of its union of power and brevity: Effie's forceful strength of character is communicated unequivocally within the stringent confines of the short story genre.

Another way Doyle subverted Gothic tradition is by using "The Yellow Face" as an issue tale, a story that condemns a widespread societal problem. Rather than confining himself to the expected Gothic modes of sensationalism and romanticism, he moved beyond them to address and condemn prejudice based on skin color. Effie Munro's history includes marriage to a man of color in the southern United States at a time when such unions were of dubious legality in America and strongly frowned upon in England, and automatically resulted in societal excommunication. Instead of upholding these traditions, "The Yellow Face" presents interracial love as a natural and desirable choice. Additionally, the existence of the child Lucy presents Grant with the ultimate test of his loyalty to ingrained prejudice versus the primacy of his love for his wife and her family. The fact that he wholeheartedly rejects prejudice in favor of love, while Holmes and Watson watch approvingly, shows Doyle's own progressive views on the subject and provides a compelling example for his Victorian readers.

As the above points make clear, a great deal of what makes "The Yellow Face" great has relatively little to do with Sherlock Holmes, but another of the story's greatest merits is its depiction of one of its detective's rare failures. Given the facts as presented to him, Holmes concocts a story to suit them—a horrifying tale of bigamy and blackmail. Instead, he's confronted with a story centered on love: of a woman for her husband and her child, and then of a man for his wife. Holmes victorious is a common thing in the Canon, and his response to it becomes expected and repetitive. His attitude to failure, because of how rarely it is depicted by Doyle, is far more revelatory of his character. Watson and the reader see a man who is humbled by his miscalculation but not vindictive, who would obviously rather witness a happy ending than be proved correct by horror and tragedy.

In their rush to sanitize and modernize elements of "The Yellow Face" that make them uncomfortable, postmodern readers often miss the beauty in a tale lovingly crafted by Doyle to be chillingly and authentically Gothic, while, at the same time, elegantly affirming progressive attitudes toward gender and skin color. The bow tied around this gift is the short but poignant insight into Holmes's unexpectedly gentle and unpretentious attitude toward his own failure. "The Yellow Face" is an example of its author at the height of his creative powers and remains a classic deserving of commendation among the Canon's stories.

Amy Thomas (Fort Myers, Florida) is the author of *The Detective and The Woman* Sherlockian mystery series, blogs at girlmeetssherlock. wordpress.com, and is a member of the Baker Street Babes podcast.

THE ADVENTURE OF
THE STOCK-BROKER'S CLERK

MICHAEL DUKE

"Nothing could be better!" exclaims Sherlock Holmes at the outset of this canonical tale, published in March 1893. And indeed it is unique and wonderfully clever, although the attentive reader may confuse this story's plot with that of "The Red-Headed League" (published August 1891) or "The Three Garridebs" (October 1924). In each case, a naïve dupe is lured away from his usual station to allow nefarious activity to take place where he should have been.

"The Stock-Broker's Clerk" seems a failure on Holmes's part: he gallops off to Birmingham, Watson in tow, while all the action takes place back in London at the financial firm of Mawson and Williams. A watchman is killed. Holmes and Watson, and the clerk who is the centre of the tale, Hall Pycroft, only learn the full story by reading a newspaper. Holmes is no rational superman here, it would appear, but an impetuous bumbler. Hall Pycroft is one hundred pounds better off, Beddington and his brother are secured, apparently by chance, but Holmes, until the very last, is "biting his nails" and "staring blankly out of the window". Ah, there's the cunning sleight of hand of the author.

But wait! The Holmes of this case trusts the official police: a seismic event, and Sergeant Tuson and Constable Pollock apprehend the main thief and murderer by themselves. Holmes, for the one and only time in the Canon, has deliberately not been on the scene and has trusted the official police with the denouement. In "The Red-Headed League", by contrast, Holmes sits in the cellar of the vault with Watson, a policeman and the bank manager to catch John Clay. That's risky business—Clay is a smasher and a murderer; the bank manager is being put in harm's way quite unnecessarily. And "The Three Garridebs"? Watson is actually shot while trying to capture the villain. Holmes and Watson are on the scene, risky or not. But not here! Note that generally a sergeant would not be on the beat, but the story has Tuson on hand to see "Pinner" with his carpet-bag come down the steps of Mawson and Williams at 1.20 p.m., and there is also a constable conveniently nearby. So a tipoff from Holmes has clearly occurred and the malefactor is arrested. Holmes still worries whether the police will be up to the task, hence Watson's misread observation of his nail biting and staring out of the window "blankly". But his trust is not misplaced.

The story takes place at a critical time for trust in the police. In 1888, Jack the Ripper carried out the horrible Whitechapel murders of working girls, prostitutes. Trust in the police plummeted as they seemed unable to solve or stop the crimes. In 1893, the Literary Agent, or Watson, or maybe even Holmes himself, decided to publish this case of 1889 where Holmes manifestly trusts the official force to catch the criminal. The triumphant newspaper article which Holmes and Watson read makes this clear. Here is an example of Holmes and Watson as the defenders of Victorian morale and values in a huge British Empire under severe strain from both external and internal events.

But what about that poor "armed watchman"? He is specifically hired because of the securities worth over one million pounds entrusted to the company "for some time back", of which one hundred thousand is stolen by "Pinner". The author of this canonical story does not say it explicitly, but clearly this extra precaution actually draws attention to the firm, rather than keeping the information privy to regular, trusted employees. It's a wonderful example of ludicrously shouting "nobody look!"

There is more. The Beddington brothers, or "Pinner" as they called themselves this time, learned of this vulnerability somehow. Invoking the master consulting criminal, Moriarty, is an unnecessary, if attractive, idea. The armed watchman himself is a probable source of the tipoff. Hence killing him by a poker-blow from behind would be, not an opportunistic murder, but a deliberate act to eliminate a possible witness. Such intentional cruelty is not a common occurrence in the Canon.

What else makes this story so striking? Early on, Holmes makes a breathtakingly bold inference when he says that the neighbouring doctor's practice has not been as successful as the one Watson has bought in Paddington. His evidence: the steps of Watson's practice rooms are worn fully "three inches deeper" than his neighbour's. Both sets of rooms have been doctors' practices "since the houses were built". Suddenly we must believe that Holmes must know so much about geology and architecture that he can gauge the rate of erosion of stone steps to a nicety, and consequentially establish rate of utilisation. When were these Paddington houses built? The Paddington Estate itself was built in 1838, with cream-stuccoed terraces and grand squares. But it usually takes very ancient buildings, like medieval churches and historic houses, to have stone steps at the front door worn down three inches. Fifty years of ailing patients' tread seems scarcely enough. But Watson publishes this inference by Holmes, which seems to me to be a feint to make the reader start questioning the latter's entire work in this case, or at least be very sceptical. Poor Holmes, we think! Drawing a long bow rather than being precise, factual and logical! Wrong: this is a ploy to mislead the reader about that seemingly absurd trip to Birmingham rather than Holmes making for the main game at Mawson and Williams in London.

One other observation: newlyweds John and Mary Watson are some three months into the doctor's new private medical practice and a little more into their marriage. But it seems that Holmes is so confident that his own relationship with Watson—of some seven or eight years—will be stronger than the bonds of wedlock that he calls in on a Saturday morning and has every expectation that Watson will abandon not only his patients, but Mary as well, for a trip of unknown duration and risk to Birmingham. This rivalry, as we are bound to think of it, continues until Mary is either dead, as could be inferred from Holmes's comments in "The Empty House" ("your sad bereavement"), or carefully concealed. This possible concealment would be due to the increasing danger to her and Holmes's other friends and associates because of the villains he is antagonising. Imagine the late unlamented Professor Moriarty, or many other villains, threatening or even kidnapping Watson, Mary, or Mrs Hudson to try and prevent Holmes thwarting their criminal activities. Getting into hiding, with a different identity is an excellent plan. But in these early post-nuptial days, Mary is still in evidence, and not hidden at all.

So there are singular features of this story, and I point out the logical developments arising from it, which may colour the whole subsequent Canon, the stories set after 1891 and the Great Hiatus. Firstly, Holmes uniquely trusts the official police, and the author has played with the reader while establishing as much. The author encourages trust in the police by the readers, the great British public, at a critical time for the Empire, the unstable 1890s. Secondly, the seemingly superfluous parts of the story, including the death of the watchman, may be explained. Thirdly, the story is partly nostalgic, as the openness of the relationship between Holmes and the Watsons, especially Mary, changes after the Great Hiatus—to the extent of Mary being stated to be dead, though I think she is hidden for her own protection.

In short, "The Stock-Broker's Clerk" is very much a canonical story where, in the words of Holmes himself, "nothing could be better."

Michael Duke (Melbourne, Australia) is a founding member and president of the Sherlock Holmes Society of Melbourne, and a member of the Sydney Passengers and other societies. His Holmesian commentary has been published in *The Passengers' Log* and the book *Victorian Holmes*.

THE ADVENTURE OF THE 'GLORIA SCOTT'

WILLIAM R. COCHRAN

"The Adventure of the 'Gloria Scott'" is an engaging departure from the normal narratives found in the Canon of Sherlock Holmes. Most chronologists place the case in 1873 or 1874, eight years before Holmes met Watson in 1881; thus, the entire account is related by Holmes to Watson. So many scholars have pored over the text of the tale without observing the details that bring to bear the prime importance of this particular narrative in the saga of Sherlock Holmes. Holmes cleverly conceals his justification for relating the case when he suggests that the observation of old Trevor—"it seems to me that all the detectives of fact and of fancy would be children in your hands"—was the reason he became a detective at all. It is ironic that the great detective should use the JP's remark to seemingly boast about his powers of observation, when in fact he has failed miserably in detecting the threat posed by Hudson's visit.

Trevor's statement speaks volumes about Holmes's powers of observation, while at the same time revealing a distinct prejudice in Holmes's judgement. Although Trevor possesses great qualities and exhibits an evenhanded manner of dispensing judgement, Holmes cannot get past the fact that Trevor's library contains books he has never read. This act of hubris on the part of the naive detective reveals his assumption that one who has not obtained wisdom from books, but who has learned volumes through their experiences, must not possess great intellect. Holmes was wrong—dead wrong in this case, and as a result he failed.

Before one begins to pass judgement on Sherlock Holmes, one needs to consider that the visit was supposed to be a vacation from school. Holmes and Victor Trevor became friends under unusual circumstances while at university. It is quite probable that Victor had been friendless at the university because his father feared someone might use the son to punish the father. This fact may well be why "he invited me down to his father's place at Donnithorpe, in Norfolk, and I accepted his hospitality for a month of the long vacation." He did not go to Donnithorpe to solve any crime. It was a visit, a time to relax.

However, old Trevor wanted to examine the one who befriended his son at college. Old Trevor's curiosity about Holmes caused him to want to meet this extraordinary young man face-to-face. Holmes was cleverly lured into revealing his skills because he perceived, "The old man evidently thought that his son was exaggerating in his description of one or two trivial feats which I had performed." Thus, Holmes's ego reared its ugly head, and events were set into motion. Trevor faints when Holmes gets too close to the truth because he believed Holmes was there to reveal his past. Yet Holmes's concern proved that the JP had misjudged him. Contrary to what the detective revealed to Watson, the statement concerning Holmes's skill was not the determining factor which caused Holmes to become a detective.

At this time in his career he had honed these skills at home with his brother Mycroft, who also taught him to *not* go out of his way to verify his own solutions. It is reason Sherlock is so critical of his brother in "The Greek Interpreter," a case in which he reveals the tutor who helped him develop his skills. To the brothers, it was a marvelous game which held no consequences for being wrong. The events at Donnithorpe proved that the "game" had serious consequences if one fails to observe.

One can envisage the fledgling detective's frustration as he asks pertinent questions but his source will not provide the necessary data. One such exchange concerns old Trevor's walking stick. "You have taken some pains to bore the head of it and pour melted lead into the hole, so as to make it a formidable weapon. I argued that you would not take such precautions unless you had some danger to fear." Yet Trevor steadfastly refuses to admit he is in danger, let alone tell from whom the threat emanates. As he gains in experience, Holmes learns to walk away from any case if his instincts tell him the prospective client is withholding important facts. In cases after he meets Dr. Watson, this is precisely what Holmes accomplishes. However, in this instance, his respect for Old Trevor prevents him from refusing the case. Thus, Holmes believes he has overstayed his welcome, and returns to his London rooms where he works out a few experiments in organic chemistry for the next seven weeks.

Almost two months after Holmes returns to London, Victor Trevor seeks Holmes again because something has gone terribly wrong. Holmes must have had some reservations about returning to Donnithorpe, but the urgency in his friend's request and his reassurance—"From you I shall have no secrets. Here is the statement which was drawn up by my father when he knew that the danger from Hudson had become imminent"—spurred him to action. The document takes up more than one-third of the entire narrative, stating every detail of old Trevor's past history. Had the elder Trevor confided in the young detective from the outset, the outcome might have been different. However, it is clear that old Trevor also knew Sherlock Holmes had not fully accepted his path to become a detective. It is the reason he only *suggests* that Holmes would make a great detective. His worldly experience tells him to use caution, thus he does not say that this paradigm has yet to be accomplished.

The cryptic message contained in the little tarnished cylinder, scrawled upon a half sheet of slate-grey paper, reveals Holmes's powers regarding ciphers—it was child's play in the hands of Sherlock Holmes. While these parlor tricks which entertained his college friend reveal the skills he would need to become the supreme detective, it was still a game to him. Holmes does observe the elder Trevor collapsing in a "dead faint" at the revelation of the JA initials, but he fails to determine why old Trevor was so frightened. He is also aware that the arrival of Hudson initiates the unusual behavior of Trevor, yet once again he again does not pursue answers.

Because of what has befallen his college friend, Holmes begins to realize detective work is not a parlor game, and his neglect of minutiae was the cause of his failure. The hubris of his youth caused him not to recognize that he has failed his good friend, Victor, until it is too late. Upon the revelation of the life of his father James Armitage, young Trevor is forced to flee the country in disgrace, accepting a position on the marshy lowlands of Terai planting tea. We are told he became successful, a fact which reveals Holmes's awareness that his friend "was heart-broken." Yet, over time, Holmes realizes "that he is doing well."

As ironic as it may seem, these blunders are the essence of making this the greatest story of the Canon. Holmes's determination to not repeat these mistakes created the *raison d'etre* in the stoic student of detection that Watson meets at Bart's. For example, Holmes's successful demonstration of observation and inference garnered him a reputation. He had believed he was invincible, but the deficiencies described in "The 'Gloria Scott'" humbled him, causing him to re-evaluate the application of his ratiocinative skills. Scottish author Samuel Smiles observed: "We learn wisdom from failure much more than from success. We often discover what will do, by finding out what will not do; and probably he who never made a mistake never made a discovery." Old Trevor's remarks that Holmes should consider detective work as a profession merely made him aware of what he could become.

Between the events in this case and the fateful meeting at Bart's, Holmes was attempting to determine "how far bruises may be produced after death." He learned to leave no stone unturned in order to avoid future embarrassment. His plan was to establish a foolproof formula for gathering all of the facts before forming an opinion. Without Holmes's awakening, the world might never have known of Sherlock Holmes. In the post-Watson cases, Holmes has rectified all the mistakes exhibited in this narrative. Furthermore, the fact that Hudson proves to be a blackmailer of the first order may well have been the genesis of his disdain for extortionists in the Canon. Therefore, "The Adventure of the 'Gloria Scott'" not only should be included as the one of the best cases in the Canon, but deserves the title of "the best of the best" of the 60 adventures of Sherlock Holmes.

William R. Cochran (Carbondale, Illinois) is a Baker Street Irregular, a former editor of the *Baker Street Journal*, author of *Thinking Outside the Tin Dispatch Box* and other works, and co-founder and Master of the Occupants of the Empty House.

THE ADVENTURE OF
THE MUSGRAVE RITUAL

SUSAN E. BAILEY

In order for a story to be the best, it must display elements that are both unique and archetypical. I believe this to be true for "The Musgrave Ritual." It also contains both drama and comedy, and it provides wonderful insight into Holmes and Watson's daily life, as well as a fantastically complex mystery that is solved through both mental deduction and real nitty-gritty work. In addition, it is also the best to me for reasons of my own special interest, which I will discuss later.

I love the beginning of a Sherlock Holmes story. Many of the stories begin with an evocative scene of life at Baker Street, but "The Musgrave Ritual" has the best. A few of the physical objects that are considered essential to a depiction of the rooms at 221B are found in this story, such as the Persian slipper and the jackknife pinning correspondence to the mantelpiece. Any representation of Holmes and Watson's sitting room would be incomplete without these essential details. In this story, Watson also tells us about Holmes's unappreciated adornment of their sitting room wall with bullet-pocks in the shape of the letters VR, honoring their monarch, Victoria Regina. I think it is curious to note, as the story progresses, that Holmes is a kind of royalist in his own, perhaps ironic, way.

To my mind, any successful Holmes story must contain humor. The way in which Watson sets the scene in this case is incredibly endearing. He reveals our hero to be both a thoroughly loveable and an entirely annoying person through his sarcastic, humorous tone. Not only does Watson poke fun at Holmes by depicting him as an intolerable individual with whom to share a living space, but Holmes jibes back at Watson, showing the doctor to be comical too, as he suddenly becomes more interested in hearing a good story to publish than in having his sitting room tidied. At least we know that Watson has his priorities straight. By beginning a story in this witty manner, Watson opens our minds and hearts to adventure. Our guard is let down through laughter which allows us to become more receptive to—and engrossed in—the narrative that follows.

"The Musgrave Ritual" is indispensable to the Canon because along with "The 'Gloria Scott'," it is one of only two stories in which Holmes himself relates the course of his investigative activities before his collaboration with Watson. Thus we gain access to invaluable information about Holmes's early life and career that can be found nowhere else. Here we find that as a young man he had taken rooms in Montague Street, close to the British Museum, and when he was not in work he would spend his days at the Museum studying. (Really, wouldn't we all?)

Another remarkable feature of "The Musgrave Ritual" is that Watson is not present for the action. The same could only be said to be true of a few other stories, including "The 'Gloria Scott'," "The Lion's Mane," and part of *The Hound of the Baskervilles*. What we have instead is Watson's narration of his hearing of Holmes's case. Thus we are made to identify with Watson. Watson is our stand-in as listener, and his excitement and curiosity guides our own.

The method by which Holmes goes about investigating the mystery is thrilling to read. To achieve his conclusion he is required to utilize an impressive variety of mental tools—mathematics, botany, geography, astronomy, and human psychology. Clearly Holmes's work at the British Museum has borne fruit. As he details for Watson how he deciphered the clues, it is evident that he truly enjoys his work.

Every time I read the scene in which Holmes measures out the grounds of Hurlstone Manor with his strides, my mental image is of its depiction in the Granada television series. Jeremy Brett's expression of glee and mischief is a visual portrayal of exactly how I imagine Holmes feels in the moment. It is also apparent to me that he is having fun, prancing around the yard following a treasure map. This scene makes it easy for me to understand how, in BBC *Sherlock*, Mycroft Holmes could state that as a child, Sherlock wanted to be a pirate. In this case he has his chance to act like one.

The joy with which Holmes finds the subterranean chamber makes his revelation of its contents all the more striking. He slowly describes how the stone is lifted, the box is found within, and then the contents of the box are revealed, leaving us unprepared for the shocking discovery of Brunton's corpse. It is as if we have just heard the climax of a campfire ghost story. In my mind, I scream in surprise as though I had been watching a horror film.

The mystery itself contains components that make so many Holmes stories satisfying: an aristocratic house, a love affair gone awry, a main character afflicted with brain fever, a tragic death. What makes "The

Musgrave Ritual" unique is that the crux of the mystery is an actual historical event. Of course, to readers in the twenty-first century, the stories themselves seem shrouded in history. But it was not so to readers at the time the stories were originally published, who were reading about cases set amid their present life or in the recent past. Holmes's discovery of the crown of King Charles I brings the weight of British history and the monarchy to bear on our story. At this point we start to understand Holmes's tease at the beginning of his tale, that the relics of "The Musgrave Ritual" are themselves history. Associating Holmes with an object of true historical import magnifies the detective from being just a man to being an actor of significance within the narrative of British history. For a moment he is confirmed to be the figure of greatness that we, his devotees, have always known him to be.

Still, we could hardly say that the mystery was entirely brought to a satisfying completion, for three questions remain. What has become of Rachel Howells? Was Brunton's death an accident, or did Rachel murder him? And, as Holmes asks, why was the crown of Charles I never reclaimed by his successors? Far from leaving Holmes and his tale diminished, this lack of completion leaves the impression on us that the story continues and the mystery has not ended. I believe this is also partly the intent behind including the enigmatic and somewhat ridiculous titles of unwritten cases at the beginning of this story, as Watson often does. We feel that the present story is only a small part of something much bigger, the bounds of which cannot be reached.

"The Musgrave Ritual" is attractive to me on a personal level because I have an academic background in religious studies. Among many other things, I studied ritual in an anthropological context as a phenomenon of human behavior. In her book *Ritual: Perspectives and Dimensions*, Catherine Bell classifies rituals into six different types. These include rites of passage and political rituals, or rituals of group identity. The ritual in "The Musgrave Ritual" functions as both of these. It is a rite of passage in the Musgrave family, a text and practice that was handed down from father to son. It is also a political ritual in that it marks allegiance to the Stuart kings. In *Ritual and Memory*, Harvey Whitehouse and James Laidlaw discuss how ritual works as a preservation of memory, either personal or historical. The Musgrave ritual could also be said to operate in this way. It preserves a memory in code. Even if those who recite it and practice it no longer understand what it literally signifies, it can still be "read" to retrieve its inner meaning. It is remarkable that American Sherlockians have taken the ritual catechism in this story and used it as a metaritual of group identity. At least as far back as 1947, every year at the Baker Street Irregulars' dinner in January, the Musgrave Ritual has been recited antiphonally, that is, in a call and response method, thereby turning the ritual text into a ritual practice.

What is it that "The Musgrave Ritual" lacks? Perhaps just a pretty young woman for Watson to admire. "The Musgrave Ritual" has everything else necessary for a great Holmes and Watson story—mystery, deductions, humor, romance, brain fever—as well as features that can be found nowhere else. The story has a significant role in the Sherlockian community and it demonstrates that Holmes has an important place in history. I can think of nothing more a reader could desire.

Susan E. Bailey (Sterling, Virginia) holds master's degrees in religious studies from Harvard Divinity School and Duke University. She is a member of Watson's Tin Box of Ellicott City, Maryland, and of the Scintillation of Scions organizing committee.

THE ADVENTURE OF
THE REIGATE SQUIRES

ASHLEY D. POLASEK

In 1927, the *Strand Magazine* invited Arthur Conan Doyle to publish a list of his favorite dozen Sherlock Holmes stories. Subsequently, Sherlockians have conducted several polls to attempt to devise a list of the best tales in the Canon. The lists tend roughly to agree both with one another and with Conan Doyle, but there is one story that Conan Doyle cites that none of the published polls—those from 1944, 1954, 1959, 1989, and 1999—includes: "The Adventure of the Reigate Squires." The story has been overlooked in adaptation as well. Thirteen of the 60 stories in the Canon are not part of the surviving talkie screen tradition of Sherlock Holmes; only one of these stories overlaps with Conan Doyle's own list of his best tales, so it's worth asking why "The Reigate Squires," which the author himself favored, is thus uniquely disregarded.

There are many avenues for approaching a Sherlock Holmes story. Among the most popular are reading for the cleverness of the mystery, for the daring of the adventure, for the compelling genius of Sherlock Holmes himself, and for the beauty of the relationship between Holmes and Watson. Most stories in the Canon suit one of these approaches, or possibly two, extremely well, but few satisfy all four simultaneously; among these rare treasures is "The Adventure of the Reigate Squires."

The simple fact is this: because its mystery perhaps lacks quite the panache of "The Red-Headed League," its adventure is admittedly less gripping than "The Speckled Band," its illustrations of Holmes's genius not quite as sexy as "Silver Blaze," and its revelations about our intrepid heroes' mutual love and respect more subtle than in "The Three Garridebs," it's easy to miss the fact that "The Reigate Squires" accomplishes what none of these tales manages: it represents a rare and skillful balance of all four of these components, and is therefore among the finest stories in the Canon.

When Holmes first hears of the circumstances of William Kirwan's murder, he notes that "the crime is a very peculiar one." Beyond the murder itself, the mystery at the heart of "The Reigate Squires" is a delightful tangle. Each of the many elements that comprise the puzzle might be submitted as the most interesting seed of mystery within other, more oft-feted tales. "The Six Napoleons" and "The Abbey Grange" include unconventional burglaries as significant clues, but what could be more clever than a blind in which the criminals defray suspicion by having the local constabulary investigate their burglary of their own home? "A Case of Identity" and "The Dancing Men" include bizarre missives, but here we have the detailed incriminating correspondence from the former, with the opportunity for readers to conduct their own analysis on the reproduced evidence that is such a delight in the latter. There isn't a great deal of mystery in "Charles Augustus Milverton," but murderous retribution against intended blackmail underpins the puzzle in "The Reigate Squires." In only a few stories is Holmes forced to distinguish real clues from fabricated evidence: "The Abbey Grange" and "The Norwood Builder" famously include this additional layer of inscrutability, but only in "The Reigate Squires" do we get the pleasure of watching the villain taunt the detective before being exposed as both a fool and a murderer simultaneously in the denouement.

Of course the surprise associated with the mystery is attached to our first reading, which for most of us is lost to the mists of time. One reason why the Canon stands up to continuous re-reading is that these are not crime stories; they are adventures. We enjoy seeing Holmes and Watson face imminent danger and emerge bruised but triumphant. Our heroes are attacked bodily on several occasions; the structure of the story-telling, however, ensures that there are usually narrative layers dampening the immediacy of the danger, as is the case in the notorious fights in "The Solitary Cyclist," "The Illustrious Client," and "The Final Problem." Holmes relates his brawl with Mr. Woodley after the fact, Watson learns of the attack on Holmes ordered by Baron Gruner through the newspaper, and the good doctor is relegated to speculation as to the confrontation at the Reichenbach Falls.

We must go to the Canon's most thrilling showdowns, those in *The Sign of Four*, *The Hound of the Baskervilles*, "The Empty House," and "The Three Garridebs," to find deadly confrontations for which Watson and Holmes are both present. Lest we forget, though, there is another. Watson is conversing with Inspector Forrester when they hear "a sudden scream of 'Help! Help! Murder!'." The doctor recognizes Holmes's voice and rushes "madly from the room" to find Holmes prostrate, being assaulted by both Cunninghams. Without the doctor's timely intervention, Holmes would have become Alec Cunningham's second murder victim.

Arthur Conan Doyle's justification for including "The Reigate Squires" on his list of top twelve Sherlock Holmes stories when he might, he noted, have selected any from half a dozen others he considered of roughly equal quality, is that out of all of them, it is in "The Reigate Squires" that, "on the whole, Holmes himself shows perhaps the most ingenuity." There are easily as many people who read the Canon for the characters as for the plots. Likely many more, in fact. In "The Reigate Squires," the mystery unfolds around Holmes and Watson. Unlike the common case, therefore, there is very little backstory to recount, and Watson is present for the best moments of the investigation.

We know that Holmes would have made a fine actor, but it is only on rare occasions that Watson actually observes these skills. We would likely cite "A Scandal in Bohemia" and "The Dying Detective" as the best examples of such occasions, but consider the extent to which Holmes feigns illness to draw the Cunninghams into his trap. He fakes a fainting spell in which his "face had suddenly assumed the most dreadful expression. His eyes rolled upward, his features writhed in agony, and with a suppressed groan he dropped on his face upon the ground," and must allow himself to be carried bodily into the house. Through his pretense of feebleness, he collects evidence and creates an opportunity to acquire the incriminating note from Alec's room. While in so many cases we only hear of Holmes employing his methods, here we see it in action.

Finally, and for many readers, most vitally, "The Reigate Squires" is a tale that highlights the joy that Holmes and Watson take in one another. Because the foundation of the story is Watson nursing Holmes back to health, it shows the doctor at his medical best and illustrates Holmes's reliance on Watson's love and care. Within 24 hours of learning that Holmes is ill and in a state of nervous collapse, Watson is by his sickbed in France. So sympathetic to his friend's needs is he, that Watson sees what doctors in Lyons miss: Watson looks past the physical illness and recognizes that Holmes is in a state of depression, and it is that which the good doctor seeks to treat with their stay in Reigate.

Playfulness marks the interactions between Holmes and Watson as the latter struggles vainly to keep the former in a state of calm recuperation. Holmes's good-humored attempts to give himself over to Watson's care and best judgment lead to delightful images, such as Holmes shrugging his shoulders "with a glance of comic resignation," followed by his yawning declaration, "All right, Watson, I don't intend to meddle," when Watson warns him against interesting himself in the initial burglary. Then, when the murder case is laid at his feet, Holmes laughingly cries, "The fates are against you, Watson!" We must also not neglect one of the funniest moments in the entire Canon, in which the doctor watches his friend upset a table, sending water and oranges flying in all directions, and, to Watson's astonishment, declares, "You've done it now, Watson.... A pretty mess you've made of the carpet." Few stories in the Canon provide so many illustrations of the easy camaraderie that marks their friendship.

If you search the Canon for the cleverest mystery, the most exciting adventure, the finest instance of Holmes's ingenuity, and the most touching illustration of Holmes and Watson's friendship, you'll come up with four different stories, and none of them will be "The Reigate Squires." It is for this reason that the tale has been so unfairly passed over since Conan Doyle included it on his own list of dozen favorites. However, if instead of searching for a single gourmet dish, you elect to enjoy a smorgasbord, you will find the most delicious variety of Sherlockian flavors in "The Reigate Squires" and, like Holmes, you'll be forced to admit that "your country trip has been a distinct success."

Ashley D. Polasek (Anderson, South Carolina) holds a PhD in the study of Sherlock Holmes on screen and is a member of the Baker Street Babes, the Adventuresses of Sherlock Holmes, the Sherlock Holmes Society of London, and the Diogenes Club of Washington, D.C.

THE ADVENTURE OF THE CROOKED MAN

PEGGY PERDUE

Congratulations, dear Reader. You have made it to the best of all Holmes stories, "The Adventure of the Crooked Man." Here at last is the story that will deliver everything you want from the Great Detective.

The sterling quality of this bright treasure from the Canon can be seen from the very outset of the narrative. Instead of starting off in Baker Street, we find ourselves at the home of Watson, where we have the opportunity to acquire even more information about our dynamic duo than a standard visit to 221B could provide. What Watsonian does not relish this chance to learn who Watson is when he is at home? What Sherlockian scholar does not pause to wonder which of the doctor's innumerable wives has just gone off to bed?

Then, as always, the tale really gets under way when Holmes arrives. If we are pleased to see the personal side of Watson in the opening paragraph, we must be doubly pleased to be treated to a glimpse of the inner Holmes as well. We see the greatest mind in detection calling on a friend, just as you or I would. We love the Holmes stories in large part because they are such a beautiful testament to the value of friendship, but instances when Holmes explicitly shows his regard for Watson are not really so very numerous. Here we have a prime example. Watson is no mere flunky or tagalong in this scene. Holmes has come to Watson's house because even after his friend has married and moved away he finds that he cannot quite manage without him.

Another reason we read the Canon is that we enjoy Sherlock Holmes's flair for the art of detection. In "The Crooked Man", the deductions pile up like Christmas presents. As soon as Holmes appears on the scene, he makes a rapid series of inferences about Watson's state of mind, his brand of tobacco, his habits of dress, his lack of a gentleman visitor, the state of his medical practice, and the recent presence of a workman in the house. This is generosity on the part of our author! This is being spoiled with treats! Watson is duly impressed as well, and when he praises his friend for this *tour de force* Sherlock replies with that most Holmesian of catch phrases, "Elementary." As the two friends sit cozily smoking at Watson's hearth we can almost hear him add, "...my dear Watson."

These homely elements act as a fine foil to the adventurous and exotic aspects of the story, which are also abundant. Henry Wood's eyewitness account of the Indian rebellion of 1857 makes for exciting reading, especially when it is followed by details of his adventures in Nepal and Afghanistan. On top of all this, there is the revelation of Colonel Barclay's despicable deed. "The Crooked Man", which offers so much, would be remarkable for its nested story of jealousy and betrayal alone.

The story's adventurous side is matched, moreover, by its air of mystery. Notably, it makes use of one of the best effects in the crime fiction writer's toolbox—the locked room mystery. We all enjoy a good puzzle, and the main points of this one offer tantalizing questions for the reader: What has become of the missing key and who—or what—ran up the curtain? Naysayers may argue that Conan Doyle's use of a climbing creature in a locked room is only a rehash of Tonga from *The Sign of the Four*, and that even this is an idea that he borrowed from Edgar Allan Poe's "Murders in the Rue Morgue." Let us have done with this complaint right away. After all, it takes true mastery to play such marvelous variations on a theme, and who but Poe and Conan Doyle in concert could give English literature a police lineup consisting of an orangutan, an Andaman Islander and a mongoose?

Another classic crime fiction concept made use of in this adventure is the "fair play" mystery. Not all of the canonical stories give the reader a reasonable chance of deducing part of the mystery for themselves. Holmes acknowledges this himself when he tells Watson that the effect of his "little sketches" depends upon his holding back "some factors in the problem which are never imparted to the reader." As if in answer to this, we are later provided with many pertinent facts about the alleged murder at the Barclay residence, including details about the room's open window. As well, given the description of the animal and the tale's Indian elements, it would even be possible for first-time readers to guess the name of the animal that Wood kept in his mysterious box.

That is not to say that it would have been easy for the story's Victorian readers to make the identification, because most English and American readers would have had little experience of South Asian fauna in person or in print. Indeed, Henry Wood's furry companion seems to have been the first significant appearance of such a creature in English literature. It is not, however, the most famous. That honor surely goes to the titular mongoose in Rudyard Kipling's story "Rikki-Tikki-Tavi", which was published in *Pall Mall Magazine* in November of 1893, three months after "The Crooked Man" first appeared in the *Strand*. Perhaps the Holmes story was even part of the inspiration for Rikki-Tikki-Tavi, in which case we can add to our tale's perfections the honor of having played a role in the development of this beloved children's tale. This may seem a grand claim, but support for the idea of Kipling as a fan of Conan Doyle's writing can be found in a manuscript letter from him held by Toronto Public Library's Arthur Conan Doyle Collection (November 11, 1894).

The more you read "The Crooked Man", the more you find to love. What else would you add to the ideal Holmes story? Peculiar footprints? This tale has them. A train journey out of London? Check. A beautiful woman prostrated by brain fever? Check. This story that has it all is also one of only three that mention the Baker Street boys, a.k.a. the irregulars. In this case we have Simpson acting for Holmes, allowing us some room to hope that *A Study in Scarlet's* Wiggins was not in attendance because he had found a regular job.

It is a truism that the business of crime fiction is to bring order out of chaos, and the resolution of "The Crooked Man" is also deserving of much praise. The twist to the tale is that there has been no crime at all except for the very old sin committed by Colonel Barclay himself. The Colonel has died of apoplexy brought on by his own guilty conscience. Victim and criminal are neatly combined into one person, and we are assured that no bad deed goes unpunished. This moral gains additional gravitas when Holmes makes the connection to the Biblical tale of David and Bathsheba, giving the reader a pleasing sense of having dipped into theology as well as crime fiction. At the story's conclusion, we learn that no charges will be laid against any innocent person, because the police have correctly determined the cause of death, even though the full details of the event remain beyond their understanding. As friends of Sherlock Holmes, we must be additionally gratified that this time the deliverance of his own brand of justice does not require that our hero commit misprision of felony.

In "The Adventure of the Crooked Man," Arthur Conan Doyle seems determined to bring out his best material as he deftly combines lively writing with weighty themes. When this tale of friendship and adventure is over, we can close the book with great satisfaction, knowing that we have just read the perfect Sherlock Holmes story.

Peggy Perdue (Toronto, Ontario) is curator of the Toronto Public Library's Arthur Conan Doyle Collection, a Baker Street Irregular and Master Bootmaker, a notable Sherlockian traveller, speaker and socialite, and an adventurous cook.

THE ADVENTURE OF THE RESIDENT PATIENT

MARGOT NORTHCOTT

Caveat time: this is not the most thrilling story in the Canon, even if you're medically inclined. Sure, there's some standard episode-of-*House-M.D.* seizure-faking, and a murder most foul, but at its core there's not much by way of mystery or stakes. Normally, Holmes's involvement in a case is brought to a satisfactory conclusion when his deductions lead to the bad guys getting caught, disaster being averted, etc. In "The Resident Patient", the disaster happens anyway and Holmes merely deduces the circumstances of the crime. It's not really a whodunit because the mystery isn't solvable by the audience, we're just along for the ride. It's more of a dunit.

That being said, "The Resident Patient" was an early favourite of mine. During my childhood read-through of the Canon, Watson's first-person *mise-en-scène* stuck out as a hallmark Sherlockian Moment, wherein Sherlock Holmes seemingly develops psychic powers:

> It had been a close, rainy day in October. Our blinds were half-drawn, and Holmes lay curled upon the sofa, reading and re-reading a letter which he had received by the morning post....
>
> Finding that Holmes was too absorbed for conversation, I had tossed aside the barren paper, and leaning back in my chair, I fell into a brown study. Suddenly my companion's voice broke in upon my thoughts.
>
> "You are right, Watson," said he. "It does seem a very preposterous way of settling a dispute."
>
> "Most preposterous!" I exclaimed, and then, suddenly realizing how he had echoed the inmost thought of my soul, I sat up in my chair and stared at him in blank amazement.
>
> "What is this, Holmes?" I cried. "This is beyond anything which I could have imagined."

This is one of my favourite moments between Holmes and Watson in the whole Canon. They're so married it's not even funny. When Watson questions Holmes about his *Long Island Medium* stunt, Holmes proceeds to explain how he deduced Watson's train of thought by staring at his features, "especially your eyes." After waxing poetic about Watson's face for a few paragraphs, Holmes suggests that they go for a stroll, and the pair of them spend three hours people-watching. I swear I am not making this up. They're so busy holding hands and judging everybody that they don't make it home until 10:00. They return to 221B to find a brougham waiting outside and the lights on upstairs; a case. Classic, right?

Imagine my surprise when I reread the story a few years later and found this part was missing! As it turns out, the edition of "The Resident Patient" I read as a kid wasn't the original one from the *Strand* magazine, but the version that appeared in the first British edition of the *Memoirs of Sherlock Holmes*.

Holmes's brief foray into cold reading was not originally from "The Resident Patient". The scene is scavenged from "The Cardboard Box", a story which editors of the *Memoirs* scrapped as too racy. Racy is perhaps a strong word for the objectionable content in "The Cardboard Box", but clearly Arthur Conan Doyle or his editors felt it was unpleasant enough to warrant removing the entire story from the *Memoirs*. The only part that the editors deemed worth publishing at that time was the psychic scene, which they cut and pasted into this story instead.

While the story loses some of its shine without the transplanted "Cardboard Box" introduction, it still features the beating heart of the Canon pretty prominently: the relationship between Holmes and Watson. The alternative introduction (in fact there are two versions of it) still situates us within the early years of Holmes and Watson's acquaintance, and the boys still get their three-hour evening ramble through London. Just as it is with Mulder and Scully in *The X-Files*, or Kirk and Spock in *Star Trek*, the dynamic between the two protagonists keeps the audience engaged during the occasional lacklustre tale.

The story goes on to have some really nice Watson moments, where our self-deprecating narrator makes a few spot-on deductions using Holmes's methods. When Holmes takes one look at the brougham outside and announces that a general practitioner (not long in practice) has come to seek their help, Watson helpfully dissects Holmes's swift and unexplained deductions for the reader without missing a beat. Later in the case, when Watson suggests that perhaps their client has concocted the whole strange story for a nefarious purpose, Holmes responds with an amused smile and reassures Watson that his first thought was the exact same thing. He's a little condescending about it, but by his standards he's being downright lovely. In other stories Holmes is such a colossal jerk about Watson's deductive reasoning skills that it makes you wonder how they're friends in the first place. This story is one of the times where the audience gets to see how much the characters genuinely enjoy each other's company.

Interestingly, Conan Doyle included "The Resident Patient" on his own "Top 19" greatest hits list. Granted, he ranked it 18th out of 19, but it's worth mentioning because it represents a unique insight into Conan Doyle's fantasies about London. Holmes's client, Dr. Percy Trevelyan, is a bright young graduate of the University of London. He won a prestigious award in medical school, and he runs a flourishing practice in the expensive Cavendish Square district, where London's top specialists keep their offices. It reads a bit like escapist fiction for Victorian doctors.

In the story's set-up, Trevelyan explains how he lucked into an unusual arrangement with a patient named Blessington. Blessington offered to put them both up indefinitely near Cavendish Square as long as Trevelyan agreed to run a practice downstairs and turn over most of the profits. This arrangement suits them both for a few years until Blessington's past (as a member of a bank gang who sold out his compatriots for a lighter sentence) catches up with him. While Blessington meets a gruesome end and his murderers are presumed to have drowned while fleeing the country, everything seems to work out reasonably well for Dr. Trevelyan.

In 1891, Conan Doyle attempted to set up a practice as an eye specialist not far from Cavendish Square, but after just three months he abandoned the venture—presumably because the rent was too steep and the patients too few, and to concentrate on literature. He might have wished for a wealthy resident patient to solve all his financial woes, as Dr. Trevelyan had. Although "The Resident Patient" is not necessarily the best Sherlock Holmes story, I am confident that it is the best sugar daddy wish-fulfillment fantasy Conan Doyle ever published.

Margot Northcott (London, Ontario) is a music teacher, and a founding member of the Cesspudlian Society of London, Ontario. She also hangs out with the Bootmakers of Toronto and the Stratford-On-Avon Sherlock Holmes Society.

THE ADVENTURE OF THE GREEK INTERPRETER

BILL MASON

Fully twelve years into the partnership of Sherlock Holmes and John Watson, the good doctor had "never heard him refer to his relatives and hardly ever to his own early life." Even among readers who had not considered the question, Watson's revelation of such ignorance in the opening lines of "The Greek Interpreter" must have raised more than a few eyebrows. Anyone would just assume that two men living in the same rooms for a dozen years would know all there was to know about each other's life and background, But Watson had been no better off than the legions of enthusiastic readers of the two novels and 21 short stories about the great detective that had already appeared. For them, Holmes was a hero without a history, a man who had stepped into fame without accounting for his background, a solver of mysteries who himself was a mystery.

All of that was changed abruptly by "The Greek Interpreter." The introduction of Mycroft Holmes, the disclosure of his very existence, was a bombshell. The reverse side of the Sherlock Holmes coin had finally been seen, an event of import not unlike the first glimpse of the dark side of the moon, And, at long last, to the delight of the reading public in the *Strand Magazine*, Holmes became something more than just a thinking machine who solved his cases in a calculating and coldly logical manner. He was a real man, after all.

When "The Greek Interpreter" was presented to the public in 1893, the popularity of Sherlock Holmes stories was at its zenith. By this time, Holmes himself was a celebrity, and with celebrity (in 1893 and in the present day) comes a public demand for intimate details. Personal privacy is sacrificed to the insatiable curiosity of the masses. Knowing, or at least sensing, this, Conan Doyle consciously decided to address the need. He deviated from a basic formula that, by this time, was familiar to his legions of readers.

The opening statement is actually a declaration of intent, of purpose, for writing this story at all. Holmes's "reticence," we are told, "had increased the somewhat inhuman effect" he produced. Holmes was "a brain without a heart... deficient in human sympathy." So "The Greek Interpreter" was designed to fix a problem, and did so.

Watson might as well have commented, as did Capt. Renault to Rick Blaine in *Casablanca*, "I must say, Holmes, you are becoming quite human." The importance of this humanization of Holmes cannot be overstated. "The Greek Interpreter" is the foundation upon which the entire Sherlockian mythos is built. Without it, Holmes might have remained a two-dimensional literary device—a problem solver, but not a believable person.

Consider the appearance of Mycroft Holmes on the Sherlockian stage, the revelation that the two brothers were descended from "country squires" on one side and a family of exotic French artists on the other, the almost juvenile observational competition between the brothers, the indirect but unavoidable images of a childhood, a home life, parents. All of this mitigated that "somewhat inhuman effect" which Holmes had produced in previous tales. Without "The Greek Interpreter," Sherlock Holmes could never have become Vincent Starrett's "man who never lived, and yet can never die."

Of course, the story certainly can also be cherished for the abundance of grist provided for the Sherlockian's mill. Two of the greatest quotations of the Canon can be found here: "I hear of Sherlock everywhere since you became his chronicler," and "Art in the blood is liable to take the strangest forms." Wonderful problems, perfect for the Great Game precisely because they are ultimately unsolvable and open to eternal debate, are to be found as well: the actual relationship of the brothers Holmes to the artist Vernet, the location and identity of the Diogenes Club, the inexplicable failure to protect Mr. Melas (a victim in this story), the nature of the "property" that the Kratides possessed that was so important, just how that newspaper clipping came to be sent from Buda-Pesth.

To be sure, the "adventure" itself is nothing remarkable. Sherlock Holmes accomplishes nothing, really. He allows himself to be hamstrung by a bumbling Scotland Yard bureaucracy. He and Mycroft actually enable the murder of Paul Kratides. A huge amount of information attempting to explain the case is crammed into just one paragraph at the end, almost as an afterthought.

But none of this matters. Conan Doyle knew what he was doing. Even though he had already resolved in his own mind to carry through with his threat to kill Sherlock Holmes and move on to "better things," which he did only three months later with the publication of "The Final Problem," Conan Doyle was providing a background story for his most famous character. In many ways, this was necessary to carry out his nefarious plot against Holmes. How much better to provide the biographical details in "The Greek Interpreter" than to insert them in some sort of obituary awkwardly appended without proper context to the account of the struggle at the Reichenbach Falls.

Conan Doyle already had produced an important literary innovation: a serial character who appeared in numerous stories in a familiar setting. This new idea was readily adopted by other authors, and it set the tone for popular entertainment to the present day, and not only in short stories and novels. Every serial television program, from sitcoms to dramas, owes a debt to the Holmes tales, especially to "The Greek Interpreter," which went one step further with the humanization of the hero. All of the other Sherlock Holmes tales may, and do, flesh out that very real person; but at some level, each and every one of them must be considered in the context of this story.

For giving Sherlock Holmes a background story, for making him "quite human," for providing the raw materials to make him a real person, a man with a family and with a past, just like all of those who loved reading about him, "The Greek Interpreter" stands above any other single story in the Canon.

Bill Mason (Greenbrier, Tennessee) is a Sherlockian lecturer of note, and author of *Pursuing Sherlock Holmes*. A Baker Street Irregular and Master Bootmaker, he is also Head-Light (president) of the Beacon Society, founder of the Fresh Rashers of Nashville, and a member of the Nashville Scholars of the Three-Pipe Problem.

THE ADVENTURE OF THE NAVAL TREATY

BONNIE MacBIRD

Of the many arguments against Conan Doyle's presumed view of women as the weaker sex, perhaps the most piquant is to be found in "The Adventure of the Naval Treaty". Featured in it are one of the strongest females in the Canon—the understated Annie Harrison, who is grace under pressure incarnate—and one of the weakest males, the mousy hysteric Percy Phelps, her fiancé. This couple's bond beggars belief, but they make for a colorful combination, and a fascinating tale.

But that touch of feminism is just the tip of the gigantic ice cube in this refreshing gin and tonic of a story. It provides us not only a cracking good mystery, but also delicious insights into both heroes. It illuminates with humor Watson's schoolboy past, and with unabashed emotion, a bit of Holmes's philosophy.

As for the latter, we have Holmes's famous "lighthouse" prophecy at the end, and possibly one of the most puzzled-over moments in the Canon, that odd brief soliloquy on the rose. But that's the gin, and before we get there, let's look at how this story delivers up the fizzy tonic of its many classic moments.

For the eccentric Holmes, there is "you've come at a crisis, Watson," the chemical experiment that means "a man's life," and a later image of him jotting notes on his shirt-cuff. For rapid-fire Holmes, we are rewarded with his concise putdown of Forbes, an initially unfriendly copper who about-faces so fast the wind whistles off the page. For man-of-action moments we have our unarmed hero overcoming an armed bully: "He looked murder out of the only eye he could see with when we had finished." For pure "feels" and a touch of bromance, "The Naval Treaty" delivers Watson worrying about Holmes's injury—"You are not wounded Holmes?" (as indeed he was, and even bleeding in the Granada dramatization).

And for the theatrical, impish Holmes, we are rewarded with the solution—and the outrageous presentation of the rescued document served up for breakfast on a domed plate to the frenzied relief of Phelps. This follows the oft-quoted description of Mrs. Hudson and her breakfast, forever dividing Sherlockians into the two noisy camps of "Mrs. Hudson was a Scot", or "Hell, no."

For the cerebrally inclined (and aren't all Sherlockians?) "The Naval Treaty" offers us a sparkling piece of reasoning, particularly about the ringing bell and the nature and circumstances of the theft. Thus it delivers the intellectual pyrotechnics we expect from Holmes, but also illustrates Watson's sleight-of-hand in this respect.

Some claim that the Canon always presents all the clues to you, the reader, so you can figure it out with Holmes all along—a common misconception. In this tale, however, the final nail in the coffin (Harrison's motive) is actually discovered off the page, and Holmes's wrap-up surprises us as well as his friend and client. (Additionally, much of the corroboration for Holmes's theories is collected by others, the police and their unnamed women helpers).

Watson delivers the facts in the order that best serves the storytelling, and so this trick usually passes notice. The presentation of the solution here is so dramatically satisfying that we gulp it down with pleasure. Who could ask for more from a single story?

It's fun to infer Doyle's philosophy from his writings, and here the story flashes us a satisfying glimpse of the naked author, er, literary agent. Note Watson's detail about his shared schooldays with the insufferable Percy: "it seemed rather a piquant thing to us to chevy him about the playground and hit him over the shins with a wicket." One can well imagine a similar scene at Stonyhurst—the adventurous, athletic Doyle, confronted with a smarmy, privileged whiner and responding this way. But Watson (and Doyle) are essentially kind men at heart, and it is this generous world-view that is one of the most endearing qualities of the Canon. Watson's disgust at Percy is softened by his actual response to his old schoolmate's cry for help; he brings Holmes into the case.

Doyle's and Watson's natural dislike of the uppercrust is tempered by the willingness to see past the generalization—Lord Holdhurst for example is "that not too common type, a nobleman who is in truth noble." Watson/Doyle have a gentleness in their strength that is one of the strongest attractions for this reader.

Many of us delight in the science of the Canon. That Doyle/Watson stayed *au courant* with the discoveries of the day turns this into great fun. But this story contains a moment of questionable science, graphology, which occasionally pops up along with other discounted "sciences" such as craniometry, phrenology, and physiognomy.

But, back to the wonderful deduction and those two non sequiturs. As a whodunnit, "The Naval Treaty" delivers the goods. The key in scientific method is to find the right question to ask. Here, it is: Who rang the bell and why? No wet footprints indicate a cab, therefore a deliberate visit. After eliminating the commissionaire, his grotesque wife, and Percy's officemate, Holmes narrows the explanation to an impulse grab by this visitor, or a collaboration with Percy, the bell being a ruse to clear him of suspicion.

But the treaty does not surface in the intervening weeks and so the second theory breaks down. After the attempted break-in at Briarbrae, Holmes has his man but still needs a motive to close the case and to satisfy his curiosity. Of course, Holmes figures it all out before Watson, as mentioned, saving his reveal for a moment of pure theatre.

And now to the story's rare moments of philosophy, the gin to our gin-and-tonic. These provide the real kicker. In this reader's view, both the rose and the lighthouse moments point to Holmes the rational optimist rather than faith-driven mystic. Others disagree. And that brings up one of the great delights of reading Sherlock Holmes: there is enough mystery to the man himself to allow each of us to feel justified in our deeply personal confirmation biases.

Let's look at that hotly debated "rose" moment. Holmes has abruptly broken off questioning Percy and has launched into a poetic ramble, which seems a complete non sequitur. Does this brief soliloquy point to a deep spirituality on Holmes's part? Les Klinger mentions that Baring-Gould noted its similarity (and echo) of the "lilies of the field" passage in scripture, Matthew 6:28, 29. Admittedly, there is resonance there. And Holmes is clearly up on his Bible, as evidenced elsewhere. But Klinger also mentions John Lubbock's monograph "Proof of color vision in bees", 1882. Any budding apiarist worth his salt would know well that the color and scent of the flowers is hardly an "extra" as they are precisely what attracts bees.

I incline away from the rose moment as evidence for Holmes's wholesale belief in religion. While we know he attended church in college, I see evidence of agnosticism throughout Canon. His unwillingness to presume, to theorize in advance of the facts, is paramount. By pointing out that nature is stunning in its beauty, and doesn't "need to be" (wrong as he is here about the rose), Holmes acknowledges that good in the world does not have to have a reason. This eliminates the notion of a God who minutely directs traffic. And if there is a God who creates good for no reason whatsoever, then S/He is not essentially a punitive entity.

Therefore this might be a roundabout effort at offering comfort to his client.

Here's another theory: At that point in the investigation, Holmes, trapped in that stifling sickroom, might very well just have needed a break and decided to step away from this frustrating case and its whiny protagonist. Perhaps he contemplated a rose as a form of instant meditation, possibly to cleanse his palate for a renewed bout of thinking.

Sound crazy? Stay with me. I am privileged to know several people who are widely regarded as "world class thinkers", and every one of them has a similar strange habit. My late friend, the genius Marvin Minsky (Father of Artificial Intelligence), used to break off in the middle of conversation to move to the piano and improvise a fugue. Great minds are well known to touch into beauty or art as a way of refilling the well. Some paint, some play music (Holmes and his violin come to mind), some walk in nature. You may argue that many of us with less prodigious gifts also take nourishment from nature and art, but it is peculiar to these geniuses that they break off quite abruptly from whatever they are doing to do so. It looks wacky, but it's so ubiquitous among them that this explanation does, in fact, fit.

My final theory is that Holmes goes off on a tangent just to mess with the incredibly annoying Phelps. He is not above teasing. We then laugh at Miss Harrison's "touch of asperity" when she questions if he's making any headway on the case. In writing parlance, this is called "hanging a lantern on it".

The second random moment of philosophy happens on the train back to London where Watson gloomily notes the ugly factory-like schools being built for the rising armies of poor children. He sadly implies this is a band-aid solution to an expanding social wound. By contrast, Holmes sees in these brick monstrosities nothing less than lighthouses, "beacons of the future" which will "lead England to a brighter tomorrow." Those are the words of an optimist. (My husband, computer pioneer Alan Kay, notes that minds that are used to tackling big and difficult problems are by nature optimistic. Not that they share a uniformly sunny view of human nature, but rather a belief that solutions to big problems exist and the scientific method is the surest path to them.)

These philosophical forays are relatively rare in the Canon and yet there are two of them in this one story, almost stuck like raisins into a gin and tonic. Why? If you will allow me further speculation, perhaps Doyle felt that at the story's greater length (it is the longest in the Canon by far), readers might want a little more meat. He did famously consider his Holmes stories inferior to the serious endeavor of a novel. One might even wonder if Doyle was responding here to critics or fans (as Moffat and Gatiss are so aggressively criticized for doing in their modern remix of Holmes). Who knows? Writers are sensitive beings, even blade straight, steel true ones.

In sum, while you may not agree with my theories, I think we can agree that "The Naval Treaty" provides the fizzy fabulousness of a tightly constructed mystery, and the tantalizing intoxicant of a glimpse of the philosophical Holmes. So let's raise a glass to one of the greatest stories in the Canon.

Bonnie MacBird (Los Angeles and London) is a novelist and a former screenwriter, actor, and producer with three Emmy awards. A member of several Sherlock Holmes societies, she founded the Sherlock Breakfast Club in Los Angeles. Her first Holmes novel, *Art in the Blood*, has been translated into 14 languages; she is at work on a sequel.

THE ADVENTURE OF
THE FINAL PROBLEM

JIM HAWKINS

"The Final Problem", an adventure to end the adventures of Sherlock Holmes, is unique among the Canon of sixty stories, and is one of my favorites for several reasons. In it we see Arthur Conan Doyle plotting to rid himself of his detective creation because Holmes has become a major impediment to his desire to do "more serious literary work." In a 1927 newsreel interview, Conan Doyle admitted his dilemma: "I've written a good deal more about him than I ever intended to do, but my hand has been rather forced by kind friends who continually wanted to know more. And so it is that this rather monstrous growth has come out of what was really a comparative small seed." With the publication of "The Final Problem" in the December 1893 issue of the *Strand Magazine*, Conan Doyle hoped this twelfth serialized story about Holmes and "his rather stupid friend Watson" (Doyle's own words) would be his last.

Four aspects of "The Final Problem" have always delighted me: Watson's *devotion* for Holmes, never so clearly or fully expressed; the impassioned *dialogues* and soliloquies delivered by all three major characters, Holmes, Watson, and Professor Moriarty; the *diversion* of the plot from the usual plan of action; and of course, the seeming *death* of Sherlock Holmes, a scheme long in the making by Conan Doyle, but a complete surprise to both readers and editors of the *Strand Magazine* in 1893.

In previous Holmes stories it is evident that Watson was in awe of Holmes's skills and intellect, but here we see the depth of Watson's *devotion* and admiration for his recently departed friend. Watson's accounts of his adventures with Holmes point out the frustrations and rewards of being both his friend and biographer. Holmes can be an intellectual snob and bully and a know-it-all. With his constant complaining about Scotland Yard, bumbling detectives and shoddy police work, Holmes could be a very unpleasant man to be around much of the time. In "The Final

Problem" Watson, it seems, has forgiven Holmes all his eccentricities and unkind remarks, closing this final story with praise for Holmes, as "the best and the wisest man whom I have ever known."

The impassioned *dialogues* and soliloquies penned by Doyle for this story are among the most memorable in the canon. An example is the oft-quoted opening of "The Final Problem": "It is with a heavy heart that I take up my pen to write these last words in which I shall ever record the singular gifts by which my friend Sherlock Holmes was distinguished." You can almost hear the groans of *Strand Magazine* readers as they read these ominous words. They looked forward eagerly to each new adventure of Holmes and Watson, and were not ready to give them up, even if Holmes had to be resurrected from his untimely death, an idea that Conan Doyle finally adopted himself after feeling a definite pinch in his income.

Another classic soliloquy from this story is Holmes's description of Moriarty. Speaking to Watson, he says: "You have probably never heard of Professor Moriarty?... He sits motionless, like a spider in the center of its web, but that web has a thousand radiations, and he knows well every quiver of each of them. He does little himself. He only plans. But his agents are numerous and splendidly organized. Is there a crime to be done, a paper to be abstracted, we will say, a house to be rifled, a man to be removed—the word is passed to the Professor, the matter is organized and carried out."

At the dramatic encounter between Holmes and Moriarty at 221B Baker Street, Doyle introduces into detective fiction one of the greatest dialogues ever between criminal and detective. An excerpt:

> "You evidently don't know me," said he.
> "On the contrary," I answered, "I think it is fairly evident that I do. Pray take a chair. I can spare you five minutes if you have anything to say."
> "All that I have to say has already crossed your mind," said he.
> "Then possibly my answer has crossed yours," I replied.
> "You stand fast?"
> "Absolutely."

Later in the conversation, Moriarty begins to threaten Holmes with a famous speech: "You crossed my path on the 4th of January, on the 23rd you incommoded me, by the middle of February I was seriously inconvenienced by you, at the end of March I was absolutely hampered in my plans, and now, at the close of April, I find myself placed in such a position through your continual persecution that I am in positive danger of losing my liberty. The situation is becoming an impossible one." Moriarty warns that "If you are clever enough to bring destruction upon me, rest assured that I shall do as much to you," and Holmes counters that "if I were assured of the former eventuality I would, in the interests of the public, cheerfully accept the latter."

"The Final Problem" is not an adventure story like any other in the Canon. Since it is Watson's recounting of Holmes's suicidal struggle with his greatest foe, the story takes an unusual *diversion*, and Conan Doyle does not follow his normal plot progression. Holmes usually comes to his conclusions early on in the story, makes sure of his theories with specific data, then exposes the culprit or plot without (sometimes in spite of) the assistance of police or local detectives. He then explains to all how he did it. In "The Final Problem" Holmes is not present to give that final explanation, so it is left to Watson to fill in the details, some of which are supplied in the farewell note Holmes leaves behind.

Undoubtedly the most distinctive aspect of "The Final Problem" is the seeming *death* of Holmes when he and Moriarty, locked in mortal combat, fall hundreds of feet into the bottom of the Reichenbach Falls. For years Conan Doyle had planned to rid himself of Holmes, feeling that the time spent on these detective stories kept him from creating more substantive literature such as his historical novels, *Micah Clarke* (1889) and *The White Company* (1891, the same year as the first six "Adventures of Sherlock Holmes" in the *Strand Magazine*). Doyle goes to great lengths to make his destruction of Holmes seem inevitable and unavoidable. For this purpose he creates Professor James Moriarty, "the Napoleon of Crime," and sets up Holmes's final heroic act with these words of Holmes to Watson: "He pervades London and no one has heard of him. That's what puts him on a pinnacle on the records of crime. I tell you, Watson, in all seriousness, if I could beat that man, if I could free society of him, I should feel that my own career had reached its summit." By "summit" Doyle's underlying meaning is "end," the last time he ever has to deal with Sherlock Holmes.

"The Final Problem" is not a mystery cast in the model of any of the earlier stories, but it is most certainly Holmes's greatest adventure—a journey to his "death" at the hands of a menace to the world. Holmes's note, written to Watson just before his final meeting with Moriarty, is really a final statement from Conan Doyle to his readers. It is his final solution to his greatest problem, Sherlock Holmes. "I am pleased to think that I shall be able to free society from any further effects of his presence, though I fear that it is at a cost which will give pain to my friends, and especially, my dear Watson, to you. I have already explained to you, however, that my career had in any case reached its crisis, and that no possible conclusion to it could be more congenial to me than this."

It turned out, of course, that "The Final Problem" was not so final after all, but even if it had been (and some argue that it should have been), it is still a most enjoyable story with Conan Doyle at the top of his game. It stands as one of the finest stories in the Holmes Canon, one that I enjoy again and again.

Jim Hawkins (Nashville, Tennessee) became a member of the Nashville Scholars in 1987 and helped establish their website (nashvillescholars. net) and their discussion group WelcomeHolmes. He has worked for Southwest Airlines since 2001, and as a flight attendant since 2005.

THE HOUND OF
THE BASKERVILLES

ANASTASIA KLIMCHYNSKAYA

The Hound of the Baskervilles is perhaps the most famous of the Sherlock Holmes stories. It is certainly the most famous novel, and with good reason: if one were to choose a single story that perfectly embodies the cultural significance of Sherlock Holmes, then as well as now, this would be it.

The novel recounts how Watson and Holmes travel to Dartmoor to investigate the mystery of the "Hound of the Baskervilles," a legend of a fantastic hound that has been reportedly killing members of the Baskerville family. The murder they unearth was, instead, motivated by the desire for an inheritance. In short, *The Hound* is a story in which the rational Sherlock Holmes is pitted against the supernatural, in the form of an ancient legend and a familial curse. This trope, or theme, of the ultra-rational Sherlock Holmes confronting the unexplainable supernatural is one of the most popular in Sherlockian adaptations, pastiches, and retellings, returning again and again in every form and genre conceivable. And unsurprisingly so: it gets at the heart of what Sherlock Holmes *means*, what he stands for.

Sherlock Holmes is not just a man of rationality, he is a symbol of it—a perfect embodiment of the Victorian mentality of science, progress, and modernity. From a cultural standpoint, he is both a man of his time and yet timeless, representing the positivism and rationality of the Victorian period as well as of our own. Through his approach to solving cases, he makes use of the latest science and technologies. He uses many forms of forensic and scientific investigation, such as fingerprinting, just as they were in their infancy. He's constantly writing telegrams, making use of a Victorian mail system whose deliveries happened twelve times a day, and taking trains (the advent of the rail system starting in 1830 being a major aspect of British industrialization). Newspapers (a form of mass media made possible by industrialization and mass literacy), encyclopedias, and reference books abound in the Canon. In short, as Michael Saler has so aptly pointed out in *As If: The Literary Prehistory of Virtual Reality*, Holmes represents and celebrates "the central tenets of modernity adumbrated at the time—not just rationalism and secularism, but also urbanism and consumerism."

And, most significantly for this novel, throughout the Canon, he consistently rejects supernatural explanations in favor of rational ones, thus embodying the skepticism and rationality that modernity values so highly. The first chapter of *The Hound of the Baskervilles* sees Dr. Mortimer present Sherlock Holmes with the old and terrifying tale of the Hound, which Holmes rejects: "If Dr. Mortimer's surmise should be correct, and we are dealing with forces outside the ordinary laws of Nature, there is an end of our investigation. But we are bound to exhaust all other hypotheses before falling back upon this one." Here he echoes a sentiment that he has stated numerous times before, that the supernatural does not exist. "No ghosts need apply," he tells Watson in "The Sussex Vampire." A modern man *par excellence*.

However, if Holmes is the embodiment of modern skepticism, science, and rationality, then his greatest enemy is never Professor Moriarty (who is, after all, a man of flesh and blood, and, being a professor of mathematics, capable of the same logic and rationality as Holmes). Rather, the greatest threat to a man who is also a symbol of rationality and positivism is that which is, by definition, irrational and unexplainable: the supernatural. Thus, *The Hound of the Baskervilles* is arguably the novel that gets most aptly at the essence of why Sherlock Holmes has remained so popular and so significant in the cultural imagination. As writers and readers, we cannot stop challenging the very nature of Holmes and what he represents—whether via adaptations of the novel itself or in crossovers between Sherlock Holmes and the Lovecraft universe. We challenge Holmes again and again in order to be proven wrong by him, to be shown, again and again, that science and reason can and will triumph over the unexplainable. Every time Sherlock Holmes confronts a ghostly hound, an eldritch horror from the deep, a ghost, a man risen from the dead, or any of the other myriad monsters of fantasy, and every time he provides a rational explanation for it, he proves once again that reason will out, that rationality is a meaningful approach to the world, because the world is explainable and understandable via human reason.

"And yet there should be no combination of events for which the wit of man cannot conceive an explanation," Holmes says in *The Valley of Fear*, and *The Hound of the Baskervilles* takes that statement to the extreme, tests it to see if it holds in even the most seemingly inexplicable of explanations. It remains the first ("The Sussex Vampire" and

"The Devil's Foot" are the two other canonical stories that pose similar problems, but were written later), and possibly the best, embodiment of this perennial theme of the rational confronting the supernatural. It is certainly the most sustained canonical exploration of this confrontation and, written at the turn of the 20th century, a landmark text of modernity.

What makes *The Hound of the Baskervilles* such a perfect embodiment of this confrontation between rationality and the supernatural, between modernity and those things that pose a challenge to it, is the way that Doyle draws on the Gothic novel. The Gothic is a genre that, since its emergence, has set up dichotomies that reflect social fears: the old and the new, the institution and the individual, reason and superstition. Its mysterious castles, convents, and haunted mansions were often representative of the institutions within them that were to be feared: tradition, religion, feudalism, and the crumbling and decadent nature of the structures themselves reflected fears of decadence and decay, individual, familial, and social. Significantly, in the late Victorian period, Gothic fiction moved its setting from these haunted castles in the countryside to the city, as metropolises produced by industrialization and urbanization became a new site of fear and concern. A genre of the urban Gothic arose, embodied by three of the most famous novels of the period, *Dr. Jekyll and Mr. Hyde, Dracula*, and *The Picture of Dorian Gray*.

The Hound of the Baskervilles, however, rejects this ideology of the urban Gothic, returning instead to the more traditional Gothic novel—a rejection voiced by Holmes himself in "The Copper Beeches":

> "Good heavens!" I cried. "Who would associate crime with these dear old homesteads?"
>
> "They always fill me with a certain horror. It is my belief, Watson, founded upon my experience, that the lowest and vilest alleys in London do not present a more dreadful record of sin than does the smiling and beautiful countryside."

And, in fact, this again bears out both the role of Sherlock Holmes in Victorian society and the nature of the late Victorian city: according to all statistics, violent crime was *falling* in cities in Britain at the end of the nineteenth century. Thus, much of the Canon is not actually about crime, and when wrongdoings do happen, there is always Sherlock Holmes to clear them up and restore civilized order to the Imperial metropolis. That is, when crimes happen in the city: much of the time, crime is relegated to rural spaces, such as in *The Hound of the Baskervilles*, or, if it makes its way to the city, its source is on the edges of the British Imperial map (India, Australia, and America play almost the same role as Dartmoor in this sense). That is why, perhaps, Sherlock Holmes and London are so intertwined in the cultural imagination: both are bastions of rationality and progress, of civilized order.

Thus, rather than choosing the city as a site of fear and decay, *The Hound of the Baskervilles* sets up a neat dichotomy in which the city, civilized, technological, and advanced, is juxtaposed with the country (Dartmoor) as the site of irrationality, superstition, and backwardness. The novel is then a confrontation, via the characters of Sherlock Holmes and Doctor Watson, between these two opposites, and as such, a confrontation between two attitudes, two ways of life, two ideologies: positivist rationality and irrational superstitions. It is no mystery which one wins out in the end, but the interest lies in the way the book journeys towards this endpoint.

The first few chapters of the novel are therefore emphatically founded on establishing the civilized rationality of Victorian London, where Holmes is both surrounded by and embodies rationality, technology, and progress. Within the first chapter alone, Holmes deduces the details of Mortimer's life from his cane, consults Watson's Medical Dictionary to confirm his findings, has a debate with Dr. Mortimer about phrenology, dates the document Mortimer brings with him to the 18th century by observation alone, and makes use of the manuscript (an authenticated historical document) to confirm the legend of the Hound. Even as the story begins to unfold with mysterious events (a figure in disguise following Sir Henry Baskerville, the disappearing boot), the modernity of Victorian London, and the scientific nature of Holmes's methods, is on full display: Henry Baskerville is followed in a hansom cab, a warning letter is sent to him using newsprint (a symbol of mass literacy), and Holmes immediately recognizes the font and type used, as he is familiar with the technological details behind the printing of newspapers.

The London of the first few chapters thus forms a stark contrast with the rest of the novel, which draws upon practically every trope of the Gothic novel available—evoked explicitly so that they can be laid to rest by Holmes himself. It is via the force of this contrast, and the weight of Gothic literary tradition, that the confrontation between rationality and the supernatural gains significance, as Holmes, the incarnation of modernity, lays to rest centuries of mystery and superstition in the form of literary history.

The most obvious of these tropes are evoked with the first appearance of Baskerville Hall and the moors, which one cannot help but compare to Edgar Allan Poe's *The Fall of the House of Usher*—a story that neatly encapsulates the entirety of the Gothic genre within the span of twenty pages. (Poe, of course, was a significant influence on Doyle, in particular via his Dupin stories). His tale begins thus:

During the whole of a dull, dark, and soundless day in the autumn of the year, when the clouds hung oppressively low in the heavens, I had been passing alone, on horseback, through a singularly dreary tract of country; and at length found myself, as the shades of the evening drew on, within view of the melancholy House of Usher. I know not how it was, but, with the first glimpse of the building, a sense of insufferable gloom pervaded my spirit. I say insufferable; for the feeling was unrelieved by any of that half-pleasurable, because poetic, sentiment with which the mind usually receives even the sternest natural images of the desolate or terrible.

The narrator's approach to the ill-fated House of Usher, where he looks upon "the bleak walls... the vacant eye-like windows... rank sedges... decayed trees... with an utter depression of soul," is not unlike Watson's approach to Baskerville Hall, as he is affected by the "gloomy curve of the moor, broken by the jagged and sinister hills." Watson finds the landscape desolate and bleak: "to me a tinge of melancholy lay upon the countryside, which bore so clearly the mark of the waning year." Such evocations of death and decay abound, until the very house glimmers "like a ghost." To add more Gothic weight to the landscape, one might consider that it is also not unlike the evocations of the wild, windswept moors of *Wuthering Heights*, another Victorian Gothic novel. Doom, gloom, fear, and superstition abound, with Watson's romantic constitution naturally affected by it.

And yet every aspect of this gloomy, Gothic mansion has an eventual explanation: the wailing Watson hears is the actual crying of Mrs. Barrymore, the mysterious light on the moor is not a fairy or sprite but the flesh-and-blood convict Selden, the reason why the moors are so dangerous is the treacherous Grimpen mire into which one can fall and sink (a perfectly scientific phenomenon). Most importantly, the legend of the Hound of the Baskervilles, which is irrevocably tied to the mansion itself—just as, in Gothic fiction, ancestral curses tend to be tied to the structures of the families living with them—is put to rest by Holmes himself, in full view of the reader, who watches the revelation that the Hound is nothing more than a dog with phosphorus painted on it to make it glow.

Another trope of the Gothic that is evoked only to be laid to rest is that of the portrait. Mysterious, terrifying portraits abound in Gothic fiction: the most obvious is the eponymous picture of Dorian Gray, though Oscar Wilde's protagonist also loves to stroll through the "gaunt, cold" picture gallery of his ancestors and contemplate genealogy, decadence, and decay. That trope is evoked immediately upon Watson's arrival at Baskerville Hall, where "a dim line of ancestors, in every variety of dress, from the Elizabethan knight to the buck of the Regency, stared down upon us and daunted us by their silent company." And yet, rather than remaining gloomy and foreboding tropes of the Gothic, the portraits rather become an explicit solution to one of the mysteries of the novel: Holmes, upon looking at the portrait, is able to ignore the "trimmings" and see the portrait as a "criminal investigator," so that what appears to be a pictorial piece of evidence into the "doctrine of reincarnation" (another Gothic trope) becomes a rationalization and solution of a seemingly supernatural mystery.

This use of the Gothic, and of the theme of rationality confronting the irrational, also explains one of the more questionable aspects of the novel: the fact that Holmes is missing from a large part of it. Of course, of the canonical four novels, only one *doesn't* have a huge digression that doesn't even involve Holmes. Nonetheless, Holmes's absence and separation from Watson for a large portion of the narrative is something often questioned by readers. It is, however, incredibly fitting for the larger aims of the story: part of the effectiveness of the novel lies precisely in the way that Dartmoor and Baskerville Hall affect Watson, and thus the reader. Watson himself confesses, "I have tried to make the reader share those dark fears and vague surmises which clouded our lives so long and ended in so tragic a manner." True to his nature, Watson is being rather melodramatic, but he really has been working as hard as he can to make the reader share in the irrationality, fear, and superstition that is the purview of the Gothic novel—so that, when each supernatural mystery is revealed and explained by the rational Holmes, it creates the greatest effect via its contrast. Affected as we have been by Watson's Gothic mood, the practically Messianic appearance of Holmes, standing on the foggy moors and providing a purely scientific explanation of the legend of the Hound, is the ultimate triumph of rationality and positivism over the fear and superstition that the novel has so carefully built up.

This, then, also explains why Holmes recurs so often in science fiction (*Star Trek* is a particularly excellent example, where Holmes is Spock's ancestor, and the thinking and reasoning machine Data often re-enacts Holmes stories on the holodeck). Science fiction, as a genre, is that which rationalizes the magical: it takes those things that seem seemingly supernatural, such as space and time travel, teleportation, and invisibility, and provides technological and scientific explanations for them. In fact, science fiction scholar Eric Rabkin even traces science fiction back to a subgenre of the Gothic made famous by Ann Radcliffe, the Gothic *expliqué*, in which the seemingly supernatural is always rationalized at the end. As landmark science fiction author Arthur C. Clarke has stated, "any sufficiently advanced technology is indistinguishable from magic," and indeed, in a modern society in which technology advances at an exponential rate, the innovations on every hand soon begin to look like magic.

And Sherlock Holmes, as the pinnacle of rational modernity, is the one who transforms that magic into science and rationalizes it, reminding us that the inevitable march of progress means that those things we have considered supernatural, magical, and unexplainable will be made possible and explainable by the power of the human mind.

Anastasia Klimchynskaya (Philadelphia, Pennsylvania) is a doctoral candidate in comparative literature at the University of Pennsylvania, focusing on the intersections of 19th century science and literature. She is the winner of the 2013 Morley-Montgomery Award and co-founder of Philadelphia's Ancient Order of Free Sherlockians.

THE ADVENTURE OF
THE EMPTY HOUSE

WILLIAM A. WALSH

We would reside in a vastly different and diminished world if the events of April 1894 had not occurred and prompted Dr. Watson, once again, to put pen to paper. Violet Smith would have faced protracted misery, rather than wedded bliss ("The Solitary Cyclist"). Lady Eva Blackwell would have suffered social humiliation and a cancelled wedding ("Charles Augustus Milverton"). Far more telling, a European war might have commenced earlier ("The Second Stain"), or Imperial Germany might have entered the Great War with submarines built around the Bruce-Partington plans, as well as possessing detailed information about British armaments, naval signals and other critical military information ("His Last Bow"). The reduction of the Canon to a mere 30 tales, arguably, constitutes the greatest loss we would have suffered absent the sudden return of Sherlock Holmes. For this reason alone, "The Adventure of the Empty House" stands as the greatest of Watson's records.

It earns and deserves the title of the single greatest tale in the Canon for several reasons. The essence of great literature rests in a story's ability to appeal on multiple levels while it endures through time, and this story meets that criterion. In baseball terms, "The Empty House" stands out as a five-tool tale. The story immediately appeals because it possesses all of the critical elements of a Sherlockian story. Watson's recounting also provides insight into the relationship between Holmes and Watson, while offering information with Holmes's usual directness. The tale further excels because Watson details the return of Holmes in a straightforward manner. Finally, "The Empty House" exceeds all other stories for Sherlockians because it is the single richest vein for research in the Canon. From the Great Hiatus to Holmes's fine collection of M's, no other story provides the same opportunity for research or speculation.

"The Empty House" comes fully furnished with all of the critical elements of a Sherlockian tale. The case commences with an unsolved murder baffling Scotland Yard and involving a body in a locked room. Enhancing the mystery, no one heard the shot that killed Ronald Adair, and an examination of the interior of the room and the area outside the house fails to offer a clue explaining how the murderer achieved his feat. The victim's family status and the potential association with various London card clubs overlap the tale with the higher levels of society, while the presence of money on the table before the victim is suggestive.

Watson's narrative contains the small, expected elements of a Holmes mystery and resolution. Holmes and Watson pass through London in a hansom cab, with Watson bringing his service revolver to the confrontation. Holmes assumes a disguise in the story, providing yet another example of his ability to fool everyone except Irene Adler. The introduction of a bust of Holmes, to create a false silhouette and draw out the killer, adds another novel twist and confirms that "age doth not wither nor custom stale [Holmes's] infinite variety." Typical of the outstanding tales, Holmes provides a classical reference, observing that "Journeys end in lovers' meetings," with the capture of Colonel Moran, and then he and Watson retreat to Baker Street to recount and connect the details of the case.

The tale also involves a signature villain. Holmes is not battling against a cheating student, love-motivated scientist or jellyfish, but confronts the second most dangerous man in London, best shot in India and trusted lieutenant of Professor James Moriarty. (While most readers view Moran as the murderer that Watson describes, his personal history and achievements on behalf of the Crown have prompted an argument that he continued to serve the Queen, and Mycroft Holmes, as a spy within Moriarty's criminal regime.) Brave enough to crawl into a drain in order to kill a man-eating tiger, the colonel had the brains and ability to escape suspicion and arrest for years, even after Holmes had pulled together all of the necessary details for the criminal trial of the century and the conviction of the wicked colonel ("The Final Problem"). This villain possesses an equally unique weapon, a hand-crafted air gun capable of executing a kill from a distance in silence. The weapon is a technical marvel that Moriarty commissioned specifically for the colonel. The combination of man and weapon proved sufficient to banish Holmes from England for three years, something no other antagonist accomplished.

Delightfully, "The Empty House" embraces the friendly antagonism between Holmes and Scotland Yard. Inspector Lestrade returns, and his officers are so efficient in their undercover stakeout that even Watson immediately identifies them in their hiding-place. While Lestrade expresses his pleasure at having Holmes back in London, the detective offers a back-handed compliment over the Molesey Mystery. Holmes's congratulation of Lestrade for the capture of Adair's murderer, moreover, contains the disdain for the Yard's detectives essential to the byplay in the best of the canonical stories: "Yes, Lestrade, I congratulate you! With your usual happy mixture of cunning and audacity you have got him."

The adventure also provides a rare glimpse into the Holmes-Watson relationship. Watson confirms the impact that Holmes had on his life at the outset, noting his own efforts to duplicate Holmes's analytical approach to crimes during the intervening years and even how he remains attracted to crime scenes, three years after the passing of his friend. Then, with that friend's sudden return, Watson experiences a "sudden flood of joy, amazement, and incredulity which utterly submerged my mind." Holmes, in turn, is solicitous of his friend's well-being, apologizing for the impact of the disclosure and noting that the one thing he needed to restore a sense of order was the presence of his old friend in the opposite chair in their room on Baker Street.

In detailing the return of Sherlock Holmes to London, Watson's handling of the event merits appreciation and congratulations. Certainly, modern screen writers would benefit from adopting Watson's approach (take note, script writers responsible for "The Empty Hearse"). Rather than a convoluted tale, or a suggestion that the confrontation at Reichenbach never occurred, or that some bargain between Moriarty and Holmes was struck, Holmes provides a rational explanation of his escape, a vertical climb, while glossing over the subsequent three years. (Nicholas Meyer may have had the escape from Reichenbach in mind for a critical scene in *The Wrath of Khan* in which Spock notes that Khan "is intelligent, but not experienced. His pattern indicates two-dimensional thinking." The Enterprise is then moved vertically for a critical kill shot and escape.) As old friends do, the pair then step right back into their partnership and work together to solve the murder and apprehend the villain.

Finally, its outstanding quantity of trifles separates "The Empty House" from all other published cases; it provides a wealth of opportunity for canonical studies. For Holmes, we learn that his study of baritsu aided his survival. The trip along Manchester Street and Blandford Street leads us to Camden House and is the primary source for pinning down the location of 221B Baker Street. Details from the story give the student the best available clues concerning the pair's living space. Once back inside, Watson covers the presence of all the old landmarks within the flat. From chemicals to Persian slipper, Watson offers the essential items within the sitting room. Regrettably, although we learn that Watson lives within walking distance of Hyde Park, he decided to hide from his readers the location of his home connected with the untimely death of Mary Morstan Watson.

For individuals who enjoy pondering the unrecorded cases or drafting a pastiche, this case also stands out as a gold mine. Holmes makes passing references to Parker the garroter, Morgan the poisoner, Matthews, and Merridew, along with the unsolved murder of Mrs. Stewart. Likewise, the Great Hiatus provides a three-year gap that demands conjecture, speculation, or frivolous suggestions to fill the time. Indeed, Holmes's offered explanation makes no sense. (If he determined before Moriarty reached the base of the falls the value of Moriarty's three henchmen believing him dead, then that strategic approach died minutes later when Moran attempted to dislodge Holmes with rocks. So, what was the true reason for the Great Hiatus?)

Ultimately, "The Empty House" excels all other tales simply for our pleasure in reading the story, the joy in discovering that Holmes survived his confrontation with the professor, and the recognition that, with Holmes and Watson once more reunited, we will have many more stories to enjoy.

William A. Walsh (Cortlandt Manor, New York) is an environmental law attorney, a Baker Street Irregular, and a member of the Adventuresses of Sherlock Holmes, the Three Garridebs, and the Hudson Valley Sciontists.

THE ADVENTURE OF
THE NORWOOD BUILDER

VINCENT W. WRIGHT

If you take a look at the Contents pages in the front of the two volumes of William S. Baring-Gould's *The Annotated Sherlock Holmes*, you will see that quotes or taglines have been added under the title of each story. A quick count of the 60 shows that 35 are quotes or sayings from Holmes, 18 are from Watson, three are from other people, Mycroft has one, and "The Boscombe Valley Mystery" doesn't have anything at all.

Do the math and you'll see that leaves two. And whom are the quips for those attributed to? The answer: Inspector G. Lestrade. The titles that feature his remarks below them are *A Study in Scarlet* and "The Adventure of the Norwood Builder."

A Study? The first case as a team? Now that's a pretty big deal. Does that imply that using Lestrade for "The Norwood Builder" means it's a big deal, too? Well, he certainly seemed to think so, telling Holmes toward the end of the case, "I don't mind saying... that this is the brightest thing you have done yet." (That's not the entire sentence, but it is the most important part.)

For the record, the tale, the second one in *The Return of Sherlock Holmes*, is a good story. Holmes and Watson are visited by John Hector McFarlane, who is being accused of murdering someone for an inheritance, and burning the body. There is a decent case against him, but Holmes thinks that something is amiss. While Lestrade takes the accused into custody, Holmes sets out to investigate the case in more depth. What he finds convinces him the young solicitor is innocent, though the very confident Lestrade believes differently.

A trip to the residence in question gives Holmes the proof he needs to wrap the case up and exonerate McFarlane, even with the appearance of even more seemingly damning evidence against him. Holmes knows that the suspected deceased is *not* deceased, and that the house has a hidden room. Once he reveals the "dead" man, Jonas Oldacre, Lestrade realizes that he has again been bested by the Master. Oldacre claims it was all just a practical joke, but it is revealed that it is all a big love triangle kind of thing.

This isn't exactly a classic hidden doorway or secret passage case. There's no creaking staircase that leads to a dark and dank dungeon, or a cobweb-covered torch-lit hallway behind a bookcase. However, it's close enough. Holmes knows the man is in the house somewhere, and after a careful examination of the dimensions of each floor knows exactly where. He could have easily used the line "because I knew [he] was nowhere else" in this case and it would have been true. (It wasn't true in "The Second Stain," where he did use it, but you get the point.)

I doubt anyone has ever placed this story on a list of bests or favorites, and it's known that Arthur Conan Doyle didn't. In fact, when the Baker Street Irregulars were polled in 1944, "The Norwood Builder" was close to the bottom of their list. One has to wonder why, though. It has a number of the elements that go into a good Holmes tale—the opening scene at Baker Street with the client, the deductions about them by Holmes, Lestrade and his smugness, Holmes out gathering data, the trip to the scene of the crime, and the solution that no one was expecting.

On top of all of that we have Watson seeming to be getting better at figuring out Holmes's logic with his deductions. There is also more information about Holmes's relatives. And we get a rare mention of Professor Moriarty.

Now, if all of those weren't enough to convince you this is a good yarn, then let us talk briefly about dactyloscopy. You know, fingerprint identification. At the time of this case, probably in 1895, the world was still toying with the notion of fingermarks being usable in criminology. However, Lestrade seems to be ahead of the game when he asks Holmes if he is aware that no two thumb-marks are alike. Holmes, not surprisingly, says that he has read something of the kind. The curious part of the conversation is when Lestrade says, "I leave it to any expert in the world whether that is not the mark of his thumb." A quick look at the history of fingerprinting shows that in the mid-1890's there weren't very many experts around on the subject. In fact, they could likely be counted on one hand—and half of them were being laughed at by the police community as scientific fools. Still, it's an interesting glimpse into the future of forensics and helps remind us of Holmes's place in the development of those practices.

I am among those who do not count this among their favorite stories. I like it, but it doesn't really have that spark that makes me gasp in awe. It's clever, yes, but it seems to fall short in the excitement category. I certainly wouldn't place it near the bottom of a complete list, more like somewhere in the middle. Chronologically it doesn't cause any problems, and for someone like me who is interested in that sort of thing that does help raise it a few points on the scale.

Perhaps it's the things that don't get examined more that cause its unexceptional feel. For instance, how long does it take a body to be wholly consumed by a bonfire? What are the other theories that Holmes had come up with so early in the case? (He only revealed one.) Also, why does Watson allow the part of the story about Holmes failing so badly at Blackheath into the text? He could just as easily have converted the conversation with McFarlane's mother into a success and left out the parts where Holmes admits he found nothing of use.

In the big picture that is the Canon, one might consider this story to be light reading at best, in the presence of so many fantastic adventures. But, it does have its moments, and it definitely isn't unworthy of one's time.

Vincent W. Wright (Indianapolis, Indiana) is creator of the Facebook site Historical Sherlock and a 20-year member of the Illustrious Clients. He has been hooked since discovering *The Annotated Sherlock Holmes* while in high school and seeing Jeremy Brett in the Granada series.

THE ADVENTURE OF
THE DANCING MEN

RANDALL STOCK

While "The Dancing Men" may not be a great case for its detective, it is a great Sherlock Holmes story. As a case, it sees Holmes fail to protect his client, who ends up dying, and the killer gets only a jail sentence. But as a story, it consistently ranks among the best Holmes tales.

Arthur Conan Doyle was pleased with "The Dancing Men." He called it "a strong bloody story" in a 1903 letter to his editor, and in 1927 placed it third on his list of the best Holmes tales. Readers have also ranked it highly. A 1944 BSI poll put it fifth, and *Baker Street Journal* and *Sherlock Holmes Journal* polls from the 1950s and the 1980s rated it ninth and seventh. My own comprehensive 1999 poll, described in the winter 1999 *Baker Street Journal,* also placed it ninth. The average of all these polls, adjusting for their scoring methodology, ranks "The Dancing Men" as the seventh best story in the Canon.

So why is it rated so highly? Conan Doyle cited the originality of its plot, but that's both vague and misleading. The main events of this tale are essentially a mashup of "The Noble Bachelor" and "The Five Orange Pips." In the former, an American woman's prior romance ends with disastrous results for an English gentleman. In the latter, Holmes fails to protect his client when a mysterious message from an American criminal leads to the death of the innocent Englishman.

Even the centerpiece of the story, the stick-figure cipher, is not wholly original or unique in the Canon. A children's magazine carried a stick-figure cipher in 1874 that very much resembled the one in "The Dancing Men." Conan Doyle admitted in *The Magic Door* (1907) that all "cryptogram-solving yarns trace back to his [Poe's] 'Gold Bug'." Holmes also deals with codes and ciphers in a number of other cases, including "The Gloria Scott," *The Valley of Fear,* and "The Red Circle."

Despite that, the stick figure cipher remains a highlight of the story and offers one of the purest intellectual puzzles in the Canon. To solve the cryptogram messages, you don't need to sift through the story or wait for Holmes to point out something that Watson didn't observe. Barring typographical errors in your book (and a couple by Conan Doyle on his original manuscript), you are on an even footing with the detective.

Conan Doyle's inspired description of the cipher as "dancing men" makes it especially memorable. His use of that phrase in the story's title insured that the cipher remains top-of-mind for all Sherlockians. You might not recall the codes and ciphers in other Holmes stories, or even the critical deductions from some tales, but you do remember those dancing men.

A great story needs a great opening, and this tale delivers on all fronts. We get delightful character sketches, a bit of humor, and an impressive deduction. Holmes's chemical investigations remind us he is a Victorian-era techie. He lectures "with the air of a professor," and his deduction about Watson not investing in South African securities highlights his intellect and insight.

Watson quickly emerges as predictable and, depending on your preferences, either as a bit dim or as a sly humorist. After first assuring Holmes he will do no such thing, he declares "how absurdly simple" in response to Holmes's explanation of the deduction. At the same time, we learn that Watson plays billiards, has a friend named Thurston, and needs to ask Holmes for a key in order to retrieve his own checkbook. Conan Doyle establishes both of his main characters and engages the reader in a mere 500 words.

He also fills the story with two major puzzles rather than one, and weaves them together in a rather elegant fashion. The first involves solving the cryptograms, while the second relates to the locked-room killing of Hilton Cubitt. That second mystery, which includes an excellent analysis of the crime scene and some fine deductions, could practically stand by itself as a respectable Holmes story.

As with the cryptograms, the reader has a fair chance to solve the locked-room problem. You get a complete description of the crime scene and witness testimony. Holmes even points out the smell of gunpowder in the top floor passage, letting the careful reader anticipate his later revelations.

In a nice touch, Holmes uses the killer's own secret cipher to lure Abe Slaney into a trap. This echoes a similar tactic in "The Five Orange Pips" when Holmes sent pips to the killer. However, in "The Dancing Men," the message extends the suspense of the story, letting Holmes explain how he solved the cipher before the climactic capture of Abe Slaney.

Clever phrasings also make a Holmes story memorable and special. Here we have a counterpoint to "elementary" with Watson's "how absurdly simple," as well as "every problem becomes very childish when once it is explained to you." While it may not match the dog in the nighttime, Holmes's conversation with Inspector Martin nicely encapsulates the Holmes style:

> "By George!" cried the inspector. "How ever did you see that?"
> "Because I looked for it."

Part of the ongoing appeal of the Holmes tales is their sense of tradition and justice. We hear that in Inspector Martin's advice to Abe Slaney: "'It is my duty to warn you that it will be used against you,' cried the inspector, with the magnificent fair-play of the British criminal law."

Finally, "The Dancing Men" includes its own contribution to the aphorisms and epigrams that tend to personify Sherlock Holmes. Poe conveyed the concept in rather florid prose in "The Gold Bug," noting "it may well be doubted whether human ingenuity can construct an enigma of the kind which human ingenuity may not, by proper application, resolve." Conan Doyle expresses this rather more concisely and memorably as "what one man can invent, another can discover."

Admittedly, the story has its shortcomings. Some key plot points involving Abe Slaney and Elsie Cubitt do not withstand close scrutiny. For that matter, none of the characters except for Holmes and Watson are especially memorable. Yet the story as a whole overcomes these limitations by including the requisite elements of a Holmes classic. It opens at 221B with a flashy, curtain-raising deduction. It carries on with two mysteries that play fair with the reader and showcase convincing deductions and puzzle-solving. Some strong quotations add their own special appeal. But in the end, it is the cipher, and most particularly, the description of the symbols as "dancing men," that raises this story above the others and makes it so memorable.

Randall Stock (Mountain View, California) is a Baker Street Irregular, author of many papers about Arthur Conan Doyle rarities, an authority on manuscripts and first editions, and the producer of the website The Best of Sherlock Holmes (www.bestofsherlock.com).

THE ADVENTURE OF
THE SOLITARY CYCLIST

LISA BURSCHEIDT

In this essay, I will briefly argue that "The Solitary Cyclist" is the best Sherlock Holmes story. I think it is the best because it has all the ingredients of a successful mystery and also all the ingredients of a successful Sherlock Holmes story. In no particular order, these ingredients are as follows:

1. Violet Smith—a damsel in distress who turns out not to be. If ever there was a client who made An Impression at 221B, it's Violet Smith. Upon first seeing her, Watson describes her as "tall, graceful and queenly." Though, as we all know, the good doctor is always attentive to the charms of the fairer sex, this is a rather exuberant statement even by his standards.

But Violet Smith also possesses a myriad of inward qualities in addition to her outward charms. Apart from the ones that Holmes points out—that she is a musician and that she keeps herself healthy by cycling a lot in the open air—we also soon learn that she is spirited, resourceful, and intelligent.

Throughout the course of the story, she navigates a dangerous world mostly by herself. Though she calls on Holmes for help and writes to him regularly with updates on her situation, which becomes more and more precarious as the story goes on, we never hear about him or Watson replying to her. Watson is sent to Farnham to look into the situation, but by the time he gets there, Violet Smith has already got to a point where she has decided that it is time for her to take action as the men are dragging their feet—cue her chasing her mysterious "suitor" on her own bicycle. In this, she resembles another Violet from the Holmes canon—Violet Hunter in "The Copper Beeches". Miss Hunter takes it upon herself to explore the mysterious and forbidden rooms in the house where she works as a governess and get to the heart of the mystery that she feels her employer must be hiding from her. Violet Smith takes fate into her own hands in the same fashion. You go, Miss Smith, you go.

2. A plot that plays fair with the audience. The notion of "playing fair" with the audience is a great challenge in mystery writing. There is a fine line to be walked between giving the game away too early and keeping your cards so close to your writerly chest that the audience has no chance of even trying to figure out whodunit. Holmes is notorious for withholding information, and so many of the stories are closed to the readership's participation: we watch in awe as he deduces his way to a solution, but we are not an involved party in the process. Though, of course, there is always the possibility that Watson wanted to make Holmes appear smarter than he really was and erred on the side of withholding information to the point where the game becomes impossible for the readership to play.

"The Solitary Cyclist" is fairer to the readership in this respect. We get enough facts about the case at the beginning and through Violet Smith's subsequent missives to be able to make our own guesses and inferences as to what may be going on. A shady ex-priest? Proposals of marriage? Two men as rivals for the affections of the same woman? Something isn't right here, and it's not hard for us to put together where it all may be going, though the final solution still holds some shock value.

3. The setting. We all love the coziness of 221B Baker Street, and we accept Holmes as a *genius loci* of 19th century London. But the case can be made that with Holmes, as with much in life, the fun starts outside the comfort zone. Whether a case takes Holmes and Watson to Dartmoor, Germany, or indeed Farnham, some of the most interesting stories happen when they are taken outside their familiar environment. Tying in the previous comments about playing fair with the audience, I believe there's something about Holmes being unable to call on such familiar help as Scotland Yard, the Baker Street Irregulars, or his own encyclopaedic knowledge of London that puts him on more of a level with us as the audience and leaves him in a position of relative vulnerability and uncertainty. We enjoy watching the great mind at work, but we get so used to the notion of Holmes as a person who can solve any mystery put in front of him that it's good to be reminded that much of his omniscience results from being in a space where he can move with ease and confidence.

4. Action! There is lots of action throughout the Canon, but the dramatic showdown at the end of this story stands out in its abruptness and brutality. There are plenty of crimes in the Canon that aren't really crimes, and many instances in which Holmes takes justice into his own hands and lets people off the hook. Woodley, by contrast, is truly disgusting and deserves everything that's coming to him.

5. *It almost goes terribly wrong.* Closely related to the last point, there is a real sense of peril towards the end of this story. By the time "The Solitary Cyclist" is reached, halfway through the Canon, the image of Holmes as a man who can solve anything is cemented in readers' minds. But, as this case illustrates, Holmes gets things wrong—and sometimes, this has terrible consequences. He does not take Miss Smith's case seriously enough early enough, and by the time he realises what may be at stake, it is almost too late. He can do little except serve as transport for Mr Carruthers, who delivers the final blow (or rather shot) that brings down Woodley, the villain of the piece, and then stick around to explain the plot to the audience. It certainly isn't his finest hour, but it's something that is important and vital to see, and something that makes him very human.

We learn in the postscript that the criminals are punished, the good people rewarded, and the world is once again put back as it should be. This closure lies at the heart of what makes mystery writing and reading so satisfying, and as such, it is one of the finest examples of pay-off in the Canon.

In summary, this story combines everything we love about Holmes and Watson with everything we love about successful mysteries. It is a great example of what Arthur Conan Doyle was able to achieve at his best, and it should be read and appreciated more than it is.

Lisa Burscheidt (London, England) hails originally from Germany. She is a member of the Sherlock Holmes Society of London, and is also part of the Baker Street Babes group, creating the web's only all-female Sherlock Holmes podcast.

THE ADVENTURE OF
THE PRIORY SCHOOL

DENNY DOBRY

In the opening of most of the canonical tales, we find Sherlock Holmes and Dr. Watson resting comfortably in their cozy Baker Street sitting room. Typically, a new adventure is blandly introduced and our heroes set out to do their thing. However, exceptions to this blueprint can be found in the beginning of several cases: Alexander Holder's madman's antics in the street and head-banging in the sitting-room in "The Beryl Coronet," Steve Dixie's abrupt intrusion at Baker Street in "The Three Gables," and in "The Abbey Grange," with Holmes's discourteous awakening of Watson with "Come Watson, come! The game is afoot."

Arguably, however, the most dramatic entrance in all the cases is found in "The Adventure of the Priory School," as Watson proclaims: "I cannot recollect anything more sudden and startling than the first appearance of Thorneycroft Huxtable, M.A., PhD, etc." In the first paragraph of this story, Holmes and Watson find Dr. Huxtable, in Watson's words, "this ponderous piece of wreckage… prostrate and insensible upon our bearskin hearthrug." Sherlock Holmes, of course, is both startled and surprised by the scholar's intrusion and subsequent prone posture. After all, he is not accustomed to seeing his clients in this position until after he has presented them with his invoice.

This opening to "The Priory School" is so attention-grabbing that the distinguished Sherlockian scholar Vincent Starrett combined it with the opening of "The Beryl Coronet" to jumpstart his memorable pastiche, "The Unique Hamlet," published in 1920. With imitation being the sincerest form of flattery, Starrett was obviously impressed with the effectiveness of the bumbling entrances of both Alexander Holder and Dr. Huxtable in capturing the reader's attention.

After Huxtable's startling invasion of the Baker Street sitting room, the reader witnesses a surprising departure from a time-honored canonical ritual. In no less than twelve stories, someone offers brandy as an aid to overcome a physical ailment. Although Watson produces the canonical cure-all to revive the distinguished educator, Dr. Huxtable refuses the brandy and requests "a glass of milk and a biscuit." Apparently Watson didn't take this remedy seriously, since the brandy cure resurfaces a number of times in later cases, and there is never any mention of Watson carrying around a supply of Lorna Doones in his medical bag.

Readers of the Canon have shared with Watson the frustration and annoyance of Holmes's wont to conceal facts and evidence until the end of the case, and then presenting his findings and solution in a flamboyant and dramatic fashion. Watson has repeatedly reported Holmes returning to Baker Street after a jaunt about London, often in a disguise, without revealing what he has discovered. Watson can only deduce that Holmes was successful if he returns in a "chipper" mood or that his outing was a complete failure if he appears crestfallen. In the latter case, Watson surely would have dreaded Holmes trying to drown his sorrows by playing his violin.

In "The Priory School," however, we find a different Sherlock Holmes. Although he has several solitary reconnaissance expeditions, upon his return, he is quick to bring Watson up to speed on his findings. Whereas Holmes's methodical way of proceeding can never be doubted, the details of his progress or setbacks are most often hidden from the reader and Watson. Not so in this tale! From the time Holmes pulls out his notebook to actually take notes, a canonical rarity in itself (isn't that what Watson is for?), Watson and the reader can follow along with the discovery of clues and the implications that they have for the case. When the significance of a clue is not obvious to Watson, Holmes helps him along: "Well now, Watson, how many cows did you see on the moor?" (Surprisingly, Watson didn't counter that the cows could have been in the barn, but then the absence of cow plops would have been conclusive.)

Because of his involvement in the play-by-play of the solution, unlike the norm in many other cases, Watson comes away feeling that he partnered with Holmes rather than simply serving as a "conductor of light" or someone with "a remarkable power of stimulating genius without actually possessing it." The two companions work side by side in solving the mystery, and Holmes never belittles Watson's intelligence. Although not as dramatic as the scene in "The Three Garridebs," when Holmes reacts powerfully to the shooting of Watson, "The Priory School" effectively demonstrates the friendship and partnership between Sherlock Holmes and his colleague.

In this investigation, in particular, Holmes and Watson certainly had their hands full. Some of the stories in the Canon have no crimes committed at all, such as "A Case of Identity," "The Yellow Face," and

"The Missing Three-Quarter" to name a few. "The Priory School," however, has a variety of offences to entertain the reader. The primary crime, of course, is the kidnapping of Arthur, Lord Saltire, by his stepbrother James Wilder. This villainy is the only juvenile kidnapping case in the Canon. Additionally, we are treated to a crowded charge-sheet:

- the murder of the German master, Heidegger, by Reuben Hayes
- complicity to murder, by James Wilder
- conspiracy to commit a kidnapping, by Mr. and Mrs. Hayes
- aiding and abetting a felony, by James Wilder through warning Reuben Hayes to escape
- aiding and abetting a felony, by the Duke of Holdernesse by yielding to Wilder's plan to allow Hayes time to escape
- aiding and abetting a felon, by the Duke by not turning in his stepson to the authorities
- aiding and abetting felons, by Sherlock Holmes and Dr. Watson by not turning in the Duke and his stepson.

Certainly Inspector Lestrade could have added to the crime list had he known the whole story, but as is, "The Priory School" may be the most crime-ridden short story in the Canon.

Perhaps a fitting ending to this adventure would have been Holmes crying: "Come, Watson, come! The game was a cloven foot!"

Denny Dobry (Reading, Pennsylvania) is a retired professional civil engineer, the Gasogene of the White Rose Irregulars of York, and the creator and proprietor of a widely admired 221B Baker Street re-creation in his basement.

THE ADVENTURE OF BLACK PETER

CARLA COUPE

"The Adventure of Black Peter" is a gem: the perfect Sherlock Holmes story. In its eight-thousand-and-some-odd words, it contains all the best Holmesian tropes, including a villain you love to hate, an unusual (and disturbing) means of death, a convoluted plot that hares off in unexpected directions, Holmes being brilliant in contrast to the well-meaning but rather dim Scotland Yard detective, and a satisfying end.

Despite Moriarty and Milverton, few stories have such a thoroughly repellent villain as this one. Peter Carey is the former captain of a sealing ship called the *Sea Unicorn* (whose very name conjures up images that could be viewed as portents of its captain's future method of death). Appropriately known as Black Peter, he is a nasty drunk, a wife- and child-beater, and as we discover later in the story, a thief and murderer as well, with an explosive temper and a suspicious soul. His demise, skewered on the end of a harpoon, is particularly gratifying, and the reader can't help but feel a certain sympathy with whoever killed him.

When the story begins, Watson takes some pains to place the case in a specific year—1895, a meaningful date for all Holmes *aficionados*—and remarks on the "curious and incongruous" cases they had encountered so far. He paints Holmes as a man who is a slave to his curiosity and enthusiasms, who only takes on cases that have "strange and dramatic qualities which appealed to his imagination and challenged his ingenuity."

Holmes is apparently involved in an investigation and for some unknown reason is calling himself "Captain Basil." Watson notes the tantalizing fact that Holmes maintains five bolt-holes throughout London where he can assume disguises as necessary, which of course leads the reader to speculate about where these places are located. As Watson breakfasts, Holmes returns from some errand, carrying a "huge, barbed-headed spear," and proceeds to regale Watson with a detailed description of his efforts trying to harpoon a dead pig. This leads to some comradely banter:

> "I have satisfied myself that by no exertion of my strength can I transfix the pig with a single blow. Perhaps you would care to try?"
> "Not for worlds."

One can imagine the heartfelt forcefulness of Watson's reply!

Of course there is a Scotland Yard presence with young Stanley Hopkins (who shares the same initials as Sherlock Holmes—is that a coincidence?), "for whose future Holmes had high hopes." Holmes is in tip-top form here; when Hopkins relates the story of Peter Carey's murder for Watson's edification, Holmes immediately brings up the obscure clue of the tobacco pouch, which Hopkins dismisses. Taking a contrary position, Holmes says: "if I had been handling the case I should have been inclined to make that the starting-point of my investigation."

Rather than heeding Holmes's advice and perhaps saving himself later grief, Hopkins continues his explanation, while Holmes interjects comments on certain pieces of evidence that will turn out to be instrumental in solving the case. Readers can see that Holmes is "detecting," but like Hopkins, most will have to wait for the denouement before understanding the importance of each clue.

Poor Hopkins tries to use Holmes's methods but makes a right mess of things, and to make matters worse, he fails to pick up on the clues Holmes brings to his attention. But in a slight twist, at one point Hopkins introduces a new piece of evidence and throws a spanner into the works: "Sherlock Holmes's face showed that he was thoroughly taken aback by this new development." However, he handsomely admits this to Hopkins and instead of dismissing it, adds this new information to his collection of facts. Holmes's actions are a perfect example of his investigatory strength: his insistence on building his reconstruction of the crime based on the facts, rather than choosing facts that support a favored theory.

There are moments when Watson shines, too. When Holmes, Hopkins, and Watson travel to the murder scene, he sets the stage and provides a bit of local history in a lovely paragraph. Even Holmes appreciates the local scenery. After investigating the location of the murder and while waiting to ambush a suspect, he says: "Let us walk in these beautiful woods, Watson, and give a few hours to the birds and the flowers."

"The Adventure of Black Peter" is a nicely convoluted case, featuring two disparate threads that, like two of the main players, overlap by coincidence with disastrous results. As expected, Hopkins takes the more straightforward path to solving the murder and arrests a suspect, but Holmes is "disappointed in Stanley Hopkins," for he has arrested the wrong man.

Once Holmes has teased out all the threads to his own satisfaction, he arranges a revelatory meeting with Watson and Hopkins in attendance. We meet three seamen, including one Patrick Cairns, whose "fierce bull-dog face was framed in a tangle of hair and beard." The three are there at the behest of Captain Basil, already established as Holmes's *nom-de-espionnage*. It's clear that Holmes was ahead of Hopkins by leaps and bounds even before Watson's account begins.

Holmes, deft showman that he is, solves the case with his usual flourish and reveals that Patrick Cairns is the murderer. Holmes handcuffs Cairns and only succeeds in subduing him with the help of Hopkins and Watson. Indeed, it takes the press of Watson's revolver against Cairns's temple before he stops struggling.

Once restrained, Cairns provides the case's backstory; when Carey was captain of the *Sea Unicorn*, he rescued a man from a foundering yacht, then murdered him and stole a box of valuable securities. Cairns covertly witnessed the murder and now, down on his luck and in need of money, visited Carey in order to force him to share his ill-gotten gains. Carey, drunk and belligerent, attacked Cairns, who killed him in self-defense. His confirmation of Holmes's deductions not only frees an innocent man, but allows the stolen property to be restored to its rightful owners.

In an agony of self-abasement, Hopkins immediately apologizes: "I should never have forgotten, I am the pupil and you are the master." Let's hope he remembers his words the next time he works with Sherlock Holmes.

The story winds up satisfactorily for all save Carey and Cairns, and in a throw-away line to Hopkins at the end, Holmes hints at further investigations in this case: "If you want me for the trial, my address and that of Watson will be somewhere in Norway—I'll send particulars later."

How very Holmes!

Carla Coupe (New Market, Maryland) is an editor for Wildside Press. Her pastiches have appeared in *Sherlock Holmes Mystery Magazine* and *Sherlock's Home: The Empty House*, and one, "The Book of Tobit," was included in *The Best American Mystery Stories of 2011*.

THE ADVENTURE OF CHARLES AUGUSTUS MILVERTON

BETH L. GALLEGO

In the opening paragraph of this, the best of all their canonical adventures, Watson promises to tell us of "an absolutely unique experience" in his career with Holmes. What follows is less a detective story than a screwball heist caper chock-full of action, drama, and humor. It features a villain we love to hate and a stellar moment in the friendship we simply love. Each twist of the plot overturns our expectations. The normally reserved Holmes is moved to passionate speech. The war-wounded Watson proves surprisingly athletic. The heroes turn to crime to thwart a shameless criminal, only to have their scheme interrupted by a mysterious woman on a mission of vengeance.

Let's begin, as the story does, with the eponymous blackmailer, who by the end seems to well deserve his gory demise at the hands of his unnamed victim. Milverton is one of the most memorable villains Holmes ever faces (arguably second only to a certain professor of mathematics). Holmes calls him "the worst man in London", which is saying something, given Holmes's familiarity with the city's less respectable occupants. As Holmes continues, comparing Milverton to a "slithery, gliding, venomous" serpent, Watson notes, "I had seldom heard my friend speak with such intensity of feeling."

What is it about Milverton that provokes such loathing? What makes him more repulsive than a murderer? Why does his "heart of marble" and the way he "at his leisure tortures the soul and wrings the nerves in order to add to his already swollen money-bags" fill Holmes with disgust? These questions are never precisely answered within the narrative, providing a rich opportunity for creative fans to fill in their own ideas of the possible origin of Holmes's contempt for Milverton. Meanwhile, we know that Holmes focuses on the very passionless nature of Milverton's crimes. Holmes cares about the victims, especially those vulnerable upper-class women who rely on their reputations to secure their futures. Milverton cares nothing about the actual sordid secrets in which he trades, only about the money his threats will bring him. He plays a long game with no fear of prosecution, as those he singles out "dare not hit back", lest their "own ruin must immediately follow". A target refusing to meet his terms becomes "a severe example" that will only encourage future victims to pay whatever he asks. Even when he loses, he wins. He can easily afford to sit back with a smile and wait for the next opportunity.

As if his smug attitude weren't enough to get under Holmes's skin, Milverton presents no puzzle, no enigma, no challenge to Holmes's intellect. There is no mystery to solve. Holmes has been hired as a negotiator, not an investigator. For a man who hates being bored above all things, this commission for Lady Eva can hardly be an enticing task. So, naturally, when the brief negotiations do not go Holmes's way, he quite literally leaps into action, jumping out of his chair and attempting to grab the incriminating letters from Milverton's pocketbook. Being chided by the blackmailer for being unoriginal as well as foolish has to hurt.

Once Milverton departs, the story really picks up steam. Holmes spends just half an hour in thought—he doesn't even bother to light a pipe!—to hatch a plan drawing on his dramatic talents. It's a superbly theatrical moment when he disappears from the sitting room and reappears in his new persona (complete with pipe this time). A remarkably short period of time—"some days"—later, he tells a shocked Watson that he is engaged to Milverton's housemaid, but that the romance is merely a ploy to gain access to the house. He quickly distracts Watson from consideration of that ethically shady maneuver by announcing that he intends to burgle said house that very night. He hasn't solved a mystery; he's planned a heist.

Watson immediately imagines his friend caught in the act, publicly disgraced, and, worst of all, "at the mercy of the odious Milverton." Once Holmes convinces him of the necessity of this action, though, Watson simply asks, "When do we start?" What follows is one of my favorite canonical passages.

> "You are not coming."
> "Then you are not going," said I. "I give you my word of honor—and I never broke it in my life—that I will take a cab straight to the police station and give you away unless you let me share this adventure with you."

Watson will not allow Holmes to take on Milverton alone. Both of them will go, or neither.

A brief, but necessary, note on chronology here. This story was published in the middle of the series later collected as *The Return of Sherlock Holmes*, but its place in the complete chronology is uncertain. Some scholars argue that it happened in the early years of the partnership; others maintain that it took place sometime after Holmes's return from his supposed death at the Reichenbach Falls. A full discussion is outside the scope of this essay, but I am inclined to agree with those who would place the story later, in 1899 or 1900, when Watson's experience of losing his dearest friend would still loom large in his mind and color his response. He will not let Holmes go toward certain doom alone again. If it all goes horribly wrong, they will at least be companions in misery.

Exactly how Watson will assist Holmes during the burglary is unclear, but he does bring homemade black silk masks and his own rubber-soled tennis shoes to the endeavor. (That he owned those shoes is a curious thing. Shoes with vulcanized rubber soles, also called "plimsolls" or "sand shoes", were hardly everyday wear for the typical Victorian Londoner. Not to mention that tennis seems a curiously physical form of recreation for someone carrying a Jezail bullet around in one of his limbs.) Cleverly disguised with the masks, they make their roundabout way into Milverton's study, where Watson waxes particularly poetic in his descriptions. He casts the two of them as knights errant, referring to the safe holding the various letters collected for blackmailing purposes as a "green and gold monster, the dragon which held in its maw the reputations of many fair ladies."

He finds himself rather enjoying their illicit mission: "The high object of our mission, the consciousness that it was unselfish and chivalrous, the villainous character of our opponent, all added to the sporting interest of the adventure." As in a good fairy tale, when the hero breaks into a dragon's hoard, they are the most chivalrous of burglars. It is a shame, really, that the two have to leg it over a wall instead of galloping away on valiant steeds.

Before they can make their flight from the house, though, they have to escape the study, where Milverton nearly catches them in the act. Fate appears to be on the side of the men hiding behind the curtains, however, as one of Milverton's victims appears, surprising everyone. After a wonderfully dramatic speech, she empties a revolver into the man and promptly exits the scene. The villain thus dispatched, Holmes and Watson take the opportunity to complete one more significant task and prove that while Holmes may believe he "would have made a highly efficient criminal", he doesn't truly have the heart for it. Rather than just grab Lady Eva's letters and run, he takes precious minutes to lock the door and cast all of Milverton's blackmail materials into the fire.

Having saved the reputations of an untold number of fair damsels, they finally dash from the scene, pursuers hot on their heels. Every good tale of adventure needs a chase sequence.

After all that, the mood needs lightening, and Holmes can't resist a bit of fun at the expense of both Lestrade and Watson. Told that a witness described one of the burglars as "a middle-sized, strongly-built man—square jaw, thick neck, moustache, a mask over his eyes", Holmes says that "it might be a description of Watson!" An amused Lestrade agrees. Watson, perhaps less amused, keeps his feelings on the matter to himself. Not since Stamford's initial exclamations in *A Study in Scarlet* have we been given any canonical details of Watson's appearance, making this moment a precious one indeed.

The story is a rollicking yarn, filled with intense action leading to a satisfying end for a repugnant villain. Watson is loyal and true, the perfect counterpart to this dramatic and expressive Holmes. The thread of their unwavering friendship runs through every exchange, reminding us of the central relationship that draws us back to the Canon again and again. It is a perfect example of Holmes and Watson as an inseparable team, and that is why it is the very best adventure of all.

Beth L. Gallego (Los Angeles, California) is a children's librarian, "Boy in Buttons" or leader of the John H. Watson Society, and a member of the Curious Collectors of Baker Street, the Sub-Librarians Scion, and the Beacon Society.

THE ADVENTURE OF THE SIX NAPOLEONS

REGINA STINSON

Anyone who has read the entire Canon can hardly have failed to appreciate the many virtues that put "The Six Napoleons" at the top of the canonical heap. This story is replete with every enchanting treasure the reader could hope for. In fact, I can think of few other stories that offer such a plethora of those characteristics Sherlockians have come to know and love about the sacred writings. We are treated to smashed busts, an apocryphal tale, a murder, a Holmesian aphorism, a famous pearl and a number of colorful characters. There are also several elements that are exclusive to this tale, making it a unique and invaluable contribution to the series.

As an example of how important a seemingly trifling incident can be, Holmes tantalizes us with an incidental mention of the unrecorded chronicle regarding the Abernetty family and how the dreadful business was first brought to his attention "by the depth to which the parsley had sunk into butter upon a hot day." What reader can resist a desire to learn the details of this intriguing sequence of events?

The use of plaster busts of Napoleon is genius. Holmes leads us on a delightful treasure hunt as he follows each clue. There are a few bumps along the way to keep things interesting, but eventually Holmes succeeds in his goal of discovering how many busts are involved, who owns them, where they are located and (most importantly) why they are being smashed. We're also treated to a demonstration of Holmes's logic as he explains that the reason one of the busts was carried away before being smashed was that the bust-smasher was looking for something and he needed to be near a light.

Lestrade plays a key role by bringing the matter to Holmes's attention. Certainly, one the most delightful features about "The Six Napoleons" is the relationship that has developed between Holmes and Lestrade since they first began working together. Instead of the competitive one-upmanship exemplified by "It is Lestrade's cock-a-doodle of victory" ("The Norwood Builder"), or the implied sarcasm in "You are right, you do find it very hard to tackle the facts" ("The Boscombe Valley Mystery"), we read: "It was no very unusual thing for Mr. Lestrade of Scotland Yard to look in upon us of an evening, and his visits were welcome to Sherlock Holmes." The two men have come to know one another pretty well by this time. So much so, in fact, that Holmes was able to read Lestrade's thoughts as easily as he could read Watson's:

> "Anything remarkable on hand?" he asked.
> "Oh, no, Mr. Holmes—nothing very particular."
> "Then tell me about it."
> Lestrade laughed.

Additionally, Holmes invites Lestrade to sleep at Baker Street in preparation for an all-night vigil during which they plan to capture Beppo (a courtesy he neglected to extend to John Openshaw in "The Five Orange Pips," although it might have saved his life). At the conclusion of the tale, there is no attempt on Lestrade's part to grab the glory as he's done in the past, in *A Study in Scarlet*. On the contrary, Lestrade gives one of his most eloquent speeches praising Holmes and telling him how proud they are of him at Scotland Yard. Clearly, something has changed in this relationship since its commencement. What began as a working relationship has developed into genuine friendship. In no other story do we witness this level of camaraderie between the two.

Furthermore, Lestrade serves as a comic foil. His propensity to completely overlook the significance of the busts makes us smile. While Lestrade plods along his merry way searching for the identity of the victim, Holmes further confuses the Scotland Yard detective by asking him to tell Mr. Harker that he believes the bust-breaker to be a lunatic and to advise Harker to include this information in his newspaper column. After the article is published, Holmes regales us with one of his delightful aphorisms: "The press is a most valuable institution, if only you know how to use it."

Throughout the course of the investigation Holmes spends only a brief time interviewing people, yet each character has a distinct personality that makes them seem real to us. Newspaper reporter Horace Harker is so mortified at having a murder take place on his front steps that he can't gather his thoughts to write about it. The photo of a baboon-faced man that was discovered in the murdered man's pocket leads Holmes to stout, red-faced Morse Hudson, who launches into a tirade about anarchists, Red Republicans and Nihilist plots. Hudson is the first to identify the photo as "Beppo," an Italian workman. At "Gelder & Co." we're introduced to the big, blond German owner whose otherwise gentle demeanor is suddenly transformed at viewing the photo of Beppo, exclaiming, "Ah, the rascal!" And at Harding Brothers, the brisk little emporium owner is able to provide the final pieces to the puzzle: the names of the people who own the remaining busts, Josiah Brown and Mr. Sandeford.

It's refreshing to see that Watson has grasped the fact that Holmes hopes to catch Beppo in the act of smashing one of the last remaining busts. While it is unclear whether or not Lestrade has made this connection, he does score on one point. Lestrade has tracked down the identity of the victim, Pietro Venucci, and discovered his association with the Mafia, for which he earns a round of applause from Holmes that appears to be genuine. Again, we see a very different Holmes/Lestrade relationship. The mention of the Mafia is unique to this story, as well.

The night-time vigil at the home of Josiah Brown keeps us on the edge of our seats. As if to reinforce his simian appearance, Beppo's movements are described as "swift and active as an ape." Lestrade brings the handcuffs, Watson his revolver, and Holmes his loaded hunting-crop, which in this story we learn is his favorite weapon. Creaking gates, dark lanterns, smashing busts, tiger-like attacks and finally handcuffs follow—the capture is complete, but Lestrade still fails to fully comprehend the significance of the busts. Holmes claims there are some features to this incident "which make it absolutely original in the history of crime."

The final act of this captivating drama is truly unique to the Canon and without a doubt the most outstanding. Only Holmes knows what is about to be revealed. He lures Mr. Sandeford, the owner of the final bust, to his apartment, pays him off and sets the stage. Once again, we are on the edge of our seats as Holmes lays out the tableau, picks up his loaded hunting-crop and smashes the final bust to smithereens. *Voilà!* With appropriate flourish, Holmes displays the famed black pearl of the Borgias, which elicits applause from his audience, Watson and Lestrade. Here is one of the rare moments in the Canon when Holmes is clearly touched by emotion.

After a detailed explanation as to how he unraveled this complex case, Holmes is again emotionally moved by the heartfelt compliment Lestrade bestows. Although it is brief, and a moment later Holmes is all business as usual, it warms our hearts to witness the human side of Sherlock Holmes.

Regina Stinson (Royal Oak, Michigan) is a Baker Street Irregular and a member of the Adventuresses of Sherlock Holmes, as well as founder and still Gasogene of her local Sherlockian society, the Ribston-Pippins. She recently began making and selling Sherlockian jewelry and gifts.

THE ADVENTURE OF
THE THREE STUDENTS

RACHEL E. KELLOGG

People who love Sherlock Holmes come to the stories in a variety of ways. Many have seen a film or television adaptation of The Great Detective before ever reading the text. Some people pick their interest up through less conventional methods such as a play, a cartoon, or following a favorite actor into an adaptation. Others read stories in school and fall in love. Many times people start with *The Hound of the Baskervilles* (by far the most famous story) or another story with unusual features, such as "The Speckled Band" or 'The Dancing Men". However, I wish to make the argument that, if you want to introduce the Canon to a new reader, you should start with what I consider to be the best, most typical and emotionally accessible short story, "The Three Students".

It is, first of all, one of the better-written stories. From start to finish, "The Three Students" takes place in less than twenty-four hours, the action unfolds logically, and the clues are at least partially helpful to a reader trying to decide "whodunit." The story neither closes with startling abruptness (as does "The Yellow Face"), nor wanders into self-indulgent, seemingly pointless digressions ("The Country of the Saints" in *A Study in Scarlet*). A reader new to the Holmes stories, but perhaps unfamiliar with some vocabulary or with Victorian England, will especially appreciate the smooth pacing and clear writing.

Beyond ease of reading, two principles make "The Three Students" the best story to start with. It contains many character and narrative elements that become familiar to devotees of the Canon, and is emotionally accessible and relatable to the ordinary, modern reader.

"The Three Students" takes place in that most typical Sherlockian year, 1895. This year is widely recognized as one of the greatest in Sherlock Holmes's career; it is a year after his return from the Great Hiatus, and he is at the height of his powers with many years of work left. Famed scholar Vincent Starrett even immortalized it in his poem "221B," noting that "it is always 1895." Other significant cases set in 1895 include "The Solitary Cyclist" and "The Bruce-Partington Plans".

Another typical Arthur Conan Doyle plot device is the Very Agitated Client. This is an effective introductory element he uses to bring the reader into the emotional heart of the story; we know the case will be a Big Deal because the client is desperate and confused, in need of Holmes's sharp intellect and experienced wisdom. We have sympathy for the client in such distress, and eagerly await Holmes's response. The Very Agitated Client shows up in many stories: the King of Bohemia (who wears a mask and attempts to use a fake name) and headmaster Thorneycroft Huxtable (who faints in front of the fire at Baker Street) are two dramatic instances. "The Three Students" begins with the introduction of the tutor, Mr. Hilton Soames. Watson describes him as a man "of a nervous and excitable temperament" who, on this occasion, has achieved "such a state of uncontrollable agitation that it was clear something very unusual had occurred." Thankfully he neither comes in disguise, nor collapses on the hearthrug.

As with most Sherlock Holmes stories, this one gives a fine example of Holmes's grasp of obscure information with his discourse on the pencil shavings left behind by the cheating student. This quality of Holmes is one of his most famous (and most parodied). From familiarity with non-native jellyfish in "The Lion's Mane", to monographs on 140 types of tobacco ash in *The Sign of Four*, Holmes is a fount of knowledge that eludes the average person. His reasoning from the pencil shavings as to the size of the remaining pencil, the uncommon type of it, and the size and bluntness of the perpetrator's knife speaks to his focus on seeming trifles and ability to make deductions from them.

Another frequent step in Holmes's process sees him leave Watson and run off on his own to do research or investigation. In "The Three Students", he leaves early in the morning (when he investigates the university track at 6 a.m.); in another case, such as "The Beryl Coronet", he may be out very late to investigate a scene or to speak with a witness. These researches often require a costume, as in "A Case of Identity" and "A Scandal in Bohemia".

Perhaps an underestimated feature of Holmes's personality is his very dry humor. It's on display in many stories, memorably in "The Devil's Foot" ("That is what you may expect to see when I follow you"). In "The Three Students", two such moments stand out. Holmes asks Soames if he has any reason to suspect one of the three students more than the others. Soames demurs: "One hardly likes to throw suspicion where there are no proofs." "Let us hear the suspicions," says Holmes. "I will look after the proofs." The joke, of course, is that the Greek examination "proofs" are a major part of the evidence that Holmes examines to find a solution.

Holmes's second moment of humor in this story, which would be taken at face value by one who was unfamiliar with the other stories, is when he playfully chides Watson for his bad habits. "By Jove! my dear fellow, it is nearly nine, and the landlady babbled of green peas at seven-thirty. What with your eternal tobacco, Watson, and your irregularity at meals, I expect that you will get notice to quit." Of course we know from various stories that it is Holmes who smokes too much, eats too little, and drives his landlady crazy (by shooting up the walls, performing messy chemistry experiments, and so on).

Although Holmes's quirks and personality are a major part of why the stories remain so popular today, many new readers may find the more elaborate language tough going, and the unfamiliar late Victorian cultural norms and assumptions may also be an obstacle at first. However, "The Three Students" has several things that make it emotionally relatable or accessible to the modern reader new to the Canon. It is set in "one of our great university towns," and a university setting is filled with potential for drama and different types of characters, with its own unique culture that can still seem familiar to many readers even if they have never attended university. And even those who never attended college understand the seriousness of being caught cheating on a school exam. While the stakes are lower than in many other Holmes stories, it is still something inexperienced and younger readers can relate to.

Another moment in "The Three Students" allows the modern reader to connect with the story. As in several other canonical tales, this one has a dramatically remorseful perpetrator, who "bur[ies] his face in his hands," and "burst[s] into a storm of passionate sobbing." Any normal person who had committed a crime, small or large, might certainly be overwhelmed by Holmes's ability to unmask the truth seemingly out of thin air, and the reader can certainly understand those feelings and picture their own reaction in such a situation.

A third relatable element is that Sherlock Holmes, for all his supposed "coldness" and "pure reason," has a tendency to judge and release criminals on his own, if he feels that it's the right thing to do. In "The Blue Carbuncle" he lets a thief go because "it is just possible that I am saving a soul." In "The Abbey Grange" he pronounces Watson a "British jury" and himself a judge, acquitting Captain Crocker. This pattern also shows up in "The Three Students;" young Gilchrist has shown himself to be remorseful and to have already excused himself from taking the examination, so Holmes wishes him well in his upcoming position with the Rhodesian police: "Let us see, in the future, how high you can rise."

The reader, who has undertaken a journey with Holmes, is able to see the big picture as he does, and have sympathy for those unfortunate souls who find themselves caught up in events.

In this story, in short, Arthur Conan Doyle brings together quality writing, many of Holmes's personal characteristics and common canonical plot devices, and emotional connection. All of these allow the modern reader to become immersed in the story, and they are why I believe that "The Three Students" is the best starting point for the new reader of Sherlock Holmes.

Rachel E. Kellogg (Fort Wayne, Indiana) has worked in higher education for several years, teaching English and working in student affairs. She first met Sherlock Holmes at a young and impressionable age by watching Jeremy Brett, and quickly dived into the Canon, abetted by her parents.

THE ADVENTURE OF THE GOLDEN PINCE-NEZ

ALEXIAN A. GREGORY

Asking a dedicated Sherlockian to pick his favorite story is akin to asking a father to pick the daughter he loves the most—a dangerous and disagreeable task. But at least in the Sherlockian case one can rest assured that there will be no hurt feelings on the part of the ink-and-paper non-nominees.

I've been a Sherlockian since the ripe old age of seven when I first read the Canon. I can honestly say that "The Golden Pince-Nez" is one of my short story favorites. This is so because it contains a number of "must-have" mystery story elements all neatly and expertly packaged within its pages.

Let's start with the title: "The Golden Pince-Nez," French for "pinch nose." That artifact brings us squarely into the age of Victoria's elongated reign so beloved of Sherlockians. No one uses such an item today. But back then it was *de rigueur* for the middle-class gentleman. (I've always assumed that the male aristocrats favored monocles.) Attached to a hole in the lapel of a jacket by a black silken cord, the pince-nez was always at hand to be perched on a man's nose as he perused the *Times* from the comfy environs of a luxurious wing chair at his smoky male-only club, or as he scrutinized a will in his barrister's book-lined boardroom. What gentleman wouldn't look elegantly elite or ponderously pensive when sporting spectacles like these? Obviously women wore them as well, as the story reveals and as we can see from old photographs.

One of the delightful highlights of this story is the long series of highly accurate deductions that Holmes makes about the wearer of this pince-nez. He reconstructs her with the same professorial precision that would be displayed by an anthropologist recreating an entire early hominid skeleton based upon the characteristics of a single bone. Holmes may speak casually, but he shines at his deductive and ratiocinative best in this *demonstratio ad oculos*.

The reader sails between the two Pillars of Hercules to enter this adventure. First we have Watson's maddening allusions to several unrecorded cases involving a red leech and a banker, the Addleton tragedy, an ancient British barrow, and the arrest of Huret the boulevard assassin, with the Order of the Legion of Honour for Holmes as its outcome. What heaven-ensconced saint wouldn't agree to a short sojourn in the infernal regions in exchange for detailed knowledge of these cases?

Then there is the second pillar, the horrific weather, "a wild, tempestuous night," as Watson calls it. The rain beating down upon Baker Street is the mighty menacing meteorological messenger portending some horror about to break in on the manly coziness of 221B. This counterpoint between the horrid weather outside and the serenity within provides the anticipatory tension and the dramatic overture to this case. The boundary line between the wet and wild weather without, and the dry and tranquil warmth within, is breached by Stanley Hopkins. He brings the torrential weather inside in the form of his "shining waterproof."

My next gem is the name of the scene of the crime, Yoxley Old Place. Along with Baskerville Hall and Pondicherry Lodge, there is a certain *je ne sais quoi* about this name which inevitably excites keen expectation on my part. Perhaps it's the name's redolence of venerable medievalism which engenders this feeling. Does the stately name suggest a history—bloody, sad or triumphant—of eras gone by?

The issue of names then brings me to the villain of the piece, Professor Sergius Coram. This name is doubly peculiar and mysterious. He is Russian, yet neither his given name nor his surname is so. My Latin dictionary defines "coram" as "openly, publicly." The wily white-haired old Professor is neither. He lives a very isolated existence, rarely leaving his house, and never departing his property. He prefers to stay entombed amidst his learned tomes. Did he take his pseudonym Coram as an ironic joke? Sergius, meanwhile, is the Latin form of the name Serge. In Russian it's Sergei. Why does Anna use the Latinized form in addressing him? Is she knowingly going along with his Latin pseudonym for some obscure reason? Even the mysteries of his decidedly non-Slavic name make this story fascinating.

I'm no cognoscente of the history of the mystery story. But it has always seemed to me that it was the English who invented the genre of the country house murder mystery. Let's face it, a murder committed in an English country house has a much more attractive patina for us than a murder in, say, a country house in Norman, Oklahoma. This is true even if the details of the two crimes are of the same horrific and mysterious caliber.

The Yoxley Old Place crime is indisputably an English country house murder. That alone makes this story attractive for the reader. And what country house murder would be complete without a secret passage, or at least a fine old hidey-hole? "The Golden Pince-Nez" certainly has the latter, as our killer makes a dramatic appearance from its cobwebby recess.

The back story to this adventure is the doings of revolutionaries in faraway, semi-medieval, autocratic Russia. While not too much is revealed about the Brotherhood, there is still enough there to add to the pathos of this tale.

Finally, there is the dialectic between the sociopathy and the scholarliness of Professor Coram that adds a rich texture to the story. On the one hand he is a remorseless evil man who has allowed an innocent man to languish in Siberia. On the other hand he is a devoted scholar who studies the Coptic Church of Egypt, a highly esoteric field of historical study. These studies threaten, according to his boast, to "cut deep at the very foundations of revealed religion." My own studies of the history of the Coptic Church have convinced me that Coram was out to prove that many of the central tenets developed in early Christianity were direct adaptations from the polytheistic Egyptian religion. So a man who had betrayed political revolutionaries in Russia was preparing to make a religious revolution in England in the field of early Christian historiography.

Exotic Egypt makes another, if fleeting, appearance in this story. It occurs in the name of Coram's custom cigarette maker, Ionides of Alexandria. How did Coram come to know of him? Had Coram ever been in Egypt when doing his research on the "Coptic monasteries of Syria and Egypt"? I should like to have known a bit more about this chap, Ionides of Alexandria! Coram says he orders 1,000 of his custom-made Alexandrian cigarettes every fortnight. That means he smokes three-and-a-half packs every single day. He is a human chimney unequaled in the Canon.

Holmes tangled with very few criminals who were genuine intellectuals or scholars. We might mention the pathological pathologist Culverton Smith, the lepidopterist Stapleton, and not least in this Hall of Intellectual Invidiousness the mathematical Moriarty. But to my mind no sociopathic intellectual rises to the scholarly heights, or is as well limned, as Professor Sergius Coram of Yoxley Old Place.

The most dramatic element in the story is the suicide of Anna. This is unique in the Canon. In "The Stock-Broker's Clerk" and "The Retired Colourman," Holmes stops attempted suicides. In "Thor Bridge" he shows that what was an ostensible murder was actually a successful suicide. In "The Veiled Lodger" he talks a woman out of committing suicide. But in no story, other than "The Golden Pince-Nez," do we see a successful suicide being committed before our very eyes. This is high drama indeed.

This, then, is the bright mosaic of literary elements which Doyle artfully crafted into this masterpiece of detective fiction. It's a tale for all the ages which will never grow stale, even upon numerous re-readings.

Alexian A. Gregory (Verona, New Jersey) owns more than 400 copies of *The Hound of the Baskervilles* in 46 languages. He is a Baker Street Irregular and produces the annual alphabetical listing of investiture names of BSI members; he has also written about such Sherlockian topics as the Coptic religion.

THE ADVENTURE OF
THE MISSING THREE-QUARTER

DAN ANDRIACCO

Like Charles Dickens before him, the author of the Canon excels at word-portraits of minor characters. Nowhere is that exemplified better than in "The Adventure of the Missing Three-Quarter," starting with the overwrought client. The exuberant personality of Cyril Overton precedes him to Baker Street in the form of a frenetic telegram: "Please await me. Terrible misfortune. Right wing three-quarter missing; indispensable to-morrow. – Overton." This Overton turns out to be "an enormous young man, sixteen stone of solid bone and muscle, who spanned the doorway with his broad shoulders and looked from one of us to the other with a comely face which was haggard with anxiety." Perhaps not surprisingly, this admirable physique and handsome phiz belong to an athlete, a rugby player for Oxford. As Holmes notes, this is the sleuth's first professional involvement in amateur sport, which he calls "the best and soundest thing in England."

Overton pours out a long-winded appeal for help "with extraordinary vigour and earnestness, every point being driven home by the slapping of a brawny hand upon the speaker's knee." He expresses what Watson calls "naïve astonishment" that Holmes has never heard of Cyril Overton or Godfrey Staunton, the missing three-quarter: "Good Lord! Mr. Holmes, where *have* you lived?" (One wants to cry, "221B—everybody knows that!")

The young giant, "more accustomed to using his muscles than his wits," gives an account of Staunton's disappearance that Watson edits for us to remove "many repetitions and obscurities." The resulting narrative plus Q&A with Holmes provide not only a clear statement of the case, but an introduction to the next significant character. Overton accurately characterizes Lord Mount-James, the missing man's wealthy uncle, as "an absolute miser." (We cannot know, alas, whether it is equally accurate that—as Overton has heard—the gout-ridden nobleman "could chalk his billiard cue with his knuckles.")

A short while later, in the missing Staunton's hotel room, Lord Mount-James makes a memorable entrance into Dr. Watson's narrative:

> "One moment—one moment!" cried a querulous voice, and we looked up to find a queer little old man, jerking and twitching in the doorway. He was dressed in rusty black, with a very broad brimmed top-hat and a loose white necktie—the whole effect being that of a very rustic parson or of an undertaker's mute. Yet, in spite of his shabby and even absurd appearance, his voice had a sharp crackle, and his manner a quick intensity which commanded attention.
>
> "Who are you, sir, and by what right do you touch this gentleman's papers?" he asked.

Steven Doyle, a notable Sherlockian and publisher of the *Baker Street Journal*, once commented to me that the Canon has both jerks and villains—and that the two are not synonymous. "The Missing Three-Quarter" has no real villain in the criminal sense, but Lord Mount-James is certainly a real jerk. With his heir missing, his chief concern is that he not be stuck with the bill for finding the lad. "Don't look to me for a penny—not a penny! You understand that, Mr. Detective!"

With a mischievous twinkle in his eye, Holmes disingenuously suggests to Lord Mount-James that perhaps a gang of kidnappers made away with Staunton in order to get information about his uncle's home and treasure. The old man turns white at the thought and makes a comical about-face in his attitude toward Holmes: "I'll have the plate moved over to the bank this evening. In the meantime spare no pains, Mr. Detective! I beg you to leave no stone unturned to bring him safely back. As to money, well, so far as a fiver, or even a tenner, goes, you can always look to me." Note that, despite the change in demeanor, he is still a jerk.

When the trail takes Holmes on one of his rare visits to a university city, clearly identified as Oxford for a change, he encounters a more rounded character with a larger role in the story. Upon first reading, one likely suspects Dr. Leslie Armstrong of being a jerk *and* a villain, like that more famous physician in the Canon, Grimesby Roylott. But we eventually learn that he is neither, just an overly protective father-figure.

Again Watson pens a strong description of this "thinker of European reputation in more than one branch of science." Perhaps not accidentally, the phrase recalls a certain mathematics professor whose treatise on the binomial theorem, written when he was just twenty-one, "enjoyed a European vogue." Writes Watson: "Yet even without knowing his brilliant record one could not fail to be impressed by a mere glance at the man, the square, massive face, the brooding eyes under the thatched brows, and the granite moulding of the inflexible jaw. A man of deep character, a man with an alert mind, grim, ascetic, self-contained, formidable—so I read Dr. Leslie Armstrong."

Armstrong greets Holmes frostily: "I have heard your name, Mr. Sherlock Holmes, and I am aware of your profession, one of which I by no means approve." Holmes has not been treated so rudely since, well, since Lord Mount-James. Armstrong goes on to say that the detective is wasting Armstrong's time, which could be better spent "writing a treatise." (Aha! we think—a treatise!) Nevertheless, the physician/scientist submits to questions from Holmes, alternately stonewalling and lying in his responses. When a furious Armstrong finally ejects Holmes and Watson from his house, Holmes bursts out laughing. Earlier, he had laughed at Overton and chuckled at pulling one over on the young woman at the telegraph office. Clearly, he is having a good time on this case.

As early as *A Study in Scarlet*, Holmes chafed at the lack of a worthy opponent. He pays Armstrong the highest possible compliment, therefore, when he says, perhaps with Armstrong's treatise-writing in mind: "I have not seen a man who, if he turned his talents that way, was more calculated to fill the gap left by the illustrious Moriarty." But *has* the doctor turned his talents that way? It certainly looks that way for most of the story. When Holmes follows Armstrong's carriage on a bicycle, Armstrong gets out and confronts him. The next day, he sends Holmes a letter politely telling the latter to buzz off. "An outspoken, honest antagonist is the doctor," says Holmes. His admiration only grows when he finds out later that Armstrong "has certainly played the game for all it is worth" by taking his carriage on a detour to throw Holmes off his scent. (It is literally a scent, though it is not literally Holmes sniffing it; more on that later.)

In their final scene together, after the tragic death of Godfrey Staunton's secret wife, Armstrong gives Holmes a tongue-lashing. Within minutes, however, Holmes sets him straight as to the sleuth's role in the case. In a quick turn-around reminiscent of Lord Mount-James, Armstrong wrings the detective's hand and proclaims him "a good fellow." Armstrong's account of Staunton's story, though not meant to exculpate his boorish behavior to Holmes, nevertheless makes it clear that he acted out of affection for the athlete, not his own selfish interests. He isn't a jerk, after all! We and Holmes have misjudged him, just as he admits misjudging Holmes.

Cyril Overton introduced the case, Lord Mount-James provided a little drama and comic relief, and Dr. Leslie Armstrong ultimately led Holmes to the missing three-quarter. There is, however, one more character to be considered: Pompey the draghound. Most Sherlockians will find it almost impossible to think about this story without remembering the iconic Frederic Dorr Steele illustration of an Americanized Holmes (*à la* William Gillette) in a deerstalker cap holding the noble animal on a leash. "Pompey is the pride of the local draghounds, no very great flier, as his build will show, but a staunch hound on a scent," Holmes assures Watson. And so he proves to be. "The dog sniffed round for an instant, and then with a shrill whine of excitement started off down the street, tugging at his leash in his efforts to go faster. In half an hour, we were clear of the town and hastening down a country road." Pompey is one of two great trackers in the Canon, the other being Toby in *The Sign of Four*, "an ugly, long-haired, lop-eared creature, half-spaniel and half-lurcher, brown-and-white in colour, with a very clumsy waddling gait."

These four players in what many aficionados of Mr. Sherlock Holmes would consider a lesser adventure demonstrate the author's masterful ability to create memorable characters even when the tale itself is perhaps not of the first rank.

Dan Andriacco (Cincinnati, Ohio) is a recovering journalist, and the author of *Baker Street Beat: An Eclectic Collection of Sherlockian Scribblings* and the Sebastian McCabe and Jeff Cody mystery series.

THE ADVENTURE OF THE ABBEY GRANGE

MEGHASHYAM CHIRRAVOORI

As you browse the Sherlockian Canon, there's no dearth of stories where Sherlock Holmes stumps you with his mind-blowing deductions. Holmes's deductions in "Silver Blaze", "The Bruce-Partington Plans", "The Cardboard Box", "The Red-Headed League" and way too many other stories are superb. But how many stories can you find in which Sherlock Holmes behaves like a real, relatable human being—a person who makes mistakes, forms judgements based on prejudices, and gets fooled by what other people try to tell him?

A select few. And out of those stories, how many can you find in which despite behaving exactly as you or I would, and being just another fallible dude, Holmes bounces right back, introspects, realizes his foolishness and then comes up with eye-popping deductions that steal the show?

Exactly one: "The Abbey Grange".

I still remember the shock I experienced when I read this story for the first time. It's not as though no other Holmes story has a twist. "The Norwood Builder" has a stunning twist and so do "The Boscombe Valley Mystery" and "Thor Bridge". But the reason I found the twist in "The Abbey Grange" to be the most shocking was the extent to which I had started relating to Holmes—in a way I never could relate to Holmes—in other stories. I admired Holmes, respected him, was in awe of him—but in "The Abbey Grange", for a short while, I had started seeing him as a friend, before he turned the story on its head. Which made the twist so shocking and real.

You see, in this story Holmes ignores the glasses with dregs in the beginning even though he notices them. He knows the burglars couldn't have come at 11 p.m., couldn't have struck again a fortnight after their last haul, couldn't have pulled off the bell-pull or hit Lady Brackenstall to stop her from screaming—or even killed the man, Sir Eustace

Brackenstall. He knows there's something fishy right away. And yet, he genuinely believes the beautiful Lady Brackenstall's story and closes the case.

Holmes doesn't act like Mr. Know-it-all here. For once, you as a reader don't need to identify with Watson; you can sail in the same boat as Holmes. You can be with him every moment as he fights his intuition. As he's rattled by whether his gut feeling should be heeded. Before he risks it and takes the plunge.

While other stories may be mind-blowing because of Holmes's powers, "The Abbey Grange" is a beautiful rendition of the humanness of Holmes... along with some bow-inducing deductions we haven't even touched upon yet.

Just as only being *über*-clever makes Holmes unrelatable at times, making Holmes only human would make you question: Where the deuce is the Sherlock Holmes I know in this story? Ah, but in "The Abbey Grange", there is the Holmes we know too—and in full measure! The Holmes who's the master of deductions? That one.

As soon as Sherlock Holmes spots the three wine glasses on the mantelpiece, he sees something Watson and Hopkins can't see. "And yet you must admit that the three glasses are very remarkable, Hopkins. What, you see nothing remarkable!" He says that in his typical cryptic style. Then, later, he proves that there were only two glasses used for drinking wine and the third one was faked by adding dregs to it. After all, why otherwise would only one glass have all the dregs of wine and the others not have any?

Since Lady Brackenstall insists that all three glasses were used in front of her... she's lying.

And that deduction turns the story upside down, because everything we've assumed till now is false. Brilliant!

And then there's the torn bell pull. Holmes displays his usual obsession for details when he climbs the massive mantelpiece to find that one end of the torn bell-pull's rope is frayed while the other isn't. Why should one end of any rope be frayed and not the other unless it was cut clean, and then made to look like it was ripped by manually fraying the other end? Which means yet again that Lady Brackenstall is lying and that the waters are deep and murky. And yet again, it's as clean and flawless as any other amazing deduction in the Canon.

So, you see, "The Abbey Grange" has no dearth of those cool deductions we all love. It doesn't leave out Holmes's outstanding powers, it just adds more flavours to Holmes without taking anything away.

Arthur Conan Doyle is not a very verbose writer for the time period in which he wrote. But if you look at "Wisteria Lodge" or "The Naval

Treaty" or even *A Study in Scarlet*, there are times when the story proceeds at quite a leisurely pace. Not so in the case of "The Abbey Grange".

I recently read this story for the *n*th time and was surprised that despite having read it so many times before, I just raced through it to the end, before I could say to myself, "Wait, I know all this. Let me skim this portion." There couldn't be any skimming. It's that crisp. And that racy. Right from the first line, you delve straight into the story. There's no long-drawn meandering about the weather or the lack of cases or anything at all. As Holmes himself puts it in the story—not a word! Not a word is extra or unnecessary. Not even one.

In fact, just three lines into the story, you have one of the most exciting Sherlock Holmes quotes of all time:

> "Come, Watson, come!" he cried. "The game is afoot. Not a word! Into your clothes and come!"

And that's exactly how the whole story is. Exciting! Not a word can you breathe till the tale is done.

Yes, you see a human Sherlock Holmes making mistakes in "The Abbey Grange". Yes, you see an awe-inspiring Sherlock Holmes making spectacular deductions. But the icing on the cake is yet another Holmes that you don't often see: a warm-hearted Sherlock Holmes.

Holmes has the culprit eating out of his hand in the story, but he doesn't say, "I got my kicks solving the case. I don't care what happens to the killer." Instead, he carefully assesses the culprit's intentions. When he realizes that Captain Crocker (the killer) did what he did to protect Lady Brackenstall, and that he acted nobly and gracefully throughout, Holmes takes the law in his hands. He lets the Crocker dude go in style! I'd say that this display of Sherlockian compassion is a fitting ending to a brilliant tale.

Holmes even adds a touch of the dramatic as he acquits Captain Crocker, appointing Watson as the jury and himself as the judge. So, just in case we were missing that typical Sherlockian pizzazz in this story: that's there too!

If you've ever had a satisfying five-course meal, then you know what "The Abbey Grange" offers: everything. There's excitement from the word go, lots of fumbling from the Holmes who never fumbles, some spell-binding deductions, and to top it a beautiful display of empathy by Sherlock Holmes. Plus some more icing of Holmes's love of drama at the end.

What more could you ask for?

And that is exactly why, if there were an award ceremony for Sherlock Holmes stories, this is the award I would give "The Abbey Grange": The Most Underrated Sherlock Holmes Story.

Meghashyam Chirravoori (New Delhi, India) is the creator of SherlockHolmes-Fan.com, where he delves into anything related to Sherlock Holmes that piques his interest, from limericks and jokes to the origin of the word "Sherlock".

THE ADVENTURE OF
THE SECOND STAIN

MARY LOVING

"The Second Stain" is the greatest and one of the most exciting stories in all of the Sherlock Holmes Canon. I offer as ultimate proof this statement by the greatest authority on the Sacred Writings: none other than the author himself, John H. Watson, MD, who in "The Naval Treaty" stated this about "The Second Stain": "No case, however, in which Holmes was engaged has ever illustrated the value of his analytical methods so clearly or has impressed those who were associated with him so deeply."

Another important, although secondary, authority was the Literary Agent, Arthur Conan Doyle, who chose to include this story when compiling his own list of the twelve best stories of the Holmes *oeuvre*. One can only assume his working relationship with Dr. Watson gave him additional insight unavailable to the serious scholar, and certainly to the casual reader. That he did not rank this story first in his list only diminishes his otherwise excellent contribution to the Sherlockian scholarly body of works.

In spite of these unimpeachable authorities, however, I will endeavor to prove that "The Second Stain" is the greatest of all of the Sherlock Holmes stories, using the criteria set down by the first, and in the opinion of many the greatest, Sherlockian scholar, Monsignor Ronald A. Knox, who, in his seminal essay "Studies in the Literature of Sherlock Holmes" gave future scholars a means by which to rank the worthiness of the stories of the Sherlockian Canon. Knox developed eleven criteria for evaluating any Sherlock Holmes story. He allowed that in some stories these might be in a different order but in no way suggested they should not be included. In my evaluation I will list those here along with how that particular criterion was fulfilled in "The Second Stain."

Proömion, a homely Baker Street scene. Rather than the usual domestic scene being placed at the beginning of the tale, Dr. Watson wisely decided that he wanted to introduce their clients and the case right away, to give the story the proper tone of urgency. However, not wishing to disappoint his readers by leaving it out altogether, he decided instead to share with us a scene where he and Holmes discuss the case after their illustrious clients leave, during which Holmes, his mind already on the problem of the missing letter, determines that one of three known international spies was likely to have been the recipient of it. This cozy yet exciting scene also affords Watson the rare treat of surprising Holmes by relaying the news report of the murder of one of those suspects, Eduardo Lucas, which adds to the complication of the case.

Exegesis kata ton diokonta, the client's statement of the case. Were there ever more illustrious clients? We have none other than Lord Bellinger, the Prime Minister, and the Right Honorable Trelawney Hope, Secretary of State for European Affairs. Other stories may have had similar or more illustrious clients, but seldom did they deem to visit Baker Street themselves (such as in the story titled "The Illustrious Client"). Here they bring the problem of the missing volatile letter to the Master Detective personally yet decide to withhold the contents of it. Holmes knows that he is brilliant, but he cannot make bricks without clay, so he only agrees to take the case after they give in to the threat that they will be turned away if they cannot trust him fully.

Ichneusis, or personal investigation. Holmes spends the next few days going back and forth from Godolphin Street to Baker Street investigating the circumstances of the crime. We can also assume Holmes was ensuring the other two spies, Oberstein and La Rothière, were not involved in spite of their distance from Whitehall Terrace. Watson observes Holmes's restless mood and assumes he was not making much headway in the case, at least nothing he cared to share with Watson. Watson monitors, and also shares with the reader, press reports of the Lucas murder to keep us abreast of that connected and lurid investigation.

Anaskeue, or refutation on its own merits of the official theory of Scotland Yard. Typically the police will present their evidence to Holmes who then proceeds to pick it apart and list all the things they missed. In this case it is not possible for the police to even have an official theory because they are unaware of the missing letter. Their focus is entirely on the Lucas murder, but even there they seem to be unsure, as they rush to judgment, arrest the valet then release him after he presents an alibi. Holmes did not need to lift a finger to dispute the theories of the "Yarders" because the Parisian police did that for him by investigating the insane Mme. Fournaye, thus solving a murder that would have otherwise remained unsolved.

The first Promenusis (exoterike), which gives a few stray hints to the police, which they never adopt. At first glance it would seem this criterion is only partially fulfilled when Holmes suggested that Lestrade challenge MacPherson about his dereliction of duty in allowing a visitor to be present alone at the crime scene. And although Lestrade apparently negates this criterion by actually taking the hint Holmes provided, because the pompous Inspector had absolutely no understanding of the reasoning behind it I think we can allow for a fulfillment of the spirit of this criterion.

The second Promenusis (esoterike), which adumbrates the true course of the investigation to Watson alone. Again, we must allow that the spirit, rather than the letter, of this criterion is fulfilled by Holmes allowing Watson to be witness to the developments and the eventual denouement of the case rather than have it told to him at some later time.

Xetasis, or further following up of the trial, including the cross-questioning of relatives, dependents, etc., of the corpse (if there is one), visits to the Record Office, and various investigations in an assumed character. Holmes and Watson's visit to Godophin Street followed by their visit to Lady Hilda is all that was needed in order to come to the correct conclusions about the disappearance of the letter. In this case no disguise by Holmes was needed other than his seeming nonchalance and "suppressed excitement" in the presence of Lestrade and awareness of the second stain on the floor.

Anagnorisis, in which the criminal is caught or exposed. Had Lady Hilda not visited Baker Street, Holmes might not have made the connection between her and the "mysterious woman" who reportedly visited Lucas the night of his death. Finding the empty compartment in the floor in Lucas's home showed Holmes he was on the right track, but showing Lady Hilda's photograph to MacPherson confirmed the true culprit in his mind and gave him all he needed to confront her directly and demand the return of the letter and an explanation.

Second Exegesis (kata ton pheugonta), that is to say, the criminal's confession. Lady Hilda, seeing no other way out, decides to confess her role in the crime. She throws herself on Holmes's mercy by explaining that her only motive was to prevent her husband from discovering he was not her first love. Holmes believes her, and as he has done before in the cause of love ("The Abbey Grange" and "The Devil's Foot"), he decides not to expose her guilt, thus making himself an accessory after the fact. But he knew a greater good—preventing a war—was served by shielding her from personal and legal consequences.

Metamenusis, in which Holmes describes what his clues were and how he followed them. Often Holmes will explain how he came to the conclusion of a case, but here is another instance where only the spirit of this criterion is followed. Not only is Watson allowed to witness the chain of events as they happened, he deliberately chose to structure the story in the same manner so as to invite the reader along to the exciting conclusion.

Epilogos, sometimes comprised in a single sentence. Occasionally Holmes will quote a famous writer in summing up a case; here he decides, perhaps in relief, that a little sardonic humor is needed. As the Premier said, "How came the letter back into the box?" Holmes wittily replied, "We also have our diplomatic secrets," making this a fitting end to this brilliant case and story.

And there we have it—eleven criteria and eleven reasons why "The Second Stain" is the greatest story of the Canon. And if it's good enough for Monsignor Knox, then it should be good enough for us.

Mary Loving (Minneapolis, Minnesota) discovered Sherlock Holmes by watching Basil Rathbone's *Hound of the Baskervilles* on the late, late show. A member of the Norwegian Explorers of Minnesota, she is one of the leaders of their monthly study group and editor of their social media.

THE VALLEY OF FEAR

JENNIFER LIANG

Among the stories of the Sherlock Holmes Canon, *The Valley of Fear* has a special place. Like *A Study in Scarlet*, it is a two-part novel, composed of a mystery story as the first part and a second story that explains the characters and the context of the mystery. However, what makes *Valley* stand above all other stories of the Canon is its "completeness". The level of detail in this novel goes above all others in developing character and developing backstory. It leaves little need to speculate about character motive, history, or the plot itself; it has a sense of completeness that goes beyond that of any other story in the number of different elements from different genres.

The Valley of Fear starts as a typical Holmes story that is strong enough to be an excellent drama on its own. However, the addition of the second part gives a twist to the mystery that Holmes could not have reasoned out on his own. Having so many elements in both stories that make it more than just a mystery, make the novel so much more engaging. Elements of romance, tragedy, drama, action, and even a little humor put little flashes of fun into an otherwise suspenseful and dark tale.

I present a picture of the beginning of a typical Sherlock Holmes story. It starts quietly, the two men eating breakfast. Eventually, a visitor will arrive with the promise of a new adventure. False clues and lies cloud the story, which the men pursue until, eventually, the truth comes out. As repetitive as it is, this formula is as comforting as Inverness capes and deerstalker hats. The setup is so familiar that it makes the contrast more striking when, in this remarkable instance, the mystery transitions into the second story. Furthermore, the second story gives the mystery a special twist because the puzzle, or at least the identity of the culprit, can actually be solved without using the clues given in the story.

Canon stories in which it is possible to solve the mystery are always better than ones in which the key to solving the mystery is some detail that Holmes figured out without telling Watson, or something that would have been common knowledge in 19th century England but is not in the modern world. Being able to try to match wits and logic with Holmes on fair terms makes the story much more engaging, and *The Valley of Fear* is most certainly one of those.

In many mystery stories, the solution can hinge on an assumption that the author has tempted the reader to make but which turns out to be false: in "The Beryl Coronet", for example, it is already assumed that Arthur was the guilty party when it was actually the least likely suspect who was the culprit. The same goes for "The Boscombe Valley Mystery", in which the reader is led to believe that James murdered his father even though the situation is contradictory to that conclusion. "A Case of Identity" is another story that is possible to reason out, but parallels *The Valley of Fear* in its simplicity. The reader assumes that the fiancé is some trickster who has not been introduced yet, but all the important characters involved have in fact been introduced, so it must be one of them.

Here in *The Valley*, working out the mystery hinges on the assumption that the man initially shot and dead at the beginning of the story is John Douglas, and that the murderer is someone who has not been found yet. Initially it seems that the murderer must be an outside suspect, because of clues such as the boot mark on the window, and the explanation that someone must have gotten into the house while the drawbridge was down and hidden in the house until his chance arrived to kill Douglas. The card inscribed "V.V. 341" furthers this assumption that it was someone involved with Douglas's past. The next clue, which could go both ways, is the missing wedding ring. So presumably the murderer had a connection to Douglas's wife, and was American judging by the next clue, the gun manufactured by the Pennsylvania Small Arms Company. Moreover, a bicycle was found in the bushes, and it seems sure that the criminal abandoned the bicycle on his way to safety. So the clues point to someone with a connection to Douglas's past involvement with an organization with the rubric V.V. 341, a connection with his wife, and a background in America. Additionally, the murderer must have had a connection to both the wife and Barker that made them override their loyalty to Douglas and help the murderer escape. However, nobody has been presented in the story who would fit this description.

The other possibility is that the guilty person was someone who was not an outsider, leaving it to be either Barker or Mrs. Douglas, or the two together. The only real evidence that this is a possibility is that the timing of events given by both witnesses doesn't make sense. They were seen laughing together by Watson, which although it is suspicious, is not a usable clue. As Holmes says, they could be involved in a conspiracy, but to what end seems unknown.

The bicycle belonged to Hargrave, who could have possibly been the murderer, but it doesn't make sense that he would be that person since he has never had any connection with Mrs. Douglas, and so his guilt would not explain why the wedding ring was missing. He has no connection with Barker either, for that matter. The only person mentioned in the story who fits all clues that are not circumstantial, such as the bicycle, is Douglas himself. Although it is possible that he might have committed suicide, this was already disproved by the sergeant and MacDonald. Assuming that all the clues are there, and that there is no hidden background information that Watson has not been told by Holmes, and if Holmes is correct about a conspiracy afoot, it would fit the circumstances that Douglas himself was the culprit and somehow faked his death. It would remain to be seen how the second body with the same tattoo was obtained, but at least a faked death would be the most elegant explanation, rather than an outside murderer or a plot by Mrs. Douglas and Barker.

Another asset that makes *The Valley of Fear* the best story of the Canon is the supremely well-done characterization. This novel goes into depth like no other story and illustrates the complexity of the people involved in the mystery. Unlike the short stories, where there can be only glimpses of insight into the cosmos that is the lives of the other characters, *Valley* is very thorough in personality detail. The characterization of Birdy Edwards, in particular, is well-done; he is arguably one of the most complex characters of the Canon. As John Douglas, he is characterized as an enigmatic figure by his neighbors, he is popular and generous, he was said to have been well involved in the community, he proved himself to be utterly fearless by entering a vicarage during a raging fire that the fire brigade deemed hopeless. As John McMurdo, he is revealed as someone from whom anything can be expected. At first introduction in the second story, he bursts out in rage at two policemen for giving some advice on the company he keeps. He is variously said by other characters to be unpredictable, good-humored, being of many talents including singing, as noted by both Watson and in the second story, playing instruments, telling stories, and obviously being quite charming. He charmed Ettie into loving him with "his glib Irish tongue, and his pretty, coaxing ways" even though Ettie already had Teddy Baldwin as a suitor.

Birdy Edwards is a truly fantastic and devoted liar, having managed to infiltrate a fraternal organization like the Scowrers, commit criminal acts, keep up with this double life, and above all, keep everything a secret from his lover and his closest companions in the area. He is clearly a man strongly committed to his goals and sense of justice. He must be a strong character to have gone along with all this criminal activity, especially to have made and learned how to use his own coining molds to create counterfeit money and yet not succumb to the criminal lifestyle.

Moreover, he is a charismatic man, able to inspire extreme loyalty. The initial mystery implies as much, since Barker and his wife are willing to lie to the police to put up this charade of a murder, and since Mrs. Douglas apparently was prepared to flee with him after the case was closed. The second story completely validates these speculations on his background, but puts the characteristics and story in a different light.

Another notable character is Boss McGinty himself. Although he is a side character, he is also given an interesting personality and cause for sympathy. He is described as "a black maned giant", with fine features and "noble proportions" and a face that shows "strength, and courage, and cunning" behind the latent evil. Although he is a fierce and commanding leader, he finds it amusing to have Birdy talk to him in an insolent manner at their first meeting. Moreover, he has a philosophical leaning about the nature of government. He's clearly established how he stands with the police by the way he talks to the officers who enter the saloon. His words mock them: "What are you but the paid tool of the capitalists hired by them to club or shoot your poorer fellow?" As the leader of the organization, it shows his confidence in himself as the better form of government. Although he may rule with fear and coercion, he sees himself as defender of the common man, although there is also evidence that he is just as corrupt. He is "a high public official, a municipal councillor, and a commissioner of roads"—he bridges the underground world and that of the official government—but he has apparently neglected public works, bribed auditors, and gotten his way through blackmail. Furthermore, he uses the money for his own profit, expanding his saloon and buying himself jewels and clothes.

The Valley of Fear is also the story in which we find out the most about Moriarty, aside from "The Final Problem". It characterizes the Professor in such a way that shows how he is a foil to Boss McGinty. Holmes says that, "In calling Moriarty a criminal you are uttering libel in the eyes of the law—and there lie the glory and wonder of it!" Inspector MacDonald also comments on Moriarty after having investigated the man. After making special inquiries, he cannot find anything and seems to think that the whole business with Moriarty is a silly conspiracy. So excellent is Moriarty's ability to delegate work that he has managed to completely separate himself from the crimes he has administered. This is a stark contrast to Boss McGinty, who not only straddles two worlds but is well known in both. Also unlike Boss McGinty, Moriarty is well accomplished at both of his "jobs". The face that he turns towards the world of respectable society is so clean that he is free of reproach. Moreover, he is a celebrated author who is viewed in the mathematics community as unable to do wrong. And yet, Holmes accuses him of being the character behind international crime. In contrast to Moriarty, McGinty clearly neglects the duties of his job as a government official and makes it obvious that he does more for the Scowrers through his saloon that he owns and continuously expands.

Another interesting character is Ettie Shafter. She seems to be the simple daughter of an upstanding man, but she seems to attract the attention of men who have more questionable values than her own father, such as Teddy Baldwin. She is also a romantic, judging from how she was willing to run away with Birdy, despite all of the dangers that it might pose and the awareness that she may be on the run for the rest of her life. Even though she feared and despised Teddy, she had no way of knowing if her life with McMurdo would be the same or even worse, since both are members of what seems to be a fraternity that commits criminal activity, and McMurdo is the one who is on the run from the law. Moreover, since his true identity was a secret, anything he told her about himself could have been a lie. Still, that she was willing to leave behind her home to marry a mysterious stranger says a lot about her personality.

The depth of the characters make *The Valley of Fear* memorable, but they also drive multiple plots that keep the story dramatic and interesting. The more plot a story has, the more room there is to create interest. Therefore, the multiple subplots also make this work rise above all others in the Canon, because within this two-part story are so many stories of so many people. The first part's mystery introduces the complexity which is to come in the second part. The main plot of the second story is that of McMurdo, a charming counterfeiter and murderer running from his old life to a new one in Chicago, and attempting to establish himself as a leader and member of society. Running alongside that story is the love of Ettie and McMurdo, who are kept apart by so much. The father, a rival suitor, and McMurdo's own chosen career as a criminal all do much to keep the lovers apart, but their love struggles to survive anyhow. Meanwhile, the third plot of Birdy Edwards as a threat to the Scowrers makes its way towards the end of the second part of the story, only to be twisted as McMurdo is revealed to have been Birdy Edwards. Best of all, all of these stories resolve in an elegant manner. *The Valley of Fear* is so cleverly written because the mystery part provides both the introduction to the characters and also the conclusion to the second story.

Thus this novel has an interesting synergistic effect of one tale making the other better. The tale of Birdy Edwards provides the background for Holmes's mystery, and the mystery gives a conclusion to the story of

Birdy Edwards. The mystery could no doubt have been solved without the background information of how John Douglas came to England and settled in as a country gentleman; it was not necessary to elaborate on the story of how he infiltrated a criminal fraternity or why he was being sought out. However, having the background gives the plot more drama and turns. To read the story of Birdy Edwards as a stand-alone story is also a possibility, giving the reader more insight into the interesting characters of Holmes's mystery and a chance to explore more than just how Watson sees them.

Another aspect which makes this adventure so interesting, indeed the best of them all, is the depth of detail in which it describes Vermissa. The gloominess of the environment sets the tone that connects the events. Unlike other stories, this one gives details about everyone else who lives in the area and even the topography of Vermissa Valley. Vermissa's main industry is, of course, mining, and it's said explicitly in the story that the miners made good money, and yet the area itself is neglected.

> "The town showed a dead level of mean ugliness and squalor. The broad street was churned up by traffic.... The sidewalks were narrow and uneven. The numerous gas-lamps served only to show more clearly a long line of wooden houses, each with its veranda facing the street, unkempt and dirty."

McGinty evidently collects a great deal of money, but steals it and uses it for himself instead of using it for public works. For example, the park that is said to be a popular destination for people in the summer is also said to be dilapidated and not well kept. So the formal government has little care for the city's public works, but the group with the monopoly on violence, the Scowrers, have no formal power to take care of the city either. It is interesting to note that Scanlan says that Vermissa Valley is where the order flourishes most, which implies its power within the community.

This story is especially brilliant because it illustrates one of the few times that even though Holmes was an excellent detective and solved the case with every detail in place, the outcome was undesirable. Although Holmes is the protagonist in the Canon, it makes a story interesting when he ultimately contributes to the problem instead of finding a solution to make the situation better as he usually does. Instead, in this instance, Holmes solves the case but ultimately makes the larger problem worse. If he had allowed the mystery to go unsolved, John Douglas would have probably been able to escape with his wife and delay his capture for another long while, especially as the plan was to move to Africa where Moriarty may have fewer connections than in Europe or America. The sequence of events was already set in motion before Holmes even began his investigation. Moriarty had already been consulted by American gangsters to seek out Douglas. The faked murder of Douglas seemed unsolvable by the local detectives, as their theories pointed towards an outside criminal involved in Douglas's former life in America. Given the number of false clues, the conclusion without Holmes probably would have been that the crime involved a gangster from America seeking vengeance. However, since Holmes had solved the case and proven that Douglas had faked his death, it led the local police to make him stand trial for the killing of the man actually sent to kill Douglas. As the setting is in a small village in the countryside, this kind of event probably garnered much attention and reached Moriarty. Thus, Douglas had no chance of escape because of Holmes's involvement in the case.

In the end, Holmes managed to uncover a plot that was part of a fantastic story spanning two continents and a series of conspiracies. This novel is so complex that the nuances of the story could only be expressed well by close attention to detail. This quality makes *The Valley of Fear* stand alone as a gem with the most well-fleshed characters and a prime example of how to build a world that exists beyond just Holmes himself. It creates interest on so many levels, as it engages with the mystery and presents situations uncommon to the rest of the Canon, such as villains who have escaped Holmes and richly layered background stories. Either of the two stories could stand alone in its completeness, but the synergistic effect of having two excellent stories complete each other make *The Valley of Fear* the best of the Canon.

Jennifer Liang (Brownsville, Texas) is known in and out of the Sherlockian world for the natty clothes, including Victorian attire, which she makes herself. Her home societies are the Parallel Case, the Noble Bachelors, and the Harpooners of the Sea Unicorn, in St. Louis. She works as a hospital pharmacist.

THE PREFACES

CHRISTOPHER REDMOND

Not part of any of the sixty stories, but certainly part of the complete Sherlock Holmes, are the one-paragraph Preface to His Last Bow, signed by "John H. Watson, M.D.", and the two-page Preface to The Case-Book, signed by Arthur Conan Doyle.

The other collections of short stories had not had prefaces of any kind, but the stories in *His Last Bow* had been published in scattered fashion over some years, and Watson (or ACD) must have felt that it would be helpful to explain the circumstances under which they were being collected in book form in the fall of 1917. At the same time he gave readers much of the still scanty information we have about Sherlock Holmes's retirement: his "occasional attacks of rheumatism" (how unlike the Holmes of our imaginations!) and his residence "five miles from Eastbourne", where he engages in "philosophy and agriculture". Interestingly, this brief report does not mention bees.

ACD's longer Preface is a different thing altogether. It first saw print when the *Case-Book* was published in June 1927, and finally achieves what the author had tried repeatedly in the past, saying farewell to the authentic Sherlock Holmes. It has some slight echoes of ACD's much longer essay "Some Personalia About Mr. Sherlock Holmes", written for the *Strand* magazine ten years earlier, when it seemed that the saga had at last been wound up with the publication of "His Last Bow". (At least five of the 60 stories show evidence of being unsuccessful attempts at ending Holmes's career.)

Far more than "Some Personalia", however, the 1927 Preface is a poetic tribute to Sherlock Holmes from his earthly creator. Its only parallels in the canonical stories are Watson's grief-stricken last sentences in "The Final Problem" and the parting conversation between Holmes and Watson in "His Last Bow". ACD, nearing the end of his own life, and confident in his Spiritualist beliefs about the continuation of life after death, forswears "repeated farewell bows" and consigns Holmes to "some fantastic limbo for the children of imagination". Then, after briefly tracing some bibliographical details (and getting one of the dates wrong), he writes, more truly than perhaps he knew, that Holmes "began his adventures in the very heart of the later Victorian era."

Then he bids "Farewell to Sherlock Holmes! I thank you for your past constancy, and can but hope that some return has been made in the shape of that distraction from the worries of life and stimulating change of thought which can only be found in the fairy kingdom of romance." Romance, indeed, and the reader comes to the end of this 600-word message breathless and thrilled.

The Preface to *The Case-Book* would be followed just three years later by Christopher Morley's "In Memoriam: Sherlock Holmes", charming and in spots eloquent, and still in use as a preface to *The Complete Sherlock Holmes*. In 1933 came Vincent Starrett's *The Private Life of Sherlock Holmes*, with the spine-tingling final paragraph of Chapter V that Starrett later formed into his sonnet "221B", and in 1946 "The Implicit Holmes", the greatest of Edgar W. Smith's many great gaslit editorials in the *Baker Street Journal*. Other deathless words have been written about Sherlock Holmes too, such as the final sentences of William S. Baring-Gould's *Sherlock Holmes of Baker Street*. But these Prefaces that are themselves part, or almost part, of the Canon have, and will always have, a pre-eminent place.

Christopher Redmond (Waterloo, Ontario) is the author of *A Sherlock Holmes Handbook, Lives Beyond Baker Street*, and other books, and editor of the Sherlockian.net website. He is a Baker Street Irregular and a Master Bootmaker, and former editor of the Bootmaker magazine, *Canadian Holmes*.

THE ADVENTURE OF WISTERIA LODGE

MARK HANSON

What do you like in a Sherlock Holmes story? Atmosphere? Memorable characters? A mystery that deepens? International intrigue? Conspiracies? A deep plot for revenge? A rival for Holmes? All these can be found in "Wisteria Lodge". No wonder, then, that it is the greatest of the Sherlock Holmes stories!

It's the second-longest short story of the Canon (after "The Naval Treaty"), and originally appeared divided into two chapters, "The Singular Experience of Mr. John Scott Eccles" and "The Tiger of San Pedro". The title "Wisteria Lodge", which was introduced only when it appeared as the first story in the collection *His Last Bow* in 1917, has remained memorable ever since then—for a reason.

The story begins conventionally enough. Recall the telegram Holmes receives: "Have just had the most incredible and grotesque experience. May I consult you? Scott Eccles." Holmes thereupon asks Watson to define "grotesque". The good doctor suggests "strange, remarkable", but the great detective, as usual, freely corrects him: "There is surely something more than that, some underlying suggestion of the tragic and terrible... the word puts me on the alert."

This conversation foreshadows much of what is to come in the story, from the pair's "cold and melancholy" walk from their hotel to Wisteria Lodge, to some of its macabre contents: the shrunken human/monkey figure, the white cock savagely torn to pieces, the charred (lamb or kid) bones, and the pail of blood. These grotesque voodoo images not only add to the atmosphere and tone of the story, but cast an ominous suspicion over the now-disappeared residents of Wisteria Lodge. The haunting, beastly, devilish description of the cook who sneaks back to the estate also adds to this ominous mood of the story.

The brutal ambush and violent bludgeoning of Señor Garcia can also be described as "grotesque", but the real monster of the piece is the Tiger of San Pedro himself—Don Juan Murillo. We never meet this culprit, but we hear stark accounts of what an angry, violent, ruthless despot he is.

An interesting feature of the "Wisteria Lodge" investigation is how early Holmes reveals his thoughts on the case. After the police leave with Eccles, the Great Detective shares with Watson his conclusion that their conservative, reputable client was merely used by his host, Mr. Aloysius Garcia, as a pawn for a potential alibi. An alibi for what, though, still must be uncovered.

While this aspect of the case may have been cleared up for us, several others take its place. There's the cryptic note Garcia receives on the night he is entertaining Eccles: "Our own colours, green and white. Green open, white shut. Main stair, first corridor, seventh right, green baize. Godspeed. D." Who sent such a note? What is the purpose of the meeting? Holmes proceeds with this clue in his more usual, private manner. After he discovers the house in the note to be High Gable, leased by a Mr. Henderson, we then wonder about the relationship between Henderson and Garcia—and their respective households.

There is also the mystery of the residents of Wisteria Lodge. If the host required an alibi from John Scott Eccles, why is he now dead? Where did the other two people in the house disappear to? Why did the cook return under cloak of night? What was the purpose of the voodoo ritual in the house?

The client, John Scott Eccles, not only finds and hires Holmes but recounts his "grotesque" story in front of Inspector Gregson of Scotland Yard and Inspector Baynes of the Surrey Constabulary. The fact that the policemen arrive together is significant. Gregson, whom we've met before, is described here as "energetic, gallant, and, within his limitations, a capable officer". Inspector Baynes is new to us. He is the highlight of this story and the main rival of Sherlock Holmes here. (I should note here that in the Granada/Brett production of "Wisteria Lodge", Gregson does not appear, and Baynes does not have to share that spotlight.) When Baynes describes his side of the investigation, Holmes compliments him no fewer than three times—for his careful examination of the house that led to the crucial discovery of the note to Garcia, for his examination of the note, and for being "very prompt and business-like in all that you have done". Holmes later describes Baynes as "excellent" to Watson.

Still, Holmes and Baynes openly compete during this investigation, each pursuing his own methods. One could argue that Baynes actually gets the upper hand on Holmes. At one point, he certainly has the upper perch. It is Baines's ruse with the capture and false arrest of the cook that emboldens Don Murillo and his party to flee since they think they are no longer under suspicion.

Holmes's agent, John Warner, Henderson/Murillo's fired gardener, does, however, rescue the kidnapped Miss Burnet/Signora Victor Durando based on the detective's instructions. Her rescue is crucial to the story since she's a witness to the actions of the Tiger of San Pedro as well as being aware of the details of the revenge plot against him.

After Baynes explains his effective ruse, Holmes compliments him: "You will rise high in your profession. You have instinct and intuition." Earlier the great detective had told the appreciative Inspector that "Your powers… seem superior to your opportunities [in Surrey]". Such praise is unprecedented in the Canon. Holmes normally uses the police for their reach, resources, or brute strength, and he is usually critical of the lack of imagination in his police counterparts. Not here. Not with Inspector Baynes.

A great appeal of the Sherlock Holmes stories, of course, is to attempt to solve the mystery and match wits with the great detective. With Inspector Baynes of the Surrey Constabulary, we have our champion.

Fellow Sherlockian, I hope that you, like I, now have a deepened appreciation for "The Adventure of Wisteria Lodge". It's the best—a story with dramatic atmosphere, international flavour, mystery upon mystery, and unique characters—particularly a most worthy rival detective. The next time you find yourself seeking lodgings in Surrey between Esher and Oxshott, ask the local land agent if Wisteria Lodge has been let.

Mark Hanson (London, Ontario) is a file clerk and a Twitter denizen, not to mention a proud member of the Cesspudlian Society, London's Sherlock Holmes sodality.

THE ADVENTURE OF
THE RED CIRCLE

DAVID LEWIS

"Attenta, Attenta, Attenta, Pericolo!": "Beware, Beware, Beware: Danger!" With these words, we start to unravel the tangled skein that leads us to Italian secret societies, Pinkerton agents, a couple of titillating hints at other cases, and a thrilling adventure which leads to the rescue of a not-quite innocent couple, but also to one of the great monsters of the Canon.

The penultimate short story collection, *His Last Bow*, was published in 1917, though the stories started appearing from 1907 (1892 if we include "The Cardboard Box"). The collection shows a re-energised Conan Doyle producing some of the very best stories of the Canon. Apart from the eponymous story, the collection boasts, among others, "The Dying Detective", "The Bruce-Partington Plans", "Wisteria Lodge", and the best of them: "The Red Circle." Why best? Any true fan won't prefer the obvious ones: that's too easy. And besides, a true fan sees the quality in the lesser-known stories. Some stories mature, like a Stradivarius violin, becoming richer and subtler and mellower with age.

"The Red Circle" is one of those. Dismissed by William S. Baring-Gould, who gives it just a footnote in his 1963 biography of Holmes and only 14 annotations in the 1967 *Annotated Sherlock Holmes*, and barely given more attention since, it's really one of the most important short stories of its time. It also shows, definitively I think, why Holmes is relevant still in the 21st century and beyond. (At the time of writing we're still easily in the first fifth of the 21st century. I trust a later editor of this volume will update to the 22nd century when applicable.)

Why is this the story that not only ranks as the best Holmes story, but stands out as one that shows Doyle's perspicacity? Well, firstly, it's a great story. But look at how it's structured. A great story is nothing without the telling. Doyle knew how timing worked: look at those chapter breaks in *The Hound of the Baskervilles*. "The Red Circle" demonstrates

Stephen Moffat's assertion that Doyle invented television. Not only does he have the same repertory and a complete story, but that break between the two halves is exactly where a good editor would put the commercials.

The other obvious thing that I think gets missed is the story's attitude to nationality. As many have pointed out, Doyle anticipates mafia fiction: here we see the seeds that blossom into *Scarface*, *The Godfather*, *Goodfellas*, *The Sopranos* and on and on. But what many commentators have missed is Doyle's attitude. The Italians are the baddies, but they are also the good guys. Doyle loved using exotic criminals, but also understood that it was people who were criminals, not nationalities. Gorgiano, known by several nicknames, including the chilling Death ("Morte" in Italian) is as satisfying and as awful as any of Doyle's rogues.

Only Rudyard Kipling surpasses Doyle in his empathy and understanding of non-British peoples. While Gorgiano is as repulsive as any of Holmes's crooks, Emilia and Gennaro Lucca are three-dimensional real people. They are not token Italians but people of Italian descent who happen to have fallen into trouble. Compared to, say, "Sapper" or even Dorothy L. Sayers, where olive-skinned people are all untrustworthy, Doyle is able to indulge his penchant for mystery. They start off suspicious, but are well and truly cleared. Also, Holmes rescues them not because he is inherently superior (or at least not more inherently superior than he is to anyone else) but because his instincts and his professional curiosity are piqued.

Doyle, as is well-known, believed in the more civil tenets of chivalry—"The Red Circle" shows Holmes at his most chivalrous. Watson assures us it is not just flattery but kindness that makes Holmes take the case for poor Mrs. Warren. It is also Doyle's chivalry which allows us to empathise with Emilia; and of course, Holmes, who walked down those mean streets decades before Philip Marlowe did, is never as chivalrous as when he realises who Emilia is dealing with. Watson is also enough of a gentleman to correct Emilia's grammar without losing the flavour of her story, or making her seem less smart or more primitive. This, given the attitude of many British writers well into the twentieth century, is remarkably progressive.

The story is full of thrilling events: it seems long for Doyle. In fact, it's a little shorter than the average. Yet it is so action-packed, the two parts are far more satisfactory than one. It never drags, though, and there are no dead spots. Holmes is particularly scintillating: the opening scene with Mrs. Warren is, to me, even more satisfying than that with Mortimer in *The Hound of the Baskervilles* or any of the many with Watson. The simplicity of the drama is effective: Holmes lays down his gum brush to accept the case. At first he is so taken with his scrapbooking he is quite prepared to send poor Mrs. Warren on her way, but when the brush goes down, he is hooked—as are we all. (One should note here that the gum brush is not for dental hygiene but the brush that applies the glue for the clippings. Holmes isn't so rude as to clean his teeth in front of a guest.)

Watson himself has hardly been more descriptive. Every detail lives in real time. He places us there, right next to Holmes, as if he was helping us reminisce. Each location is described in that way that never detracts from the action but lets us know exactly where we are and why we are there.

Doyle also uses real organisations—the Pinkertons, and the Carbonara—giving an element of real life, though he hides them enough so that a reader can suspend belief to let the story unfold. I've long admired the telling of the ritual of the Carbonara, in an obvious set up: the red disc unfolding in Gennaro's hand is just perfect. Doyle knows it's predictable, but he is a deft and skillful craftsman. The inevitability of it becomes the point of the story, not a badly hidden plot twist.

"The Red Circle" was first published in 1911, when Doyle was at his height, and this story, dismissed by so many, shows it. He may have reached these heights before and might again, but here he hits the pinnacle of his powers. The tragic story of the Gennaros is his best.

David Lewis (Sydney, Australia) is Bosun of the Sydney Passengers. He has given many public lectures on Holmes (and other crime fiction and Victorian-Edwardian adventure fiction). He is also a professional musician and historian who lectures in popular culture, popular music and roots music.

THE ADVENTURE OF
THE BRUCE-PARTINGTON PLANS

JULIE McKURAS

In 1927 the *Strand Magazine* printed Sir Arthur Conan Doyle's list of his twelve favorite Sherlock Holmes short stories. Conan Doyle ranked "The Bruce-Partington Plans" in fourteenth place as he didn't think it best represented "high diplomacy and intrigue." The 1954 and 1959 polls, recorded in the *Baker Street Journal*, moved this story to seventh position. Randall Stock's survey of 1,400 scholars was printed in the December 1999 *Baker Street Journal*; there, it ranked in eleventh place overall, with surveyed Irregulars ranking it in ninth position. While "The Bruce-Partington Plans" thus has always been a favorably regarded short story, I don't believe it has been given the recognition it deserves.

Eighty-nine years after Conan Doyle's list, I decided to survey one person—myself. My results placed this story not only at the top of the "high diplomacy and intrigue" category but also first overall among the short stories. Some 121 years after the November 1895 adventure took place, it remains an ageless example of the adage that the more the world changes, the more it stays the same.

The story begins in the familiar and comfortable setting of 221B Baker Street while outside "the greasy, heavy brown swirl" condenses in "oily drops upon the windowpanes." A bored Holmes comments: "See how the figures loom up, are dimly seen, and then blend once more into the cloud bank." The scene is set for intrigue.

It's not long before brother Mycroft's telegram arrives, stating the necessity of conferring about "Cadogan West." Mycroft, "the most indispensable man in the country," and other government officials are concerned about the recovery of the Bruce-Partington submarine plans as well as the possibility that the press might learn about their loss, a problem that concerns governments to this day. At Mycroft's urging, and with his own curiosity aroused, Holmes takes the case. Theories abound as to why the likely suspect Cadogan West stole the papers and how his lifeless body came to rest in the underground rail system. Subsequent inspection rules out a number of options while serving up new theories involving foreign agents. The unexpected death, or suicide or even murder of Sir James Walter, custodian of the plans, raises more possibilities.

We get to see Holmes's deductive powers at work in this case; and his theorem that "when all other contingencies fail, whatever remains, however improbable, must be the truth" is a welcome addition to any story. It doesn't take very long before the scene of the crime is located, the criminals apprehended and the plans recovered. All is right with the world and Holmes even gets an emerald tie pin from a "certain gracious lady" as a reminder of the adventure.

I believe what sets "The Bruce-Partington Plans" above the other tales is that this single short story has government bungling, murder, scandal, espionage, betrayal, and dysfunctional family issues. What's not to love in one adventure packed with so many elements? The reader is also given additional insights into Holmes as well as his relationships with Mycroft and Dr. Watson. How could anyone fail to rate this story number one?

The solution to the theft rests not only with who stole the plans, but how they were stolen. Government hubris comes into play here. The plans were kept "in an elaborate safe in a confidential office... with burglar-proof doors and windows" under the watchful eye of Sir James, who has an ironclad alibi. All involved with the project, including Cadogan West, are trustworthy. Senior clerk Mr. Sidney Johnson confidently relates that theirs was "as efficient an office as any in the Government service." The room and the personnel are the best the government can offer.

Unfortunately, this *might be* the best that the overconfident government can offer. When asked if there are watchmen in the building Johnson responds "There is; but he has other departments to look after as well." The singular watchman's duties include other offices. Holmes later discovers that anyone could look into the secure room from outside because the shutters "hardly met in the centre." Cadogan West's fiancée relates his belief that "we were slack about such matters...it would be easy for a traitor to get the plans." Government ineptitude plays a large part in making this theft possible.

Another aspect of this case is espionage. Foreign spies make rare but interesting appearances in the Canon. Foreign agent Oberstein makes his second canonical appearance here (the first is in "The Second Stain") and while we aren't informed about his motives, be they patriotism or greed, we know he will do anything to keep his own secrets. Oberstein's criminal partner is Colonel Valentine Walter, who proves he's more concerned with his reputation and ultimate ruin over his "Stock Exchange debt" than he is for what it might do to his brother's career and on a larger scale, to his country. With the preparation needed to steal the plans, such as copying the keys, it's obvious it wasn't a spontaneous crime.

I'm also intrigued by what we learn about Holmes. Examples of his sense of humor are rare, but in this case he bursts out laughing, cites his own sudden hilarity and even chuckles. We also have an opportunity to see more of his areas of expertise beyond criminal investigations when he loses himself in a monograph which he had undertaken upon the "Polyphonic Motets of Lassus."

Another interesting point is his relationship with Watson. He clearly shows how much he respects and trusts the good doctor, even stating, "I will do nothing serious without my trusted comrade and biographer at my elbow." When Holmes finds it necessary to break into Oberstein's lodgings, Watson agrees that they must do it, indicating his total trust in Holmes's judgement. Holmes shakes his hand and as Watson wrote, "for a moment I saw something in his eyes which was nearer to tenderness than I had ever seen."

As for Mycroft, there is always an underlying intellectual rivalry between the brothers. But as with Watson, Mycroft has implicit trust that his younger brother will solve the crime. He might even have a concern for his younger brother's retirement interests when, in describing the theft, he states "As to the Admiralty—it is buzzing like an overturned bee-hive."

What I find intriguing about this story is that both brothers prove themselves to be as capable as anyone else of human error. When Mycroft makes his appearance at 221B Baker Street he describes the Bruce-Partington submarine plans as "the most jealously guarded of all government secrets"—yet "I thought everyone had heard of it." I believe we see a spark of imperfection in Mycroft's reasoning if he believes that something everyone knows might still remain top secret. One of my favorite lines in the story occurs when Colonel Valentine Walter enters the Caulfield Gardens address. Expecting Oberstein, Holmes is surprised by Walter and announces "You can write me down an ass this time, Watson… This was not the bird that I was looking for." He is willing to have his mistake recorded in Watson's writings.

In this tale we have the unusual situation that two brothers are involved in the solution of a crime involving two brothers. It is a study in opposites in several ways. The Holmes brothers trust and respect each other, each willing to do whatever is asked of them by the other. The Walter brothers are, sadly, a different situation. One wonders if Sir James could have helped with Valentine's debt or if poor money management was an ongoing source of friction. Valentine Walter betrays his brother and his country and in some manner is connected with the death of Sir James. Whatever the back-story is for the two brothers, Colonel Walter proves himself to be that sibling everyone abhors, the one who always finds someone else to blame for their own problems. When captured, he states he has no allegiance to Oberstein and tells his captors "He has been my ruin and my downfall." Obviously Walter bears no responsibility!

The murder of Cadogan West and theft of the plans have come at a time of crisis for the government. Mycroft only refers to Siam, but annotators point out the multitude of world-wide problems that existed. Christopher Morley, writing in *Sherlock Holmes and Dr. Watson* about the stories' general appeal, observes: "It is not strange that in our recent years of turmoil and dismay there has been so keen a nostalgia for the shape of things gone by." We look on this case not only with a nostalgic eye but also with a contemporary desire for someone as capable as Sherlock Holmes, a man aware of his own mistakes and that of others, a man unerringly loyal to his brother, his comrade and his country, to solve such matters of importance. I believe that "The Bruce-Partington Plans" exemplifies this—and that is why I rate this story as number one.

Julie McKuras (Apple Valley, Minnesota) is a former intensive care nurse and a devoted grandmother. She is a Baker Street Irregular, edited the BSI Trust newsletter, is one of the Adventuresses of Sherlock Holmes, was a long-time president of the Norwegian Explorers of Minnesota, and is active with the Friends of the Sherlock Holmes Collections.

THE ADVENTURE OF
THE DYING DETECTIVE

NANCY STOTTS JONES

"The Adventure of the Dying Detective", out of the entire Canon, is the brightest star. This truly theatrical adventure unfolds to be a tale of poison and treachery. And how does one undo a poisoner? Shakespeare himself has shown us in his greatest play: Hamlet hides in plain sight, disguising himself as a sick man to disarm those around him in order to expose the treachery of his uncle the King. The trick was to make the performance utterly convincing. Hamlet's was bravura. So is Holmes's.

Holmes is our Hamlet, addressing the task of bringing a poisoner to justice. What he devises is to put on what Hamlet described as an "antic disposition." Baker Street is a disheveled sick room, a masterpiece of set design. He baffles poor Mrs. Hudson who, at the outset, describes Holmes's apparently piteous condition with the same distraught misery with which Ophelia described Hamlet's bizarre behaviour: "what a noble mind is here o'erthrown." Like Ophelia's father, Polonius, Watson is also completely convinced that Holmes is far gone. He laments the "disorganisation of his mind. Of all the ruins, that of a noble mind is the most deplorable," an echo of Ophelia's lament.

Polonius sought only to understand and somehow ameliorate Hamlet's condition, but for his troubles he endured barbarous treatment by Hamlet. In a similarly savage fashion, Holmes regards Watson's anxious solicitations with "venomous eyes" and sadistically responds, "If I am to have a doctor whether I will or not, let me at least have someone in whom I have confidence." Though Holmes is often mean-spirited with Watson, this cruel barb is beyond Holmes's sometimes cavalier treatment of his friend. Then, having put the knife in, he turns it: "after all you are only a general practitioner with very limited experience and mediocre qualifications." This outrageous treatment of his friend is unwarranted for a man who not only distinguished himself in the Army medical corps but was a graduate of the medical school of the University of London, if not

Edinburgh, where Arthur Conan Doyle himself was trained. However much he is cut by this barb, Watson generously accepts it as the ravings of a delirious man.

Holmes's explanation to Watson that he is suffering from a "coolie disease from Sumatra" which is "infallibly deadly, and… horribly contagious" is accompanied with violent spasms and outcries. His performance is elaborate, but Holmes understands, just as Hamlet did, that such excess sells the deception. He exhibits one other violent spasm accompanied by outcry when Watson picks up a curio from the disarrayed mantel—"a small black and white ivory box with a sliding lid… a neat little thing"—upon which Holmes gives a "dreadful cry… a yell… a horrible scream." These physical symptoms are no less consistent with his behaviour hitherto; however, this is a genuine response of alarm at the danger this box presents to the unwitting Watson, and it is this genuine reaction which adds verisimilitude to the previous false one.

The crisis depends upon eavesdropping. Like Polonius, Watson discovers the truth while hidden in the room. Fortunately for Watson, Holmes's plan is cleverer than Hamlet's, so he does not become a casualty of the complicated game. After the villain's arrest, Holmes explains the necessity of convincing both Mrs. Hudson and Watson of the desperate nature of his illness because he knows that, among Watson's talents "dissimulation finds no place." If Watson had known the truth he would not have had the skill "to impress Smith with the urgent necessity of his presence." Only Inspector Morse was privy to the trap Holmes set—Horatio to Holmes's Hamlet.

The trap he sets for Mr. Culverton-Smith is ingenious. The man is utterly convinced, as Watson is, of Holmes's fatal condition—indeed he is in a position to verify that Holmes is a goner. Holmes plays this scene with the skill of a great thespian, inducing the villain to bring him water, a match and a cigarette, and to turn up the gaslight. This final request signals Smith's undoing, of course: Smith has truly been gaslighted! These are elements of film noir worthy of Hitchcock: the deft interweaving of truth and fiction, the enticement into a clever trap, and even a "McGuffin": that nifty little box which occasions an ironic bit of dialogue about witness boxes and coffins is a lovely noir device. The seemingly Shakespearean tragedy played out in the first scene of the story is dramatically counterbalanced by the delicious melodrama of this film noir climax.

This very theatrical performance is made more satisfying in the denouement, a charming domestic scene involving a glass of claret and some biscuits. Now we are backstage, as it were, watching the great performer review his own performance. Holmes spends some time cleaning off the vaseline, belladonna, rouge, and beeswax with which he had contrived his ghastly visage: the "hectic spots" on his cheeks, bright eyes sunk in dark hollows, and the cold sweat of a deadly fever. As a master of disguise, Holmes has suited the words to the actions as Hamlet urged the players to do in Act Two. Holmes is a true method actor: "The best way of successfully acting a part is to be it," he says to the entrapped man. Sir Laurence Olivier, one of the greatest Hamlets of the British stage (and a legendary aficionado of elaborate stage makeup), would have absolutely approved.

Inducing the villain to confess within earshot of a hidden witness is an excellent dramatic device which Holmes successfully used again in "The Mazarin Stone". Such a remarkable story, in which all are fooled by a master director, in which Holmes never even leaves his rooms, in which echoes of Shakespearean tragedy and Hitchcockian film noir resonate to commend Holmes's skills as actor and director, is a unique and memorable experience for the reader, for the audience, for the spellbound victim of Holmes's masterful performance.

Nancy Stotts Jones (Stratford, Ontario) is a teacher of English and philosophy, a flautist, and a member of the Stratford-On-Avon Sherlock Holmes Society.

THE DISAPPEARANCE OF LADY FRANCES CARFAX

THIERRY SAINT-JOANIS

The best story of the Canon is definitely "The Disappearance of Lady Frances Carfax". When I was a young boy, with very limited knowledge of English, my "froggy" eyes were hopelessly attracted by the word "Frances." France? The woman named Carfax was probably French because it was so close to Arronax, from Jules Verne's *Twenty Thousand Leagues Under the Sea*, which I had previously read. Touché! Furthermore, an attractive part of the story takes place in my "douce France"; and also in Switzerland, in Lausanne, which is to say the French-speaking part of the country. And the supporting characters are Marie Devine, the French maid, and Jules Vibart, the guy who cried "Un sauvage—un véritable sauvage!" "Jules Vibart", it sounds so French.

The name of my country—France!—appears more in this story than in any other. France is mentioned once in "The Red-Headed League", "The Final Problem" and "His Last Bow", twice in "The Stock-Broker's Clerk", three times in "The Priory School" and "The Empty House", six times in "A Case of Identity", but no fewer than 27 times in this tale. All right, I know, it is in fact "Frances", a woman's name, but... *cherchez la femme*! Frances comes from old French "Franceise", the feminine form of "Franceis", from late Latin "Franciscus" ("Frankish"). It is frank, as well as my country name, and it means "free". It makes sense in the context of the story because Holmes's purpose is indeed to deliver Frances.

"Lady Frances Carfax" was published in December 1911 in the *Strand* magazine and the *American Magazine*. In the manuscript, the name was "Maria Carfax", before it was switched to "Frances Carfax." Maria or Frances? What did Doyle have in mind? Maybe his sister Annette, whose full name was "Anne Mary Frances", who died in 1890 in Lisbon, where she was employed as a governess. A fatal destiny on the Continent!

I love to see Holmes in France, wearing a French disguise, speaking French. The British detective was fluent in my language, thanks to his maternal grandmother, a Vernet, from the French artist's family. Holmes likes to quotes French authors. We know he worked for the French government ("The Final Problem") and received the Legion of Honour ("The Golden Pince-Nez"), but here we see him in action in France, disguised as a "French ouvrier". In Montpellier, our man needed to speak perfect French to be able to play the role of a real worker among other French people. Indisputably he spoke French, but a standard French or did he have an accent? And which one? An English one? A French accent from the South? In Montpellier, to become part of local culture, a regular worker needs to speak with a native accent and to use some specific words not used in the Paris area. Montpellier is the heart of the Narbonne-Nîmes area, where Holmes already spoke a lot of French some ten years earlier in "The Final Problem". The correct accent here is "languedocien", an Occitan dialect spoken in rural parts of southern France. It is considered as a basis for Standard Occitan. It is, of course, a trifle, but there is nothing so important as trifles: Montpellier's "languedocien" (Oriental) and Narbonne (Meridional) accents are different. Anyway, it seems elementary that Holmes spoke French with a specific accent, but certainly not a British one. Otherwise nobody would have accepted his presence as an *ouvrier* at the cabaret in Rue Trajan.

By the way, how did he pronounce the word "Montpellier"? In Standard French, because of two "L" after the "E", it would be "Mont(pé)llier" with a phonetic "e" (like in "hey"). But common usage is "Mont(peu)llier" with a phonetic "œ" (like in "bird"), as it would be if there was only one L ("Montpelier"). In the immediate area, people used to say "Mont(pé)llier" because the name comes from "montpéyé" in Occitan. Here maybe we have a clue to clear up the case of the two orthographies used by Watson to name the French town. In *A Study in Scarlet*, it is Montpellier; in this tale and in "The Empty House" it is Montpelier, with a missing L. While writing the novel, Watson maybe remembered what he had learned in school about French geography and got the orthography right. But, when writing "Lady Frances Carfax", he is back from the town where he heard Holmes and the local residents saying the town name with an irregular local accent and many more others, in Lausanne or Paris, giving it an alternative accent. This experience led him to keep the "œ" option and, logically, eliminating one letter L to conform with French grammar rules (which are not always logical). *Voilà tout!* (He could not have relied on advice from Arthur Conan Doyle either; the literary agent had encountered a one-L Montpelier, the capital of Vermont, in 1894 as he visited Rudyard Kipling.)

"Lady Frances Carfax" was not in Doyle's list of his "twelve best short stories" in 1927, or the January 1944 Baker Street Irregulars list (it received no votes at all). It was number 40 in 1959 in the *Baker Street Journal* poll and 42 in 1999 for the Study in Sherlockians poll. Why? It offers smart deductions such as the Turkish baths. As an investigative journalist, I like in particular its lesson about methods of investigation: the bad way (Watson on the Continent) and the good one (Holmes with Green). There is friendship, when Holmes saves Watson from being choked by Green's hand. There is action: kidnapping, jewel theft, a lady in danger and two heroes to save her, a pursuit by cab. Breathless suspense. Lots of travel, through many countries (France, Switzerland, Germany). And love affairs between Green and Carfax ("there never was in this world a man who loved a woman with a more whole-hearted love") and between Marie Devine and Jules Vibart. *Affaires de cœur*, and my heroes save France(s)! Who needs more?

But there is more! A pinch of *risqué*? (Pardon my French.) There are naughty passages for all tastes: A French maid (Marie Devine). An unshaven French *ouvrier* (Holmes) "with a cudgel in his hand." Turkish baths. A car... fax? Missionary no less than three times! Sticks ("Are you armed?" "My stick!"). An unconscious naked woman surrounded by men, in the last act. *Partie carrée*? White-slave trade and rape? ("The only story in the Canon that demands a serious consideration of that specifically sexual crime," wrote Chris Redmond in *In Bed with Sherlock Holmes*.)

May we focus on the "unshaven French ouvrier"? Why is he unshaven? And what is that cudgel? I always considered the "cudgel" shown by Alec Ball in the *Strand* illustration ridiculous. What is such a big club good for? It is not the design I visualized when I first read the text. Remembering Watson's mention that Holmes was "an expert singlestick player", I imagined this weapon as a singlestick, also sometimes referred to as "cudgel-play", when used to simulate a broadsword or a sabre.

The Rue Trajan incident will ever stay in my mind as my "Sherlockian deflowering". In 1993, a few months after I created the Société Sherlock Holmes de France, I joined the Sherlock Holmes Society of London team in Montpellier for a stopover during their "France in the Blood" pilgrimage. Here I played a witness watching Holmes (Philip Porter) rescuing Watson (Tim Owen) for an "unannounced re-enactment" of the canonical street fight. *Magnifique!* Driven by a lyrical impulse that only a Sherlockian meeting can raise, I wrote the lyrics of the official anthem of our society, to the tune of the Marseillaise:

Aidons Watson contre Philip Green
Même si le coupable est Shlessinger.
Étrangler John, ça c'est un crime.
Défendons-le avec vigueur,
Défendons-le avec vigueur.
Étendons raide, l'infâme barbu,
Avant même que Sherlock n'intervienne.
Il va bientôt lui tomber d'ssus,
Un gourdin, instrument de sa haine.
Aux armes, Quincailliers…

Last but not least, I love this tale because it opens to other literary myths: Dr. Shlessinger's London place is "dusty and moth-eaten" with a coffin hiding an un-dead woman named Carfax, like Dracula's London residence ("Carfax Abbey")! Holmes cannot leave London because of an unidentified "Old Abrahams in such mortal terror of his life". I've found it! Professor Abraham Van Helsing, vampire hunter! *Coup-de-maître. Bon sang!* "C'est parti, mon kiki!" (my French for "The game's afoot!").

Thierry Saint-Joanis (Saint-Sauvier, France) is founder and president of the Société Sherlock Holmes de France (since 1993), a Baker Street Irregular, a member of the John H. Watson Society and the Sherlock Holmes Society of London, and co-editor of several websites including sh-whoswho.com.

THE ADVENTURE OF THE DEVIL'S FOOT

DIANE GILBERT MADSEN

"The Adventure of the Devil's Foot" was Conan Doyle's ninth favorite Sherlock Holmes story, and it's one that always draws me back to read again and again. Why? Because we find a Sherlock Holmes we see nowhere else in the Canon—a Holmes under duress and a shadow of his usual self who handles this case like no other, leaving us with some intriguing questions.

The inauspicious beginning is significant. Holmes has been ordered by Dr. Moore Agar, his Harley Street physician, to flee London and the familiar setting of 221B Baker Street to "lay aside all his cases and surrender himself to complete rest if he wishe(s) to avert an absolute breakdown." Holmes's strange choice for his rest cure is the remote, foreboding Cornish landscape, rife with a history of devils and hints of the supernatural.

When a murder is committed on the Ides of March, Holmes is powerless to resist jumping into the "Cornish Horror" case. It is engrossing to watch Holmes veer from his customary razor-sharp focus as he tries to use "the Method" to unearth pertinent facts in this case. Holmes, so adept at ferreting out important information, doesn't shy away from questioning servants in other tales. But here, he suspends his usual thoughtful procedures and fails to sufficiently interview Mrs. Porter and the "young girl who looked after the needs of the household," both of whom are on the scene and potential eyewitnesses. Holmes never speculates they could be involved or have knowledge of the crime, so he omits them as suspects and never asks the pertinent questions. He tells Watson, "I am very sure that our material has not yet all come to hand," but in his state of mind, he seems to avoid facts rather than search for them.

Although the Vicar, Mrs. Porter and the young girl all know details of Brenda's affair with Sterndale, Holmes doesn't learn until late in the story that Sterndale's relationship as cousin to the Tregennis family and as Brenda's lover is at the heart of this mystery and of paramount importance. He's left in the dark and never finds out how long the affair has been going on, how often Sterndale visits Cornwall, the length of each visit, if Brenda visits Sterndale's house, their future plans, and whether they have recently quarreled. He tells Watson, "There is a thread here which we have not yet grasped, and which might lead us through the tangle." But instead of going in hot pursuit of this thread, Holmes again acts strangely, abruptly halting his investigation and taking time off "for the pursuit of neolithic man."

Uncharacteristically, he also seems oblivious to the fact that Dr. Leon Sterndale hid the truth in their first meeting. Sterndale doesn't reveal his affair with Brenda, doesn't explain why he can't obtain a divorce, and most notably, withholds information about the Devil's Foot root, valuable knowledge to Holmes and the police. Holmes investigates Sterndale, but only cursorily and not meeting his usual standards. He doesn't determine Sterndale's marital status, the whereabouts of his wife, whether he has children, and when he's last seen his wife. Most elemental of all, Holmes doesn't investigate Sterndale's finances.

Adding to these omissions, Holmes fails to contact the Tregennis family solicitor to follow the money trail and identify who inherits. If Mortimer doesn't, then he has no motive for murder. If Sterndale is Brenda's beneficiary, then he has a monetary motive for killing Mortimer to eliminate the Tregennis family. Other members of Sterndale's family may also have a financial motive to eliminate the entire Tregennis family.

Holmes completely overlooks Sterndale's wife, who might have wanted to seek revenge on Brenda or cover up the scandalous love affair between cousins. Holmes says that women are not to be entirely trusted—not the best of them. Yet in this tragic love triangle where I expect Holmes to *cherchez la femme*, he fails to do so. Mrs. Sterndale never even makes his list of suspects.

Holmes never clarifies why Mortimer lodges at the vicarage instead of the family home. Perhaps Mortimer disapproves of his sister's love affair with Sterndale—reason enough for Brenda to take Mortimer out of her will and name Sterndale. And Holmes dismisses Mortimer's statement about an intruder in the garden, someone who could have been Sterndale himself or his wife giving a signal to the "young girl" to put the poison in the fire. Who would notice the girl tending the fire? Or maybe it was Sterndale who climbed onto the roof and dropped the poison he brought back from Africa into the fire, not knowing Mortimer had left. We see these other possibilities and wonder why Holmes does not. Holmes's failure to establish the facts leads to his failure to consider alternate solutions to the case.

One point of particular interest to me is that Holmes dismisses Mortimer Tregennis's demeanor—usually an important factor in Holmes's observations upon which he bases his deductions. Mortimer seems more innocent than guilty. According to Watson, Mortimer is "agitated," his hands twitching, his dark eyes bright. Mortimer's "pale lips quivered as he listened to the dreadful experience which had befallen his family." He is distracted, afraid and in shock. Whatever we think about him, it is illogical that he would commit this crime under the nose of Sherlock Holmes. Mortimer was under no time pressure to act. He could easily have done the deed after Holmes and Sterndale were long gone, and avoided placing himself in jeopardy. I wondered how Mortimer, a provincial Cornishman, was able to deceive Holmes during their tea with the Vicar. Holmes's exceptionally keen brain, the hallmark of all his adventures, fails him here.

We question why Holmes overlooks, misses and fails to confirm relevant data. We must conclude that the reason Holmes believes Sterndale over Mortimer Tregennis, and finds Mortimer guilty before he eliminates every other explanation, is that Holmes was profiling both men, and in this Victorian profiling, Mortimer Tregennis comes up short.

Holmes typecasts Dr. Sterndale as an imposing golden warrior explorer, a law unto himself, versus Mortimer Tregennis, a brooding, thin, dark, spectacled creature with a stoop. I feel that this overt typecasting is the real reason Holmes doesn't delve into Sterndale's private life. But how can Holmes be certain of Sterndale's real motive for murdering Mortimer Tregennis without a thorough investigation? The Sherlock Holmes method we expect would have looked for evidence and eliminated every other explanation before concluding that Mortimer must be the murderer. Shockingly, Holmes makes his deductions absent any of this information.

Evidence abounds that Holmes was not himself but was having the "absolute breakdown" Dr. Agar predicted. The Sherlock Holmes we know never would have proclaimed that "Mrs. Porter may be eliminated. She is evidently harmless." He would definitely have questioned the young servant girl to find out who she was and what she knew. He overlooked getting information on Sterndale and the Tregennis family estate because his acute nervous breakdown rendered him unable to see the importance of obtaining these details. Watson provides evidence to support this when he describes Holmes's behavior going from "red-hot energy" to "tense and silent, his eyes shining," rushing from "the lawn, in through the window, round the room, and up into the bedroom." Then he "rushed down the stair, out through the open window, threw himself upon his face on the lawn, sprang up and into the room once more."

Although we have seen how Holmes actively investigates crime scenes, in this tale Watson describes his behavior as manic. The final confirmation that Holmes succumbed to his doctor's fears and is indeed undergoing an absolute breakdown and not thinking logically is the Devil's Foot root poison experiment Holmes undertakes. After nearly killing himself and Watson, Holmes admits, "it was an unjustifiable experiment."

Does Holmes ever grasp that thread "which might lead us through the tangle?" In assessing all the clues and how Holmes handles them, it is apparent that instead of trying to avoid a complete nervous breakdown, Holmes jumps into the fray and precipitates it. In this state of illness, Holmes misses several alternate solutions to this mystery. He forgets to Beware the Woman Scorned, he forgets to follow the money, and he never considers that Sterndale may not be the hero Holmes profiles him to be. If an alternate theory of the case is correct, the ultimate result of his emotional breakdown is that Holmes lets a self-confessed, cold-blooded murderer escape justice.

I feel that Doyle's earlier attempt to kill off Sherlock Holmes might explain the author's antipathy toward his hero here. This tale is unique in that we see a Sherlock Holmes subject to human frailty and therefore far from the top of his game. I think this interesting twist with the challenge it affords readers to emulate Holmes's method is the reason Doyle named it one of his favorites, and why I enjoy it so much.

Diane Gilbert Madsen (Cape Haze, Florida) is the author of *Cracking the Code of the Canon: How Sherlock Holmes Made His Decisions*, the DD McGil Literati Mystery Series including *The Conan Doyle Notes*, and a Sherlockian two-act play, and is a member of the Pleasant Places of Florida.

HIS LAST BOW:
THE WAR SERVICE OF
SHERLOCK HOLMES

THOMAS DRUCKER

The thirteenth book of Euclid's *Elements* is devoted to the topic of polyhedra. The last proposition of the book (the eighteenth) includes the demonstration that there are only five Platonic solids. This proposition is taken to combine beauty and depth in such a way that commentators have suggested that the whole preceding edifice was designed simply to lead to that culminating proposition. In the same way "His Last Bow", the latest of the Holmes stories as measured by the date of the action, is the adventure that brings Holmes's public career to a fitting close.

The appropriately concluding features of the story include the scale of the opponent and the importance of success. In previous adventures Holmes has foiled Professor Moriarty, much to the benefit of the citizens of London. He has also retrieved the Bruce-Partington Plans, the Naval Treaty, and a letter from a certain foreign potentate. All of these cases that resulted in saving the state are a reminder of the seriousness with which Holmes took on issues for the benefit of the government. Still, they were on a smaller scale than his efforts to defend England against the dangers of the war that was still raging when the story was first published.

The scale is also represented by the amount of time that Holmes had given to foiling the efforts of Von Bork. Professor Moriarty describes Holmes as having been involved in pursuing him for several months. Holmes claims to have devoted two years to achieving the goal of infiltrating Von Bork's network, ranging over several countries and at least two continents. One can only hope that Holmes's bees were being looked after while he was obliged to spend so much time away from the Downs.

It is worth recalling that, in the earlier stories about Holmes, he was inclined to be rather disparaging about Scotland Yard and society at large. At the end of *A Study in Scarlet*, after all, Holmes displays a lack of concern for being hissed at by the public. As the character of Holmes develops over the decades, he becomes more at home in society and less inclined to treat its pillars as made of salt. Even though we do not hear about the recognition that he received for his work described in "His Last Bow", one suspects that the government was suitably appreciative.

The style of the story is as sparkling as any other. Altamont, according to Von Bork, "seems to have declared war on the King's English as well as on the English king". The cigar ends are compared to the "smouldering eyes of some malignant fiend". As the Baron's car is started by the chauffeur, it "shivered and chuckled". By the end of the story, Holmes warns Von Bork against the dangers of shouting for help by saying, "My dear sir, if you did anything so foolish you would probably enlarge the too limited titles of our village inns by giving us 'The Dangling Prussian' as a signpost."

Beyond these typical literary touches, the last paragraph of the story deserves especial notice. Watson's taking Holmes's remark about the east wind literally gives Holmes the chance to look back at his years of association: "Good old Watson! You are the one fixed point in a changing age." What follows is a Holmesian text which it is difficult to forget, no matter what newer challenges confront us: "There's an east wind coming all the same, such a wind as never blew on England yet. It will be cold and bitter, Watson, and a good many of us may wither before its blast. But it's God's own wind none the less, and a cleaner, better, stronger land will lie in the sunshine when the storm has cleared." Such lines need no commentary. On the other hand, it's worth noting that the story ends with a slightly more offhand quip from Holmes, as a reminder that he is entitled to a break after his two years of service.

There are no similar concluding lines to a Holmes story other than in "The Final Problem". At that point Watson invokes the memory of Socrates and Plato by echoing the concluding lines of the *Phaedo*, referring to Holmes as "the best and the wisest man whom I have ever known". The lines that bring *His Last Bow* (the book as well as the story) to a close are an obituary, not only for a man, but for a way of life. The lines from "The Final Problem" also do not have the concluding twinkle in the eye that makes "His Last Bow" so effective a mixture of the somber and the light.

Many of the familiar characters from other stories do not make an appearance in "His Last Bow". We do not see the Scotland Yarders, and Mycroft is not mentioned among those in the government who persuaded Holmes to undertake the task. Even Mrs. Hudson only appears if she is identified with the Martha who has been Holmes's agent within the Von Bork household. Holmes refers to Professor Moriarty and Colonel Moran, but the story is a swan song, not just for Holmes but for the

Holmes-Watson partnership. Perhaps the third-person narration of the story is intended to give Watson the chance to take more of a bow than he would be entitled to if he were writing himself.

Two years before "His Last Bow" appeared, John Buchan published *The Thirty-Nine Steps*. In that novel he introduced a character (Richard Hannay) who would continue to appear in Buchan's novels over the years. Hannay devotes some stirring days to foiling the efforts of a German spy ring in action that is set just before the outbreak of the war. The novel concludes, "But I had done my best work, I think, before I put on khaki." In a similar spirit, Watson may have gone off to join his old service, but it is hard to think that he can have done anything in the war offering more inspiration to his countrymen than joining Holmes in taking a last bow.

Thomas Drucker (Whitewater, Wisconsin) is a professor of mathematical and computer sciences at the University of Wisconsin Whitewater, and has been an active member of the Hounds of the Internet, the Notorious Canary Trainers of Madison, and other Sherlockian societies.

THE ADVENTURE OF THE ILLUSTRIOUS CLIENT

LEAH GUINN

When I was twenty-one, I fell in love with an unsuitable man. He was unsuitable for many reasons, not all of them readily apparent to a young woman with little experience and an intense desire to be loved. He was tall and thin and distinguished, if not exactly handsome. He was nine years my senior, from another country, with so much more experience of life and the world than I believed I possessed. He smoked, often lighting one cigarette off the other while he talked about poetry and politics and played Simon and Garfunkel on his stereo. He never wore jeans, and showed me how to properly iron a shirt. I was a small-city girl with heavy family responsibilities who wanted more—more excitement, more romance, more *life*. This man offered all of that to me with his rich accent, sandalwood incense, and gentle hands.

Reader, I was a fool.

And I did not marry him.

But some years later, when I was forty-three and barreling through the Canon for the first time, I turned a page and saw my own face.

Well, not precisely. Holmes describes Violet de Merville as having an "ethereal other-world beauty." I have only been slightly pretty on my best day, but everything else was there: the deep devotion to a fascinating, older man from a foreign land, the concerned friends and family who know there is *something* wrong with him, their pleas and ultimatums to a young woman who, instead of listening to them, believes *him*, loves *him*, chooses *him* above all else. Of course, by this time, I was also a parent and, like Holmes, felt a desperate need to slap the silly girl—that the Granada version shows her as a bit of an ice maiden just makes one's palm itch even more. It is also quite a human thing to despise others for making the same mistakes you've made yourself, but over time and successive readings, I began to see, perhaps, a different side to the general's daughter.

Violet de Merville had just come of age in a society where, even (or especially) as an upper-class woman, her options in life were quite limited. She may have had her own money, but that gave her security, rather than freedom. She ran her father's household, and was expected to marry well, whether or not love entered into the picture. Lovely as she was, she doubtless had many suitors, but they must not have been very appealing. We don't get the sense from either Holmes or Sir James Damery that she was enamored of Baron Gruner's fortune, so she was not marrying to have pretty things, or to secure her family's financial stability. Instead, looking closely at those "abstracted" eyes, we might deduce that she's bored. The Austrian nobleman, with an "air of romance and mystery," coupled with his gentility, sophistication, and apparent affection, promises to rescue her from her dull everydays, to bring her wider worlds and deeper passions. Set next to the awkward young men who shambled through her father's drawing room or stepped on her toes during a waltz, the Baron is everything her inexperienced, still girlish heart yearns for. Any blemishes on his past, any suspicious actions—all of those can be explained away as malicious slanders. Those which cannot be brushed aside only add to his mystique; he has lived a daring, non-conventional life, but he has reformed, *is* reforming, and she longs to support him as a good wife should. Despite what her father and his powerful friends say, what Holmes tries to tell her, and what the haggard, shrill (and probably jealous) woman screams at her, she is already married to him in her heart, and this is what gives her the strength to stand against all of them. After all, how can she truly be a woman if she is still an obedient girl?

The parallel would be exact if von Gruner were a fictional version of my boyfriend, but he isn't. Although my ex had a very free and easy relationship with the truth, he was not a sociopath. Nor are most Canon villains. Mr. Blessington has a sordid past, but it haunts him. Sarah Cushing, Jim Browner, and Josiah Amberley are warped by passion and jealousy; they don't use people as things so much as they hold on too tightly. Still, every once in a while, Holmes matches wits against an enemy whose crimes ooze with the dark triad of narcissim, Machiavellianism, and psychopathy. Professor James Moriarty is one. Isadora Klein is likely another. And then, of course, we have the Baron.

Adelbert Gruner is, to me, one of the most realistic villains in the Canon. Anyone who lives long enough and leaves the house will eventually meet him. He (or she, obviously) might not be rich, he might not be suave, but he is self-centered and entitled, and sees other people solely as obstacles or means to an end. Over time, he has refined his methods to the point that the men and women he manipulates don't realize what's happened until, as Kitty Winter says, they are "ruined." He doesn't need to be this way; people are able to achieve happy romantic lives and some measure of financial gain without hurting anyone. The Baron is a wealthy man (although his business deals are "shady"), and he obviously has no problem attracting women. In Edwardian society, he could even marry and have a series of mistresses, as long as he was discreet about it. There is no discernible motive for his murdering his first wife, and no reason why he should wish to marry Miss de Merville. One suspects that, as he "collects women," he saw in both of these women a challenge—the chance to acquire someone who made herself as difficult to obtain as a set of rare Ming china. If he has to marry a woman like that, he will, but (unlike his actual cups and plates) he won't be able to keep her locked in a case, and he'll grow bored. Eventually, he'll want to clear her space on the shelf. Violet de Merville is unable to see this, because all of the love she has ever encountered in her young life has been genuine, and her own devotion is true. Her father has kept her safe, and as wise as she believes herself to be, she cannot see evil when she holds its hand and hears it tell her she is beautiful.

There are many reasons why I believe "The Illustrious Client" to be the best story in the Canon. It's very cleanly written, even by Conan Doyle's high standards. It features Holmes and Watson working together and alone, and shows the deep friendship between them, even if they are no longer flat-mates. For those of us who like seeing Sherlock Holmes as a human being, rather than a "calculating machine," it provides glimpses of both his emotional warmth (when he is thinking of Violet "as I would... a daughter of my own") and physical vulnerability. We get an element of danger, and Holmes has ample opportunity to be clever as he manipulates a master manipulator, first through the press, then with the supreme temptation of a little blue saucer. I've always loved Holmes's lack of regard for the social structure of his time, and we see both sides of this on display as he has no problem dismissing Sir James and his "client" should their case not suit him, and treats Kitty Winter with concern and respect. Finally, although justice is done in the Canon by shipwreck, prison sentence, or snake, it seems particularly apt here. The Baron has lost his ability to collect any more women and, if he is blinded, to enjoy a china collection as well. There is some debate as to whether Holmes was as unaware of Kitty Winter's plan as he claimed, but he doesn't seem all that torn up about it, and neither does the British justice system. We don't have Miss de Merville's reaction, but it's likely that, after the initial shock and pain of learning who her fiancé really was, she was grateful for the second chance she received, and abashed at what she had put her loved ones through. One hopes both she and Miss Winter got past any anger they felt, to realize that they have both been given a gift: the ability to see the world with (at least) one less illusion.

Often, it must be said, Holmes's cases seem a bit fanciful. Sure, people send cashiers cheques to Nigerian princes, but few people are going to believe that copying a dictionary in longhand is a valid way to earn money. As poignant as "The Creeping Man" is, ape hormones are not going to allow anyone to scale walls, and it's really difficult to believe that Mary Sutherland, however short-sighted, could not recognize her step-father. "The Illustrious Client," however, stuns me with its reality, particularly the way in which Conan Doyle could handle the topic of sexual perversion so subtly. It's easy, given the séances and fairies and Viking costume, to imagine that Sir Arthur was a gullible, fanciful man; he was, in fact, an experienced man of the world who had doubtless seen a good deal of its darker side. By the time he wrote "The Illustrious Client" he was in his sixties, and well-acquainted with human nature. His Victorian reticence kept him from discussing all he knew—*Memories and Adventures* is hardly a tell-all—but his observations and understanding come through in his stories where, perhaps, they matter more.

"Only the things the heart believes are true," we read, nodding, because Vincent Starrett's beautiful words tell us that it's important to believe in Sherlock Holmes and a world in which it's always 1895. In the end, however, the lesson of "The Illustrious Client" and all of the Canon is that illusions only bring misery in the end. The truth lies, not in our hearts, but all around us, and only when we can see and accept it will we be wise.

Leah Guinn (Fort Wayne, Indiana) is a member of the Illustrious Clients of Indianapolis and, with Jaime N. Mahoney, the author of *A Curious Collection of Dates: Through the Year With Sherlock Holmes*. In her spare time she has a husband and three children.

THE ADVENTURE OF THE BLANCHED SOLDIER

RICHARD J. SVEUM

There are only two stories in the entire Canon that were written by Sherlock Holmes, and only one, "The Blanched Soldier", records a case undertaken before he retired to beekeeping in Sussex. Why is that important and what makes this story so unique that it is critical to our understanding of Sherlock Holmes and Dr. Watson? We the readers get the story directly from the Master, Sherlock Holmes, with some insight into his mind and emotions, and without Dr. Watson's additions hiding the actual facts behind a curtain of false words and possible misinterpretation of events. We see that the great Sherlock Holmes can be lonely and self-pitying and that he believes this mystery is "the strangest happening in my collection." I believe that the strange happening isn't really that strange, but is really about friendship and love.

The case report surprisingly starts out with Holmes referencing Watson. "The Blanched Soldier" appeared in 1926 and takes place in 1903, so there is a sense of looking backward reviewing his diary and records. Holmes calls Watson "exceedingly pertinacious" and accuses Watson "of pandering to popular tastes instead of confining himself rigidly to facts and figures", but after taking pen in hand he admits that "the matter must be presented in such a way as may interest the reader." Before starting the case he gives two further complimentary observations about Watson:

> If I burden myself with a companion in my various little inquiries it is not done out of sentiment or caprice, but it is that Watson has some remarkable characteristics of his own, to which in his modesty he has given small attention amid his exaggerated estimates of my own performances. A confederate who foresees your conclusions and course of action is always dangerous, but one to whom each development comes as a perpetual surprise, and to whom the future is always a closed book, is indeed an ideal helpmate.

Holmes then goes on to quote from his notebook from January 1903 and states, "The good Watson had at that time deserted me for a wife, the only selfish action which I can recall in our association." For canonical scholars this gives an exact date for Watson and a wife recorded by Sherlock Holmes, which would be more reliable than anything written by Watson. So in this unique case, Holmes is alone without his "ideal helpmate."

The Master then takes the reader behind the curtain and reveals his methods. "It is my habit to sit with my back to the window and to place my visitor in the opposite chair, where the light falls full upon them. Mr. James M. Dodd seemed somewhat at a loss how to begin the interview. I did not attempt to help him, for his silence gave me more time for observation. I have found it wise to impress clients with a sense of power, and so I gave him some of my conclusions." The client began to believe that Holmes, "a wizard," knew everything about the case without being told. We the reader then get the story directly from Dodd just as Holmes heard it, without the filter of Watson's interpretations and faulty memory. Any interruption of the narrative annoyed the teller until he reached the end. Holmes then speaks to us, the "astute reader", believing that we would have few difficulties in its solution since there are a limited number of alternatives to get to the "root of the matter", and then, despite calling it elementary, goes on, "there are points of interest and novelty about it which may excuse my placing it upon the record. I now proceeded, using my familiar method of logical analysis, to narrow down the possible solutions." After only five brief questions it appears that Holmes has solved the case. We the readers are left puzzled. Dodd was then told that Holmes would go back with him to Tuxbury Old Park in Bedfordshire, but needed to clear up some other cases first.

"The Blanched Soldier", as written by Sherlock Holmes, refers to a case that "my friend Watson has described as that of the Abbey School" which involved the Duke of Greyminster. The reader is given a peek at Watson's curtain when Holmes reveals the true name of the school and aristocrat that Watson hid with the made-up "Adventure of the Priory School" and the Duke of Holdernesse. Why Watson was with Holmes for the case of the Abbey School but not present for this case is unclear. We also hear about an unrecorded case involving the Sultan of Turkey that had grave political consequences but that was unknown to Watson or at least never mentioned by him.

The action begins when Holmes and Dodd pick up a mysterious "grave and taciturn gentleman of iron-gray aspect" on their way to the Euston train station. Holmes inserts: "The narratives of Watson have accustomed the reader, no doubt, to the fact that I do not waste words or disclose my thoughts while the case is actually under consideration. Dodd seemed surprised, but nothing more was said, and the three of us continued our journey together." The trip was undoubtedly socially awkward without Watson. Holmes asked another question of Dodd so that the unnamed companion could hear Dodd describe the ghostly white color of his friend Godfrey Emsworth.

Upon their arrival at Tuxbury Old Park, Holmes has the elderly gentleman stay in the carriage. Holmes and Dodd enter the house and Holmes describes his act of knocking his hat off the hall table so he could smell Ralph the butler's gloves as they "passed on into the study with my case complete." It might be complete for Holmes, but we readers are left in the dark. The tension builds as Dodd and Holmes confront Colonel Emsworth, who threatens to shoot Dodd and tells Holmes, "I extend the same warning to you. I am familiar with your ignoble profession, but you must take your reputed talents to some other field. There is no opening for them here." After failing to have a private word with the Colonel, Holmes writes one word on a loose sheet of notebook paper which causes the Colonel to collapse in a chair, amazed that the detective has discerned the ruse. Holmes and Dodd then get the whole backstory from Godfrey Emsworth himself. The final delightful twist is that the austere old mystery man who accompanied them turns out to be the great dermatologist Sir James Saunders, who is indebted to Holmes and stays behind to examine Godfrey.

The case concludes with Holmes gathering everyone in the study. As they await Sir James, Holmes speaks fondly of his Boswell: "Here it is that I miss Watson. By cunning questions and ejaculations of wonder he could elevate my simple art, which is but systemized common sense, into prodigy. When I tell my own story I have no such aid." The logical process "starts upon the supposition that when you have eliminated all which is impossible, then whatever remains, however improbable, must be the truth." Watson has quoted the old maxim before, but in "The Blanched Soldier" we have Holmes in his own words go through the logical steps and rule out crime and insanity before arriving at leprosy. When Sir James returns, he pronounces a new and more hopeful diagnosis of pseudo-leprosy or ichthyosis.

As Holmes began his lifelong friendship with the war-injured Watson, the friendship between Dodd and Emsworth began as mates in the irregular Imperial Yeomanry, Middlesex Corps, fighting in the Boer War until one is injured. Dodd, who has been called out by the Colonel for his "infernal pertinacity," uses a frontal attack upon Godfrey's father to find out about his "chum" and says about his own pertinacity, "You must put it down, sir, to my real love for your son." Some might inject here the love that dare not speak its name, but I believe that Holmes selected the case to show the missing Watson the true meaning of their friendship.

"The Blanched Soldier" is the best tale written by Sherlock Holmes and is valuable to our understanding of the entire Canon because it shows both how Watson clouded and hid certain facts and how much friendship and love existed between Holmes and Watson.

Richard J. Sveum (Minneapolis, Minnesota) is a physician and a Baker Street Irregular, as well as president of the Friends of the Sherlock Holmes Collections at the University of Minnesota Libraries and a board member of the Norwegian Explorers of Minnesota.

THE ADVENTURE OF THE MAZARIN STONE

JACK ARTHUR WINN

The brightest and most valuable jewel in our Sherlockian Canon is "The Mazarin Stone". This case is an almost complete synopsis of Holmes's personality, relationships, work method, and surroundings. I can now say that I have read this story more times than any other and am still surprised at the number of facts it contains.

The drama is intense. No other story has Holmes in mortal danger from beginning to end. "The Final Problem" comes to mind, but there are moments of respite there. Also this case seems to show Holmes on the verge of a shift or even breakdown. He taunts a man who is very capable of killing him and plays a weird prank on an important nobleman. His constant sarcasm is quite out of character to those who know him, but to a first-time reader he would just come across as a wise-ass.

There are several clues that point to this being a pivotal moment in Holmes's life and career. This story is exceptional as being one of only two stories written by a third person intimate with Watson, Holmes, and their affairs, probably Watson's literary agent Dr. Arthur Conan Doyle. It is also one of two stories where Holmes is under constant threat of deadly danger. This tale is unique in having Holmes, in order to foil his opponent, appear in three places at once. He is in the bedroom as a fiddle-playing record, and in the window as a wax effigy, whilst in reality moving between the two.

A case that takes place entirely in Holmes's rooms, it is the ultimate in armchair detection, in the style of Mycroft. Holmes is in constant danger from an airgun, from the count's weighted stick and his pistol, and from a pugilist who wants to pugil him—altogether a very serious situation told in a light, almost playful way. This is because total confidence in Holmes has been quickly established for the reader. With chess-like moves, with his suave handling of Count Sylvius, "with something half protruding from the pocket of his dressing gown", Holmes never hesitates and takes decisive action to outwit and control two very dangerous men whom he has cornered.

We learn in this thumbnail sketch about the untidy first-floor Baker Street rooms, "the starting point of many an adventure". There are scientific charts, the acid-stained chemical bench, a violin, pipes, tobacco and cigars, the coal scuttle and our beloved gasogene, mentioned only here and in "A Scandal in Bohemia". There are Mrs. Hudson, Billy, Scotland Yard, and Dr. Watson with all essentials described: Watson, the honest man of action, brave, steadfast, reliable and a true friend; the Yard, much used for backup so our hero need not sully a clean collar; Billy, a youngster keen and smart, tutored by Holmes like the Baker Street Irregulars.

Billy is also one of those wonderful mysteries in the Canon that help make this a special story. Are there two Billys? Does Billy have a bad memory? Maybe Billy was born February 29? And Mrs. Hudson, who is the vehicle for one of Holmes's great lines: "When will you be pleased to dine, Mr. Holmes?" "Seven-thirty, the day after tomorrow." Does it get any better than that? Dog in the night? Well, we are now on a par with "Silver Blaze", "A Scandal in Bohemia", and "The Final Problem", and I may as well add "The Empty House". Such august company!

The description of Holmes is complete in this *Case-Book* study. It is a summary of Holmes's character from the entire Canon and is really the only story you need read to understand this Zen-like protagonist. He is instantly shown as lonely, isolated, saturnine, a great detective who works non-stop irregular hours. Tenacious, like a hound upon the scent of creosote. A brain with no distraction from a digesting body. Impatient, brave, "always knows whatever there is to know". Holmes plays the violin, is a master of disguise, is sarcastic with a "perverted sense of humour", to quote Lord Cantlemere. In this case he speaks of an "unrestrained enjoyment of the present". Be in the now, our new-age banner! It is a broad view coming from a Victorian detective. He is described as a master chess player who smiles at danger and, like Mr Spock, does not bluff. Holmes is shown as being comfortable within the circle of the Prime Minister and Lords of the realm, is on familiar terms with the police, and has criminals picking up his parasol.

There is a supernatural aspect to Holmes that I have often observed, and that is well illustrated in this story. When threatened, he seems to grow taller, his eyes become "two menacing points of steel". He sees "to the very back of his opponent's mind". It reminds me of legendary beings in Tolkien's *Lord of the Rings*. These are attributes of mythic proportions. The Count compares Holmes's powers to those of the devil. I don't know what that means, but it sounds formidable. All of this in one of the shortest stories within the Canon.

The case itself is almost beneath mention. A jewel, a theft, a cranky lord, a cop, the end. What is so important about this case? A jewel, a theft, a cranky lord, a cop, *a reward*, the end. Lord Cantlemere states, "We are greatly your debtors." Here is the money for retirement and a bee farm. Holmes knew that sooner or later an airgun, falling bricks or a two-horse van would do their job. One cannot play with edged tools forever and not cut one's dainty hands. Maybe he noticed that he was getting a little too arrogant or even a bit reckless. Time to do something purely intellectual and for the benefit of greater mankind. Have you ever read about bees? You should. They are unique upon the planet, and a worthy study for a genius. Holmes lives on, thanks to "The Mazarin Stone". One of sixty great yarns.

Jack Arthur Winn (Stratford, Ontario) is a structural impressionist painter, a classical double bass player, and organizer of the Stratford-On-Avon Sherlock Holmes Society.

THE ADVENTURE OF
THE THREE GABLES

BRAD KEEFAUVER

To fully understand why "The Adventure of the Three Gables" might just be the best story of the original sixty, one must first remember John H. Watson's humanity. From a 2016 vantage point, some ninety years after its publication, we now know both Dr. John Watson and his friend Sherlock Holmes as legendary figures, beloved paragons of male partnership, and so much more. But once, like every other man or woman of myth, they started out as mere humans. And it is in "Three Gables," that we see Watson's humanity most prominently displayed.

In the opening to the story, that racially troubling scene that causes many a reader to discount all of "The Adventure of the Three Gables," Watson writes: "I don't think that any of my adventures with Mr. Sherlock Holmes opened quite so abruptly, or so dramatically, as that which I associate with The Three Gables." This is Watson himself telling us that the opening moments of the story hit him hard. He doesn't give us the dates of this case, but it feels like an older Watson and an older Holmes. And this older Watson, while paying a social call on his friend, basically gets the crap scared out of him. A huge criminal bursts into 221B Baker Street like "a mad bull." There is "a smouldering gleam of malice" in his eyes, and Watson calls him "terrific," as in the archaic meaning "causing terror." And after the home invasion is done, Sherlock Holmes, ever the too-cool one, even chides Watson a bit for grabbing a fireplace poker in preparation to defend himself and his friend.

Consider all of that for a moment. John H. Watson, former soldier, former assistant crime-fighter, has a moment of real fright when a strong, younger man bursts in on a pleasant normal moment in his life. If ever there was a scene in the Canon where we see the need for a bit of *Rashomon* storytelling to show it from a different point of view, this is the one. Watson was plainly scared, a bit ashamed of his own reaction, and trying a bit too hard to downplay it in his published account, turning the authentically frightening Steve Dixie into a comic figure.

This scene's strong racist overtones had troubled Sherlockians for many years before we found out that Watson's friend and literary agent, Arthur Conan Doyle, had attempted similar racial stereotype comedy in an unpublished play entitled "Angels of Darkness." And since Doyle had placed Watson as a character in that very play, one might imagine that Conan Doyle shared it with his friend at some point early in their relationship. Both "Angels" and "Three Gables" are a bit troubling to us now, but in putting them side-by-side, we can sense more clearly that, like embarrassing grandparents, Watson and Doyle were definitely products of another, less kindly era. And in writing Steve Dixie the way he did, Watson could well have tried to downplay the moments of utter panic he first felt when he encountered the "mad bull" of a man, using something he had seen Doyle use before.

This literary attempt by Watson to transform a terrifying personal experience into something less harmful also transforms what might be the best story in the Sherlock Holmes Canon into something less harmful as well. "The Adventure of the Three Gables" has within it some razor-sharp components that have their edge completely dulled by that opening attempt at minstrel comedy. One obvious example is the fact that the most powerful female character in the Sherlockian Canon appears in this story and is never given her full due by fans. Isadora Klein is a more successful version of Irene Adler. She doesn't just beat Sherlock Holmes—she basically buys him off. "There was never a woman to touch her," Holmes states plainly, a line we conveniently forget in our Sherlockian fan-love of Irene Adler. Isadora Klein has not only made her way in a Victorian man's world, she has conquered it. She flees from no man, and even more than that, she uses men as her toys.

Toys, and tools, as well, for Klein has no problem bringing criminal gangs into her affairs, and here is where we see another point in favor of "Three Gables" as the most amazing story of the Canon: Sherlock Holmes directly confronting gangland London. When Holmes brought down Professor Moriarty's syndicate in "The Final Problem," we saw very little of how he actually dealt with that particular campaign against organized crime. In "Three Gables," we see him using intelligence he has been slowly amassing on the Spencer John gang to take them down when he has the time. This is Sherlock Holmes as we rarely get to see him—not bored and picking up an isolated case, but a Sherlock Holmes completely immersed in London society and looking to take apart its criminal element piece by piece.

Sherlock Holmes knows not just about gangs, but about Douglas Maberly's celebrity. He works with Langdale Pike, the "receiving-station as well as the transmitter for all the gossip of the metropolis." And while many have seen Holmes's merely telling Mrs. Maberly to have her lawyer spend the night to protect her as a flaw in Holmes's work on this case, it is actually a strong indicator of just how close to the peak of his career Holmes was at that time. He is triaging his casework, and has to delegate the protection of clients. With Moriarty safely at the bottom of Reichenbach Falls, Holmes is back and determined to clean up the rest of London—or as much as one man can do.

I have always found myself to be unnaturally fond of the stories found in *The Case-Book of Sherlock Holmes*. It is the most sensational of the collections, and I believe there is evidence that its contents are the true tin dispatch-box cases—tales selected for publication that Watson wrote up but did not want us to see, published after his death. While the prospect of the world silently losing Watson sometime after 1917 brings an even more somber light to certain lines in the story "His Last Bow," the light it shines on the accounts in *The Case-Book* is something else entirely.

And it is that light, through a lens of history and humanity, that keeps us aware that yes, we have evolved enough to take offense when offense is needed, but also to look upon our fellow mortals with a more understanding eye as needed as well. And in that light, what do we see? Well, maybe that "The Adventure of the Three Gables" is one of the best, if not *the* best, story in the Canon.

Brad Keefauver (Peoria, Illinois) is the author of *The Elementary Methods of Sherlock Holmes* and was editor of *The Holmes and Watson Report*. He blogs at SherlockPeoria.net, where many of the Sherlockian world's iconoclastic ideas first appear.

THE ADVENTURE OF
THE SUSSEX VAMPIRE

CARLINA DE LA COVA

The previous chapters of this book have argued why each Sherlock Holmes story is the best. The current chapter continues this tradition by convincing the reader that "The Sussex Vampire" is the best tale in the Sherlock Holmes Canon. Many literary, historical, and Doyle-centered autobiographical arguments could be made to support this claim. The reference to vampires should cement its status as the best Holmes story, along with its combination of topics that still resonate in Sherlockian fandom. These include the infamous Giant Rat of Sumatra, the "Gloria Scott" and "Matilda Briggs", and the use of canines in forensic detection. However, I argue that what makes "The Sussex Vampire" the best story in the Canon also includes other factors, from Sherlock Holmes's rational nature throughout the narrative to the power cultural and Victorian beliefs had on the perception of persons deemed "exotic," "foreign," and "the other" by Victorian British society.

Most importantly, however, what makes this one different from other stories in the Canon, and more exciting, is the possible presence of vampires. The sensational title alone suggests a supernatural presence entangled with the occult, intrigue, and vampirism, as well as paganistic/demonistic/hedonistic murder(s), gone amuck in the quaint English South East. Ironically Sussex is the same county, with its rolling South Downs and stunning views of the English Channel and Beachy Head, where Sherlock Holmes retired in 1903 or 1904.

Published in 1924 and set in 1896, this tale is one of twelve stories that compose the *Case-Book of Sherlock Holmes*, and thus one of Holmes's last cases at 221B Baker Street. It has emerged as the strongest narrative in the later Canon that echoes the attitudes and characterizations in the *Adventures* and *Memoirs of Sherlock Holmes*. Holmes's rationalism and logic prevail in the tale. As Christopher Redmond points out in *In Bed with Sherlock Holmes*, it brings Holmes's "famous rationalistic posture" to the forefront. The detective vehemently dismisses the super-natural and expresses his frustrations: "What have we to do with walking corpses who can only be held in their grave by stakes driven through their hearts? It's pure lunacy.... The world is big enough for us. No ghosts need apply." Whilst Holmes's empirical and rational nature rejects the supernatural, vampires, and ghosts, at the time Arthur Conan Doyle penned these words, he was a strong follower of spiritualism and remained so until his death.

Holmes's logical nature is not the only highlight. A glimpse into Watson's past is provided by the concerned husband and father who requests Holmes's assistance: Robert Ferguson, twice married and twice a father. The only personal introduction he provides is through Watson, who "played Rugby for Blackheath when I was three-quarter for Richmond." Little solid biographical information exists about Watson prior to his life with Sherlock Holmes other than his Scots origins, the existence of a troubled brother, his graduation with a medical degree from University of London in 1878, and his service in the Second Afghan War, including his injury in the Battle of Maiwand (July 27, 1880). This information about Watson's athleticism and Ferguson throwing Watson during a match provides a delightful insight into the doctor's past. If Watson played rugby for Blackheath, an amateur rugby club founded in 1858, this suggests he was associated with the area in his youth and young adulthood. It also provides a parallel with Doyle who, as a young man, played football as a keeper for Portsmouth Association Football Club.

There are other reasons why "The Sussex Vampire" is the best story in the Canon. Robert Ferguson's desperate narrative provides Holmes with witness evidence of child abuse and vampirism. Ferguson requests the detective's help in unraveling the behavior of his wife, who has twice physically assaulted Robert's oldest son, Jack. "Jacky," fifteen years old, is Ferguson's first-born and only child from his deceased wife. Jack is described as a "very charming and affectionate youth, though unhappily injured" by a childhood accident that resulted in permanent impairment of his mobility; he suffers from a "weakened" or "twisted spine" and walks with a limp. When asked why Mrs. Ferguson struck Jack, Robert is unsure, but states, "None save that she hated him" and "struck him savagely. It is the more terrible as he is a poor little inoffensive cripple.... You would think that the dear lad's condition would soften anyone's heart."

More alarming, however, is Mrs. Ferguson's actions toward their infant son, whose neck she was observed "biting" twice. A puncture wound in the baby's neck and the wife's blood-covered mouth resulted in the belief that Mrs. Ferguson was sucking her infant's blood, hence the dramatic title and vampiric overtones. Ferguson desperately seeks Holmes's assistance as his wife will not discuss the issue. Here we reach one of the key reasons why this tale is the best one in the Canon. Not only is Ferguson a distressed husband who feels he is "bound to protect and help" his wife, but Mrs. Ferguson is portrayed as very independent. Like other Sherlock Holmes stories, such as "The Yellow Face", this one has a strong-willed female protagonist who is fiercely protective of her family and refuses to distress her husband by telling him the truth.

However, what makes Mrs. Ferguson different from other canonical women is her South American origins. She becomes the exotic other, often referred to as "very beautiful." Even Watson refers to her eyes as beautiful and "glorious." Conversely, it is stated that her Peruvian origins and her "alien religion always caused a separation of interests and of feelings between husband and wife"; there were aspects of her character that he could not "explore or understand." These statements are important as they illustrate the sociological and anthropological concept of otherness, broadly defined as the marginalization of persons considered different or outside what is demarcated as the norm in society, because of physical appearance, cultural beliefs, or religious practices. Othering is usually ethnically, religiously, gender, and/or disability-based and associated with discrimination. Therefore, referencing Mrs. Ferguson's foreign birth and alien religion implies that Robert's wife is viewed by his peers as outside of Victorian cultural norms. Even Robert invokes his wife's exoticism when he states that she is very "jealous with all the strength of her fiery tropical love." This suggests that he sees her as "the other" and external to his definition of cultural normality (i.e., white Anglican Victorian Britain). Thus, Mrs. Ferguson's exoticism and poorly understood cultural practices, which are incomprehensible in the context of British culture, result in her ultimate othering and labeling as a "vampire." Ironically, this is consistent with historical and anthropological evidence of purported vampirism. Those who were foreign, disabled, and ill with tuberculosis and other wasting diseases were often persecuted as vampires as their differences deviated from societal norms.

Despite being called a vampire, Mrs. Ferguson remains strong, defiant, and loyal to her husband. She sacrifices her feelings and reputation rather than break his heart with the truth. It takes Holmes's logic, not prejudiced by cultural differences (or exotic beauty), to force Robert Ferguson to face reality. Holmes does so with little forensic analysis. He rationalizes the environment, the "crime scene," and the behavior of the Ferguson household. We watch the master's mind examine every small detail, including the recently crippled dog, Carlo, the South American weapons, the empty misplaced quiver, and lastly teenage Jack, who displays his affection for his father with the "abandon of a loving girl." However, it is Jack's disgust as Robert holds his infant son that puts the final stake in the Ferguson vampire. Holmes forces Mr. Ferguson to see and observe that a bleeding wound may be sucked for reasons other than blood consumption, including drawing poison. Thus, the truth of Jack's attempted murder of his infant half-brother is revealed and Mrs. Ferguson, who has been a strong, "very loving, and a very ill-used woman", is vindicated.

Jack proves to be a disturbed adolescent with sociopathic tendencies. His attempted murder of his own flesh suggests complex emotional issues beyond the "cruel hatred" Holmes describes. Whilst Robert saw good in his son and partly pitied him for his impairment, Holmes aptly states that Jack's love for his father and deceased mother became distorted and maniacally exaggerated, and may have resulted in the teenager's actions. It seems likely that Jack was jealous not only because of the attention his little brother received, but because the infant was everything he could not be: healthy, complete, normal, and the new center of his father's attention.

Whilst all of these elements, including a borderline sociopathic murderous teenager, make "The Sussex Vampire" the best story in the Canon, its overarching message continues to resonate. Much like the works of the modern horror writer Clive Barker, we learn that perhaps the real monsters in society are not the others, or those who are foreign and different from us; they are individuals like us, much closer to us—or they *are* us.

Carlina de la Cova (Columbia, South Carolina) is an assistant professor of anthropology at the University of South Carolina, with a research interest in forensic anthropology, Victorian medicine, and Watson's suggestion that the human femur has an "upper condyle". She also serves as a deputy county coroner.

THE ADVENTURE OF
THE THREE GARRIDEBS

TAMARA R. BOWER

"The Adventure of the Three Garridebs" begins typically enough. Watson recounts from the comfort of 221B Baker Street the timing of the adventure he is about to relate. "I remember the date very well, for it was in the same month that Holmes refused a knighthood," the reason for which is another tale that may be told in due time, but not today. The story we are about to hear is of course one of those singular, recherché cases that fill the Canon. It borrows and improves on its ruse from at least two of the earlier tales, "The Red-Headed League" and "The Stock-Broker's Clerk," in which a windfall appears out of nowhere to be claimed if only its hopeful beneficiary can be extracted from his place. "The Naval Treaty" also provides a clever twist on the notion of treasure hidden right under the characters' noses.

Nonetheless, the story has several strengths. First, Holmes's split-second deductions uncover the lies and fraudulent motive of "rain-maker" John Garrideb. This Garrideb attempts to persuade and then bluff Holmes off the case; Holmes deftly appeases him, but not before leading him into several telling revelations. He has not, as he claims, advertised in the agony columns, nor was there ever a Dr. Lysander Starr for him to know. As Holmes says, "Touch him where you would he was false." Second, and far more importantly, for many Sherlockians this story is the greatest entry in the annals because it is the most profound example of Holmes's affection for Watson. But it comes at a cost.

The opening of "The Three Garridebs" contains an epigram, referring to that awful occurrence. Watson speculates that the mystery "may have been a comedy, or it may have been a tragedy." What Watson leaves out is the possibility that this is a love story. Absent are the likes of erstwhile love interests Irene Adler or Mary Morstan, or devoted couples such as Hilton and Elsie Cubitt or Percy Phelps and Annie Harrison. Indeed, the chief characters are somewhat lackluster. John Garrideb, ostensibly American, arrives garbed in what Holmes calls an English outfit "with a year's wear." Likewise, the elderly Nathan Garrideb is odd yet agreeable. The relationship between these two is tenuous, less familial than predatory. For readers, the Garridebs' entanglement in this telling of a Publishers Clearinghouse Sweepstakes gone awry may drive the story, but the lasting theme for Sherlockians is the love that circles those two figures at the heart of every adventure, Holmes and Watson.

Borrowed though its plot is, and without as much deduction as one may see in, say, "The Musgrave Ritual" or *A Study in Scarlet*, yet "The Three Garridebs" is near and dear to "shippers" of every stripe—those fans of Sherlock Holmes who interpret aspects of the stories to imply or demonstrate a relationship between its characters. Some shippers want to see Holmes with a woman, some with Watson, and some argue for a simple but strong friendship. It falls to Watson, who often gives us reason to ponder. In "The Red-Headed League," Holmes says of Watson, "This gentleman, Mr. Wilson, has been my partner and helper in many of my most successful cases." High praise for a friend.

Another example of Watson's breadcrumb trail lies in "A Scandal in Bohemia," one of the most extensively shipped of the stories. Many Sherlockians rest happily in the knowledge that Holmes loved the siren at the center of that story, Irene Adler. Watson seems to concur, saying that "there was but one woman to him, and that woman was the late Irene Adler, of dubious and questionable memory." Even William S. Baring-Gould paired the two.

Likewise, thanks to the pivotal scene in "The Three Garridebs," many shippers see strong evidence for a romantic relationship between the Great Detective and his Boswell. As they are portrayed in the BBC's *Sherlock*, the pair even have a portmanteau: in the online *Urban Dictionary* they are Johnlock. Certainly, the two move hand-in-hand through this story, from the opening tête-à-tête with the imposter to the denouement at 221B Baker Street, and the climax is as much about what happens to Watson as it is about catching the criminal.

You may point out that Watson has a wife, proving that he is not gay. In *The Sign of the Four*, he meets, proposes and is accepted by Miss Mary Morstan. The exchange between Holmes and Watson on the subject, however, is instructive. Holmes "groans," and says, "I feared as much.... I really cannot congratulate you." A stung Watson asks why, and is told that while Mary has "a decided genius" for their work, "love is an emotional thing, and whatever is emotional is opposed to that true cold reason which I place above all things." If that were not compelling, Holmes adds, "I should never marry myself, lest I bias my judgment."

Is that a spanner in the works, or is it a declaration that he will never be closer to anyone than to Watson?

This is far from the only, or even the first, time Holmes constructs an imaginary roadblock that makes romantic shipping problematic. You will remember that in "A Scandal in Bohemia" Watson famously pronounces Holmes immune to affection, let alone love. The most distal of fans is surely familiar with Watson's claim that "all emotions, and that one particularly, were abhorrent to his cold, precise but admirably balanced mind." Can you hear the chorus of "the gentleman doth protest too much"?

One shipper has a keen response to the problem of Watson's marriage. The online scribe of *With Love, S.H.* says, "Over the next twenty years, Holmes and Watson would engage in a brief, but passionate affair, ending with Watson's marriage to Miss Mary Morstan. We have speculated throughout this series that, on several occasions, Watson had separated from Mary and moved back into Baker Street. It is reasonable to assume, then, that Holmes and Watson's physical relationship continued throughout Watson's marriage." Indeed, Watson returns many times to Baker Street.

Another writer on the subject of Holmes's love life is Cathy Camper. On the *Lambda Literary* website, an online literary review dedicated to lesbian, gay, bisexual, transgender and queer literature, she says, "Like many single unmarried adults, Holmes's sexuality gets questioned. The first nudge-nudge-wink-wink always points to gay, though as often as not it may mean a person is bisexual, asexual, complicated or just plain lonely." And Holmes is inimitably complicated.

We know that Holmes's complex mind fascinates Watson. In the account of their early days from *A Study in Scarlet*, Watson both deplores and celebrates his new friend's knowledge in a list entitled "Sherlock Holmes—his limits." Ten academic items appear on the list, but only two indicate proficiency. Social and interpersonal skills appear on the list not at all. Watson throws it into the fire. Holmes is a puzzle to the doctor, who clearly wants to get to the character of the man. As soon as he tosses his list, he observes, "I had begun to think that my companion was as friendless a man as I was myself. Presently, however, I found that he had many acquaintances, and those in the most different classes of society." Friendship, Watson seems to be saying, is what really matters.

I, too, vote for friendship. Wherever one roams in life, it is the one relationship that—without strings to tie it down—outlasts all others; the road of companionship for Holmes and Watson begins in 1881 and continues decades into the next century, through the Great War. I am also convinced by what we know of Holmes's methods and Watson's integrity as his biographer that, were there a romantic relationship, we would have been informed.

Instead, we witness Holmes's dedication to Watson many times in the Canon. He insists to the King of Bohemia in "A Scandal in Bohemia," to Jabez Wilson in "The Red-Headed League," and, of course, to John Garrideb in "The Three Garridebs" that Watson must be an accepted co-confidant. There are none more surprised by Holmes's affection than Watson, who tells readers at the outset of the story, "you shall judge for yourselves." On whichever side of the fence one falls, we all come to the text behind the arguments like the parched desert wanderer to the oasis:

> My friend's wiry arms were around me and he was leading me to the chair.
>
> "You're not hurt, Watson? For God's sake say that you're not hurt!"
>
> It was worth a wound—it was worth many wounds—to know the depths of loyalty and love which lay beyond that cold mask. The clear, hard eyes were dimmed for a moment, and the firm lips were shaking. For the one and only time I caught a glimpse of a great heart as well as of a great brain.

And that—enduring affection—is why "The Three Garridebs" is one of the finest and best-loved stories in the Canon.

Tamara R. Bower (Houston, Texas) is a writer, former journalist, and co-founder of the Studious Scarlets Society, as well as a member of the Original Tree Worshippers of Rock County and the John Openshaw Society.

THE PROBLEM OF
THOR BRIDGE

DAVID MARCUM

"The Problem of Thor Bridge" was first published, split into two parts, in the February and March 1922 issues of *The Strand* (in Britain) and *Hearst's International Magazine* (in the United States). The *Strand* illustrations were provided by A. Gilbert—quite Paget-like, but sadly missing a deerstalker—and for *Hearst's* by G. Patrick Nelson, who showed a much more Frederic-Dorr-Steele-as-influenced-by-William-Gillette Holmes. The manuscript, now owned by the Karpeles Manuscript Library, furnishes several alternate and curious titles, including "The Second Chip", "The Little Tin Box", "The Problem of Rushmere Bridge", and "Thor's Bridge".

In 1927, this story was collected, along with the other final eleven Holmes narratives, into *The Case-Book of Sherlock Holmes*. This collection has had a contentious history, not least in copyright litigation, and has been viewed by many as something Arthur Conan Doyle generated chiefly for money. It has been dismissed as being of lesser quality, with the opinion that some stories don't quite reach the mark. However, "Thor Bridge" stands out for many reasons.

The story has been adapted a number of times for the media. Films include the 1923 version with Eille Norwood (Holmes) and Hubert Willis (Watson), an unfortunately lost BBC television adaptation with Peter Cushing and Nigel Stock (1968), and the often-viewed episode with Jeremy Brett and Edward Hardwicke (1991). Radio broadcasts have occasional variations from the original text, including the addition of a Brazilian servant, Cesar, in the 1940's Rathbone versions—the script for this one is available online. An Edith Meiser script was adapted for the newspaper comics in 1954 by artist Frank Giacoia.

The narrative sets the story on October 4 and 5, with no year given. In the original two-part version, the action splits between the two days, with our heroes resuming their investigation on the morning of the second day, at the start of Part II. Most chronologists agree that this is a later case, set in 1900 or 1901. Being a manic chronologist, I choose 1900, as adjudged by William S. Baring-Gould in his *Annotated Sherlock Holmes* and other works.

In this tale, Watson is again living in Baker Street, and Holmes is identified by his Boswell as "my famous friend". Perhaps this fame allows Holmes to remain completely unintimidated by the initial bullying bluster of his client, Neil Gibson, the Gold King. At one point, Holmes says to Gibson, "Some of you rich men have to be taught that all the world cannot be bribed into condoning your offences." Before Gibson arrives, however, Holmes and Watson are given a précis of the man by his estate manager, Marlow Bates, who describes the magnate and former Senator as "a villain—an infernal villain." These strong words perhaps explain why Holmes sets the tone immediately by asking Gibson a loaded question almost guaranteed to cause an eruption. Holmes calmly faces down Gibson's threat—"No man has ever crossed me and was the better for it"—as he did Dr. Grimesby Roylott years earlier: "So many have said so, and yet here I am." This is Holmes in perfect form, in command of any situation.

This case is interesting in that, unlike a crime in a small controlled area, the events of this mystery take place in the open, on a bridge. Also, there are very few characters, rather than a plethora of suspects from whom to choose. Other than the manager Bates, the Gold King, the arrested governess, and the police sergeant, the only other mentioned individuals are the deceased and a secretary, Ferguson, who does nothing except to tell Bates (off-stage) of Holmes's possible involvement in the matter.

After Gibson is suitably chastened, the facts are laid out, and Holmes and Watson travel to the scene of the crime. Holmes meets with the accused, Grace Dunbar, who apparently shines with such goodness that Watson writes of her "innate nobility of character which would make her influence always for the good." Holmes is seemingly impressed as well. After hearing Miss Dunbar speak just a little over a dozen words, he tells her, "After seeing you, I am prepared to accept Mr. Gibson's statement both as to the influence which you had over him and as to the innocence of your relations with him." Then, after hearing the rest of her narrative, he springs up, telling her that, "With the help of the god of justice I will give you a case which will make England ring."

There has been some theorizing that Miss Dunbar was, in fact, guilty after all, leading Holmes by the nose to her manufactured solution as she points out the damage to Thor Bridge: "But what could have caused it?" she asks him, speaking of the chip in the stonework of the bridge.

"Only great violence could have such an effect." A test was conducted in 2005 by members of the Illustrious Clients of Indianapolis, in which they demonstrated on film that a gun used as described in the story would be pulled by a weight over the side wall of a bridge. Unfortunately, their experiment does not determine whether a chip would actually be knocked out of the stone on the way.

A few latter-day scholars seem to think that there was more going on with Holmes's explanation than Watson revealed—either that Holmes and Watson willingly participated in a false solution, or that Holmes was fooled. June Thomson even suggests in *Holmes and Watson* that Grace Dunbar was the third Mrs. Watson, whom he married in 1902, leading to a massive whitewash. However, I maintain that all is as described, there was no collusion between Gibson and Dunbar, and, in fact, Holmes brilliantly solved a very clever crime. I also trust Holmes's instincts: if he felt that Miss Dunbar was innocent based on his sole meeting with her, then so she was. He is, after all, Sherlock Holmes.

The story is notable for its modern (for the time) love triangle, wherein Doyle (the literary agent) was symbolically represented as Gibson, a powerful man with a wife to whom he was tied (his first wife, Louisa), while being in love with someone else (Jean Leckie, later to be Doyle's second wife). It is noteworthy that Holmes is quite critical of Gibson's actions, even as Gibson tries to explain and excuse them.

"Thor Bridge" has a modern procedural feel to it, rightly so, considering that it was published in 1922. Except for his amazing reconstruction of the events at the bridge, there are none of the deductions that one usually expects. Most of the story is dialogue, and the usual "he said" indicators are generally missing. Holmes interviews not one but three individuals for their accounts before making a physical examination of the scene, and amazingly enough, this part, with the description of the famous experiment at the bridge, occupies only seven of the final twelve paragraphs of the story.

This tale has a number of important extras. It is the only tale to have "The Problem of" in the title. It is one of the few cases where Holmes visits a prisoner in jail (the others being—although some visits take place off-stage—James McCarthy, Arthur Holder, and "Hugh Boone".) It is one of only three stories that specifically mention Billy the pageboy by name. It provides the only mention of the solitary plane tree that graces the yard behind 221B Baker Street. It is one of just three places that provide Watson's middle initial, the other two being the reprint statement at the beginning of *A Study in Scarlet* and the "Foreword" to the collection *His Last Bow*.

"Thor Bridge" is where Holmes famously states that "My professional charges are upon a fixed scale. I do not vary them, save when I remit them altogether." This, too, is where he says, "We can but try", a rallying-cry used only one other time, in "The Creeping Man", the very next story to be published.

But to me, a crazed missionary of the Church of Holmesian Pastiche since 1975 when I first discovered Holmes at age 10, the most important part of this adventure is its beginning: "Somewhere in the vaults of the bank of Cox and Co., at Charing Cross, there is a travel-worn and battered tin dispatch-box with my name, John H. Watson, M.D., Late Indian Army, painted upon the lid. It is crammed with papers, nearly all of which are records of cases to illustrate the curious problems which Mr. Sherlock Holmes had at various times to examine." As a reader and collector of thousands of traditional pastiches, I recognize that, in some way or other, they all come from this magical, bottomless, wizard-box with Watson's name on top. If for no other reason than telling us of the tin dispatch-box, I would argue that "Thor Bridge" is one of Holmes's finest hours.

David Marcum (Maryville, Tennessee) has collected thousands of traditional Holmes pastiches including novels, short stories, radio and television episodes, movies and other items. He has written many such stories himself, and edits the continuing *MX Book of New Sherlock Holmes Stories*. He is a civil engineer.

THE ADVENTURE OF THE CREEPING MAN

BARBARA RUSCH

At first blush, this story appears at worst rather silly, at best quite conventional. A tale about an elderly professor who has suddenly assumed the attributes of a monkey? Is Arthur Conan Doyle putting us on? Is this some kind of pastiche, or a satire, which might well have been called "The Creepy Man"? It certainly follows a prescriptive formula: our hero and his trusted companion are comfortably ensconced at 221B discussing matters of mutual interest, a client relates a strange tale which Holmes finds intriguing, they travel to the scene to investigate, a theory is formulated which only he perceives, all is made clear through deductive reasoning, and the narrative ends as a cautionary tale. Just another weird tale from the grotesque and lurid *Case-Book*—not much else to this crazy story, right?

Oh, so wrong. For if we excavate a little deeper, we come to realize that this is the most thematically significant tale of the Canon—in fact, a morality play and philosophical treatise which grapples with the most controversial scientific, theological and ethical questions of its time.

Pantheism. "When one tries to rise above Nature," Holmes observes, "one is liable to fall below it," one of his most memorable aphorisms and not the first time he evokes nature as proof of a higher power. In "The Naval Treaty" he expounds upon the loveliness of a moss rose: "Our highest assurance of the goodness of Providence seems to me to rest in the flowers." Here he goes even further, invoking nature not just as evidence of a higher order, but as its standard-bearer, a universal benchmark for moral behaviour. What is this but an endorsement of scientific pantheism, the belief which equates God with the laws of the universe and the forces of nature, indivisible and sacred, essentially proclaiming that God *is* nature, not just a manifestation of it? It is man's responsibility to conform to its laws, not set himself above them.

Darwinism. It is no accident that the serum Professor Presbury injects into his veins derives from the glands of the langur monkey. The tenets of Darwinian theory were still being fiercely debated 63 years after the publication of *The Origin of Species* in the year Conan Doyle was born. This story is one of several in the Canon which pits science against superstition. For fundamentalists who believed strongly in man's exceptionalism, these theories posed a huge threat, and in some circles still do. If man is nothing more than a product of evolution, what does that imply about our relationships with each other, to the lower primates, and to God?

Holmes's rant ends with a warning: "There is real danger there—a very real danger to humanity. Consider, Watson, that the material, the sensual, the worldly would all prolong their worthless lives. The spiritual would not avoid the call to something higher. It would be the survival of the least fit. What sort of cesspool may not our poor world become?" This comment, suggesting that Holmes believes in the Cartesian duality of human nature, however inconsistent that may be with the tenets of pantheism, seems to be a strong endorsement of social Darwinism. And indeed, Presbury does undergo a horrible transformation, crouching in the attitude of a frog, conjuring up the image of a creature emerging from the primordial ooze of creation, then morphing into a monkey, following the Darwinian evolutionary trajectory, though in reverse, a devolutionary path, just as Holmes predicts. Far from this being a subject of farce, the tale becomes, much like Presbury himself, a metaphor for the sexual, psychological and moral angst of its age. The story seems to anticipate the famous Scopes Monkey Trial, which took place two years after its publication in 1923, placing Darwin's evolutionary theory at the centre of a disputatious dialogue, and making "The Creeping Man" as relevant as any tale in the Canon.

Sexuality. But perhaps Holmes's admonition is more an indication of his own state of mind, his own priorities or lack of them, than a true moral indictment. Is man to be regarded as depraved for attempting to prolong healthy sexual activity into old age? Had Presbury been searching for a cure for heart disease or arthritis, two ailments also associated with the aging process, would Holmes have been equally unsympathetic? Surely justice must be tempered with compassion, though his casual dismissal of the exigencies of others speaks more loudly to a man devoid of sexual identity than to any moral imperative. After all, calculating machines and automatons do not require sex or companionship. He appears to be implying that there are limits to scientific inquiry, sexual deficiencies not falling within them. I wonder what Holmes made of Freudian theory, which was exploding at the time, or is it just sexuality in the aging male that he finds so distasteful? In this case, Holmes seems to be a bit of a creeping man himself, creeping back to the dark ages. Many of the Holmes tales revolve around the consequences of inappropriate or illicit relationships, but no others deal with the subject in as honest and forthright a manner.

Drugs and Dogs. The danger of drug use is a persistent theme in the Canon. From the opium dens of Upper Swandam Lane in "The Man with the Twisted Lip" to the Devil's Foot Root which destroyed an entire family, Conan Doyle was ahead of his time in alerting the world to its perils. In Holmes's mind, Lowenstein's injections are no more than dangerous pseudo-science. Of course, when it comes to accepting or rejecting scientific facts, Holmes has his own peculiar methods. Strange that he cannot see the folly of his own weakness for cocaine, but he is, despite our adulation, a man, after all.

Here we have another curious incident of a dog in the night-time, though unlike the canine in "Silver Blaze," Roy actually does something, once again providing an important clue to solving the mystery. Some years ago, the late Rabbi Steven Saltzman posed the question of whether Professor Presbury, when in his monkey state, was a human being at all, which he defined as having an inner life. But by that definition, those suffering from dementia might not qualify as human either. Nor is it just his physical bearing that's changed so dramatically, his crawling, swinging gait, his thick, horny knuckles dragging on the ground and his inexplicable urge to climb trees. As his daughter Edith expressed it, "It was not my father with whom I lived. His outward shell was there, but it was not really he." It is precisely this absence of humanity which Roy seems to sense as well. Whether Presbury retained some vestige of humanity is a matter for debate. But equally important, what other tale could spark a conversation on what constitutes human identity?

Literary Genres and Allusions. Where most of the Holmes tales follow the established conventions of the detective/mystery story, "The Creeping Man" is a mingling of genres. Certainly it contains elements of Gothic: unexplained horrors in the dead of night, an atmosphere of madness, perceived danger to a vulnerable young woman, secrets harboured within a spooky old pile, the transmogrification and depredation of a distinguished scholar into animal form, bad science and dangerous experimentation with deadly potions—this tale has it all.

Presbury is described as "some huge bat glued against the side of his house… his dressing gown flapping on each side of him," eerily reminiscent of no less a Gothic superstar than Bram Stoker's Count Dracula, the darkest manifestation of repressed sexual desire. Of course, as in all

Sherlock Holmes stories, the paranormal is explained away with the aid of impeccable deductive reasoning.

But the story also contains important elements of science fiction, which tends to mingle scientific fact and prophetic vision. Edgar Allan Poe, the inspiration for much of Conan Doyle's Gothic as well as his detective fiction, wrote of a trip to the moon. And while defying physical laws, science fiction generally has a basis in scientific fact. As it happens, rejuvenation treatments were actually being developed at that time by a Russian-born surgeon named Serge Veronoff, who was injecting animal glands and tissue from monkey testicles into men suffering from what we would today call erectile dysfunction. Nor was Conan Doyle the first to delve into this highly charged subject. Oscar Wilde's Dorian Gray's lust for eternal youth robs him of his eternal soul. Even more pronounced, Presbury evokes Robert Louis Stevenson's Mr. Hyde, the loathsome, Janus-like counterpart to eminent scientist Dr. Jekyll, who injects himself with a powerful concoction of drugs, his higher intellectual self subverted to his inner demons, with the inevitable devolution into madness and depravity.

All these anti-heroes, metaphors for the duality of human nature, end in a hideous moral descent reflected in an appalling physical decline, the Frankenstein monster concealed just beneath the surface, which cannot be contained by its creator. Such is the tragic inevitability when good men turn to the dark side—literary models for the eternal struggle between good and evil.

Conclusion. And so what might appear as a ridiculous story is at the crux of some of the most burning philosophical, psychological and scientific issues of the day, a fascinating discourse at the core of the human condition and an exploration of man's folly in his attempt to be god-like. For all these reasons, "The Creeping Man" is not just the best tale of the Canon; it is the most important.

Barbara Rusch (Thornhill, Ontario) is a Baker Street Irregular and a Master Bootmaker. She lectures and writes on subjects related to Victorian social history and the legacy of its printed heritage, and is a collector of ephemera and other artifacts of the 19th century.

THE ADVENTURE OF
THE LION'S MANE

JACQUELYNN MORRIS

Nearly all of the Sherlockian Canon comes to us by way of John H. Watson, MD, which means that the Holmes we know is primarily filtered through—and limited by—Dr. Watson's perceptions and perspective. Though he has done his best to share the Great Detective with us, nothing could bring us closer to Holmes than Holmes himself. What makes "The Lion's Mane" the best story in the Canon is that it is one of only two cases chronicled by Sherlock Holmes. For an aficionado of Holmes, this story is much like that special gift a child awaits on Christmas morn, but unlike the impatient child we get to unwrap this gift carefully, savoring every glimpse of what lies within. Though it will not be a gift of sweets or toys, it will be something for which we have wished through all the other fifty-five stories and four novels. We will witness who Sherlock Holmes is from the inside, through his own words.

Our first clue regarding the interior world of Sherlock Holmes comes in his beginning statements. He relates that this case was "as abstruse and unusual as any I have faced in my long professional career." No matter what Watson may have said about any of Holmes's cases he recorded, this case is the one which Holmes feels particularly triumphant about having solved.

On only rare occasions has Watson seen proof that Holmes is more than a thinking machine, that a true heart beats within that detached and analytical exterior. When Holmes writes, "the good Watson had passed almost beyond my ken," and "my house is lonely," we hear in his words more than a little melancholy for his dear friend. It must have touched Watson deeply as he read those words, as it touches us. Holmes reveals more of a sentimental streak with regard to Maud Bellamy. He writes that she has "a composed concentration which showed me that she possessed strong character as well as great beauty," and, "Maud Bellamy will always remain in my memory as a most complete and remarkable woman." Coming from Sherlock Holmes, that is nearly a love sonnet. One wonders if Miss Bellamy supplanted Irene Adler as The Woman in Holmes's heart and mind in his later years.

There are many clues to be sorted out in this case. A man has died under mysterious circumstances and all he could say before his death was to shriek, "The lion's mane!" Curious marks upon his back, a dry towel by the water's edge, an ill-tempered mathematician and rival to the deceased for the affections of a lady, that lady's controlling father and brother, a rather dim inspector—Holmes must sort through it all and make sense of it, and we get to come along for the ride.

Inspector Bardle says at a point in this story, "I wish I could see what was in your mind, Mr. Holmes," but we find that we are privy to Holmes's thought processes and his astute observations, as well as his moments of doubt. He takes us with him as he discusses the "murder" with Inspector Bardle, with his pal Stackhurst, and when he questions Bellamy and Murdoch; we see through his eyes the beach and the clues it holds; we hear his theories and his struggles to make sense of the great mystery of McPherson's death. Holmes brings us into the workings of his great mind, and it is all—and even more than—Watson has led us to believe.

This Holmes is not the Holmes of "The Yellow Face". There is no need for Watson to whisper "Norbury" in his ear to remind him to not become over-confident about his powers. Holmes's mind processes and re-processes what he has seen and heard. At one point he feels that the victim's death was by "some human hand," and "suspicion, vague and nebulous, was now beginning to take outline in my mind." Though Murdoch seems the logical choice for the guilty party, Holmes is not convinced. "In all my chronicles the reader will find no case which brought me so completely to the limit of my powers," he says, and continues with, "even my imagination could conceive no solution to the mystery." He confesses his mind was filled with racing thoughts, and he attempts to help us see what being inside his head is like when he relates his struggle to being "in a nightmare in which you feel that there is some all-important thing for which you search and which you know is there, though it remains forever just beyond your reach." Rather than a nightmare for us, though, a delicious excitement overtakes us as we know we are about to see what has been concealed beneath all the Christmas paper and ribbons. We will be there at the very moment when Holmes solves his most challenging case.

It is "a little chocolate and silver volume" from Holmes's personal library which brings Holmes, and us, to the solution of the mystery of the death of Fitzroy McPherson. Holmes admits to being "an omnivorous reader with a strangely retentive memory for trifles," and it is what that little book contained which answered all the questions, explained all the clues, and led to the killer of McPherson.

It came to me, as I was bringing this essay to its conclusion, how very much like Holmes's deductions are the processes through which we go in writing about him. How many false starts and wandering paths have we taken before our premise begins to take form? How many pages have been written that we ultimately discard, as Holmes does with his suspicions about Ian Murdoch? For a time we exist within that same nightmare with Holmes, searching for that which we know is there, so near and yet so far. How many of us, in reading obscure little books and immersed in research, have found that some odd reference or faint memory at long last brings us to where we need to be? Though it may not be J. G. Wood who makes it all fall into place for us, we share that moment of discovery, that "Behold! The Lion's Mane!" exclamation Holmes gives when everything has fit together like a wondrous puzzle.

And this is the gift which "The Lion's Mane" gives to us, the gift for which we have all yearned—to see inside the great brain of Sherlock Holmes, and to know that, in many ways, we are not so unlike him after all.

Jacquelynn Morris (Laurel, Maryland) is a Baker Street Irregular, the organizer of an annual Sherlockian symposium in the Baltimore area, A Scintillation of Scions, and a long-time member and former Gasogene of Watson's Tin Box. She has previously been published in the BSI Manuscript Series volume *The Wrong Passage*.

THE ADVENTURE OF
THE VEILED LODGER

JAIME N. MAHONEY

Hesketh Pearson once said, "We feel we know everything about [Sherlock Holmes], yet we want to know much more about him. We badly want to meet him." Meeting Sherlock Holmes—even figuratively—is a loaded proposition, however. It can mean many different things. For one reader, it may mean simply wanting to occupy the same space as the Great Detective, to be able to hear him speak. For others, meeting Sherlock Holmes may mean playing the role of Dr. Watson, and being able to accompany Holmes on his many adventures. For still others, it may mean wanting to *be* Sherlock Holmes, to wear the deerstalker and stun with both deduction and insight.

In the Canon, however, wanting to meet Sherlock Holmes often meant needing help, and hoping he would provide it. There is plenty of evidence in the stories that Sherlock Holmes would provide help if the case was interesting enough, if it stimulated him intellectually and was somehow unique. Holmes could be brutally cutting and dismissive if he thought a problem was beneath his well-honed abilities, no matter how desperate the potential client was. The burden of proof was on the client to *earn* Sherlock Holmes's help, to prove that he or she was somehow worthy of it and that their problem would not disappoint. Clients often approached the Detective during an already arduous time in their lives, and the added difficulty of assuring one of the most imperious men in London that they would not waste his time seems unfair indeed.

But Sherlock Holmes is not always so demanding or particular. He does not always require complicated contortions from his over-wrought clientele, or a doctoral-level thesis defense, in order to take on a case. More than any other story in the Canon, "The Veiled Lodger" stands apart in demonstrating that Sherlock Holmes could be compassionate and humane with no ulterior motive, with no obvious benefit to himself. This story is evidence that he would provide help simply because he could, because he could recognize the signs of an individual in deep distress, and most importantly, that such things mattered to him.

The opening paragraph of the story contains a note about the Detective's sensitivity: "The discretion and high sense of professional honour which have always distinguished my friend are still at work in the choice of these memoirs, and no confidence will be abused." As readers, we are so used to having Watson reveal all to us, tantalizingly hinting at the possibility of even more scandal and intrigue, that we occasionally forget that Sherlock Holmes knew things that could never be told—not even as a whisper in the darkest corners of the darkest rooms. We forget the cases that could cause total ruin and heartbreak if they were known, but Sherlock Holmes did not. "The Veiled Lodger" displays Sherlock Holmes as uniquely sensitive from the outset. He is tactful and diplomatic where readers might expect him to be blunt and impulsive.

This tale also sets itself apart from the rest of the Canon in that there is no mystery to solve, no vexing little problem to unravel. Holmes comes to Eugenia Ronder's side hoping to find the solution to an unsolved case that has long intrigued him, but in the end, there is no work for him to do. Rather than providing some essential clue, Ronder lays everything out on the table. There is nothing for the Detective to do except listen. And that he does well, considering that she offers no intellectual challenge. She is not a member of a royal family, and she does not have any hidden submarine plans, or an ancestral legacy of a spectral hound. Eugenia Ronder is an average person who once—as she quickly reveals to Sherlock Holmes—had a bad day at the circus. It is true that he once had a professional interest in her case, but that all seems to fade away in the face of her utter despair and desolation.

Once Eugenia Ronder begins to tell her story, Holmes says not a single word, asks not a single question, until she is fully done. When he finally does react, it is in an unexpected and extraordinary way. According to Watson:

> We sat in silence for some time after the unhappy woman had told her story. Then Holmes stretched out his long arm and patted her hand with such a show of sympathy as I had seldom known him to exhibit. "Poor girl!" he said. "Poor girl! The ways of fate are indeed hard to understand. If there is not some compensation hereafter, then the world is a cruel jest."

This is not to say that Sherlock Holmes had not shown concern for clients before, but this is a far cry from the man who once (albeit unknowingly) sent a client out to his death in "The Five Orange Pips", or who would later try to badger a battered woman into trusting him in "The Abbey Grange".

Even more unexpected, however, is the climactic scene of "The Veiled Lodger". According to Watson, as he and Holmes turn to leave, Holmes hears something in Ronder's tone which grabs his attention and gives him pause. "Your life is not your own," he said. "Keep your hands off it.... How can you tell? The example of patient suffering is in itself the most precious of all lessons to an impatient world." This impassioned plea is unlike any other in the Canon—if only on the basis that Holmes is *pleading*. The passage could easily be read with desperation. Holmes took the time to hear what Eugenia Ronder left unsaid, and then he begs her to step back from what cannot be undone.

"The Veiled Lodger" is thus a study in understanding. Eugenia Ronder's value ultimately lay, not in what she could do for Sherlock Holmes, but in what he could do for her. She does not matter to him because of any one thing, but simply *because*.

As readers, there is one thing we desire most when reading the Canon, when we ponder our metaphorical meeting with the Great Detective. It is what we desire more than speaking with him, learning from him, or even *being* Sherlock Holmes. What readers desire most of all is the knowledge that if we came to Sherlock Holmes with a problem, he would help us. Even more than just help, we search the Canon for the reassurance that he would *care*. That he would not forget us, and that we would matter. This tale is that reassurance, which makes it the most important story in Canon—and the best.

Jaime N. Mahoney (Gaithersburg, Maryland) is co-author of *A Curious Collection of Dates: Through the Year with Sherlock Holmes*, proprietor of the Sherlockian blog "Better Holmes & Gardens," and a member of Watson's Tin Box.

THE ADVENTURE OF SHOSCOMBE OLD PLACE

BOB COGHILL

"The Adventure of Shoscombe Old Place" is the best of all of the sixty Sherlock Holmes stories. Except that it is not. It would be disingenuous of me at best to even suggest it, and anyone reading that first sentence would be correct to disregard anything else I had to say about it. It is not the best story. Not by a long shot. But, like every single Sherlock Holmes story I have read, it is my favourite at the time of reading.

Yes, while I cannot in good conscience argue that it is the best story, I can argue that "Shoscombe Old Place" is my favourite. It is my favourite story because of what we continue to learn about our heroes, Sherlock Holmes and John H. Watson. It is my favourite story because it bridges the past and the future. It is my favourite story because it is a story of good people. All of the characters, with the exception perhaps of Mr. Norlett, come off as doing the right thing.

The story starts in Baker Street, as all good stories should. The relaxed way in which Holmes and Watson discuss the case at hand shows clearly how close the two collaborators have become. Holmes recognizes Watson's strengths and experiences in naming him, "my Handy Guide to the Turf" and Watson demonstrates a fine knowledge of the background of Sir Robert Norberton and of Shoscombe Old Place. Holmes is pleased with the capital "thumb-nail sketch". He has much of the information he needs to solve the case even before his client, the trainer John Mason, shows up.

In this, the last of all the stories written (1927), we see that Watson continues to have trouble with money. When we first meet him in *A Study in Scarlet*, he was "spending such money as I had, considerably more freely than I ought." And now, he is still paying "half my wound pension" on racing. Good old Watson, "one fixed point in a changing age." Similarly, as always, Watson is quick to jump into the case with Holmes and assume any role assigned, in this case one of two weary

Londoners, "famous fishermen", off to the little halt-on-demand station of Shoscombe fitted out with all the gear the role would require.

Holmes is able, as usual, to gather information from the locals, in this case Mr. Barnes, the local innkeeper. It is a skill he has used frequently, and once again we are impressed with his ability to gather valuable information without seeming to want or need it at all.

This story moves the detection of crime into the future. It is the only one in which a microscope makes an appearance at Baker Street. While microscopes had been in existence for a few hundred years, they only became fine-tuned in the late 1800s, and their use in the detection of crime was relatively new. Police use of microscopy was in its infancy; as late as 1920, "there are today not more than six or seven such qualified police microanalysts in the civilized world," as Albert Scheider wrote in the *Journal of Criminal Law and Criminology* in that year. Holmes may have not been the first to use the microscope in solving crimes, but he, as in most things, was ahead of the curve.

The story not only reaches into the future with the use of modern technology, it stirs up the past in the vivid descriptions of the chapel and the crypt on the grounds of Shoscombe Old Place, "so old that nobody could fix its date." The atmosphere created by Watson's words of the "dark, damp, lonely place" are every bit as gripping as were the descriptions of the moors of Dartmoor in *The Hound of the Baskervilles*.

There is no villain in "Shoscombe Old Place". Its characters all turn out to be pretty good people. The main characters and the secondary ones alike show themselves to be acting well, or at least morally and decently, despite Holmes's doubts when he says, "As to the morality or decency of your conduct, it is not for me to express an opinion."

The client, James Mason, brings his concerns to Baker Street because he cares about Sir Robert and his sister, Lady Beatrice. Old Barnes the innkeeper gives a home to Lady Beatrice's spaniel. Stephens the butler expresses his concern about what he thinks is Lady Beatrice's excessive drinking, and later is willing to go with Mason to the crypt in the night, even though they ended up "quaking in the bushes like two bunny-rabbits". The maid Carrie Evans perfectly understands the situation and comes to Sir Robert's aid the best way she can. And Sir Robert's behaviour is an indication not of guilt, but rather of grief.

Sir Robert's affection for his sister continued after her death, and his treatment of her was respectful—and, in his situation, necessary. Lady Beatrice, who shared his tastes and loved the horses as much as he did, would not have condemned him. Sir Robert did not do what he did easily. He could not sleep at night. His "eyes are wild," reported Mason. His nerves were shot. Lady Beatrice was devoted to her brother and would not have had him give up this one shot at solving his financial problems. The most serious claim against him in the case is that he had, like Watson, been "spending such money as I had, considerably more freely than I ought." And if we can forgive Watson, we can forgive Sir Robert.

"Shoscombe Old Place" is my favourite story because once again, Holmes shines, not only in solving the mystery but in using wisdom and judgment in withholding his opinion of the case until the time is right and the story can end happily. He introduces himself to Sir Robert with these words: "My name is Sherlock Holmes. Possibly it is familiar to you. In any case, my business is that of every other good citizen—to uphold the law."

This is the last case written by Watson and so contains the final words of Sherlock Holmes: "It is nearly midnight, Watson, and I think we may make our way back to our humble abode." And so the case ends as it begins, at 221B Baker Street, a fitting end to a fine story.

Bob Coghill (Vancouver, British Columbia) is a retired teacher and archivist, a Baker Street Irregular, and a Master Bootmaker, renowned for introducing children to Sherlock Holmes. Since 2013 he has been travelling the world, meeting Sherlockians and adding friendships as he goes.

THE ADVENTURE OF
THE RETIRED COLOURMAN

ELIZABETH BARDAWILL

There is much merit in the tale of the retired colourman, which is considered by many to be the single worst Sherlock Holmes story ever penned. However, I would argue that the seemingly weak plot and two-dimensional villain are clearly a masterful and still relevant medical warning to his vast audience—and thus Arthur Conan Doyle's best story. At this point in his career, Doyle knew he reached a very large and diverse reading public, and could not resist using Holmes to educate his audience about threats even more sinister than Moriarty.

First let's recap. In "The Retired Colourman", Holmes's client, Josiah Amberley, is a 60-something wealthy gentleman who seeks the consulting detective's advice on what appears to be a case of his fickle wife running off with his treacherous friend. They have allegedly disappeared with Amberley's cash and bonds. Watson describes Holmes as being in a melancholy and philosophical mood on the morning the case begins, and that melancholy mood sets the tone for the tale. Asked for an impression of Amberley, Watson sums him up as a "pathetic, futile and broken creature". Holmes responds "Exactly, Watson. Pathetic and futile. But is not all life pathetic and futile? Is not his story a microcosm of the whole? We reach. We grasp. And what is left in our hands at the end? A shadow. Or worse than a shadow—misery." Holmes is being rather a Debbie Downer here, but isn't the author really just setting the stage for this sad last story of the Canon?

As the tale progresses, Amberley is described in bold, garish tones. He is not just ugly but malformed and abnormal. His back is curved, both his legs are "spindly", and Holmes even observes that one leg is artificial. Amberley's deeply lined face and grizzled hair are to be expected in a man over 60, but Doyle broadly hints at other underlying physical and mental health issues. He later underscores the character of Josiah as miserly, niggardly, jealous, unpleasant, combative, argumentative and decidedly unhygienic. Even his home is described as "dingy" and "slatternly".

It is important to note that this story takes place in 1899. Holmes is now using telephones to communicate with Watson. The characters stand on the edge of a dying era, both figuratively and literally. Doyle, and writers such as Dickens before him, were aware of the many detrimental health effects of the industrial revolution and unlicensed chemists. Pea-soup fogs brought on by burning soft coal, cholera-infested city wells, and unregulated drugs and quack potions are only a part of your average Victorian's toxic troubles.

While at first glance "The Retired Colourman" seems a lackluster effort of rehashed plot devices, it seems obvious to me that Amberley has been painted as the poster child for heavy metal poisoning. The chief clue lies in Amberley's past vocation, recorded in the title of the story. Josiah Amberley had worked for decades making artistic paints. He most certainly would have been in regular physical contact with the chemical compounds that were widely used to sate the Victorian passion for vivid colours. The new chemical dyes were used in everyday items from dresses to house paint. The factories that produced them were unregulated; the shops that sold them, either unaware or the dangers or uncaring. Even as the dangers of these products became known, politicians resisted taking steps to protect the British public in deference to protecting the British pound. Deadly chemicals, and all the pretty things they were used for, were just too lucrative.

Historian Suzannah Lipscomb's BBC documentary "Hidden Killers of the Victorian Home" notes that two of the most potentially lethal items in Victorian homes were wallpaper and painted children's toys.

> The introduction of oil and gas lamps, and the abolition of window taxes, meant that, for the first time, the Victorian middle classes could put deep, vivid colours on their walls. There was a particular fashion for wallpapers in Scheele's Green, a brilliant, long-lasting green which was made from copper arsenite and therefore, unbeknownst to many consumers, potentially poisonous. *The Times* estimated that Victorian British homes contained 100 square miles of arsenic-rich wallpaper. Brightly coloured Victorian children's toys were commonly painted with lead paint. Children are always likely to put their toys in their mouths, and lead paint was sweet to taste—but one flake could be enough to poison. Lead attacks the nervous system: even mild lead poisoning can cause encephalopathy and damage a child's development.

Amberley would have spent years absorbing such lethal compounds as copper arsenite and white lead, absorbing them through the skin or inhaling the dust. Long-term exposure to just these two poisons made him the perfect vehicle for Doyle to illustrate the many horrific physical and neurological symptoms of what can only be graciously termed a mass poisoning. This stuff was everywhere. Signs and symptoms of lead poisoning include high blood pressure, abdominal, joint and muscle pain, decline of mental functioning, headaches, memory loss, and—very relevant to this story—aggressive behavior and mood disorders. Long-term exposure to arsenic is related to hypertension-related cardiovascular disease, cancer, stroke, headaches, confusion and diabetes.

Arsenic-induced diabetes would explain Amberley's missing leg and other physical abnormalities, while lead poisoning would have contributed to his depraved and highly paranoid state of mind. One need only think of the ill-fated Franklin Expedition and their new-fangled canned food—badly soldered with lead—to understand how even a few years of heavy metal exposure can take a terrible toll on the mind.

Chemically induced or not, Amberley's dramatic 'Evil to the Core' presence paints him as the most unsympathetic of characters with few redeeming qualities. However, I believe Doyle, clever fellow that he was, meant for the most deductive reasoners of his audience to strip off the melodramatic wallpaper down a few layers and look for the real story here.

The major clue that Amberley has been chemically poisoned is his use of green paint to disguise the smell of gas. Undoubtedly Amberley used one of the most common paints on the market, Scheele's Green, which was used for wallpaper and wall paint, and to dye cotton and linen. The paint itself stank, but the fumes would permeate arsenic into the very air you breathed. By the end of the century the detrimental side effects of Scheele's Green were well known. Queen Victoria was alerted to its dangers as early as 1879, when a royal guest suffered terrible illness from spending the night in a room hung with the arsenic-saturated wallpaper. She eventually was convinced of the danger and ordered it removed. However, these chemicals were so popular, and generated such huge profits, that Parliament did not to regulate or stop their manufacture. It wasn't until consumers began to shun these products that safer alternatives were found.

Holmes, after breaking and entering Amberley's house, deduces the murder of Mrs. Amberley and Ray Ernest by suffocation by gas—another common and deadly hazard in the Victorian home. When confronted by Holmes, Amberley attempts to kill himself with an unidentified white pill. That he was prepared for suicide seems bit odd considering that Amberley was convinced he'd pulled off the perfect murder. Perhaps the pill was not originally intended for himself. Having poison on one's person is not unusual considering you could buy almost anything over the counter, including radium, cocaine, arsenic power, morphine, and laudanum, to name a few.

The real point to "The Retired Colourman" is Doyle's effort to raise awareness of the dangers of the many poisons that lurk in plain view. The villain was not so much Josiah Amberley, but the insidious industrial toxins that deformed him into a raging, paranoid madman.

And this is the best Holmes story because in many ways, nothing has changed over a century later. We are Josiah Amberley. Despite our awareness of carbon emissions, dying oceans and the toxic plastics, we dally with them daily. We continue to mentally paint over such unpleasant ideas lest they be bad for business. No wonder Holmes left London to live with bees. It's just lucky he was able to do so before neonicotinoids were invented.

Elizabeth Bardawill (London, Ontario) has been an avid Sherlockian since 1980. A Toronto Bootmaker in her youth, she is now a member of the Cesspudlian Society of London. Several of her short crime stories have appeared in *Spinetingler* and *Storyteller* magazines.

Made in the USA
Lexington, KY
25 February 2017